EDITED BY ANGELA ESCHLER

CURSED COLLECTIBLES ANTHOLOGY
COPYRIGHT © 2019 PROLIFIC INK LLC

Twenty-Five Dollars and no Residuals © 2019 D.J. Butler

Red in the Hood © 2019 Joy Auburn

The Ledger © 2019 Martin L. Shoemaker

Sleight of Hand © 2019 Jessica Guernsey

Cold Logic © 2019 John D. Payne

Judge Not © 2019 Jen Bair

Twist of Fate © 2019 Karen Pellett

Djinn in Tonic © 2019 Steve Ruskin

This one is Special © 2019 Tanya Hales

More Than You Bargained For © 2019 Lauren Lang

The Seventh Strike © 2019 Frank Morin

Haunting at High Noon © 2019 Mike Jack Stoumbous

The Empath © 2019 Kelly Lynn Colby

True Reflection © 2019 Jace Killan

Chastening © 2019 Jo Schneider

Diamond in the Grave: A Goblin Star Story © 2019 Gamaliel Martinez

Other Side of the Tracks © 2019 Martin Greening

Moving On © 2019 Chris Abela

Just One of those Days © 2019 A.J. Mayall

The Parandada © 2019 Heidi A. Wilde

The Garden Party © 2019 Shannon Fox

The Bad Ju-ju Cruise © 2019 Lauryn Christopher

Requiem © 2019 Mark Leslie Lefebvre

Published by Prolific Ink LLC
in collaboration with Audiobook Publishing, LLC
and Eschler Editing.

Cover Art by Novae Caelum

Anthology Curated by Jace Killan

Print and ebook designed by Prolific Ink LLC
www.prolific.ink

ISBN: 978-1-69688-537-9

All rights reserved. No part of this book may be reproduced or transmitted in any form or by any electronic or mechanical means, including photocopying, recording or by any information storage and retrieval system, without the express written permission of the copyright holder, except where permitted by law. This novel is a work of fiction. Names, characters, places and incidents are either the product of the author's imagination, or, if real, used fictitiously.

All profits go to the Don Hodge Scholarship Fund.

for Lisa

COLLABORATORS

Many thanks to those that have helped on this project through writing, editing, proofing, and layout:

Tina Albrecht, Joy Auburn, Ashlin Awerkamp, Jennifer Bair, D.J. Butler, Jodi Christensen, Lauren Christopher, Kelly Lynn Colby, Tamara Copley, Michelle Corsillo, Beth Curtis, Melissa Dalton, Nichole Eck, Angela Eschler, Lindsay Flanagan, Shannon Fox, Daniel Friend, Fulvio Gatti, Martin Greening, Jessica Guernsey, Tanya Hales, Holly Heisey, Dan Hilton, Dick and Meg Jensen, Stan Johnson, Jace Killan, Mia Kleve, Arlene Kwaw, Mark Leslie, Kristin Luna, Gama Ray Martinez, A.J. Mayal, Robert J McCarter, Rebecca McKee, Shawn McWhorter, Adrianne Montoya, Frank Morrin, James A. Owen, Harrison Paul, John D. Payne, Karen Pellett, Mary Pletsch, Michele Preisendorf, Jenny Rabe, Jessica Roberts, Steve Ruskin, Renee Scandalis, JoAnn Schneider, Maddie Senator, Alan Smith, Shaun Smith, Wayland Smith, Mike Jack Stoumbos, JoSelle Vanderhooft, Cassidy Wadsworth, Stephen Wendell, Heidi Wilde, and Angela Woiwode.

CONTENTS

Foreword		viii
Don Hodge Memorial Scholarship		xi
D.J. BUTLER	Twenty-Five Dollars and no Residuals	1
JOY AUBURN	Red in the Hood	15
MARTIN L. SHOEMAKER	The Ledger	43
JESSICA GUERNSEY	Sleight of Hand	55
JOHN DAVID PAYNE	Cold Logic	71
JEN BAIR	Judge Not	91
KAREN PELLETT	Twist of Fate	101
STEVE RUSKIN	Djinn in Tonic	121
TANYA HALES	This One is Special	141
LAUREN LANG	More Than You Bargained For	159
FRANK MORIN	The Seventh Strike	173
MIKE JACK STOUMBOS	Haunting at High Noon	187
KELLY LYNN COLBY	The Empath	209
JACE KILLAN	True Reflection	225
JO SCHNEIDER	Chastening	239
GAMA RAY MARTINEZ	Diamond in the Grave: A Goblin Star Story	245
MARTIN GREENING	Other Side of the Tracks	259
CHRIS ABELA	Moving On	273
A.J. MAYALL	Just One of those Days	291
HEIDI A. WILDE	The Parandada	309
SHANNON FOX	The Garden Party	325
LAURYN CHRISTOPHER	The Bad Ju-ju Cruise	339
MARK LESLIE	Requiem	357

FOREWORD

I wrote my first book when I was six. It was eight pages long and talked about two aliens that went to summer camp. I always wanted to be a writer. Years passed and I did little to pursue my dream. A friend of mine, author Colette Black, gave me some direction and encouragement. "If you're really serious," she said, "then go to Superstars." I was serious. I did go. I roomed with Don Hodge, a fun, inspiring man—inspiring for both his wit and his age. He passed away a couple years later.

Superstars Writing Seminars (www.superstarswriting.com) is an incredible resource for aspiring authors. It's a writing workshop about the business of writing. Through the years I've had the opportunity to learn firsthand from the greats: Kevin J. Anderson, Rebecca Moesta, David Farland, Eric Flint, James A. Owen, Brandon Sanderson, Jim Butcher, Jonathan Maberry, Lisa Mangum, Jody Lynn Nye, Dean Wesley Smith, and many more.

At a recent Superstars, several of us were talking ghost stories. Author Mark Leslie suggested we do an anthology—this anthology. All proceeds from this anthology are dedicated to the Don Hodge Memorial Scholarship.

We are a growing tribe of Superstars alumni. We collaborate, assist, edit, and cheer on one another's successes. We are tribe. It has taken a tribe to create this anthology. Below is a list of those who have collaborated to make this anthology what it is. A huge thank-you to each of you and to all those who read this.

Sincerely,
   Jace Killan, grateful tribe member

DON HODGE MEMORIAL SCHOLARSHIP

All monies received from this anthology will fund writing scholarships to the Superstars Writing Seminars (SSWS).

SSWS is an intense business seminar—a drink-from-the-firehose deluge of real-world information designed to help attendees better navigate the pitfalls of publishing—targeted to serious writers looking to break in or enhance their career. This seminar can be a life-changing experience.

Superstars offers scholarships each year to writers who would otherwise be unable to attend due to financial circumstances. www.superstarswriting.com/scholarships/

Scholarships are funded by sales of anthologies published by WordFire Press, Prolific Ink, and contributions from individuals. All monies received are distributed to scholarship winners in the form of SSWS registrations, without a single penny subtracted for administrative costs.

Donate directly to the fund via www.paypal.me/SSWSScholarship or pick up one of the previous anthologies:

Undercurrents: An Anthology of What Lies Beneath
A Game of Horns: A Red Unicorn Anthology
Dragon Writers: An Anthology
One Horn to Rule Them All: A Purple Unicorn Anthology

TWENTY-FIVE DOLLARS AND NO RESIDUALS

D.J. BUTLER

TWENTY-FIVE DOLLARS AND NO RESIDUALS

A feller comes in the door, ring-ding-ding. He's a man I've been looking for a long time, but of course I don't tell him.

Better it's a surprise.

The honking of cars and the growl of a bus rise in volume with his opening of the door, and then fall again when the door shuts. The city outside is so unreal at this moment it might as well be heaven.

"I'm looking for old wax cylinder recordings." The man is white, he's thin in the face and in the hands, but has a safety belt of belly fat around the waist, bobbling above a strip of canvas. Liver spots on his forearms, wisps of white hair drifting around his skull. "I heard you might have some."

He doesn't look at me. He looks up over my head.

"Some?" I chuckle. I force myself not to put my hand into my jacket pocket, though the man's arrival makes me feel drier and lighter and emptier than ever. So empty I think that if the door opened again and a breeze brought in another whiff of that diesel smoke, it might just take me on out the back door with it. "I'd specialize in the things, if I didn't think that much specialization would put me out of business. Gotta sell vinyl, eight-track, cassette, and these days, I sell a lot of CDs. Kids got no respect for the tangible manifestation of music."

"No respect at all." The feller's smile is way too broad. He's humoring me.

"No respect for the artistry of arranging a series of tracks into a definite order, though really that went out when they created randomizing order on CD players. You ever listen to Sergeant Pepper in random order?"

"It's shit."

"That's generous. An album is more than just a collection of songs, it's got a logic and a narrative of its own. 'Best of' compilations are worthless nonsense for the same reason." His smile is faltering. Maybe I'm laying it on too thick. "Anyway, you didn't come to hear me complain. You looking for a particular cylinder?"

"Really, I'm looking for masters."

I gotta be real careful now, not to give anything away, not with my words, not with my face, not with any surprise hand movements. "I got a few of those, not too many. You're talking about real collector's items."

"Specifically, I'm interested in any master cylinders recorded for Lethe Records, by an engineer named Louis Shaker."

"Shachar," I say, and regret it.

"You know the man."

I shrug. "You ain't the first person has come in here looking for Lou Shachar masters."

"Oh, really?"

Now I really need to play dumb, before the sweat starts trickling down my forehead. I laugh. "Third or fourth, maybe? Last guy came in here, oh, two years ago, I finally asked him what gives." This is all invented, nobody ever came in here before looking for Shachar masters. Gotta be careful not to over-egg the pudding.

"What did he say?"

"He said, believe it or not, that there's a story about Lou

Shachar's masters. They say that any time he first recorded a bluesman on wax, he took that singer's soul. Put it right into the cylinder."

The feller hesitates a bit too long. Yeah, he's the one I been waiting for. Then he laughs, too. "So all that crossroads at midnight stuff, Robert Johnson, Peetie Wheatstraw, whoever. Only instead of a man meeting you at the crossroads, it's the company engineer who takes your soul."

"I reckon that's about the size of it. Folks want to own a bluesman's soul. Can't say I see why, but there's no accounting for folks. Maybe they're doing black magic with it."

"Maybe they just like the way it sounds." The feller hitches up his pants. "Or maybe it's Woody Guthrie–style agitation codswallop, same kind of nonsense as is in 'Sixteen Tons.' You know why the big mining companies really had company stores, don't you? So the men wouldn't drink their whole paycheck, and their wives could have store credit and get what they needed. My name's Gary."

"I'm Charlie."

We shake hands.

"I have a collection of Shachar masters," Gary says. "There's one in particular I'm looking for."

"Complete your collection, eh?"

Gary shrugs. "I've heard rumors that Big Al Dixon once recorded with Shachar, and I read a few months ago in the catalog of an estate sale that that cylinder was sold by some collector's grieving children, in a lot with a bunch of other old music. Got there too late and no record of who bought the lot, but the sale was in town here, so I figured it's worth checking in at the vintage shops."

"Vintage shops." I chuckle. "I like that. Sounds better than 'junk' or 'secondhand.'"

"These things aren't junk."

"Yeah." My eyes tear up slightly. "You know, I heard Big Al play. He could barely hold his guitar, I doubt he knew what chord he was even on. But he sang like a foghorn, and it was worth it, just to see a man that big blowing through such a tiny mouth harp."

"I read he was a bully," Gary says. "Beat his women. Cut his manager once with a razor. The kind of guy you can really believe he sold his soul."

"Or had it stolen," I say.

Gary puts his hands in his pockets and nods. "You got such a master, by any chance?"

"I got no masters." I lean forward, resting my elbows on the counter. "Over on that wall are all the cylinders I got. Take your time, but I know my stock by heart, and I got no Al Dixon."

Gary nods. "I believe you. Thanks, anyway."

"Tell you what," I say. "I come across an Al Dixon master cylinder, how will I let you know?"

Gary produces a card. I'm hoping for an address, but all it has is a name, Gary Buchanan, and a phone number. Not even a job title, just name and phone. The phone prefix makes it a local number, at least.

Well, that'll have to do.

"What do you think it's worth?" I ask.

"For resale, I don't know," Gary says. "Maybe not much, but I already admitted I'm trying to complete my collection. Tell you what, you get me the Big Al Dixon master, recorded by Lou Shachar, and I'll give you a thousand dollars."

I whistle. "A thousand bucks for a soul? Back in the day, the going rate was twenty-five dollars and no residuals."

After Gary leaves, I close the store and clutch the cylinder with both hands. Touching the wax, feeling the grooves cut by that madman Shachar all those years ago warms me. It's the only thing that makes me feel warm these days, winter and summer alike. It makes me feel full, too. It's a blanket, a mistress, food, and drink, all at once.

It's like heroin was to me, back in the day.

It's my soul, dammit.

Too bad I didn't get an address, that would have made the whole thing easier. I try the Internet, but I'm not good at that stuff, even when I can talk one of the kids at the library into helping me, and this ain't something I can get a kid involved in. I peck out a few searches, get no results, and give up.

I'll just have to let a little time pass.

How long is not suspicious? It takes me three days to prepare, in any case. I've got a master cylinder for another record company, not one that sold race records. It's a klezmer band, but physically it looks just right, the same size and color as the blanks Shachar used.

I have a teakettle, since tea is most of what I live on these days. I boil water, and carefully steam the label off the klezmer cylinder. Then I steam the label off the Big Al Dixon master—the song is "King Snake Stomp," which back in the day really made the folks get up and shake it—and with a little yellow paste and a brush, I put the Big Al label on the polka-playing Jews.

That takes me three days of my spare time, after I lock up. But three days is too soon, Gary'll never believe I just stumbled across the master, right after he came looking, so then I wait.

Just to be sure, I start carrying both cylinders with me. Sometimes I forget I've switched labels, and mistakenly grab the klezmer. It's cold and inert to me, which is always an instant reminder.

Feeling the cold wax reminds me of that room, 211 in the Grand Hotel, on the other side of town here. To keep down the room noise, Shachar put the mic in the corner, and I huddled over it on a wooden, slat-backed chair, big fingers crawling up and down the guitar strings and harp rack gouging a hole in my neck. Shachar threw the hotel room mattress over the door to muffle sounds from outside, and told his two men not to breathe.

We were only going to get one take, he warned us, over and over again.

Thirty seconds in, if you listen to the master, you can hear one feller sneeze. Shachar was true to his word, we cut it in just the one take, sneeze and all, and that was it.

A season passes. Summer's gone — I don't miss it, I feel cold, regardless — and leaves drift down the September sidewalks when I decide it's time to call Gary Buchanan.

I've found a Big Al Dixon Lou Shachar master, I tell him. The store's closed, maybe I can deliver it to him.

He gives me an address. I can't tell whether he's surprised.

I don't recognize the address until I get to the building, and then I remember it. It's an old warehouse squatting on a bluff over the river. It stares at me as I come up the brick lane, between a meatpacking plant and a machine shop.

This was Lethe's warehouse, back in the day. I came here, the day that old mambo looked at the lines of my palms, checked the dregs in a cup of John the Conqueror root tea to confirm, and told me I had already lost my soul. I knew immediately what it must have been.

So I came here, but I got nothing for my trouble, and Lou took back his promise to make more recordings, to boot.

Twenty-five bucks for three minutes' work felt like a lot of money, back then. And I had no idea what residuals even were.

I'm only carrying the one cylinder inside my jacket pocket. Not that I've left the other behind — I never do that — but I've got it taped inside my thigh.

I walk bowlegged, anyway.

The door is buckled with age and the river's humidity, but its locks and knob are new. I knock and yell. "Mr. Buchanan!"

A dog barks, but not inside the warehouse.

Buchanan lets me in. He's practically salivating.

"Do you have it with you?" he asks. He's still looking over the top of my head.

"Like I promised." I hand the cylinder over.

He gives me a thick envelope. I put it into my pocket. Not counting the cash might look like a show of trust, but really, I don't care about the money.

Hell, if he did cheat me, I wouldn't want him to realize I found it out just now.

He holds the cylinder in both hands and smells it. "You can practically taste that chopped chord on the backbeat, can't you?"

"If you're gonna listen to it now, I'd be pleased if I could hear it with you."

He hesitates. He isn't sure he wants me to stay, which makes me more certain that I do want to stick around, but I'm not going to blow my chances by saying anything. I just hang on my own grin and wait.

"Come upstairs," he says.

Upstairs is an office space at the top of a metal staircase, with windows overlooking the entire floor. The door here is new and solid and Gary Buchanan works through three locks with separate keys.

While he's unlocking the door, I count at least two security cameras.

Inside, the room is not what I expect. I imagine office furniture as I walk in, but what I see is two tables, one with master cylinders standing on their ends in rows like chess pawns, and the other with an old player-recorder, the kind that makes cylinders and can also run them back.

"Hell of a place to keep a collection," I say. "You think every one of those cylinders is worth a thousand bucks?"

"This is Shachar's office," Gary says. "That's his machine."

"I heard he recorded in hotel rooms and bars," I say.

Gary nods. "And brothels and riverboats and restaurant kitchens. And once in a restroom in the state capitol building."

"I guess you don't want to listen to your music in a restroom, though, that it?"

Gary takes a deep breath while he thinks about his words. "In affairs such as this, things that appear to be of no consequence can matter immensely. Continuity of place. Sustained contact in the past."

"My line of work, I've talked to more than one sound nut," I say. "Excuse me, I meant audiophile. Never heard anyone say 'sustained contact in the past' mattered. I ain't confident I even know what you mean."

He gets a look in his eye, and it's the first moment I'm sure Gary Buchanan plans to kill me. "Would you like me to show you what I mean?"

I make a show of indifference. I scratch my nose with one hand, and shove the other hand into my pants pockets. I cut the bottom out of those pockets, so I can reach the other thing I've taped to my thigh, which is a long razor.

Long and sharp.

"Sure," I say.

He plugs in the machine and it comes to life with a slow buzz. I know that buzz. It had a microphone jacked into it when I first saw it, but this was Lou Shachar's machine when I first met him, when we first did business.

Gary puts the cylinder on the spindle and touches the needle to it, stepping back as the speakers crackle with lively sound.

His grin of anticipation collapses into a flat line as fiddles, horns, and a drum kick out in a raucous version of "Hava Nagilah," the musicians barely managing to hold themselves to the same tempo all the way to the end of the recording.

"That isn't it," he snarls.

He checks the label; I worry the concrete floor with the toe of my shoe. "It's Big Al Dixon on the label."

"Does that sound like Big Al to you?"

I hand the cash back over.

He stares at me without taking it. He's thinking, do I kill this old fool from the vintage music shop?

"Tell you what," I say. "I want to earn back that thousand bucks. Give me a couple weeks, I'll call everyone I know in the valley. Secondhand shops, collectors, everything. If I can get my hands on that cylinder for less than a thousand bucks, I'll bring it to you here. And if the price is higher than that, I'll tell you where you can find the cylinder yourself. Deal?"

He takes back the envelope.

I n this case, no need to wait. I come back the same night.

I bring tools from the hardware store—crowbar, drill, screwdrivers, hammer—and a mask of Winnie the Pooh, together in a grip bag with the master cylinder. I wrap the cylinder in a rag to protect it. Halloween's coming, you can buy stuff like a mask in the autumn without anyone asking awkward questions.

I walk, and I put on the Winnie the Pooh mask when I'm half a block away. This part of town is quiet at night; there's no one to see me.

The locks on the outer door are solid, but it opens outward, so it's got hinges on the outside. That's easy, I just rip the hinges out of the wood with the crowbar.

I creep up the stairs by the moonlight coming in through gaps in two of the walls. I'll be on the cameras, but that won't matter, not with the mask. I don't notice until I get right to the top of the stairs that Gary Buchanan is there waiting for me.

With a pistol in his hand.

"I couldn't be sure," he says, looking over my head.

"Sure of what?"

"Dammit, Al," he says, "one mask wasn't enough. What made you think throwing a second on over the top would help anything?"

I'm quiet for a minute. What's he talking about, two masks? Finally, I strip off the Winnie the Pooh head and toss it to the warehouse floor. "I just came to . . . I just came . . ."

"You came to listen to your own master," Gary says. "I can't let you do that."

I put my right hand in my pocket. I still have the razor taped there, just in case. I force a laugh. "Okay, you got me. Look, I do have the Dixon-Shachar master. Tell you what, you let me listen to it with you, I'll give you the cylinder. Let's call it five hundred bucks, instead of a thousand. Fifty percent discount for your trouble."

"I can't let you listen to it."

"You were going to before."

"I could tell what you'd given me was a fake. If I let you listen to the master, on the very machine that recorded it, the spell will be undone, and you'll get your soul back."

Exactly. He has me dead to rights.

"I'm going to do something else," Gary says. "I'm going to free the boy."

"What boy?" I laugh.

"You don't know?"

I shrug and chuckle. "Just you and me here, Gary. It's always been just you and me. Gary and Charlie."

He reaches to the wall and flips on the light switch. As the overhead fluorescents flicker into activity, he holds up a silver tray. It's been polished to a degree you rarely see in silver, so it's reflective, every bit as much as a mirror.

He holds it up to my face . . . and I see the face of a young man.

A white kid, really, still has freckles. Maybe twenty-five years old, twenty-six at the most.

I touch the face. "Damn." I had forgotten. How long have I been in the young man's body? I remember him coming into the shop now, saying he was traveling across the country in his grandpa's car and was looking for any old eight-tracks I had around. I remember me—in the body I had borrowed before—giving him a cup of tea.

"I'm going to take you out of that boy, Al," Gary says. "I'm going to take good care of you. You can sit right on the shelf with Robert Johnson and Peetie Wheatstraw and Doug Sims. And don't worry, I'll listen to you from time to time, when I need to, or when the mood takes me. There's no music like . . . soul music."

"Damn you," I say. "A pun? Really? At a time like this?"

I tear the razor from my thigh and step forward.

Or rather, I try to step forward. But I fail. I can't move. My feet are rooted to the metal of the staircase. Looking down, I see chalk markings on the metal. They weren't there this afternoon, I'm sure of it. There's a circle, and two triangles making a six-pointed star, and a bunch of queer markings like you might see embroidered into the wall of a gypsy's tent.

I can't move my feet.

I swipe at Gary with the razor, but he's planned for that. He steps back out of my reach and I miss.

"I'll shoot you," I growl.

"No, you won't," Gary says. "Big Al Dixon beat women. And he cut men with a razor or he kicked them, but he never carried a gun."

"Asking for too much trouble, black man carrying a gun," I grumble. I regret that policy now. I regret not having a pistol in my pocket tonight.

Gary starts chanting. I don't know the words, they ain't English.

I raise the razor to my own borrowed throat. "Stop, or I'll kill the kid."

"Now that I believe," Gary says. Then he sprays mace into my eyes.

Or rather, he sprays mace into the eyes of the kid, which feels like it's over my head, because I'm really in the wax cylinder inside the grip bag, as much as I am in the twenty-five-year-old with freckles. But I feel the mace, it catches me by surprise and I drop the razor.

"Twenty-five dollars!" I roar through my tears and through the fingers over my eyes. "How would you feel? Wouldn't you want to go free? Wouldn't you fight to get back your soul? I was tricked by the record company man, and I didn't get the kingdoms of this world—I got twenty-five dollars!"

Gary finishes his chant and picks me up. I'm just in the master cylinder now. The kid in whose body I spent the last two years—before him there was another young man, and before him another—runs away, weeping. Gary lets him go.

Gary hefts the cylinder thoughtfully. I'm screaming, but he can't hear.

"Twenty-five dollars," he says, "and no residuals."

D.J. Butler is a novelist living in the Rocky Mountain west. He is a lover of language and languages, a guitarist and self-recorder, and a serious reader. He's married to a powerful and clever woman (also a novelist) and has three devious children. D.J. has been writing fiction since 2010. He is also published under the name Dave Butler. For more information visit www.davidjohnbutler.com.

RED IN THE HOOD

JOY AUBURN

RED IN THE HOOD

CUSTOMER ONE

"Wait!" Coral waved at the taxi. "I forgot my coffee."

The car replied with a puff of exhaust. It sped down the street in search of its next fare.

"By god, if I still had two good hips . . ." Coral shifted her weight onto the curb.

On the next block, a group of teens loitered near the side entrance of a diner like a pack of stray dogs, marking their territory with spray paint. The door swung wide, nearly knocking one kid over. A young woman wearing an apron stuck her head into the morning and motioned at them to move along.

Resigned to take the woman's advice as well, Coral clutched her purse and turned to face the building she . . . *good lord*, a brief survey of the street shot her senses from mild annoyance to high alert.

Boards covered the windows and doors of most buildings like they held a secret. Between the structures, discarded paper and sacks were woven through chain-link fences like urban crochet. The diner had the only foot traffic on the block. Surely the cabbie had gotten the address wrong.

Coral flipped through her purse to double-check, but a photo slipped out instead. In it, her great-granddaughter sat on a sea-blue blanket hugging her treasured handmade doll. Coral rubbed her thumb down the girl's sweet face, never the same after the fire. The two years since felt more like ten. She drew a ragged breath, returned the photo, and pulled out her nearly completed bucket list. She hadn't meant to save the most meaningful for last, but a replacement toy had been impossible to find.

Given she'd started the list before slipping on her first pair of cheaters, the ink had long since faded between the folds. Only the most recent addition remained readable. Coral squinted through her smudged bifocals and confirmed the address jotted beside the only item not crossed off.

Most antique stores welcomed shoppers with a quaint vintage sign and charming display window of prime picks, from overcluttered attics to garage-sale castaways. Considering the neighborhood, if this place ever had a sign, someone had probably stolen it. Brick and vines framed the solid metal door. At first glance, she swore the aged hardware to be faux. Though the layers of rust and refinish revealed a more historic tale, they did little to calm her nerves. She checked the time on her late husband's watch. The clockface swallowed half her arm and told her it was a quarter after nine. Surely they were open.

The unmuffled exhaust of a passing car vibrated through her chest, reminding her to pick up the pace. She didn't come this far to get kidnapped or god knows what in some back alley. Coral reached for the shop's door handle. The hinges groaned like her knees before it rained. She prepared herself for the worst. Morning light cut a swath across the pale-green tile like a knife. But instead of screams, the majestic Latin vocals of *O Fortuna* filtered through Coral's hearing aids. The shop's woodsy musk smelled vaguely familiar. She closed her eyes and reminisced over the wooden toy chest she'd passed down years ago. Coral sighed. So many treasures lost in that blasted fire. The heavenly aroma of espresso beans roused her senses. The morning breeze pressed against the back of her blouse, urging her forward. She steadied a hand against the metal doorframe and stepped inside.

No displays, bare walls. Good heavens. This was supposed to be an antique shop? Only a single piece of furniture centered the room—an aromatic red cedar table with piles of random stuff covering the top. From here, the closest thing that resembled the doll she'd come here to get was a three-foot-tall nutcracker—missing its mouth. Her friends must have misunderstood and sent her to a repair shop.

She'd come all this way for nothing.

Her eyes watered, but as she turned to leave, a ray of sunlight shone through the side window and reflected off the crystal-beaded curtain hanging across the back wall. The room came alive with a thousand tiny lights dancing to the music. Though she'd never been a believer in signs, even after the clouds shifted and the lights faded, the hope they ignited remained. In that moment, Coral realized the beads covered an opening to a back area. Perhaps she shouldn't judge a shop by its front room.

"Hello?" Hopefully her voice would carry over the music.

When no one responded, she propped a hand on the edge of the table and leaned over as though checking if someone occupied a bathroom stall. The only legs belonged to a metal barstool across the room. Surely, she hadn't made the trip only to discover they weren't actually open.

But then, who'd left the stereo on and the coffee percolating?

She shuffled around the table. Though overdue for new glasses, she swore she'd seen movement along the back wall, between two stacks of books. Probably the clerk, but this neighborhood threatened other possibilities. Coral prepared her purse and rounded the corner, ready to go down swinging if it came to it.

On top of the stool, a small figure perched like a gargoyle. Three people could have curled inside the red, hooded sweatshirt this person had pulled over their knees. The fringed edge skimmed the bare toes tapping the seat cushion to the beat of the music—no wonder Coral hadn't seen anyone before. Resembling a cave more than clothing, the hood was draped over their head.

The person leaned over the only uncluttered swatch of desk and was sketching a series of fine lines across crisp drawing paper. As the hood bobbed in time to the orchestra's crescendo, Coral noticed the Jackie-O sunglasses skimming what appeared to be a little girl's jaw.

A smile tugged at the edge of Coral's dentures. "'Scuse me, young lady."

A peculiar grin hinted at the girl's lips. Instead of answering, she hooked two porcelain teacups around her fingers, dropped her bare legs to the floor, and in one rocket shove, wheeled the stool at the coffeepot as it finished brewing. Two pours later, she added a stream of cream into one cup and plopped two lumps of sugar into the other. Before Coral could voice that her stomach couldn't handle dairy, the girl nestled the sugar cup into Coral's open palm and said, "Don't worry, I don't usually bite."

Coral chuckled. The cup's warmth and the girl's casual manner put her at ease. "Thank you . . ."

"Poppy, like the flower."

Coral blew at the layer of swirling steam and took a sip. Hints of vanilla greeted her tongue. "My, *Poppy like the flower*, this is good."

The girl responded by guzzling hers empty.

Coral blinked through her surprise. Young girls usually chose juice over bitter coffee—even with half a cup of cream.

Poppy poured herself a second helping. "If you think that's good, try my protein shake. Does *wonders* for the body." Her fine eyebrows wagged above the rim of the sunglasses.

"Thank you, dear, but the only wonder it'd give *my* body is gas."

"That depends. If it's something you need . . ." The rest of her words were drowned out by the caffeine and orchestra's crescendo.

Coral shifted her weight to her bad hip and winced. Though the conversation proved more interesting than her favorite gossip column, her joints told her she better get back to the hotel and rest. "Well, thank you, Poppy, but I believe I'm in the wrong place."

Poppy set her empty cup beside a romance novel and lofted herself back on top of the stool.

Coral nearly spilled her coffee. The cover featured a half-naked man in a forest, holding an ax, straddling a log . . . "Oh, my. It's been a long time since I've seen a body like . . . aren't you a little . . ."

"Young?" Poppy hiked her thumb at the beaded curtain. "I keep my fountain of youth in back." They both laughed until Poppy shook her head. "A fountain sure would be easier."

"You're telling me." Not her typical conversation with a young girl, until she realized that Poppy had yet to pull her left hand from the front pocket of her sweatshirt. Something about the way the girl avoided using it told Coral she shouldn't stare.

Poppy tucked her knees back inside the sweatshirt. "How'd you hear of this shop?"

"My Canasta friends."

"You're looking for something you need."

Coral nodded but gripped her purse as if opening it might close any real potential. As much as she wanted to cross the final item off her list, the answer might crush any hope she'd had of lifting her great-granddaughter's crushed spirits. Nothing put a smile on her face like that doll. Coral said a prayer, and, with a shaking hand, she pulled the photo from her purse and handed it over.

Poppy said nothing. Her glasses and hood masked any sign of recognition.

The longer Coral stared at the photo's reflection in the dark lenses, the more the image became distorted. Her eyes burned as she watched the doll's delicate features shift into a voodoo doll. She finally forced herself to blink, only to find the photo back in her own hand. Coral yelped and flung it like a hot potato.

"Oopsies!" Poppy pounced onto the perfectly normal-looking photo. She cocked her head, then shook it. "Nope. Nope. Nope."

Coral closed her eyes. Why had she thought this place would be different?

"It's just . . ." Poppy began, "I see your love for her and how much she loved that doll." The girl fisted her hands onto her hips. "Some people think they can come in here like they own the place. They don't listen to reason, love themselves more than . . ." She scooped the photo up and slipped it into Coral's fingers. "Don't get me started. Anyway, nothing in the back has ever been loved like that. I'm sure you'll find that doll, but it's new."

Surely not. Coral held the picture closer for the girl, as if *she* were the one with poor eyesight.

"That's the one," Poppy said. Before Coral could express her relief, the girl continued. "Did your friends mention the payment?"

It pained Coral to think some would see the vulnerable girl and not pay. "They said to bring something of value." Not exactly an indication of how much the doll would cost, but she opened her wallet to show she'd brought plenty of cash.

"Someone claiming printed paper means something—when actually, it means nothing without connection." Before Coral could object, Poppy yanked out a five and waved it around. "If I were to rip this up . . . what would you feel? The same emptiness your great-granddaughter felt when she lost what was most precious to her?"

"Don't be ridiculous." Lord, the girl had some awfully mature beliefs for someone so young. Coral wondered whose beliefs the girl was repeating. Goosebumps pricked her forearms. She didn't remember mentioning the doll being lost. A shiver rattled down her old bones.

Poppy gave the money back. "What good is ten or a hundred of those to me if none hold any value to you?"

Had she come all this way only to go home empty-handed? Her purse felt heavy and pointless. It flopped against the tile.

Poppy squatted, snatched the purse, and dumped out the contents of Coral's life: wallet, bucket list, spare napkins, hand sanitizer, and three half-filled crossword books. The girl frowned, and the music hushed to a dull murmur, as if her mood conducted the melody on cue. She cocked her head and grabbed Coral's wrist to check the time.

"Careful, that—"

The girl slipped her watch off in one fluid motion. Before Coral could protest, the girl pulled her left arm from her pocket for the first time. Her sweatshirt sleeve covered her hand past her fingertips. She rested the watch facedown, about where her palm should be.

Once Coral found her voice, she said, "A wedding present for my late husband, Gerald."

"This inscription . . ."

Dull from decades of wear, even under the best lighting, you had to tilt it to read the inscription, YOURS FOREVER.

"Forever's a long time," said Poppy.

"Feels like forever since . . . that watch is the only thing of his that didn't burn in the fire." Coral leaned against the wall to keep her legs from shaking. "I guess I needed it close because losing it meant losing the last piece of . . ."

Poppy stood and took her hands. In one hand, Coral held the vitality of youth. In the other, the warm round surface of the watch pressed against her palm, surrounded by a soft sweatshirt. The material brushed her skin like a whisper.

Coral prepared herself for the coming loss. In a final squeeze of agreement, horror crawled up her spine. Hidden beneath the girl's sleeve had to be little more than bones. For someone so young to find joy in helping others, Coral hoped something good would circle back to her soon.

Poppy slipped the watch into her pocket. "Stay on the path, and you'll find what you need." She guided Coral around the table and paused before the beaded curtain. "If you stray, you'll end up somewhere you might not want to be."

Coral gave her a small smile, a promise she need not worry. She walked through the beads. They tapped against her forehead, down her arms, and as Coral entered the hallway, relief washed away her grief. She welcomed the unexpected. The building hadn't seemed this large from the street, but her mind had been elsewhere at the time.

She refocused on the moment and on the narrow strip of red carpet that stretched from her to . . . she squinted . . . tried to force her eyes to adjust . . . well, she only drove in the daytime for a reason.

Metal bowls lined the edge where the carpet met the wood flooring. Tea lights floated within. Down the path, light and shadow danced like oil and water. From the darkness, the walls revealed wonders vying for her attention, only to slip away like a fleeting thought as she passed. This place resembled a museum more than an antique shop. First-edition novels, blown-glass perfume bottles, century-old bells and lamps tempted her to get a closer look. The misleading front room finally made sense. If the wrong people learned of the valuables here, there'd be trouble. She continued forward, the plush carpet easing the pressure on her hip.

"Poppy, dear," she called back. "You really should put these in a safe or at least behind glass." No response. She'd tell the girl on her way out.

Coral followed the runner to the end and paused to catch her breath at the velvet curtain. She drew the material aside to reveal a room with hundreds of shelves filled with dolls. The shades of hair, eye, and skin color . . . all handmade, without a single generic feature.

"You made it," Poppy noted from beside her.

Coral clutched her chest. "Good lord. Where did you come from?"

Poppy held up a blender as if that answered everything. Below the sunglasses, her lips formed a petite smile.

"My goodness, child. With all these dolls to play with, you must be the luckiest girl in the world to work here for your parents."

"No, your great-granddaughter is who's lucky. She has you." Poppy propped the blender against her hip. "Now, you sure I can't get you a smoothie before you leave?"

CUSTOMER TWO & THREE

Billy held the metal door open for Jenn. She brushed her fingertips down his arm and squeezed his elbow. He loved the way she thanked him almost as much as . . . well, everything about her. The brief *tink* from the bell overhead reminded him to wipe his steel-toe work boots before tracking half the construction site across the antique shop.

One whiff of vanilla bean and wood smoke brought back memories of their first night together at the cabin, five years ago today. Smooth jazz, the kind they'd slow-danced to that night, piped through wall speakers. The shop was nothing like he'd expected—he knew zero about antiques—but everything on the wooden table appeared old and important.

"Sweetie . . ." Jenn's brown eyes, dulled from exhaustion, held no hint of disappointment when she said, "this can't be the right place." She turned to leave.

They didn't have time to go anywhere else. Coordinating lunch breaks today had nearly taken an act of God. With the double shifts she'd been working to keep the diner open, who knew the last time Jenn had sat down—she probably didn't. He wanted to get her something that would remind her that even after her toughest days, when she came home from a double shift smelling of ketchup and grease with bits of food stuck in her curls, that she'd always be the best part of his day. Billy swore if his little bro had suggested this place to mess with him . . .

He drew in a breath. Maybe he needed his own reminder to stay positive. "Give it a chance. They're probably remodeling."

Jenn checked her watch, then craned her neck as if that would help her see past the beads hanging across the back wall. "Think they're out to lunch, too?"

"And leave the door unlocked in *this* neighborhood? Probably didn't hear us come in." He doubted anyone could have over the saxophone solo.

They wandered around the table. Jenn peered in boxes while he scanned the mounds of not-so-gently used items. Everything appeared so used and loved that anything he bought would likely fall apart before making it back home. He began to think she'd been right about being in the wrong place.

After a lap and a half around the room, he concluded the only thing not piled on the desk was a bell. A drawing caught his attention, and he propped a hip onto the nearby stool. It squeaked beneath his weight as he leaned over the sketch. The maze of lines reminded him of those illusion pictures where you knew there was more to it. Once his mind separated the image into three people, any other possibilities faded. The lanky figure curled against the left margin appeared finished except for an arm. Billy couldn't be sure the sketch on the right was a person at all. A watch rested across the center drawing. Billy considered moving it to get a better look.

Jenn slid beside him and nudged the watch aside. "Whoa, creepy." She pointed to the man's eyes or lack thereof.

"Might be a shadow or . . ." Billy leaned in to get a closer view, but movement behind the beaded curtain stole his attention.

A young girl burst into the room with a wicker picnic basket swinging in the crook of one arm. When his brother had told him a girl named Poppy ran the shop, Billy hadn't considered he'd meant a *little* girl. She wore a red sweatshirt like a dress, the hood draped over her hair.

"Hi there," she piped and set the basket beside the drawing. Her stomach growled like a feral animal. "Yeah, yeah. I'm—" Another low rumble interrupted her. She pulled a blender from the basket. "Shhh. I'm working on it."

While the girl unrolled the plug, Jenn tied and retied her apron. Who knew the last time she'd stood this still? He placed a hand over hers and squeezed.

"Aww." The girl studied him through her gigantic sunglasses. "Say, have you been here before?"

"My brother came here a few months back." Billy gave Jenn's waist a little squeeze. "Said it'd be the best place to get something special for my girl here." Given his brother still found baseball cards to be special, Billy should have been more specific. He rubbed his neck, still warm from the midday sun.

"Don't worry. What you need is in the back."

"Mind if I take a peek'n see what you've got? My lunch break is already half over."

"Honey, don't go taking food from children."

Jenn chuckled then stepped beside the beaded curtain. "As in, I'd like to look around the back of the store." She twirled a strand of beads around her ring finger.

"Go ahead." The girl opened the basket's lid and dropped a scoop of ice into the blender. "Stay on the path, all the way to the end. Don't wander or you'll end up somewhere you don't want to be." The back of Jenn's apron disappeared from the room before the girl had finished.

Billy lowered his voice and leaned over the stool. "I don't have a lot of money, but—" The sharp scent of iron and copper hit his nose like a wrecking ball. "Whew!" He backed away from the basket. "Have you checked the expiration date on . . . whatever that is?"

She added ingredients like a pro. "Just an old family recipe for stew. Think of it as a protein shake but with—"

A noise from the back jarred their conversation. Poppy whipped her head toward the curtain. Her hood flipped up revealing wild, blond curls. Another creak of floorboards. Poppy spun around in her chair, grabbed his shirt, and pulled him down to her level. He couldn't see her eyes through the blackout lenses. Instead, his reflection stared back and elongated like a funhouse mirror.

"Do you love her?"

"Hhhh . . ." He tried to make his mouth work but his brain refused to focus on anything besides her trippy glasses. "Hellll . . . yeah."

"Then I can't—" Her stomach growled—or maybe it was her—and she shoved him away. "Go. Help her stay on the path."

Billy couldn't ignore her warning if he'd tried. He dashed through the opening. Beads slapped his forehead like bugs on a windshield. Her words vibrated through him like a jackhammer. His brain clicked on again, and he realized Poppy had turned on the blender.

Halfway down the hallway, Jenn stood, one foot on the brick-red carpet runner, the other on the wooden floor. His long legs closed the distance. Candlelight played across Jenn's curls. Her narrow fingers reached for something shiny on the wall, but he snagged the knot of her apron and pulled her back onto the carpet and into his arms. "Thank *God*."

"Hey now." Jenn leaned back to study him. "You okay?"

"Yeah. I just . . ." He tried to remember why he'd been so desperate to get to her. "Love you."

She motioned to her left. "Look, honey, they have baseball cards. Your brother's birthday is next month."

"Come on." He took her hand that fit so perfectly in his. "We're short on time, remember?" Besides, one glance of the rare sports memorabilia told him they'd have to stick to the bargain section in the back.

They paused at the end of the hallway. Jenn leaned into him. "And we're waiting for . . ."

"You both made it," Poppy announced beside them.

Billy yelped, then tried to disguise it by clearing his throat.

"I saw that, Mr. Overreactor." Jenn bumped his hip. "Frightened by a little girl?"

"Think so, huh?" he teased back. "Your 'window shopping' will be the death of me."

Poppy doubled over. Her curls spilled down her face.

"Are you okay?" He *knew* whatever she'd put in that drink hadn't smelled right. "We should get you to—"

The girl flung her head back in a fit of laughter.

Jenn tried to cover her mouth but couldn't hide her smile lines.

"You too? Like you have any idea what's so funny?"

"You're smiling too." Jenn slipped through the velvet curtain and screamed.

Billy flung the curtain wide and lunged in front of Jenn, ready to . . . he blinked. "What . . . why'd you . . ." The room was empty except for a few dozen small boxes displayed on glass-top tables. In the tone she'd used on him, he said, *"I saw that, Miss Over—"*

Jenn dashed to the closest table. "Oh, Billy!" She bubbled like a kid, but one glimpse inside the velvet box told him this was no candy store.

He swallowed and tried to imagine the boxes holding something, anything besides rings. He'd give an arm to marry Jenn, but dangling a room full of promises he could never afford was plain cruel. With the way they sparkled beneath the overhead lights, the least expensive one likely cost more than he made in a year. The rising lump in his throat only made it too real.

"Oh, Billy." Jenn hugged his neck then bounced over to the next table.

There had to be a way to salvage this that wouldn't break Jenn's heart. He shoved his hand into the pocket of his work jeans, found the smooth edge of his worry stone, and rubbed his calloused thumb across the worn surface.

Poppy strolled beside him and studied Jenn. The point of the girl's hood attempted to reach his shoulder. Did she work here alone? All this jewelry . . . and no guard. Where were her parents? There were child labor laws. Billy lowered his voice. "How old are you?"

Jenn sighed. "Leave the girl alone."

Instead of answering him, Poppy hopped onto the nearest table. She leaned forward until his focus switched from her to the image of himself in her sunglasses. "Are you a gentleman?" she asked.

Not even close to the response he'd expected. "I'd like to think so."

"Wonderful, then you know better to ask a lady her age." Satisfied, she sat back on her heels. "Ever been to a garage sale?"

"It's . . . been a while." Though no doubt he knew more about them than where this conversation headed.

"You find what you like, but they're asking nearly full price for something used. Why?"

He shrugged. "They're greedy. Want to get their money back."

Jenn picked up a box she'd been ogling and slipped on a ring. "Or they have an emotional attachment and don't actually want to let it go."

Billy hoped she was answering the question and not referring to the ring she'd yet to remove. "But not everyone can afford what they're asking, even if it is worth the price."

Poppy pointed to the wall. "What would you pay for that painting?"

He hadn't noticed the palm-sized splatter print on the back wall. He was gentle in case it was hers. "Ten, maybe twenty dollars."

Poppy grinned. "You're quite generous. What if I said it had inspired me to draw?"

"It'd be priceless to you, but that's not how things work."

"Just because that's how things have always been done doesn't make it the best way." Poppy tapped a finger against her cheek. "I can tell how much you love each other. Tell you what." She gestured to the room. "Trade something of value and you won't have to pay an arm and a leg."

Jenn smiled at him as if he'd given her the world. She held her left hand out for him to take. On that special finger, she now wore a tear-shaped ruby on a simple silver band.

"Ah." The girl leaned in like a secret. "That's my favorite, too." Poppy nodded like they'd struck a deal, but before he objected, she said, "So, let's see what you have of value."

Billy reached back for his wallet, but the fifty bucks he'd been saving for today now seemed like a bad joke.

"Your other pocket." Poppy held up her hand, palm up. "This isn't a robbery."

Might as well amuse the girl once more before breaking it to them both that lunch was nearly over. From his right front pocket, he pulled two mint wrappers and a receipt for insufficient funds. From the other, three dimes, a penny, and his grandfather's worry stone.

Jenn sighed and thanked the girl for her time. With only a fleeting air of disappointment, she pulled the ring from her finger and held it out for the girl.

Poppy ignored her and took the worry stone. She held it up like a precious gem, then dropped it into the front pocket of her sweatshirt. "One rock for another."

Jenn's eyes glistened. "Wait, what?"

Billy took the ring from her. "I believe I'm the one with the question. . . ." Her happy tears always made him weak in the knees, so he took one. Whatever came out of his mouth next must have been the right thing.

Jenn had him back on his feet and wrapped her arms around his neck. "Though you might need that worry stone more now than ever."

"He found his true love," said Poppy. "There's nothing to worry about."

Jenn gave him a salty kiss.

He rested his forehead against hers. "Probably shouldn't do that in front of . . ."

The girl in red had disappeared.

❧

CUSTOMER FOUR

There was something to be said about a creature of habit. Randyl hadn't planned to ghost his usual haunts, but until he landed a big score to pay off his debt, living meant lying low. Randyl had grown accustomed to others knowing what he wanted.

He huffed and tipped the plastic menu down—like playing a royal flush to an empty room. Randyl wondered if the waitress made it her habit to flit about the diner and flash her cheap engagement ring to every patron and their mother.

Randyl ran a palm down his mustache, knew it was his annoyance tell. He prided himself as a master of tells—seeing through people, hiding his true nature—but that sort of thing didn't matter here, not when he could eat a whole cow.

Did she *actually* think any of these poor saps gave a rip about costume jewelry? He unrolled his silverware. A butter knife. How quaint. He flapped the flimsy napkin like he planned to control a bull and bumped the useless utensil off the table. "Whoops." The knife clattered against the tile and stripped the buzzing diner of sound like a switch. Anyone else would take the dozen over-the-shoulder stares as a cue to apologize and scurry to pick it up. Randyl made no move. Clearly, she needed the chance to do her job.

From across the room, the waitress gave him a pleasant smile, power walked her way on over, scooped up the silverware, and replaced it with another from her apron. "Here you go. Can I get you a water?"

"Just your best cut of meat." He considered the joint, then added, "Whatever you've got that takes a real steak knife."

"How you want that cooked?"

"Ever heard a cow moo?"

She brushed her hand across the wrinkles of her apron—a clear tell that he better keep the annoyance out of his voice if he wanted his food spit-free.

Randyl eased back in the booth and flashed his pearly whites, waiting until he held her full attention.

No one could resist his baby blues.

She relaxed and pulled a pad of paper from her pocket—as if she couldn't keep a single thought in her head beyond that ring of hers. The midday sun shone through the window. She raised the pad to shield her eyes. Randyl wasn't one to get distracted by average shiny things, and that ruby refused to be ignored. His heart fluttered.

"Nice rock you've got there." Real, too. If her man's that loaded, why the hell did she work here?

"Funny you should say that. My boyfr—" She giggled and fanned herself with the pad. "—fiancé. That's exactly how he paid." She told Randyl about the shop down the block run by a little girl. He hadn't hung onto every word from a woman so intently since . . . huh, he'd have to think on that one. Paying with a *rock?* No doubt he better visit the shop himself before the girl's parents came back, and he had just the thing for payment.

"Well, congrats." He held up the butter knife. Clearly, he'd require something sharper. "Now, how about that steak? Extra bloody."

Twenty minutes later, Randyl had his tools of the trade—glass breaker, leather gloves, lock pick—in his to-go sack. He fished out a special velvet sack from his glove box, slipped it into his jacket's front pocket, and headed toward the antique shop.

He suppressed the urge to quicken his pace as he passed the

diner. Inside, the waitress dealt a round of waters to a table like a poker game. She noticed him and waved. His lips curled into a smile, and through his teeth, he said, "That's right, just out for an evening stroll. Nothing to see." Her ring sparkled beneath the fluorescents. Randyl let out a low wolf whistle and raised the to-go sack in salute.

Dusk spread across the sidewalk like it had somewhere to be. Randyl closed his coat — no sense in getting robbed. Streetlamps flicked on as he strolled into the antique shop.

The bell over the door announced his arrival like an alarm. The unexpected noise shot through his skull like it'd used his head as the clapper. He tripped over the doorframe and landed on his knees with a *thunk*.

Randyl stared at the gray-flecked tile until his ears stopped ringing. He stood and rolled with it. It'd been a while since he'd used the disarming clumsy professor persona. From his side pocket, he pulled out a pair of thick-framed glasses and slid them on.

Whiskey and unlit cigars filtered through his mustache. The tantalizing scents made him think of back rooms, shuffling cards, and stacked decks.

The only sound came from the far side of the table. *Sqreek. Reeek. Sqreek. Reeek.* The shifting whine of grinding metal made his forearm hair stand. He reminded himself that hesitation led to failure, so he headed toward the hanging beads.

There, a little girl swiveled back and forth on top a bar stool, drawing a complex picture. He couldn't imagine why she wore sunglasses this late, or inside. Maybe the kid was blind, except, even with her other hand buried in the front pocket of her sweatshirt, she drew with a careful touch. This had to be the girl the waitress spoke of — even younger than he'd expected.

Randyl cleared his throat. His gruff voice served no use here. "Hello, Little Miss. Is there an adult around?"

The stool answered, *sqreeek, reeek.*

Without acknowledging him, she dropped her pen and

reached for a tall glass of a berry-red drink. She gulped mouthfuls though the straw the way he scarfed down a choice cut of meat.

Hadn't she heard his question? Randyl wanted to grab her shoulders and shake them until she stopped that incessant swinging.

Her mouth curved into an innocent smile. "No worries. I can handle you." The girl's words held a confidence of someone well past puberty, but one look at her said otherwise.

Just her—as he'd hoped. He'd made the right call going with the professor. Randyl furrowed his brow and laced his words with an air of concern. "You're in a rough neighborhood."

She shrugged and inked the final lines of her drawing.

He got a look at it for the first time. "Are those people in . . ."

"Coffins," she chirped.

A chill wound up his spine. Something about the middle figure caught his attention. Randyl shivered as though all heat had been sucked from the room. The drawing held an uncanny resemblance to himself, only, the eyes had been replaced by two gaping holes.

Sqreeeeeek. Reeeeeek.

He had to hurry this along before the noise drove him insane. Handy that her drawing stripped any hesitation for what he had planned. Randyl snatched the velvet bag from his pocket with a flourish. "I hear you're interested in things with value."

"Not exactly. See I . . ."

The chair drowned out her chattering. He'd be thankful of that if the infernal thing wasn't also short-circuiting his brain, making it impossible to choose the best cards for this plan and . . .

SQREEEEEK. REEEEEK. SQREEE—

He grabbed the edge of the seat and squinted at the beaded curtain behind her—as if his thick glasses weren't as fake as the gems in his velvet bag. "Are you sure there's no one back there?" He paused. "I could have sworn I saw something."

Her petite brows knitted together. She turned to see for herself.

Randyl dumped the gems onto the drawing pad. "Oh, gosh." He tripped and reached out to keep from falling. Instead of the table, he caught the edge of the drawing pad, catapulting the gems into the air like a firework finale.

"How clumsy of me." He held a hand out to help, then froze for effect. "You sure there's no one else here? I swear I saw something moving." Ignoring her assurances, he said, "Do you have a back door?"

"Yes."

Perfect. "Someone could have snuck in." He squinted through the glasses again. "I doubt my useless eyes will see those gems."

"Useless?" She tsked and leaned toward him. "Hasn't anyone told you what nice eyes you have?"

Time to get away from this crazy brat. He pointed to the back. "I'll go double-check for you. Wait here."

She replied with something about the path and getting what he needed, but she need not worry her pretty hooded head, he planned to get exactly what he needed. Past the beads, one look at the hallway and Randyl almost dropped the to-go sack—that he now wished was ten times larger. Stacks of pull-tabs, rows of vintage poker chips and playing cards. Considering the neighborhood, how had no one swiped all this before now?

He stepped on the hardwood. The board beneath his polished loafer groaned its protest. Randyl froze and checked the beaded curtain for a sign of the girl. Either he could shift his weight back and try for something else, or . . . realization smacked him in the face. What did he think a fifty-pound girl would do? He chuckled and removed the glasses. Shame to cover his best feature.

Randyl started with a set of perfectly balanced straight edged steak knives. The box must have been there for a while. He huffed and blew off a layer of dust. In less than a minute, he held his heaven in a to-go sack.

Temptation itched at his neck to fill his coat pockets. He pawed at his collar and decided to leave space for the good stuff in the back. Considering this appetizer, Randyl salivated with anticipation of the main course. The girl still hadn't checked on him. Oh, to be young and naïve. All the easier for him to slip out the back. He tucked the sack beneath his arm.

Randyl pushed the heavy curtain aside and stepped into blackness. His heart rate picked up, and he reminded himself he wasn't in some back-alley, outnumbered with another deal going south. He probed for a light switch, but his fingers only found a smooth wall that extended higher than he could reach.

Randyl shuffled back the other way, searching for the curtain with his free hand, but found another wall. Where the hell was that opening? He set the sack down and felt around with both hands, careful to follow along the surface until he found the next wall, then another . . . his breath quickened, and an unexpected stench made him wonder if he'd stepped into a porta-potty.

Track lighting flickered on overhead. A pile of clothing lay on the floor beside him, like some idiot left out their laundry. On the right, a haggard man faced away, cradling something. His shirtless body swayed back and forth as if he sat in a rocking chair.

Randyl growled. The little brat had tricked him.

The man didn't seem to notice him yet, which meant he could still make it out the back door. Randyl squinted until his eyes adjusted in the dim light. He recognized his sack near the pile of clothes. With one eye on the man behind him, Randyl reached for it and rammed his fingers into something solid. His sack, filled with valuables worth ten times his debt, waited for him on the other side of a glass wall—that he swore hadn't been there moments before.

"You strayed from the path."

Randyl spun.

The little brat leaned against the back wall sipping that drink, five feet from him.

"I warrrned youuu," she sang. "I give the disclaimer to everyone. This shop . . ." She placed an affectionate hand against the bricks behind her and smiled as if she spoke of an old friend. "It helps people find what they need . . . for a price." The corners of her lips curled until her innocent face transformed into a formidable grin.

She had played him like a shark. Randyl lunged at her and nearly bashed his brains against the glass wall she stood behind. His shoulder slammed into the hard surface.

Instead of flinching, she leaned in. Her sunglasses reflected his image like a mirror.

"Look, you little brat, I paid you."

She giggled and bobbed her head side to side. "Real. Fake. Real. Fake. It doesn't matter."

Randyl pounded his palm against it—right at her smug face. Money always mattered. She walked around what he now realized was a glass cage. "Hey, little brat, you better—"

"Everyone who comes to the shop gives up what they treasure most for someone else." The girl strolled over to his to-go sack.

"Don't you touch—"

She scooped it up like a loose ball and checked the contents. She grabbed his glass breaker and twirled it like a baton. "You only care about yourself."

"Fine." He gritted his teeth. "You got your crap back. Let me out of here."

She sighed and tossed the sack to the concrete as though the priceless contents held no value to her. For the first time, she pulled her left hand from her front pocket, along with a metal scoop. She toasted Randyl with the half-empty cup. Thick veins bulged across her newly exposed hand. If he'd seen the hand alone, he would have sworn the disgusting thing belonged to an old hag.

"G-g-give . . ."

Randyl turned to see the man lean against the far side of the cage and pivot his body to face the girl. Where his left arm should have been, there was a long gash from shoulder to ribs. Blood trickled from the staples holding his puckered flesh together.

"What the hell happened to him?" Randyl barked.

The girl tipped the cup. She scooped the drink down her throat with her decrepit hand. The finger bones jabbed at her transparent skin.

"G-give . . . it . . ." The man's jaw shook. He reached out to her with his remaining arm and grabbed at the air.

The man tried to stand. Staples pulled and ripped through his skin like freshly grated cheese. He sobbed and grasped the wound. "Give it b-back!" Blood streamed over his knuckles and streaked across the concrete.

Bile surged up Randyl's throat.

The man slipped in his own blood. His face slammed into the concrete with a wet *thunk*. Randyl shuffled back in time to keep the man from splattering across his favorite pair of argyle socks. His heel caught something solid, and he tripped backward. Randyl's shoulder crashed against the floor. Black spots swam across his vision.

A blood-curdling wail vibrated through his bones. Randyl sat up like a whip. Had that come from him? His attention darted from the girl's unreadable gaze to the unconscious man, to the mound of laundry Randyl just tripped over. What the hell had—

Beneath Randyl's legs, the folds of clothing twitched. At least, he thought they had. He leaned in. The violent stench of urine and filth made his stomach heave. He re-swallowed the bits of steak and grimaced at the unconscious man. Had the guy used this as his toilet? Spread it out some and it could have been a bed . . . Randyl tapped the mound with the toe of his shoe.

A hand appeared from the folds of clothing. Long fingers reached for his argyle sock.

"Oh, God." Randyl scurried to his feet. "What the . . . ?"

The fingers recoiled and disappeared.

From where he stood, Randyl could make out the curled up form beneath a faded hoodie and jeans. A ring of red circled the upper thighs. From there to where the ankles should have been, the pants lay flat. Dirt clung to the frayed bottom edge, probably from the day the person walked in here . . .

The hair standing on the back of Randyl's neck screamed at him to do whatever it took to get the hell out of this place. He went to the girl and dropped to his knees. "Come on. You have them. You don't need me."

"You ignored my warning. Didn't stay on the path."

He pressed his palms against the glass and studied her expression, her movements—something that would tell him how to play this out. "Please, let me go."

"Everyone who comes in must give up what they value most for someone else."

"Trust me, I've never valued anything more than what's in that sack. I'll leave it all." He gritted his teeth and bowed his head. "And I'll owe you." The last thing he needed was another debt to pay. "Or, I can work for you."

"The only person you care about is *you*." She tapped the glass at his nose. "But don't you worry. You'll help me watch over this place for years to come."

Randyl refused to fold. He lifted his chin and doubled down with his baby blues.

She slurped the final sip of her drink. Her hand plumped, and the lines softened until it shifted to a child's. She hooked her new finger around the edge of her sunglasses and dropped them into the sack. Where her pupils should be, a blanket of milky film stared back at him. "My, what nice eyes you have."

. . .

Joy Auburn has a BFA, MBA, and she has ghostwritten novels for a USA Today bestselling author. In 2019, she placed Silver Honorable Mention in the Writers of the Future contest. Her short stories have appeared in several anthologies published by WordFire Press. Joy owns Prolific Ink LLC, the publisher of this anthology, and she offers an array of services in the publishing industry. For more information visit www.prolific.ink and www.joyauburn.com.

THE LEDGER

MARTIN L. SHOEMAKER

THE LEDGER

Ari Morios didn't look up as The Shape entered through the locked door of the shop.

In thirty-seven years, Ari had not once looked up at The Shape during its annual visits. The cowardice shamed him, but he didn't have the will to look at his master.

Instead, Ari remained seated on the old leather-covered barstool behind his glass-top counter, as if the books and pots and clay figures could shelter him. The bell over the door made no sound. The old clock behind the counter sounded muffled as if the air thickened in the presence of The Shape. Ari's eyes remained fixed on the black leather-bound Ledger that lay open upon the glass. He didn't have to look up. He could feel The Shape. It was time for the Accounting.

But The Shape was in no hurry. It hovered around the shop, passing from shelf to shelf as if inspecting the goods. Books, of course, but also a wide range of curios in no particular order. China dishes. Candlesticks. Pewter figurines. Geodes. A brass harmonica. A corncob pipe. Antique dolls in faded clothes. A football trophy. Onyx bookends, shaped like elephants. A golden canary cage. And more, so much more that Ari forgot his own inventory.

Occasionally The Shape paused and mumbled in an arcane language that Ari had never been able to place. He had tried to identify the language, years ago, but to no avail. The voice would not record—just as The Shape would not photograph—and Ari could only reproduce a few words of what he had heard. What little he had written down, none of his contacts had recognized. Before Scott had . . . been lost, he had claimed it was pre-human.

Scott, of all people, should have known better than to deal with Ari. Scott had tangled with and beaten demonic forces for more than fifty years. Scott should've known that there is no winning the Bargain. But Scott had wanted a few more years for his wife.

And when they want it badly enough, they all come to Morios.

"All of them," The Shape said from just across the counter, and Ari jolted. He hadn't realized it had gotten so close. If he had looked up . . .

"Go ahead," The Shape said. "You have earned the right to look upon your master."

Ari shook his head, peering even more intently at the Ledger. "He almost beat you."

"He made a very good try," The Shape said, its voice shaking the glass counter. Then in a lower tone, it continued. "He was almost amusing. He knew words and sigils that I have not encountered in over three centuries. The barrier he raised was truly impenetrable. I could not touch him."

"But you could touch Frieda."

"But I could touch Frieda. And that was his mistake. Once, she had been purer than he, truly beyond my reach. And even at the end, she belonged to the Adversary. I could not claim her."

"But because of the taint of the pestle he used to grind her medicines . . ."

"The pestle that you sold him."

". . . because of the taint, you could touch her."

"And make her scream . . . Such glorious agony . . . And I

could not take her, but neither could the Adversary. It was not her time."

"And so he broke the sigils so that you could claim him and leave her."

The Shape's laugh boomed throughout the shop, knocking a porcelain eye off the nearest shelf. "Cleverness is such a tasty vice. When I crush it and drink it, it is sweeter than the blood of a newborn babe. You maggots think that you can outwit me. If after fifty thousand years the Adversary still has not caught me, what chance have any of you?"

None, Ari knew, but he refused to say it out loud.

But he didn't have to. The Shape knew. It chuckled low in its darkness. "I especially enjoyed the look on your face. The look of shame, it suits you so well. You knew that in the end, Scott did what you could not, Morios."

Ari squeezed his eyes shut, but tears leaked out despite himself. Scott had been his friend, and The Shape had made Ari watch Scott's destruction. It often made Ari stand witness to the fulfillment of a Bargain. Just a reminder, it had said once, of your inevitable fate. And it will be sooner if you displease me.

"I shall not," Ari said quietly, as if answering the long-ago admonition.

But The Shape answered as if the pause of years had never happened. "Then you shall have more time. Enough to make any other maggot envious."

If they only knew . . . Ari thought.

"But it is time," The Shape continued. "Give me the Accounting for this year."

Ari turned from the first page of the Ledger, with its single line of text, all the way to the last. There were still five lines upon that page that had not been crossed off. Ari turned back a page. That one had three.

"Come, come," The Shape said. "I might have all eternity, but you do not."

Ari thumbed back one more page. Every name there had

been crossed off, the Bargains complete. He turned forward again.

"Here it is," he said, "the latest open page."

"Then read it to me."

Ari looked for the first open line on the page, and he checked: yes, it had a closing date. He read aloud. "William Sackrison, a bronze harp, the gift of soothing. Died May 4, at the hands of a jealous musician and former lover." As he read the line, he drew a stroke through it.

"And the harp?"

"Still in her possession." Ari paged forward, and he found her name on the last page. "Veronica Miles, Bargain still open."

"Continue."

Ari returned to the line under Sackrison's. "Adrienne Lang . . ." Despite himself, Ari's mind turned back to Lang. He had witnessed the closing of her Bargain. She had felt unsafe, had sought a weapon that would protect her against any danger in the world. But in the end, it hadn't protected her against itself. It had turned on her in a weak moment and had sliced her stomach open. Ari might have saved her by simply calling an ambulance. But he hadn't dared. He told himself that there wouldn't have been enough time anyway, and he scratched out her line.

And so he continued through the list of Bargains that had closed in the past year. Dumont Stevens, a ring to woo away the wife of a rival. Dead from despair when she committed suicide. Hannah Grace, a mirror to bring her beauty to match her name. Killed when a thief shattered the mirror. Peter Rivers, a safe that filled with gems each night. Dead in a fire, trying to pull the safe from the wall.

And these were only the deaths he had witnessed. Nearly forty of those. Threescore more he had been fortunate not to see.

When Ari was done, The Shape gave out a hum, perhaps of contentment.

"You are a most excellent servant, Morios," it said. "You have held up your part of your Bargain for another year. Another year of life I grant you."

In the earliest days, back when The Shape had still worn a pleasing human form, Ari had thanked it for each year. But now there was no pretense between them. He was a slave, The Shape was his master, and there was no gratitude to be found.

After a pause, as if waiting for an answer, The Shape continued. "In fact, you are by far the most productive of my merchants."

At that, Ari almost looked up. "You have . . . others?"

The Shape leaned close. "You are no fool. This is not news to you."

It was not. Ari had suspected. But he had not known for sure, and this was the first time The Shape had admitted as much.

"This world is very large," The Shape continued. "And populous. Nearly seven billion of you maggots now, not counting those long past. And a good number of you have delivered themselves to me long ago. Mostly through deeds, but some through words or intentions so vile that it is merely a matter of time. The Adversary has given up on them."

"And some . . ." Ari said.

"Yes, you can say it: some are just as truly committed to the Adversary as mine are to me. They're not worth my time, except when I can use them as levers, like your friend Frieda. And some, of course, are special cases. Valuable. Influencers. For those, I spare my personal attention. Even one such as I has only so much time to work. You should feel honored that I give you part of a night each year."

Ari did not answer. Honored, cursed. The word didn't matter.

"But some . . . Some are on the edge, and they can be coaxed. Tempted to fall to me with the right incentive. And so my merchants can earn a little favor in the hereafter by helping to deliver others unto me."

"Deliver, yes," Ari said. "But why do we have to witness . . . ?"

"Because I wish it!" The Shape paused as if gathering its temper. "And because you are mine to command. And because I want you to understand what you do."

Ari understood. God help them—but he could not even think that. He was beyond that help, as were they. He had witnessed enough Bargains ending to know what awaited the Bargainer. The exact form of their corporeal punishment varied from Bargain to Bargain, but at the end, there was always the rush of the flames and the shriek of pain and fear that echoed in his ears weeks after. It still echoed in his dreams at night.

The Shape's tone lightened. "Do not feel so bad. I promised you another year. As long as you fulfill your side of the Bargain, I always fulfill mine. You should know that by now."

"I know."

"And you keep it so well." The Shape paused, then continued in a more serious tone. "Do you have some secret?"

Ari shook his head. "No."

The Shape gasped. "You do! You have a secret, a . . . sales technique."

"No." Ari shook his head more firmly, desperate to evade the questions. "I just sell them what they want."

"You know . . ."

"No!"

"You . . . know . . . You understand the Bargain. That is how you snare them. You know."

Ari sank into the stool back, trembling. He couldn't. If he said the secret out loud, he could no longer deny it to himself.

"Say it!"

"The secret . . ."

"Say. It."

"The secret . . . is there are no curses. All of these trinkets and baubles. I don't even try to find them anymore. Whatever I can find in the trash is sufficient. You lied to me all along. There are no curses, there never were."

"No, Morios. There are curses. Say it. The rest of it."

"They . . . bring their curses with them. They already think they're damned. They could be saved, but they don't believe it."

"And so they come here willingly."

"They come here. And they find . . . they find a focus. Something that in their mind represents their curse, and the meager power that soothes their consciences and says they're getting something for their souls."

"Very good, Morios. All I have to do is meet their expectations, let their curse manifest in its focus."

"If they just walked away from it . . . just . . . turned it down . . ."

"They could still be saved. The Adversary would see them turn away from temptation. He would smile upon their contrition and give them one more chance. He is so fond of last chances."

"And you . . . convince them that their chances are gone."

"With your help, Morios. You are exactly what they expect."

"Yes. Curse me, I am. The wizened old man running a mysterious shop full of antiques and treasures. And pointing them . . . toward the thing they really want . . ."

"Toward the focus of their self-hatred."

"Yes . . . I give . . . a little push . . ."

"But you console yourself that they take the final steps. They sign the Ledger. That they had a choice, you did not force it upon them."

Ari remained silent. If he did not say it aloud, he could still believe the lie. For one more year.

But The Shape was cruel, as Ari knew too well. "What if I told you that they would turn away without your little push?" Ari's eyes grew wide, his head spun, and The Shape cackled. "Would that be too much for you to bear? To know that each damned one in your Ledger had your name inscribed upon their souls?"

"No. They have . . . free will."

"Yes. Curse the Adversary for that creation above all. You maggots have never known how to use free will responsibly. But yes, they have free will. As do you, Morios. Any time their souls trouble your conscience, you simply need to shutter your doors. Turn them away. And who knows what souls you might save?"

Ari said nothing.

"Well?"

In the silence, Ari heard the old clock ticking as if from a great distance.

Finally, The Shape spoke again. "Very well. I will take that as assent. Another year . . . unless you decide to close the Bargain."

Ari could feel The Shape leave, but he still did not dare look up from the Ledger. He stared at the names, particularly those that had not been crossed out yet. He wondered which he might witness next. He wondered how many more names he would add.

How long Ari sat there, he could not say. At last a tapping at the window drew his eyes up until they met those of a young blonde girl. Late teens, maybe, too young to be out on these streets at this time of night. But Ari was not her parent. Who was he to tell her?

The girl pointed down at the window, toward a string of pearls on a stand. Her pale blue eyes were wide and watery in her thin, bony face. She looked small, frail, in need of . . . protection. Not one of the curios from Ari's shop.

Ari dropped down from the stool, limping out from behind the counter and up to the door. Leaving the chain in place, he unlocked the deadbolt and pulled the door open a crack. "I'm sorry. We're closed. You should . . . You should go home."

The girl came up to the crack of the door. "But I . . . Those pearls. I want them. I . . . I can pay . . ."

Ari shook his head. What had brought a girl like this to his shop? She looked too young to be ready to give up on her soul already. Too . . . No, not innocent. Ari knew that innocence passed quickly these days. But she shouldn't be hopeless. Not this soon.

"You can't pay what these cost," he said.

"But I can. I . . ." She batted her eyes at him.

Once a younger Ari might have found that seductive. Now . . . It tore at his heartstrings. "Please . . . Go home . . ."

Ari moved to close the door, but at that instant, a breeze blew in, disturbing the dust on the shelves and flipping the pages of the Ledger back. Back to the very first page, the one with a single name, not crossed out: Aristos Morios, one Ledger.

Ari sighed. He heard the crackle of hellfire and the screams. And he unlocked the door.

Martin L. Shoemaker is a programmer who writes on the side . . . or maybe it's the other way around. Programming pays the bills, but a second place story in the Jim Baen Memorial Writing Contest earned him lunch with Buzz Aldrin. His work has appeared in *Analog*, *Galaxy's Edge*, *Digital Science Fiction*, *Forever* magazine, and *Writers of the Future* 31. He received the WSFA Small Press Award for his Clarkesworld story "Today I Am Paul," which also appeared in four year's best anthologies and eight translations. The story continues in *Today I Am Carey*, coming from Baen. Learn more at http://Shoemaker.Space.

SLEIGHT OF HAND

JESSICA GUERNSEY

SLEIGHT OF HAND

"Do you understand what tertiary means, Matthew?" the tiny man asked looking over his fashionably broad glasses.

Matthew sighed. No use trying to explain again to the uppity curator that his undergraduate degree was in art history. This guy didn't care; his name was Michel, for Pete's sake. He had a glint in his squinty hipster eyes when seeing Matthew miserable. The only reason Matthew stayed was because Imogene, his fiancée, positively purred over the new gallery in town.

One glance at Imogene beside him, one squeeze of her hand on his arm, and his heart sped up for different reasons. She was gorgeous. Beyond beautiful, left pretty in the dust. Blonde, blue-eyed, perfectly proportioned. And every inch of her was coated in designer goods. If she wanted something from "that darling antique art gallery," then Matthew would get it. Shoot, if she wanted the Ark of the Covenant, he'd battle Indiana Jones just to see her smile.

"Isn't it awe-inspiring, Matthew?" She ran one lacquered nail down the edge of the glass, then she turned that smile on him and his frustration melted into a puddle at her feet.

Awe-inspiring wasn't his first thought; more like awe-ful.

Imogene gazed into the block of glass about the size of a shoebox standing on one end. Inside was a severed, withered hand. Not a real hand, the curator had sniffed at Matthew over that question. It was wax and paint, an interpretation of a hand. A Dutch antique created decades ago by a true master of the artform. No one created work like this anymore. Michel even went so far as to claim acquiring antiques was another way to be environmentally friendly but left off that line when Imogene scoffed. Next, he used a bunch of other terms that had the woman cooing. Matthew could have told her that "tertiary" was just a fancy way of saying "mixing colors" but she might not have believed him. When Michel backed away to let them "discuss," Matthew let her beg him to buy the atrocious thing.

"I thought you wanted a painting." Matthew looked around the gallery to avoid her pout.

"Paintings are just so . . . flat," Imogene said. "This has presence."

"Why don't we see what Nathali thinks?" Matthew suggested. "It's her house, too."

Imogene slipped her hand from his arm and slinked away, the tilt of her chin showing him just how displeased she was with the suggestion. Matthew turned on his heel in the opposite direction. Now that he'd mentioned Imogene's younger sister, he wondered where she had gotten off to.

"Please don't touch. There are things here that children cannot begin to appreciate."

It was Michel's haughty tone from the back of the gallery that caught Matthew's attention. No sooner had Matthew rounded a display when the little curator nearly stalked into him, a smirk on his pinched face quickly evolving into a patronizing smile as the man swept by him. In the direction he'd come was a stack of shipping crates. And Nathali. She held what looked like a decrepit teapot.

"Where did you find that?"

She spun toward him, setting the pot down behind her with a thud. "Nothing."

Matthew grinned at her wrong answer. Imogene was constantly correcting the smaller version of herself and wasn't exactly nice about it, so he understood the twenty-year-old's reaction. Didn't help that Nathali was known to simply take things that caught her eye.

"That's a weird-looking teapot," Matthew said, peering behind her to the crate full of packing material. "And aren't you a little old for tea parties?"

Nathali smiled and her shoulders relaxed, letting the handle of her oversized and overpriced designer bag slide down to her wrist. "I was just looking at it. I don't think it's a teapot, though."

Matthew shrugged and took a closer look. Unglazed clay. More modern than the creepy hand. Definitely dirty, with a strand of stars etched around the middle and across the fitted lid.

"Matty." Imogene startled him as she slid a hand across his shoulders, pressing herself into his side. "You left me."

Her perfectly glossy lips parted and he became mesmerized. "Sorry, Mo. Did you still want the old hand thing or have you seen something less creepy that you like better?"

He knew as soon as her eyes went hard that he'd said the wrong words.

"You don't like it?" Her face turned back to the wiry curator behind them. "Michel said that Dutch antiques are the new must-have."

Matthew refused to let his eye twitch at the mix of antiques and new trends.

"And I don't have anything Dutch." Her lips returned to pouting, his previous misstep forgotten. "Not even Frederick thought to buy me that."

At the sound of her ex-fiancé's name, Matthew reached for his wallet. "We'll take it."

. . .

M atthew glared at the hand embedded in glass, now in a prominent place in their living room, over the fireplace. The same fireplace that Imogene had paid large sums of money to have gutted and replaced with a real wood chimney because gas fireplaces were "so over." The hand still creeped him out, no matter how many times Imogene told him she loved it or made a big show of telling all their party guests about it—even using Michel's favorite word "tertiary"—when they entertained last night.

As was her habit on nights they didn't have people over, Imogene was in bed just after dark, under layers of pillows and pills. He'd better bring her a bottle of water for the nightstand, or he'd be getting back out of bed to get one later.

Walking into the kitchen, he surprised Nathali at the sink. The item in her hand dropped with a thunk.

"What is that?" Matthew peered over her narrow shoulder into the sink. The dirty pot with stars around its belly lolled to one side. "Where did you get that?"

But her face told him everything. Her eyes flickered to him once, and then they refocused on the pot. Instead of admitting wrongdoing, she stuck out her little chin, just like her sister did when she refused to back down.

"You know perfectly well where I got it." Nathali turned her back to him.

"Did you steal it?" Matthew gripped the counter, surprised at his anger. She wasn't his sister; he wasn't a father-figure either. Why was he so upset?

"More like made things even," she said as she turned on the water. "Do you honestly think that zombie hand is worth what you paid?"

His anger evaporated. That slimy Michel hadn't taken his eyes off Imogene's perfectly toned backside the entire time Matthew filled out the billing information. Maybe taking a little something extra from his gallery evened the score. Besides, the pot wasn't a Dutch antique so not exactly in high demand. Matthew chuckled, earning a quick smile cast over Nathali's shoulder.

"Just don't tell your sister," he said, grabbing a water bottle from the fridge.

Nathali snorted and continued scrubbing the pot.

"Is that dirt or rust coming off?" He peeked into the sink at the swirls of red going down the drain.

"Don't know," she said. "This thing is old. The lid is covered in some gunk, too. Gonna scrape it off next."

"Hope you don't ruin it. That's an antique."

"But now I can see the pattern on it."

An electronic screech drew Matthew's attention back to the other room, like every single ringtone he had going off at the same time. His phone lay on the coffee table, the screen flashing and shifting through broken images and text.

"Weird." He reached for the phone, then jerked his hand back at the heat.

Matthew groaned. Stupid new tech. Always had bugs in it that made life difficult. The screen was black now. The sinking feeling in his gut told him it wouldn't be turning back on again. Ever.

"What was that noise?" Nathali's head showed around the corner, her long hair streaming down.

"Phone is toast." He stuffed both hands in his hair, product be damned; Imogene wasn't here to nag him about ruining the style.

"Sucks to be you," she said and then disappeared back into the kitchen.

Pretty much, he thought. Didn't Imogene say he should get one of the new matte black ones anyway? Sinking to the couch, Matthew considered going to bed early. Imogene would screech as loud as his phone if he woke her up. Maybe he ought to wait a little while longer, make sure she was asleep, before he snuck into their room with her water.

A few hours later, Nathali waved as she walked toward her bedroom, pot wrapped in a dish towel. Michael shut his laptop and leaned back on the couch. He ought to head to bed, too. He had to be up early to get a new phone.

As his eyes adjusted to the slightly darkened room, they were drawn to the glass atrocity on his mantel.

Were the fingertips . . . glowing?

He rubbed his eyes and stood. Definitely too tired if he was seeing things. Time for bed.

After turning off the lights and setting the alarm, a quick glance at the mantel showed him nothing unusual.

He walked barefoot down the hallway, Imogene's water in hand. A yawn cracked his jaw open, but the sound choked in his throat.

Someone stood in the hallway.

Too large to be either of the girls. And too dark to make out any sort of face. Matthew slammed a hand against the wall, dropping the water bottle as he fumbled his fingers toward the switch. A second later, light flooded the hall.

Nothing there.

Nathali's door was closed, as was the door to the bathroom closest to him. Matthew bent over slowly to retrieve the rolling bottle, never taking his eyes off the space in front of him. He stared a moment longer, then scoffed and hit the light switch again. First glowing fingers and now dark intruders. Matthew must be more exhausted than he thought.

Matthew sat on the bed, too keyed up now to move under the covers, laptop perched on his thighs. He tried to find information about the antique sculpture online. The artist didn't make many pieces, and most featured something buried in glass, usually a body, or at least part of one. Nothing about the freakish hand sitting on Matthew's mantel. Its title wasn't even listed under the artist's known works, which would have royally pissed him off, if he hadn't been so freaked out. Didn't help that the man died under mysterious circumstances well before Matthew was born.

He kept seeing the shape in the hallway. It stood outside Nathali's door. If it had gone inside, what would Matthew have done? What could he do?

He opened a new browser tab and typed in "dead man's hand." After scrolling through a dozen results for poker references, the phrase "hand of glory" showed up. He clicked the link. The top image looked just like the creepy hand, only this one wasn't cast in glass. A hand of glory had all kinds of stories surrounding it, and all of them made his stomach turn cold. The hand had to be cut from a hanged man, so someone who was already a criminal. Then there were all sorts of strange directions about using certain archaic herbs to pickle it and leaving the severed limb out during a particular phase of the moon. If that was done correctly, then the fingertips could be lit like candles and whoever was holding the hand could walk through walls and open any locks. After clicking through a few more articles, Matthew dozed off to dark dreams of a man with no hand slipping through the walls.

❖

"I'll miss you, too," Imogene oozed into his ear over his new phone. "But it's important to Daddy that I make these trips for the company."

Matthew couldn't argue, not when he worked for her father, too. Imogene was all about public relations, and her father's vast oil company needed all the help it could get, thanks to too many spills on their record. The board of directors might be destroying the environment, but they paid very well for his insight on new drilling locations. So Matthew put in just as many hours with chemical and geological sampling reports as Imogene did with parties and press events. Even now, his laptop sat open on the coffee table in front of him. The video from an ecology conference where the keynote denounced oil companies played in the background as

Matthew ended the phone call with his fiancée. He needed a break.

He closed his eyes and tried recalling Imogene's face when he'd kissed her goodbye. He'd been careful to not smudge her lipstick. She'd tossed him one of her smiles before disappearing into the company hangar. Matthew had watched her go, wondering what he'd miss the most: the feel of her hand in his or the smell of her on his clothes.

His phone buzzed, jerking him back to reality with a new voicemail notification. The number looked familiar, but he couldn't quite place it, so he tapped on the play button.

"This is Michel from the gallery."

At the way the twerp overly pronounced his own name, Matthew rolled his eyes. He'd made the call to the gallery late last night, wanting to know why the hand wasn't listed on the artist's page and if Dutch artists had been known to use real human parts.

The message from the curator continued but went all to crap, breaking down into garbled burps. All he could make out was something like "interpretation" and "superstitious." There was no mistaking the condescending tone. Great. At least the odious man hadn't noticed the missing pot. Matthew did not need an accusation of theft.

Matthew sent a text to Nathali, telling her they needed to talk. He hadn't seen her since last night, which was odd since she was normally begging for help with her college classes by now. As he tossed his new phone onto the couch, it screeched, the screen erupting with flashing words and mismatched pictures just like before. And this time, his computer joined in the technological death. The laptop still sat open, but now the screen was covered in pieces of what looked like every video he'd ever watched. He tried pressing keys and the touchpad, but nothing made a difference. Finally, he held down the power button until the screen went black. Sitting back on the couch, Matthew ran a hand through his dark hair, snagging his fingers on a few curls with too much product on them as the last few days of agonizing analysis melted in front of him. He smelled burning plastic.

"Whoa."

Matthew's head whipped to Nathali standing in the doorway, still in the pajamas she wore last night.

"Did you even leave the house today?" he asked, trying to not let his forehead get that crinkly disapproving look that he'd seen so often on his own father.

Nathali slumped against the doorway. "You have the worst luck with electronics."

"Seems like it lately." He turned his disapproval on the dead laptop. "I don't think you should keep that pot."

She was quiet.

"So we should probably return it."

"Can't," she said. "I broke the lid."

Matthew swallowed his sigh.

"Then you'll have to take your dad with you when you go back and explain what happened."

She made a sort of snort but then dissolved into giggles. "Sure. I even get to add 'destruction of property' to my list of stolen goods. Daddy will be so pleased his little girl isn't just a thief."

"Either you ask him to go with you or I ask him." Matthew gave her the same look he gave to the research teams who fell behind their timelines.

"Fine." She crossed her arms. "It'll only take a month and three lawyers for him to return my phone call."

"Then you'd better go make it now."

Nathali rolled away from the doorframe and disappeared back down the hall. Matthew let the frown return. It wasn't like her to stay inside all day and certainly not in the same clothes. Her hair was a mess and not even in the fashionable way. She must not have posted any selfies to her social media accounts today. He had his late night of demonic research to account for his general feeling of crappiness; what did Nathali have? Was there something in the house making them feel this way? His eyes strayed to the mantel. He shook his head and looked away. Maybe she was getting sick.

He rubbed his face and thought about going to bed. Sleeping alone was hard enough without all the extra layers of stress. Trying not to glance at the disembodied hand again, Matthew decided a fire might be just the thing. Something soothing about the crackle of real burning wood.

The fire came along nicely. He lost himself for a little while, watching the flames devour the logs. A scrape from the hallway brought him back to reality.

"Nathali?" he called. "Is that you?"

A crunch came in reply.

He pulled his feet down from the coffee table and listened, hearing small scratches. Matthew strode into the hallway, reaching first for the light switch.

Nathali leaned against the wall next to her room, her eyes rolled up into her head and her mouth gaping.

"Nathali!" Matthew raced to her side, reaching her just as she slid down to the floor, leaving a dent the size of her on the wall.

Matthew didn't know what to stare at first, the girl or the girl-shaped damage to the plaster. He called her name again, patting her cheeks like everyone seemed to do on television. No response. That's when he noticed she was covered in plaster dust. He looked back at the wall. Did she . . . did she just come through the wall?

He should call someone. Anyone.

But his phone was toast. And his laptop was fried, too. He patted her pockets, but Nathali didn't have her phone on her, either.

Landline. In the kitchen. The old phone might still work!

Matthew stood and ran back toward the kitchen. As he came around the doorway into the living room, the first thing he saw was the fire reflected in the glass block above it. The relic looked . . . unholy. The bony hand was distorted further by the glass.

Matthew turned toward the fireplace. It had to be the hand that caused all their problems. Hadn't it all started when they brought it home?

A low beep sounded behind him, followed by a soft pop. He turned in time to see the light go out on the alarm system. It was dead, too. He assumed the home automation and fire alarms were toast along with them. Suffering the same fate as his phone and computer. What about Nathali? Was she next?

Not if he could help her. Matthew had to destroy the hand. All this weirdness would go back to normal if it were gone. He had to destroy it. He reached for the hand, hefted the glass block over his head, closing his eyes from the expected shatter, and then slammed the cursed thing down on the fireplace edge. He popped his eyes open and looked down. No change. The block wasn't even cracked or chipped as it rippled back the light from the fire.

Fire.

Matthew tossed the block on top of the blazing logs. Heat ought to destroy the monstrosity.

He grabbed the iron poker and stabbed at the block and the wood, stirring it up even hotter, too hot for him. Stepping back from the heat, Matthew narrowed his eyes against the flames, watching the glass.

Around him, the ceiling lights flared and then burst.

The only light came from the fire. And still, the glass didn't change.

It wasn't hot enough.

With the poker, he pulled the block from the fire, scattering logs with it as it rolled to the rug several feet away. Matthew attacked it with the poker, smashing again and again until finally the glass cracked and broke open. He hammered away until the poker sank into the softer material of the hand. Too soft. No bones or blood. It wasn't a real hand; just an interpretation after all.

Matthew coughed. Lifting his eyes, he saw the fire blazing behind him, crawling up the curtains and nipping at the couch. The cushions caught, and flames roared and flowed, running down the couch like spilt water.

Stumbling back, Matthew coughed again. No air in this heat. He fell to his knees, crawling along the now smoldering carpet toward the door. He couldn't draw in a breath as he pulled himself along the hallway. He had to get Nathali out of here. Imogene would never forgive him if anything happened to her sister. Never.

His eyes stung so much they barely functioned and his lungs raged in his chest, but still he moved toward Nathali's form in the dark hall. Drawing on everything he had, he pulled her limp body into his arms and turned around, still on his knees, intent on the front doors.

Maybe it was the smoke or the lack of oxygen, but Matthew didn't see the man standing in front of the door until he was only a few feet away from escape.

The same size as the shape he'd seen in the hallway, this was a fully formed person, down to his ragged robes and dark eyes that glared down at Matthew. But it was the man's forehead that drew attention. In angry red lines carved into his skin was the strange star pattern that had crossed Nathali's pot.

And now this man blocked their exit.

No. Not a man. Not with that gaunt face and expression that seethed hatred. This was a demon.

Matthew slumped, dropping Nathali beside him as the flames crept along the walls toward them.

The next morning, with wisps of smoke leaking from the ruins of Imogene and Matthew's house, a petite man stood outside the gates with the other neighbors, listening to their clucking and gossiping over the young couple. He stayed to the side, not interacting with anyone, and most likely, after the body bags were carried from the house, none of them would remember him. When the fire inspector left the site carrying a cardboard box and returned to his car, Michel walked in step beside him.

"Did you recover it?" Michel asked, his tone low as he watched the line of trees beside the road.

The inspector answered with a grunt.

"Good."

Michel pressed the button on the fob in his pocket. Parked just in front of the inspector's, his car chirped and the trunk popped open. The older man slid the box inside and waited for Michel to close the lid.

"It worked," the older man said.

"I told you it would." Michel gave a hard, thin smile. "Women like that can't resist the hot new thing, and men like him would give them whatever they wanted, no matter how ridiculous. Throw in a kid known to have sticky fingers and the plan was solid."

"The hand was destroyed."

Michel shrugged. "Doesn't matter; it was only a prop. There's no record of it anyway. The dybbuk pot did all the work. The demon it houses usually just makes the people around it go crazy until they kill each other. It doesn't set fires, so that was unexpected, even if it vastly improved our timetable. Good thing we have you on our side."

Another grunt from the inspector. "I'm getting too old for this."

"Really?" Michel turned his face toward the man. "Because I have a pair of tailored men's shoes, sixteenth century, Spanish leatherwork, said to make the wearer feel twenty years younger."

The inspector's heavy eyebrows drooped over his eyes. "And what else do they do?"

Michel's smile showed teeth. "Erase your memories one by one until you forget your name, how to walk, how to speak, and then how to breathe."

"No, thank you. I'd rather protect Mother Nature without forgetting myself."

"That's fine." Michel fiddled with his vest buttons. "Overall, I'd say this was moderately successful. We got the geological wonder boy, so that will slow down their tainting of the environment. Pity we couldn't also get the PR princess. Still, we have the company's biggest financial backer as the next target. His wife is bringing him in for a tour. She's absolutely in love with all things Spanish."

Jessica Guernsey writes urban fantasy novels and short stories. A BYU alumna with a degree in journalism, her work is published in magazines and anthologies. She is a manuscript evaluator for Covenant Communications and slush pile reader for Shadow Mountain, along with providing freelance feedback. While she spent her teenage angst in Texas, she currently lives on a mountain in Utah with her husband, three kids, and a codependent mini schnauzer. Connect with her on Twitter @JessGuernsey.

COLD LOGIC

JOHN DAVID PAYNE

COLD LOGIC

Manny Vasques checked his phone. Midnight. The witching hour. It was time. He opened the door to his garage, finally ready to confront whatever it was that was haunting his food truck.

As the door opened, he was hit by a wave of faintly gasoline-scented Texas heat that reminded him of his days in the Sandbox. Not that the rest of the house was exactly cool, even at this hour. He could barely afford the rent, much less run the A/C all day. But however hot the house was, the garage was always hotter. He found the light switch in the dark and stepped in, securing the door behind him with a quiet click. Got to keep that heat contained.

He glanced over at the neat stacks of boxes on the far side of the garage, doing a quick mental inventory. Low on napkins. Again. He burned through those so fast. Well, not Manny—greedy customers who took twenty napkins and threw them all away. Come on, people!

The near side of the garage was occupied by his gorgeous new food truck, which barely fit. It was clean, classy platinum, with a sharp, black silhouette running along the side: a man seen from behind, reclining lazily in a chair, one arm stretched out with the fingers elegantly cradling a bright green pickle. Above, MAD MAN in large block capital letters. Underneath, meat loaf and more.

On any other night, he would have stopped to admire the wrap. It had cost five grand, but it was worth it. People came up to the truck to talk about it, or to take selfies with the logo. They remembered it and came back. It really was the best wrap in town. But tonight he had other things on his mind.

Manny squeezed around the front of the truck, between the hood and the shelves of canned goods. He opened the passenger side door and retrieved his Beretta M9A1 from the glove compartment gun safe. He checked the chamber and the magazine, tucked it into his pocket, and then made his way around to the back.

He unlocked the rear door, stepped into the galley, and switched on the lights and the A/C. Heat didn't bother him, but for this conversation he needed to be cold as ice, not constantly wiping the sweat off his forehead.

He pulled the weapon from his pocket and sat down on a barstool in the narrow aisle between the cabinets and appliances. He disengaged the safety and cleared his throat.

"We need to talk."

No sound but the hum of the air conditioner.

With a sigh, Manny reached over to the counter and turned the thirteen-inch Big Boy collectible figurine around so it was facing him. A handwritten sign taped to the base declared: Big Boys Give Big Tips.

"No use playing dumb." Manny kept the Beretta flat against his thigh. "I know it's you haunting my truck."

Still no answer.

"Why do you think I swapped out the sandwich press, the oven, the fridge?" He slapped the door of the new refrigerator. Well, not new. And not as good as the old one. But for now, it was perfect. "That was the last thing I hadn't checked. I've eliminated every other possibility. Cold logic, amigo. Game over."

Silence.

Manny shrugged. "Okay, güey." He lifted the pistol and aimed it at the figurine. "Don't know what this is going to do to you, but . . . let's find out."

"Put that disgusting thing away," the Big Boy said. "Gun violence is destroying this country."

The voice that came out of the chubby-cheeked tip jar was definitely male, but that didn't mean he was talking to a man. There was a lot he didn't know. Like whether the figurine in the red-checked overalls was really haunted. Like, by a ghost.

His uncle Beto, a big-time brujo back in Dallas, said there were three major possibilities for a possessed object. Restless ghost, demon, or human sorcerer playing ventriloquist—each of which had to be handled differently. Manny was prepared for all three but needed to know who he was talking to first, so he did what they taught him in HUMINT training at Fort Huachuca. He started a conversation.

"Do guns make you nervous?" He lifted the Beretta. "Is that why you want me to put it away?"

"Please." The Big Boy waved one hand dismissively. The other held up a platter with a huge burger.

That gave Manny ideas about haunted hamburgers for Halloween, but he shoved them aside for the moment. Ninety percent of interrogation, he knew, was just paying attention.

"I'm so far beyond your reach," the tip jar snorted, "it isn't even funny. What worries me is collateral damage. Do you know how many walls a stray round from an automatic weapon can punch through?"

Manny did. He hadn't fought in Second Fallujah, but he'd seen urban combat. Of course, in a successful interrogation, information flowed only one way. So he kept his face neutral. Blank.

From the conversation so far, Manny guessed it was a sorcerer doing the haunting. Uncle Beto said demons and dead people were easy to pick out—weeping and wailing, ranting about boiling blood. So this was a man. Good. But what kind of man? Time to push some buttons and find out.

Manny held up his pistol. "This isn't an automatic. It's a semi-auto." Completely irrelevant to the point about how far a stray round would travel. But the Big Boy struck him as the kind of person who couldn't pass up a pointless argument.

"I know that," the Big Boy said testily. "I can see it's not a rifle."

"It's not." Manny put the pistol down flat against his thigh again. "But most rifles aren't capable of fully automatic fire, either."

"Whatever." The fat little figurine shook its head. "Slap a bump stock on it and you got yourself a frickin' machine gun. Thirty seconds."

Manny leaned back and stroked his chin. "You've done your homework." Without a partner here to be the good cop, he had to play both parts himself. Easy enough. A little needling, a little flattery. Some threatening, an olive branch. Kid stuff.

"Yeah." The Big Boy rolled its eyes and snorted. "Not that you need a doctorate to weigh in on this debate."

Doctorate. Interesting. The only person Manny knew who used that word was his cousin Sofia, who taught at UTEP.

"What do you mean?"

The chubby little collectible heaved a sanctimonious sigh. "You gun nuts are so obsessive about the stupid little technical details. Like it matters if you call it a magazine or a clip. It kills people, that's the point."

Manny's drill sergeant and his firearms instructor would have had a few things to say in response, but it was time for a new subject.

"You care a lot," Manny ventured. "Other people just let stuff happen. Whatever. It's not their business. But you can't let it go, can you?"

The figurine gave him a squinty, suspicious glare. "What are you getting at?"

Time to get a little more direct. Manny leaned forward. "When ketchup and pickles started flying around my truck and the meat all spoiled, I thought it must be a poltergeist."

The Big Boy chuckled, his huge burger bouncing on the upraised tray.

Manny lifted a finger. "But they're malditos. Cursed. Malicious. That's not you. You're doing this for a reason. You're an altruist."

It was what every terrorist and insurgent told himself. They cared. It's what separated them from bank robbers, warlords, and drug dealers—even if they ended up also robbing banks, shaking down villagers, and trafficking drugs. Sure they killed, raped, and tortured—but only because they cared. So. Much.

"So," Manny asked, "why are you haunting my truck?"

He was not surprised to see the same self-righteous, knowing smirk on the fat plastic figurine that he had seen in countless interrogation rooms. That smug, silent smile that said, "I know what you want, but you're not going to get it from me."

But getting that information usually didn't take anything like that S&M circus at Abu Ghraib. All it took was understanding what makes people talk. In this case, his subject loved correcting people. So Manny tossed out something stupid.

"Is it because I have a gun? Is that why you put your curse on me?"

The Big Boy blew out a derisive snort.

"I think it is. I think you're fed up with all these mass shootings. All these guns, killing. And politicians doing nothing. You want to do something."

Manny could read it on those plastic lips, screwed up so tight to keep the words from spilling out. The Big Boy had something to say. He was desperate to get it out. Just barely holding it in.

A flash of inspiration hit him. "And the worst are all these school shootings. Those kids, man. Their lives are worth more than that. You know? And here I am, taking my truck—and my gun—onto campus. Into what ought to be a gun free zone."

He leaned back and gave the little plastic figurine a hard stare. It stared back. And still said nothing. But it was a different kind of silence. Not so smug, now. He had scored a point. Figured something out that he wasn't supposed to.

It wasn't the gun thing. That was nonsense. Oh, the Big Boy might have haunted him for it. But he probably never knew there was a gun in the glove compartment in the first place.

No, it was something about the school. His truck was being targeted because he parked it at the school. Why? If the Big Boy had wanted to do something nasty to UT students, he could have done a lot worse than making a mess of the food truck. Like poisoning the food.

So maybe his truck was just a target of opportunity. Which would mean that the Big Boy was somewhere close by. UT faculty? A student? One of the other food trucks? Or maybe just someone who worked across the street.

Too many options. He needed to narrow things down. Which meant he needed more information. Needed the Big Boy to start talking again.

Needed, not wanted. Because what he wanted was to kill this conversation already, to go straight to end game and shut this haunted hunk of plastic down. Which he could do. And it would be so satisfying. But it wouldn't stop the man behind the Big Boy from coming right back after him. So he had to keep talking, keep listening, keep learning.

Manny took a deep breath and leaned back, nodding his head. "When someone says 'gun free zone,' you know what I hear? Ese? White privilege, man. Privilegio blanco."

"Well, actually—"

Manny ignored the Big Boy's interjection and pushed on. "When my family first came to this country—" Four hundred years ago. As conquistadors. "—we came with nothing. Nothing but a dream."

Not true. But what would be the point in sharing his actual

life story (or his real opinions) with some anonymous jerk haunting his truck? Manny just wanted him gone.

"A dream of freedom," he continued, "and justice. But you know what we found? Not opportunity, but oppression."

Again, a lie. Nobody pushed his family around. His dad had been a hard-driving Shell Oil exec, and his mom had ruled the neighborhood ladies' garden club with an iron fist. They were the ones who did the oppressing, as Manny knew from firsthand experience. But this lie was a little easier to sell, because it was all about righteous anger. And Manny was actually angry.

"So, tell me, güero," he growled, "why you keeping this brown man down? Huh? Out of all the food trucks parked on Guadalupe, why you haunting mine?"

"This is not about race," the Big Boy hurried to say, waving the hand that wasn't holding up a giant hamburger on a tray.

Manny shook his head, pursing his lips in disgust. He made sure to fold his arms across his chest, a barrier to keep out this white figurine's racist lies. "Must be nice," he sighed, leaning back on his stool, "to be able to tell yourself it's not about race."

All just playacting, of course. In truth, he didn't think this was about race any more than it was about guns. But it was hard for Americans to keep their lips buttoned when someone accused them of prejudice—especially "woke" Americans. And this possessed piggy bank was woke as hell.

"I'm not trying to tell you what you feel," the Big Boy said, lifting one hand defensively. "Nor will I try to claim I know what it's like. I acknowledge and accept the validity of your unique experience—your truth, as you live it."

Definitely talked like a professor. Or a grad student, maybe? Damn. "My truth," he said out loud, "is this truck pays my rent. Alimony. Child support. My abuela's doctor bills. It's a game for you, but this is real life for me."

This part was actually about half true, which was dangerous. He reminded himself what Captain Bradley had taught him in Army Intelligence. Make it sound like a conversation. Let them feel like it's a conversation. But it's not. It can't be. Information is power. Get it, don't give it.

The Big Boy nodded sympathetically. "I'm not going to pretend I know your pain, but I hope you can recognize me as your ally in this struggle. I marched for fifteen-dollar minimum wage. For rent relief. Better pay and benefits for adjuncts."

This caught Manny's attention. He knew from his cousin Sofia that there was a real divide in colleges between the kind of full-time faculty who could get cushy tenured jobs and the glorified temps who actually did most of the teaching. So now the question was, did mentioning adjuncts mean that the Big Boy was one himself?

Unlikely. Even back to his first comments about collateral damage, he seemed to think of himself as unselfish. He reached down to help the little people beneath him. So, not an adjunct. Someone tenured, then? Or just on the tenure track? The Big Boy liked to play it safe. He was tenured, Manny was sure of it.

He fought back a grin. If his guess was right, he had just narrowed his pool down considerably. Even a big school like UT only had, what? A thousand tenured professors? And more than half of those he could rule out if Big Boy was a white man. He was getting closer. But still not close enough to make his move. Not yet.

"Fifteen-dollar minimum," Manny scoffed. "I own my own business. That doesn't help me, man."

The Big Boy raised his painted eyebrows. "This isn't just about you, or about me."

"Easy for you to say." He pointed at the sign taped to the figurine's fat stomach and then hooked his finger around to indicate the coin slot on the Big Boy's back. "You are literally full of money. That's some symbolism there, homeboy. You could have possessed anything in this truck, and you're occupying my tip jar. Where is your head?"

A flush of red came to the Big Boy's cheeks, which . . . How was that even possible? Then the chubby little collectible spluttered out, "We have to think bigger. This is about the greater good."

Now we're getting somewhere. Manny leaned in close. "How?" he asked. "What greater good?"

"Not just greater. The greatest good," said the Big Boy.

Manny narrowed his eyes. "Is this . . . ?" He took a deep breath and kept his finger off the trigger. "Is this a Jesus thing?"

The Big Boy shook his little plastic head. "I knew you wouldn't understand."

"I can't understand if you won't talk to me."

"You're not ready."

"Try me."

The fat little figurine stared off into space, saying nothing, rubbing its chubby chin with the hand that wasn't holding up a giant burger on a platter. The silence was maddening, but like any interrogator worth his salt, Manny knew that it was his ally. People hate silence, Captain Bradley had taught them. Wait long enough, and your respondent will fill it.

"Have you ever seen," the Big Boy began, "a blue sunset?"

Manny shook his head, slowly.

"You won't see one in Austin," said the Big Boy. "Too much air pollution. The particulates are what give you all the orange and pink. They give us sunsets that look beautiful, but what we're really seeing are the poisons that are killing us."

Manny nodded. This all sounded like total bullshit to him, but it didn't matter. The Big Boy was building to something. So Manny just let him talk.

"You get out away from the cities," the Big Boy continued. "And you see what sunsets used to look like, when the world was new. Before we came and wrecked this planet." He let an angry snort out his plastic nose.

"I was driving one summer, in the highlands of New Mexico. It was probably . . ." The Big Boy waggled his upturned fingers as if searching for words. "Nine o'clock in the evening. The sun was sinking low. There were big fluffy clouds everywhere. And nothing on the horizon to interrupt the view. Just . . . sky."

The Big Boy leaned back with a reverent sigh and tucked his thumb into the strap of his checkered overalls. "I was expecting a spectacular sunset. Intense. The kind you get out in the desert sometimes. Like some celestial cow kicked over a lantern, and now all of heaven is on fire."

The Big Boy looked at him, with that kind of smug smile that said he thought he was being funny, or clever. He wasn't. But Manny smiled back anyway and gave him a little half-chuckle.

"You know what I saw instead?" The Big Boy raised his painted eyebrows. "Blue. Blue clouds, blue sky, blue shadows on the mountains and the trees. Not that light, bright sky blue. A deep, dark, midnight blue. Almost indigo. You can see it in some old paintings, from the 17- and 1800s. But I'd never seen it before. A blue sunset. And it changed me."

Manny cocked his head slightly to one side, drew his eyebrows together, and grunted.

"It was like God, whoever or wherever she is—"

With iron determination, Manny successfully fought his eyes' instinctive roll and kept his face neutral and attentive.

"–was speaking to me." The Big Boy looked reverentially upward, the glisten of tears in his plastic eyes. Was that possible? Why not? The thing had already blushed.

"What was she saying?" Manny asked.

"I love you," the Big Boy said. "And I realized in that moment that I loved her. Mother Earth and all her children. Do you understand?"

"I think," Manny lied, "I'm beginning to catch the vision."

The Big Boy sighed in relief. "So now you see why, if we are ever to return this gorgeous green planet to its unspoiled, divine magnificence, we must do everything we can to end the barbaric cruelty of eating our fellow animals."

Manny blinked, once. This was beyond his wildest guesses as to where all this hippie-dippy new age nonsense might be leading. Meat? This stupid sorcerer was haunting his beautiful food truck because of meat?

Showing surprise now could ruin all the time he had invested in this interrogation. So he mustered all the discipline of his training, all the skill developed in his years in the field, and did what he could to keep the shock and anger off his face.

"So that's why you picked my truck?" Neutral. Calm. "Because I sell meat?"

"Yes."

And there it was. The at once disappointing and reassuring truth that most victims of terrorism are chosen essentially at random. Ninety percent of the food trucks on the street sold meat. Any of them would have worked as a target for the Big Boy. Manny hadn't been special. He'd just been unlucky. The revelation was . . . infuriating.

"That's why you spoiled all the beef in my refrigerator?"

"Yes."

"Three times."

"Yes."

"And why . . ." Manny took a deep breath. "Why you sabotaged my deep freeze." There had been more than three hundred and fifty pounds of beef in there when it had gone. Three hundred. And fifty. Pounds.

The Big Boy smiled, looking all sad and compassionate, which meant he was about to launch into the speech every violent nutjob gave when he thought he had a sympathetic ear. Oh, I'm so sorry. Oh, I had to do it. Oh, I didn't have a choice. Oh, it's not my fault I blew up that school bus.

"I'm so sorry," the Big Boy said. "For what I had to do to you. But I had no choice. You see that now, don't you?"

Pinche cabrón, you always have a choice, Manny was very careful not to say. Then with his mouth he painstakingly formed the necessary words: "It wasn't about me. It wasn't about you. It was this system. The system makes victims of us all."

The Big Boy bit his lower lip and nodded, tapping his fat

plastic chest with his fat plastic fist. Right over his nonexistent heart. Then he stuck that fist out for perhaps the most patronizing bump Manny had ever received.

"Gracias, mi hermano," said the collectible in badly accented Spanish. "Thank you for understanding."

"De nada."

At this point in a real interrogation, Manny would probably have stopped for a break. Maybe even for the rest of the day. It was getting increasingly difficult to keep his cool—not a good thing in an interrogation. Better to return your respondent to the boredom and isolation of the cell. A little wait and he'll be grateful to see you again, not just ready but positively anxious to talk.

But this was different. The Big Boy—or rather, the sorcerer who was using the figurine to do the haunting—wasn't being detained, cut off from his support network. He was at home, taking it easy. Probably some nice place close to campus, instead of a forty-minute commute away.

So Manny had to take this shot while he had it. But how to approach things at this point? He'd already tried playing tough guy, pushing buttons, guilt tripping, the silent treatment, and getting on the bandwagon. He didn't have a lot of cards left in his hand.

But it was time for end game. Time for risks. So he played the riskiest card he had left. Straight talk.

Manny took a deep breath. "So here's my problem."

"Problem?" the Big Boy asked.

"Yeah. I get what you're saying about animal cruelty and saving the planet and all that. But before I think about saving the planet, I need to pay my rent. And I've sunk my life savings into a business that sells high-end nostalgia food. Pretty hard to do meat loaf without meat."

"Then you haven't tried—"

Manny held up a hand. "Please. You think I wouldn't look into vegetarian and vegan options in Austin? Give me a little credit. That part of the market is pretty overserved right now. So I went a different way."

"That's . . . disappointing to hear."

"Tell it to the customers lining up around the block for my bacon-wrapped tenderloin loaf with honey glaze."

"Oh," the Big Boy snarled, "I will."

Manny spread his hands. "Right. Well, we can go back to you making the meat scream whenever someone takes a bite. I'll be the first to admit, that was a pretty good trick."

"Spare me your flattery."

"No, man." Manny shook his head. "I'm serious. You're a big bad brujo. You've got talent—and more importantly, you know stuff. You're read in." He pulled his stool up close to the countertop and got nose to nose with the tip jar. "But so am I."

The Big Boy snorted and rolled its plastic eyes, unimpressed.

Manny stood up, towering over the little plastic figurine. "I did six tours, man. Iraq, Afghanistan, the DMZ. I was with one of the units experimenting with the TTR and the Empath. So I have seen some spooky shit."

"You think so?" The Big Boy laughed, menacingly, and the lights dimmed to complete blackness. The only things visible inside the food truck were the tip jar's eyes, which were now glowing an ugly red. "Just wait. You haven't seen anything yet."

As the lights flickered back to life, the Big Boy jumped when he saw that the business end of Manny's drawn pistol was mere inches from his plastic face.

Not that Manny was really going to pull the trigger. For starters, he believed the sorcerer when he said shooting the Big Boy wouldn't hurt him. But even if they were face to face, what was he going to do? Murder this idiot? Okay, then what? Everybody in Indian Country bitched about the Rules of Engagement and how they tied your hands. But sometimes tying your hands kept you from doing something stupid. Protected you from blowback. You know, like life in prison. Or a date with the needle.

He put the Beretta back in his pocket and spread his arms.

"You trying to scare me, brujo? Because I've seen worse possessions at my little cousin's quinceañera."

The figurine howled with incoherent rage.

Manny folded his arms and shook his head. "Try harder, pendejo. This is 2019. The whole world is a horror show. I turn on the Saw movies to put me to sleep. I've seen Rosie O'Donnell's sex tape, man. My president is Donald Trump. You got to up your game."

With a terrible roar, the Big Boy rose up off the counter and levitated in the air, head spinning around and vomiting blood. Ectoplasm erupted from the sink, and every drawer and cabinet door in the food truck slammed open and closed over and over, producing a deafening clatter.

But Manny stood his ground. He had already removed everything from the drawers and cabinets. There were no cans to pelt him, or knives to cut him. The only dangerous thing in the food truck was . . .

The Beretta flew out of his pocket and hovered in the air, inches away from his face. The Big Boy, now back on the counter, gave him a smug, nasty smile. "Hands on your head, if you please. Nice and slow."

"Respect." Manny slowly lifted his hands and placed them on his head. "Turning my own weapon against me. That's a baller move."

The plastic figurine's smile turned even uglier. A menacing sneer, now. "Kneel."

Manny knelt, grimacing. "Trust me, you don't want to do this."

"You don't know what I want."

"I've been where you are. On that side of the gun. Thinking to myself, what now? Do I really have to do this? Isn't there some other way out of this situation?"

"You're the one who needs a way out." The Big Boy shook his head. "And I offered you one. But you wouldn't take it. You've got no one to blame for this but yourself."

Manny laughed. "Yeah, you tell yourself that."

"Shut up."

"Look." Manny shrugged. "You're putting the blame on me because you know you don't want to do this."

"Shut up."

"And I get that. Taking a life is . . ." He shrugged his shoulders like he was trying to dislodge something squirmy. "It changes you, amigo. That feeling, that memory, that guilt—it never goes away. Believe me, you don't want it."

"You don't know me," said the Big Boy.

Manny took a deep breath. He had a hand full of cards. Time to see what they were worth. "You're a white middle-aged male," he began. Most domestic terrorists were. "You live alone." Terrorists usually did. Especially those who weren't part of a larger organization.

The Big Boy laughed. "Total crap. You don't know anything."

"You're not from Texas, and even in Austin you're not sure you fit in. You care about politics. You go to protests, you sign petitions, you're active on social media."

The little painted eyebrows drew together, and a frown appeared on the fat little plastic face. Time to push it a little harder.

"Even though you're a tenured professor at UT—"

The Big Boy started.

"—you still read your student reviews. Because you care about your students, you really want them to learn." This last was a freebie. Every professor thought this about himself. "But, yeah, I don't know you."

"Random guesses."

Manny gave him a cold smile and said nothing.

"And even if you did know something," the Big Boy blurted out, "what are you going to do—call the cops and tell them you want their help to track down the man who's haunting your food truck?" He laughed.

Manny laughed, too. "I know, man, cops are useless! That's why I would take care of this myself. In person."

The Big Boy wasn't laughing any more.

"Walk away right now, brujo," Manny said quietly. "And we're good. Otherwise, next time you see me, it's going to be too late. And that's not a threat. That's a promise."

The figurine stared, incredulous. "I just wanted to scare you. But you . . ." His little plastic nostrils flared in anger, and the Beretta got even closer, hovering maybe an inch in front of the bridge of Manny's nose. "You pushed me to this. This is all you."

Manny watched the trigger slowly depress, and then there was a metallic click, loud in the silence of the food truck's galley. He stood up. The trigger kept pulling, producing click after click after click.

"What kind of idiot would bring a loaded gun to a haunting?" Manny said, shaking his head. He picked up the Big Boy figurine, which squirmed in his hands and hit him with its giant plastic hamburger.

"This isn't over!" shouted the collectible. "I'll be back!"

Possible. But unlikely. The cold, brutal logic of terrorism isn't about particular people. It's about soft targets. Manny wasn't soft.

So he said nothing and threw the Big Boy into the refrigerator his Uncle Beto had prepared with spells that would cut a possessed object off from a remote sorcerer. If it had been a real ghost, it would have gone in the oven, prepared with spells of binding and soothing. A demon would have been exorcised with the sandwich press.

He got out his phone and texted his cousins from Dallas to come pick up the refrigerator. Uncle Beto would take care of the figurine. Manny wasn't looking forward to paying off this favor, but that was a problem for some future day.

Today? He checked his phone. It was only 12:30. Handing off the fridge would take some time, and then he still had a lot of prep to do for tomorrow. But he could still get three hours of sleep in if all went well. Not too bad.

He turned off the lights and the A/C and stepped down out of the truck. He made his way over to his new (used) deep freeze and pulled out two big boxes of ground beef. The frozen beef felt pleasantly cool against his chest as he squeezed past the front of the truck. Then, he turned off the light with his elbow and pulled the garage door closed behind him with his foot. Time to get to work.

John D. Payne grew up in the American Midwest, watching the lightning flash outside his window and imagining himself as everything from a leaf in the wind to the god of thunder. Today, he lives with his wife and family in the shadow of the Organ Mountains in New Mexico, where he imagines that with enough concentration he might be able to rustle up a little cloud cover for some shade. For more information about John visit www.johndpayne.com.

JUDGE NOT

JEN BAIR

JUDGE NOT

The Intuit, Colburn, knew that if he failed to make a righteous judgment, the repercussions would certainly end his career, and quite possibly his life. He sat in judgment on the accused and, despite that, he was certain his heart was pounding louder than anyone else's in the courtyard. Most of the city had turned out to hear the proceedings. If he had presided over such a case the year before, he would have preened for months over the esteem he garnered from being so prominent in the public's eye, but today, too much was at stake for him personally.

"Are you okay, Your Honor?" The nearby city guardsman had noticed his shaking hands and sweaty face.

Colburn gave a wan smile. "Yes, of course," he said, fighting back a wave of nausea. The shadows had been dancing along his periphery for several minutes, bringing on a bout of motion sickness. He tried to ignore them and focus on the people before him. Everyone was waiting for his verdict, but he didn't know. He couldn't make a decision until he was absolutely certain. Guilty or not guilty? Oh, how he wished he had never been given that blasted gavel!

"Ah, Jonas, so good to see you again!"

"And you too, Intuit. It's good to see you're still doing well," Jonas said.

"How has trading been treating you these many months?"

"Oh, the stories I could tell you! I met the prince himself three months back. It turns out the stories they tell about him are true." He laughed.

"My wife heard at the baker's this morning that you were in town. She bought enough food to feed an army. Certainly you'll be staying with us again while you're here. You can tell me all about the prince at dinner."

"Of course," the tradesman said, smiling. Finding accommodations was simple for a master storyteller. "I wouldn't dream of keeping you from your duties. I shall come by tonight after the market closes.

They said their goodbyes and carried on with their separate businesses. Later that night, when dinner was through and tales of the prince had danced across the dinner table like memories of fairy tales, the two men sat by the fire while the Intuit's wife, Laina, cleaned the dishes.

"I wanted to repay your hospitality, Intuit. You're always very good to me. It is a precious thing indeed to have friends so willing to open their home to a lowly trader."

"Lowly trader, indeed! You sell some of the finest goods this town has ever seen, and you repay me enough by the stories you tell."

"Even so, I must insist on giving you this gift, as it is suited for no one else I know." Jonas reached into his sack and pulled out a curious wooden piece, handing it gently over to the judge. "I found it in an antique shop in Oestrich, and I immediately thought of you."

Colburn took the gavel, turning it over in his hands. Its workmanship was like nothing he had ever seen, black-brown swirled with a deep red and a pale white, as if three separate woods were somehow melded into one. Engravings, worn with age, ran down the handle, forming elegant symbols that twined with the delicate whorls. It was a thing of beauty.

"I would like to hear the evidence once more." He heard a subdued groan roll throughout the audience, and he couldn't help but scowl.

"Again, Your Honor?" asked the spokesman of the accused, forcibly polite.

"Absolutely," he retorted. "Does a man's life not hang in the balance?" he asked, thinking more of his own life than that of the accused. "Is it not right to take the time for careful deliberation by thoroughly evaluating the facts? I would not be doing the law justice if I did not make certain of my verdict before I delivered it."

He reminded himself that doing the law justice had seldom crossed his mind throughout his career. He noted the look of relief and hope on the face of the young man who stood accused. Perhaps if he studied the evidence well enough, he would be able to find a way to get justice for them both. Granted, justice for the young man may well be death, but for him it would be life. He had discovered the consequences of avoiding due diligence the hard way.

He had tried to be patient as the evidence was presented to him, though he had already known the verdict before the hearing started. The coins he had been given still jingled in his pocket. Laina's birthday was two weeks hence, and he intended to impress her with a gift that dazzled.

The farmer before him looked angry, no doubt affronted at having his name besmirched. He was about to get angrier. True, stealing a few pumpkins from a neighboring farm was a minor offense, but the farmer who owned the pumpkins wanted his neighbor out of the way, and he was willing to pay for the privilege. It would be an unpleasant few weeks for the accused, but nothing he wouldn't survive. Perhaps he would learn not to irritate his neighbors.

By the time the case came to a close, Colburn was already thinking about the fine steak he would have for lunch. He gave the verdict without hesitation as he reached for his fancy antique gavel. He pounded it on the podium, feeling a shock vibrate through his arm as he did so. He flinched a bit at the sharpness of it, but the pain lasted only a moment, quickly forgotten. The neighbor, who apparently thought his reputation would keep him from jail, began loudly protesting, asking for reconsideration. Colburn hardly heard him.

That day Colburn was robbed in the street on his way to the store. At night, he had terrible dreams in which every time he tried to buy something, the money disappeared as it left his fingers until he had none left. Leaving the store, he returned home to find that his wife had left him and that all of his furniture had been stolen by thieves. He woke to wonder if his conscience was trying to tell him something.

In the following three weeks, he took bribes for cases twice more before finally making the connection between his faulty verdicts and his increasingly unfortunate luck. The gavel . . . the shock through his arm that only happened when he pronounced false judgment . . . the bad luck. It was easy to see the pattern once he looked, and so he did what any reasonable person would do. He took the gavel home and put it in a drawer to be used no more.

The Intuit listened once again as the man, son of a baronet, insisted he had loved his wife dearly and would never cause her harm. His friends, once again, claimed likewise. And yet the murder weapon, covered in blood, had been taken from his shed and hidden under his own mattress. He had been sleeping on that same mattress when the messenger arrived at the house and spotted the wife on the floor through the window. The guards arrested the man, who had spatters of blood on his pants and shirt.

Surely he had killed her. Only, the man himself brought up good points. Why would he leave her lying there and yet hide the evidence in his own room? But then, if he were not the killer, how was anyone able to kill his wife in his own house where he slept, hide the knife under his mattress, and spatter him with blood, all without waking him? If the wife were killed before he came home, he would have seen her body as he entered the house. By all accounts, he was neither lazy nor stupid. Perhaps he was drugged? Round and round, and yet there was no way to be positive. The Intuit couldn't afford to make the wrong decision.

Despite having the gavel tucked away in a drawer at home, there was no escaping its curse. His next three cases were simple, and no bribes were offered. He was feeling confident by the time he passed false judgment again. This time he used an ordinary gavel, yet he felt the sting in his arm once again. Telling himself he had imagined it, he was too nervous to leave the courthouse, skipping both lunch and dinner. Hoping he had made it through the day unscathed, he hurried home.

Spotting the smoke that wafted on the air as he rounded the last hill, he assumed his wife was cooking. It was late in the day and far past dinnertime, but still the hope persisted until he was close enough to see the charred remains ahead of him. Laina rushed to him as she saw him approach. She had spent the afternoon gathering the neighbors, and they had already heard her account.

Colburn listened to her story, his heart growing heavier with each word. She had gone outside to hang the wash before lunch, repeatedly insisting that the sky was clear and that the sun shone cheerily. Halfway through hanging the wash she heard a brief rumble overhead and turned just in time to see a bolt of lightning streak from the cloudless blue above, like the finger of God itself. It hit the barn with a deafening crack as wood splintered. The ensuing fire burned so quickly and so hot she barely had time to let the cows out before running to get help. It had taken over a dozen neighbors the entire afternoon to wrestle the beastly flames down to smoldering embers and ash.

After Laina recounted the event, the couple walked among

the crowd, placing a hand on a shoulder here, a word of thanks there as they surveyed the mess. Luckily, if such a curse could be called lucky, the fire hadn't spread to the house. At least they would have a place to sleep for the night. Colburn gave his wife what comfort he could before leaving her to stare into the eyes of the demons that sat scowling from the ruins.

Inside the house, he walked heavily up the stairs and opened a certain drawer. Returning to the barn, he surreptitiously dropped the antique gavel into the smoldering embers, stoking the flames until they were large enough to embrace it, and left it there to burn.

The next morning, he came out to survey the ruins and found the gavel untarnished amid the pile of ashes. Horror dawning at the implications, he snatched it from the soot, stuffing it into his overcoat. He hurried to town, where he stopped to scan the area and located a horse tethered outside a tavern. He approached it, trying to be inconspicuous as he lifted the flap on the saddlebag and deposited the source of his misfortune inside, though he had few hopes that something as simple as distance would save him from it.

He had pondered his circumstances these past many months. His best guess as to how the blasted thing worked was that he had activated the curse by using the gavel in an official capacity. He imagined he could be released from the curse if the gavel was given to another judge who would then transfer the curse to himself. Only he couldn't test his theory since the gavel had left town in the saddlebags of a brown horse.

At some point, he had stopped taking bribes. That was how he learned that the curse worked whenever he pronounced the wrong verdict, bribe or no. The curse brought about an equal amount of misfortune to him as he bestowed upon the accused. He began to work hard at getting to the truth before pronouncing judgement, hoping that due diligence would be enough to save him. It wasn't.

By deliberating so thoroughly on every case that came

before him he had acquired quite a reputation. That in itself was a curse for, the more a person had at stake, the more adamant they were at having him be their judge. And the more that was at stake for the accused, the more was at stake for him.

The last case he judged wrongly, though he truly did the best he could, resulted in months of suffering. A man had been accused of beating his child, though the accusing neighbor was said to be jealous of the man's wife and was discredited by several witnesses. When he had proclaimed the man innocent, he felt the zing in his arm and knew he had chosen wrong. He quickly retracted his statement and proclaimed the man guilty.

Thinking he had avoided the curse, he went to lunch, just to be kicked by a horse, shattering three ribs. Before the doctor could show up, a loose dog had wandered by and attacked him without provocation. But the dreams were the worst. They planted visions in his head that had him thrashing through the night. His ribs had needed to be reset four times before they finally healed enough to hold through his night terrors. The dreams followed him throughout the day, as well, visions passing before his eyes that made him question his sanity, shadows that drifted like the ghosts of dead men. . . .

Evidence presented, the courtyard once again waited for his verdict. He heard their shuffling feet and impatient sighs. He stared down at the simple gavel in his hand with growing dread. He had tried doing without a gavel at all. It hadn't helped.

He had enjoyed the status of being in the public eye and could appreciate how his reputation had grown over the past year, but he had made enemies, too, of those whose bribes he would no longer accept. The price of the bribes was too high, now that he was paying that price himself.

It was only after he broke down and told his wife about the curse that a solution had come. She had worried about his strange behavior over the past weeks and hearing what ailed him, she presented a solution so ludicrously simple that he cried out at his own stupidity. "If judging people wrongly causes you so much grief, husband, then stop judging them."

He had given the city notice that this would be his last case. He would quit and look for another profession, one that didn't involve broken bones and hallucinations. He had tried his best to wriggle out of taking on this one final case, knowing the stakes would be high, but the baronet had friends in high places.

The Intuit inhaled deeply, holding it for a long moment, and consoled himself with the fact that it would all be over soon. Hopefully he wouldn't end up in the hospital for the night. Or worse yet, a grave. "I find the accused to be," he caught his wife's eye at the back of the crowd, ". . . innocent."

He brought the gavel down and waited a long moment as his eyes filled with silent gratitude at the realization that he had felt the simple vibration of wood hitting wood. It was a double proclamation, meant for himself as well as the accused man before him. Perhaps now they both would be free to live their lives, hopefully far from courtyards and judgment.

Jen Bair is a homeschooling mother of four rambunctious boys. She has spent her life being a military brat, military veteran, and military spouse. She lives . . . wherever the Air Force sends her husband, which tends to be a different state/country every two years. She has lived in sixteen different locations, including Hawaii, the Philippines, Korea, and Guam. She served five years in the Army, achieved a Master's in Business Administration, and is currently attempting to launch a writing career.

TWIST OF FATE

KAREN PELLETT

TWIST OF FATE

"Found another one for ya, bud." Harold handed his stepgrandson, Alex, a miniature Ford Fairlane.

Without looking at Harold, the towheaded young man took the burgundy car and lined it up between the Ford Coupe and the Model-T in the window display. The placement was precise, not quite fitting the cozy impression Harold aimed for in the shop. He needed the right mix of antiques and collectibles to draw in customers from the swarm of parents depositing their college-aged kids off at Antioch University for fall semester. If they didn't, he and his wife would have to close the shop and move away from Alex.

Harold rolled his shoulders back. There was no way he would do that. Marrying into a ready-made family had been full of adventures and landmines. But what he never expected was how much he'd come to adore his wife's autistic grandson.

"Wouldn't it look better over here by the Impala?" Harold asked, moving the car toward the end of the shelf.

"No." The thirteen-year-old grabbed the car, placing it back in its correct space.

Alex reminded Harold a lot of a brownie: he didn't speak much, was loyal to his family, was a brilliant helper, tended to disappear around other humans, and if you triggered one of his meltdowns—oh boy, watch out. So, if Alex said that the Fairlane needed to be on the moon, then Harold would book the next flight to outer space. He might not understand the boy's reasoning, but it was always spot on.

"Okay, bud. You're right." Harold rubbed the boy's head and smiled. His step-grandson was better than a mob of brownies any day. Harold checked the cardboard box to make sure he hadn't forgotten any other items.

"Well, hello there," Harold said as he discovered one more item.

He lifted a tiny Japanese figurine, a good luck cat, that had slipped beneath the flap of the box. He placed it at eye-level next to the matryoshka nesting doll collection.

"I think that does it." Harold's arthritic knees popped as he pulled himself to standing position. "Let's see how it looks from the outside."

Alex remained sitting cross-legged before the open case, rotating the wheels on a pressed-steel fire truck, content in his own world. Harold nodded with a smile. *That's my boy.*

The shop bell rang as Harold stepped outside and breathed in the afternoon air, still muggy from the tail end of summer. The sky shifted through a palette of pinks and oranges as the sun set behind the hills, highlighting the hints of reds emerging in the trees. One by one the black-stick lamp posts lining Main Street clicked on, creating a sphere of yellow light every 12 feet.

Harold inspected the store front from the curb. He'd have to move the dual-chime clock closer to the door. They always were a big winner with tourists. But, overall the window display looked good. In fact, if he'd put the Fairlane where he thought it should go, the entire balance of the display would look tilted.

Harold chuckled, then crouched down until he could see Alex through the window. Tapping on the glass Harold gave him two thumbs up.

Alex smirked back.

When Harold had first met Alex's grandmother, Maeve, they'd argued over a pair of 18th-century French opera glasses at an antiquity's convention in Maryland. That meeting had led to them opening Twist of Fate Antiques & Estate Sales together and falling in love. Neither had known at the time that those glasses had been cursed.

Who knew curses could bring such mixed blessings? Harold thought.

The door opened, spilling his stepdaughter on to the sidewalk like a whirling dervish. Harold turned down the volume on his hearing aids. Charlotte was a petite firecracker of energy and charisma. Being a single mother had to be hard enough, but raising an autistic teen by herself . . . well, she was one remarkable lady. Secretly, Harold preferred Alex's yin to Charlotte's yang; so much conversation could be had with a single look or an action, without having to speak a thousand words a minute.

"Thanks for covering for me, Harold." Charlotte stood on her tiptoes and kissed him on the cheek. "You're a gem. It's so much easier dealing with World War 'Ex' without spinning poor Alex into the mess. Alex doesn't deserve that."

Harold nodded, a bit flustered. Her energy made words impossible, until the cavalry arrived. Maeve emerged from the shop leading Alex gently by the hand, saving Harold from having to think of what to say. Harold smiled. Ten years together, and Maeve still looked like Betty Grable, only better. Age suited her well, though he counted a few more worry lines around her eyes.

Before he could ask Maeve what was wrong, Charlotte pulled Harold and Maeve into a group hug while Alex stepped safely to the side, content to suck on the pull string of his hoodie. Harold breathed in the honeysuckle and wood tones of Maeve's Clair de Lune perfume and hugged the women tighter. Until ten years ago, he'd been a confirmed bachelor. Now he couldn't imagine life without Maeve. Without any of them.

Charlotte's phone beeped, shattering the tender moment.

"Sorry, that's me. Come on, Alex. Time to go see Isabelle." Alex dodged around them, ripped open the door of Charlotte's yellow VW bug, and buckled himself in record time. Charlotte laughed. "He loves his occupational therapy appointments, especially if he gets to work in the pirate room."

"See ya, champ," Harold said, bending down to wave goodbye to Alex through the window.

Maeve blew her daughter a kiss.

As the bright-yellow bug drove away, Harold asked, "What's wrong?"

Maeve cleared her throat. "We received an eviction notice."

"The apartment, the shop, or both?" he asked.

"Both." Maeve leaned her head on his shoulder.

Harold enfolded his wife in his arms and held her while she cried softly. "I love you, you know," he whispered.

Maeve sucked in a deep breath, then wiped away the tears. "Yep."

Harold kissed Maeve long and deep until two teenagers across Main Street whistled and called out, "Way to go, Gramps!" Maeve pulled away, her face red as the sunset, but Harold simply yelled back, "It gets better the longer you wait for it."

Maeve slapped him on the chest. "Come on, sailor. We've got work to do. There's a client coming in tonight."

"Right." His mind became a jumble, like a shattered mirror made up of many shards, some smooth and others incredibly damaged, but pieced together they made a beautifully complex image. Harold ran both hands through his thinning hair, a habit he'd acquired as a method of shifting gears between the many facets of his life—from loving husband, grandpa, and antique shop owner, to black-marketeer of hard-to-find magical creatures. Gears in place, Harold opened the door for her.

"Which client?" he asked.

Maeve grabbed a leather folio she'd left on a table by the

door. "Helen Miller's granddaughter. She's catching a train back to Chicago tomorrow."

Harold stepped inside the door, allowing his eyes to adjust while taking a moment to savor the musty smell of the vintage clothes, dusty books, and the sweet tang of polish. When they'd first started Twist of Fate Antiques, they'd worked hard to create an atmosphere that accentuated the mystique and history of long-forgotten objects. The recessed lighting deepened the rose tones of the wallpaper and provided a calming atmosphere. That was why Alex felt safe and relaxed when he visited. It didn't hurt that it also helped soothe a client before being subjected to the transformation.

They wove their way around the displays of ornate candlesticks and past the music boxes, visually ensuring everything was in its place. Suddenly, he heard one sound, one beat, slightly out of sync from the rest of the shop and stopped. Harold turned up his hearing aide. "Miller. Over in Jaffrey?" he asked her, though his senses were honing in on the cause of the discordant sound.

Maeve slipped on the bifocals hanging from a chain to read her notes. "Hm-hm. Granddaughter's name is Ashley. Not married, as far as I can tell. An only child. And works as a graphic designer out of her home." Maeve snapped the folio shut. "So, she shouldn't be missed."

There. A small brass carriage clock along the wall ticked in a slightly syncopated rhythm to its mates surrounding it. "Which artifact did she get?"

Maeve looked at her notes and chuckled. "The opera glasses."

Over the years, he'd gotten better and better at laying his traps. Granted, breaking into homes in small towns tended to be easy—most of the elderly leave their doors unlocked. With Mrs. Miller, he'd simply slipped in through the back door after the coroner had taken her body away. He'd left the very glasses that had brought him and Maeve together perched on the dead woman's nightstand next to his business card.

Harold extracted the winding key taped to the back of the clock and opened the face panel.

"Um, hon." Maeve cleared her throat. "Is now really the best time to deal with that? I mean, depending on how things go tonight with Mrs. Miller's granddaughter, maybe we can keep the wolves at bay a bit longer."

Harold blinked. "What?"

"The landlord," she replied.

"Right." Harold grabbed the carriage clock by the handle and stuffed it inside the Burr wardrobe across the aisle.

Maeve's jaw dropped as her gaze darted between him and the wardrobe.

"It'll be safe there until I can deal with it." Harold gave her a squeeze.

Maeve kissed his weathered cheek. "It's a rare man who'll admit when he's wrong."

Harold straightened his bow tie and gestured for Maeve to lead the way. Once behind the counter, he pulled back the curtain that separated the shop from their private offices and let Maeve pass through first.

"What's the current inventory demand on the Shadow Market?" he asked.

"It's the Dark Web, honey," Maeve said in all seriousness as she slid into her desk chair and touched the inventory app on her screen.

Harold shrugged. "Shadow Market. Dark Web. *Comme ci, comme ça.*"

Either way, it was a means to an end. They had to keep the shop open. Not only was it their dream, but it allowed them to help Charlotte with Alex. Secretly, though, Harold loved the danger; there was always a risk involved in transforming humans into magical creatures for sale. Especially when the results depended on factors completely out of their control—like an individual's personality.

Harold couldn't figure out where to look as Maeve zipped

between spreadsheet, order forms, and complex computer algorithms. The faster she worked, the more her bifocals slipped down the bridge of her nose. If his glasses were falling off his nose that way it would've driven him batty, but on her, it was cute.

"At last count—two harpies, four hobgoblins, three pixies, and a griffin," she reported.

Harold's right leg twitched, a reminder that not all his knee pain was from his arthritis. He'd once matched a jewelry box to an accountant with anger management issues, and he'd ended up with a mad griffin on his hands. Two years later the scars still throbbed when a storm was brewing.

"That won't be enough to ward off the landlord, even if we could match the right individual to the right object." Maeve bit her bottom lip, scanning through the inventory lists. "Why can't magic be simpler?"

"If it were simple, everyone would be doing it." Sitting down at his own laptop, Harold pulled up his notes. "It's only the intrepid few who dare try."

Maeve cracked open the window next to her monitor, letting the cool of evening alleviate the mugginess in the cramped office. "I'm not so sure two senior citizens with a penchant for line dancing and hoarding antiques qualify as intrepid."

"Speak for yourself." Harold's voice dropped off as he found his notes on the opera glasses under *Malediction/Curses*.

The client must read the incantation through the lenses of the opera glasses themselves to effect the transformation. The five previous transformations seemed standard, though the results varied each time. "If only we could hone the vetting process to identify a person's personality before the transformation."

Maeve looked over his shoulder and ran her fingers through his hair. Her touch made him feel like a schoolboy with his first crush. She smiled sadly. "It is what it is."

Ping.

Maeve turned back to her own desktop to check on the notification alert.

Harold groaned. "Please tell me it's not another gnome. They're nasty, bite, and don't pay enough."

Harold turned around when Maeve didn't respond. "What?" he asked.

"A unicorn," she replied.

Harold nearly fell out of his chair. This could be the answer to all their prayers. One unicorn, and all their financial problems would disappear.

A flurry of motion and sound pulled Harold back to the present. Maeve paced the length of their tiny office, her hands waving in the air as she rambled. "No one has replicated one in nearly 50 years. Harpies. Pixies. Sure. But a unicorn? It's impossible."

"We could pay off our business loans," Harold mumbled to himself. "Get the landlord off our backs and pay for Alex's medical bills."

He typed in a specialized search on the Dark Web for information on unicorns. A quick read through proved Maeve right. Unicorns were rarer than dragons, and no one could pinpoint why. It didn't seem to matter the artifact used or the personality matched to the object. Harold leaned back, staring at the blinking cursor as if it held the secrets of the universe.

"How are we supposed to create a unicorn?" Maeve's voice neared hysterics. "Even trying, we risk a repeat griffin incident. What if you got hurt again? What if you'd lost your leg entirely? But $1,750,000 . . ."

Harold pulled Maeve to him and held her tight. "Breathe. We can't do anything if you pass out."

His wife's frame shook as she took a deep breath. He'd never seen her this agitated before. Maeve deserved better than the strain they'd been under of late. If a unicorn could get rid of all their problems in one blow, then come hells bells he was going to find a unicorn.

Ching. The muffled sound of the shop bell sent them flying apart like Romeo and Juliet being discovered by their parents.

"Hello?" a woman's voice called out. "Is anyone here?"

Maeve wiped her eyes. "You'd better go."

"Right. We'll figure out the whole unicorn issue after I take care of this one, okay?" Harold asked.

Maeve nodded.

Kissing her on the forehead, Harold slid through the green curtain toward the shop, feeling every bit as old as his driver's license said he was.

"Anyone here?" A dark-haired woman poked her head over the display of oriental vases near the front of the store. She wore a peach cardigan over jeans and a t-shirt with letters worn so thin Harold couldn't make out what it said. He was never a good judge of women's clothing, but her cardigan and boots looked designer, or at least like quality knock-offs. Her hair was severely pulled back in a ponytail.

I bet she's a harpy, he thought, eyeing the customer up and down. Type A personalities usually were. They were almost worse than those kids that wear their pants with the crotch down to their kneecaps. Almost.

In her ear was one of those gadgets for hands-free talking.

Harold groaned. What were they called again? Greenteeth? Bluetooths? Either way, those gadgets left him disoriented. There was no way to tell if the customer was talking to him or the disembodied voice on the phone. Clearing his throat, he waved the woman over. But she held up a finger, silencing him before he said anything.

"Don't touch a thing," she said, speaking a bit louder than necessary. "When I'm done here, we'll go out for ice cream."

Harold walked from one end of the counter to the other, checking each aisle, but as far as he could tell there were no other customers. What an odd duck.

The lady took out her ear gadget and popped it into a

shoulder bag that looked big enough to hold a wallet, a six-pack of sodas, and probably a Chihuahua.

"Sorry about that," she said as she dug through her purse. "I'm Ashley. I called earlier. My grandmother, Harriet Miller, passed away a week ago."

"I'm sorry for your loss," Harold replied.

Ashley blinked at him as if still distracted by that phone call. "Thanks. I was sorting through her affairs when I found this unusual item in her bedroom with your card. I'm hoping you might tell me a little more about it." She pulled out a worn leather case resembling the outline of binoculars, his business card strategically placed beneath the handle, and pushed it across the counter to him. Her fingers were bare of any rings.

Good sign, Harold thought. It meant she'd been divorced long enough for the ring line to disappear but not long enough to get engaged or married again. Still, he wished he had more time to confirm.

Harold flipped the brass latch, opening the case, and placed his magnification spectacles on. "Let's see what we're dealing with. Opera glasses. Mother-of-pearl. Hmm." He pulled out his tablet from the drawer under the counter and opened the appraisal app. It was all a performance, a presentation for the client, but experience had taught him that a transformation went more smoothly if he played his part.

The woman tapped her manicured nails on the counter. From the corner of his eye Harold could see her leaning from one side to another, as if trying to make sure no one else was in the shop. Which there wasn't. Harold confirmed their solitude again with a quick glance over Ashley's shoulder. He wouldn't dare transform a client if other eyes were present.

"Mmm, yes," he said, scrolling to the item in his catalog. "Lefils, if I'm not mistaken. Paris. Late 1800s." He straightened, ready for the dramatic reveal of the price tag, but Ashley was busy pacing from the specialty table to the lamps displayed across the far end of the counter. She bent, peering around corners and under the tablecloths.

"Is something wrong?" Harold asked.

"What? Oh, sorry." The woman rushed back toward the register. "What did you say?"

Maybe she's a griffin instead. It's not too late to back out now. Harold's muscles tensed. He hated the sudden pit in his stomach. What if he was wrong? But they needed the money. He'd just have to deal with whatever creature luck threw at him.

Ugh. Harold felt as if a cartoon angel sat on one shoulder and a devil on the other. He hated those cartoons, so he told his angel to shut up. "I'll give you $600. I just need you to verify that the lenses still focus."

Ashley froze, her jaw slack. "Excuse me?"

"Your grandmother seems to have taken excellent care of these." Harold held the opera glasses out to her. "They are well maintained, no scratches. These are quality French opera glasses that utilize Galilean optics with a fixed focus. As long as they still work well, I don't see any reason not to give a decent price for them."

She bit her lip, then nodded.

Harold relaxed. Step one, out of the way. Now he only needed her to trigger the spell then pray that she turned into one of the creatures on their list. Or a unicorn. Wouldn't that be nice. Harold told his devil to shut up too.

"Wonderful. Look through the lens and see if you can read that poster on the wall." Harold pointed to the 1950s advertisement poster that hung on the wall to his right, next to the dressing rooms. In reality, it was the spell that unlocked the magic and triggered the transformation.

Ashley set her purse on the counter and took the antique glasses. Turning toward the poster, she raised the glasses halfway, then paused. Harold thought she mumbled, "There you are."

Harold looked up, confused. But Ashley's demeanor had softened and her shoulders relaxed. Definitely an odd duck.

Ashley lifted the glasses to her eyes and silently read the words on the sign. A whirlwind erupted, enveloping Ashley in smoke and sparks like aerial fireworks being set off indoors.

Harold pressed the latch on the side of his register, triggering a lockdown on the shop. The illuminated OPEN sign switched off, and fire-retardant metal doors slammed down, blocking off the entire front of the store. To passersby, the shop would look closed for the night. Harold flipped open the hidden side panel on the register and reached for his tranquilizer gun, ready for battle.

The shop clocks beat faster and faster in the building chaos. He'd have to fix more than the carriage clock now.

Harold opened the chamber of his gun, removed the safety cap off a prefilled sedative dart, and slid it into the chamber. Pulling out his pocket watch, he ticked down the seconds until the transformation would be complete.

Five seconds. Four. Three. Two. One.

The swirling vortex vanished with a pop.

Every clock stopped.

In the ensuing silence, he heard a tiny scratching sound and a soft whimper.

Harold stood on his tiptoes, trying to pinpoint the sound's source in the growing haze. But then, the floorboards vibrated, sending shockwaves up the rubber soles of his loafers, and the store felt as if autumn had reversed to the intense, muggy heat of summer once again.

When the smoke cleared, Ashley was gone. In her place was a coiled figure, bluer than the ocean, lying on the shredded remains of Ashley's jeans, shirt, and peach cardigan. The creature breathed deep and slow. Once. Twice. Then it uncurled its tail and stood, radiating strength, force, and wonder in waves of heat from its scales.

In all the years he had specialized in black market sales of magical creatures on the Dark Web, he'd never once dealt with a dragon. Salamanders, yes, but not dragons. And yet, here was an eight-foot, sapphire-blue dragon in his antique store.

"Beautiful," Harold whispered.

The dragon stretched toward the ceiling, her head swaying like a charmed cobra learning a new dance. She extended her limbs one at a time, testing her new form. As Ashley-the-dragon turned, her tail hit the opera glasses where they had fallen. The artifact slid across the floor and ricocheted off an upturned table and into the dressing room.

Harold slid the chamber shut on the gun.

The dragon snapped to attention, focusing her yellow-green eyes on him. With a growl of a furnace coming to life, the creature spread her wings and sipped in a breath of air.

"Damn." Harold dove under the counter, gun in hand, as an orange flame shot over his head. The air smelled of fire, brimstone, and burnt hair.

Overhead, the emergency sprinklers activated, spurting out a sad drizzle of water before giving up entirely. Harold grabbed Maeve's water bottle and squirted the liquid all over his scalp to douse the tendrils of dragon fire clinging to his follicles.

The dragon knocked over shelves, vases, and lamps as she stumbled toward the front of the store along the wall of vintage clothes. The few chandeliers overhead clinked together, reflecting the dim shop lighting into the crystals and off her scales like a giant blue disco ball. With one swipe of her claws, the chandeliers crashed to the ground.

"Maeve, get the—" But his words were interrupted by a roar louder than a Nomad's engine. Harold immediately shut off his hearing aids.

Maeve's head peered below the curtain, her eyes wide with fear. Her lips moved, but Harold couldn't understand any of it. Maeve disappeared only to reemerge seconds later.

She held up three fingers.

Maeve slid the first item, a modified rifle, across the floor to him with perfect accuracy.

On the second signal, she sent his black case of silver-tipped darts. He opened the darts and loaded the gun. When he looked up, a paper-wrapped bundle bounced across the uneven wood, stopping inches from his fingertips. Harold pulled off the crinkled notepaper from around a red apple and read the message: poisoned.

What was she thinking?

"She's not Snow White," he yelled at her.

Whatever she was about to mouth was replaced by a silent scream and Maeve covering her head. Harold immediately dove beneath the counter just as an entire rack of vintage clothing slammed into the register next to him. Harold rolled aside to avoid the jagged pieces of broken metal and sliced his arm on a piece of glass stuck between two wooden floor beams.

Harold's knees protested as he skirted around the counter and ducked behind a full-sized cherry cabinet. Risking blown eardrums, he turned on his hearing aids and listened. The dragon sniffed the air, then moved further away. If the creature was looking for him, she was moving in the wrong direction.

Harold weighed his options, and he didn't like any of them. What he wouldn't give for a good shoulder angel at that moment.

The dragon raked her claws against the metal barrier blocking the front of the shop. Grateful for old age, Harold immediately switched back to his nearly deaf mode. Crouching into position, Harold raised the rifle to his shoulder. Lifting the sight just a hair, he focused on the weak spot under her arm and fired. The dart hit home, and the dragon roared. She spun, creating a deep dent into the metal barrier, sending candlesticks and music boxes exploding in the air as if hit by a grenade.

He dropped the rifle and stumbled backwards, landing hard on the floor. The dragon knocked over wardrobes and end tables as she barreled toward him like, well, a dragon in an antique shop. He grabbed everything within reach and threw it at her. He even threw the apple.

Harold fled for the safety of what was left of the counter but slipped on the shattered glass and slammed into it instead. His vision blurred and went dark.

❖

Was he dead? It hurt too much to be dead. Then why hadn't Ashley finished him off?

A rough cloth pressed against his forehead. Harold waited for the overwhelming explosion of sound from a rampaging dragon, but he only heard the crunching of someone moving on glass.

"Can you hear me?" Maeve asked him, her voice tinged with worry, but soft.

Harold opened his eyes, then wished he hadn't. His head ached. Light hurt his eyes. And Maeve, his Maeve, looked near death. Her hair rivaled photos of Einstein, and her face was covered in scratches.

"Thanks for not dying on me." She kissed his cheek, then helped him stand up.

"You're welcome?" he replied tentatively, looking at the chaos before him. In the middle of their decimated inventory lay a sapphire dragon fast asleep. It would take more than the money from a dragon to repair the amount of damage she'd made.

"She went down when I shot her with the gun you dropped," Maeve said, bending over to pick up the shredded remains of the woman's handbag and rifling through it.

A flurry of fabric near the poster grabbed Harold's attention. Coming out of the dressing room and holding the dented opera glasses was a young girl with short, curly hair. She couldn't be more than ten or eleven years old and wore pink stretch pants with a grey DC Girl Superheroes shirt and a red plastic bracelet on her wrist.

She looked at the sleeping dragon on the floor and tilted her head. She didn't seem afraid, but curious. "Mom-my?"

Maeve gasped. "No."

The sapphire dragon shifted toward the girl but did not wake. Harold couldn't move, couldn't think.

The girl lifted the opera glasses to her face and moved around, mimicking each move her mom made, step-by-step, as if trying to recreate a science experiment. Silently, she mouthed the words on the advertisement poster.

Maeve dove to stop her, but the magic had already triggered. A whirlwind swirled through the store, picking at the debris surrounding the girl's feet.

Smoke filled the air. Pop. Snap. Sparks flew.

The wind swirled faster and faster, tugging at the hem of Harold's slacks, but he still could not move. Maeve knocked the glasses out of the girl's hands just as the smoke enveloped them both.

Time froze. Harold couldn't breathe. Didn't dare breathe.

The first shape Harold could pick out of the smoke as the magic subsided was Maeve collapsing to the floor. Cradled in her arms was a bundle no bigger than a newborn foal, the same mother-of-pearl color as the opera glasses.

"No," Maeve whimpered as tears streamed down her face and onto the creature's head.

The foal sneezed, revealing a spiral horn of gold. Standing on shaky legs, she walked hesitantly toward the sleeping dragon. As she passed Harold a red circle fell from her foreleg.

Harold picked up a child's medical bracelet that read, "My name is Lacy. I am autistic and may not respond or be aware of danger."

The unicorn foal curled up to the dragon and fell fast asleep.

Harold glanced back at his wife. From the look in her eyes,

he could see that Maeve was as broken as the remains of the opera glasses lying next to her.

What have we done?

Karen Pellett has worked as a photographer, a business analyst, and a freelance writer for newspapers and magazines. But most of her time is spent between raising three overly brilliant (and stinkin' cute) children, playing video games with her stepsons, and the rare peaceful moment with her husband. When opportunity provides she escapes to an alternate dimension to work on her non-fiction series, Spectrum Mom, delving into the world of parenting children with Autism Spectrum Disorder, and short fiction that explores human complexity with unusual twists on perspective. Karen lives, plots, writes, and hides in the suburbs of Northern Utah.

DJINN IN TONIC

STEVE RUSKIN

DJINN IN TONIC

It was a slow Tuesday when the man from the D.A.S. walked into the Ketchum Antique Emporium.

He came in the late afternoon. I know this because the light right then was gorgeous: that early-autumn afternoon sun that filters through the front windows and casts golden rays over every inch of wooden furniture, porcelain figurine, and chipped Victorian teacup. Motes of dust hung in the air like flaxen will-o-the-wisps, floating among rusty ranch tools, die-cast toy cars, and someone's uncle's Army uniform worn at Iwo Jima.

In that light, the Emporium's worn wooden floors and mahogany-paneled walls glowed honey-brown. The rays even lit up the old photos I'd hung of the Idaho forest fires of 1910, known to history as the "Big Blowup." Illuminated in that soft sunlight, you could almost see the massive orange and yellow flames engulfing Idaho's towering pines, even though the century-old images were in black and white.

Those photos captivated me; they were the only items in the store I was never able to part with, despite repeated requests to sell them. They reminded me of the potential for natural catastrophe, even in the most serene of places. I just never expected my little antique store to be one of those places, at least not on a day as tranquil as this. But then again, I've always been a bit naïve.

With an hour to go before closing, I was putting a stash of very old cologne bottles into the counter-top case by the register. I'd bought them at an estate sale down in Sun Valley last month, and some of them still smelled nice, even after all these years.

I pried the rubber stopper out of one of them and gave it a tentative sniff. The cologne itself was long gone, of course, but there was a bit of residue at the bottom, a faint amber ring.

The overall nose was woody. Sandalwood maybe, or cedar. Bergamot was in there, too, and cardamom. It was a custom scent, hand-made for a gentleman in London, or perhaps Milan. How this bottle made its way to Idaho, I'll never know. But it was way better than the stuff the kids were dousing themselves with these days: Polo's Horse Sweat or Nautica's Damp Kelp or Calvin Klein's Paranoid Obsession. Or whatever.

I was never very good with names.

I replaced the stopper and set it alongside the other bottles when I noticed, through the opposite side of the glass case, a small man.

Very small.

How long he'd been standing there I couldn't say. But I could be forgiven for not noticing him at first. After all, the top of his head barely came up to the level of the counter. And when I say barely, that includes the white feather sticking up out of his yellow silk turban.

Yeah, I said turban. And while I didn't see him at first, once I did, I couldn't unsee him.

A few years back, an old penny arcade in Boise was unloading some of its broken and worn-out games. Classic items, all wood and brass: skee ball, pachinko, squeeze-the-grip-and-test-your-strength. You know the ones.

Included in the lot was one those upright mechanical fortune tellers. Remember those? They'd have a name like "Zoltan the Magnificent" painted in bright red circus letters across the glass, while inside was the mechanical upper body of some mustachioed gypsy-looking guy, complete with turban and puffy sleeves. You'd put in a nickel, and he'd start to wave his arms, gyrate for a bit as lights flashed in his eyes. Finally, after all the rigmarole, a little card dropped into a tray: your fortune.

You'd pick it up, anticipating something profound and oriental, the wisdom of the Old World condensed to a helpful aphorism. Instead, you'd get the most ridiculously trite advice you could imagine:

> Never burn your candle at both ends.
> Happiness is a walk on the beach.
> Call your mother, she misses you.

Well, what do you expect for a nickel?

Anyway, if Zoltan the Automaton were to hop out of his fortune-telling machine and walk into my Ketchum Antique Emporium, he would have looked exactly like the man standing —and believe me, I had to double check to make sure the little guy was in fact standing—in front of me on the other side of the counter.

"Oh," I said. "Uh, hi. How can I help you?"

"Oh? Uh, hi?" he replied, in a tone clearly calculated to imitate mine—despite the fact that his voice was about five octaves higher, and heavily accented. "I dare say you've done quite enough already."

"I have?" I didn't remember ever seeing him before, and certainly not recently. "Well, good. So, how can I help you again? Something to return, perhaps?"

"In a manner of speaking, yes," he said. I think he stamped his foot—there was a faint *pflumpf* of fabric. I leaned over the counter and saw, protruding beneath his baggy pants, two little yellow slippers, the kind I imagined court jesters wore, or maybe sultans in their harem: flat and silken, with those cute little curled-up toes.

Huh. I thought. Maybe there was a costume party later at one of the local bars . . . .

"What exactly do you need to return?"

"Not a what, a who. But the immediate question is, where?"

. . . or maybe a cannabis convention—those guys were always wearing weird hippie stuff and talking crazy talk.

"I'm afraid you've lost me, Mister . . . ?"

"Abu Jabir ibn Padishah, at your service," he said with a curt nod. "I am a field agent with the Djinn Assistance Society. No doubt you've heard of us."

"Gin Assistance? I can't say. . . ."

"Say nothing, indeed," he said, waving his little hand. "It's expected you'll want to see some ID before you confess. Here you are, then."

Confess?

From the depths of his silken ensemble he produced an ornate scroll, tied in ribbon, which he snapped open. It unfurled through the air like a yo-yo, the end of the paper stopping inches from my nose, then fluttered downward gently until it rested on the glass counter.

I glanced down, but after less than a second, he yanked it back again faster than I could blink, rolling it back up his sleeve. I'd had only the briefest glance, but I'd caught a glimpse of different languages: Arabic, Hebrew, and what looked conspicuously like Sanskrit. There was some kind of wax badge at the top, and also a picture at the bottom: a portrait in the late-medieval style that may or may not have been the little guy himself.

"Satisfied now?" he said.

I sighed. I know I'm not the sharpest bayonet in the Civil-War memorabilia cabinet, but when you work in an antique store as long as I have, you learn a few things.

Like how to spot a phony.

"I'm sorry, Mr. Abdul-Jabbar, but that wasn't even close to a real badge, or official government papers, or—"

"It's Abu Jabir," he shot back, squeaking with indignation. "And the ancient brotherhood of the Djinn Assistance Society doesn't need any badges!"

Great. A funny guy.

"Gin Assistance Society? So . . . the G.A.S.? Is that one of those organizations that help people who, you know, imbibe a little too much?"

I made the drinky-drinky gesture with my thumb and pinky. He looked at me like I was an idiot. Which, given the way he was dressed, seemed rather presumptuous.

"It's the D.A.S.," he said curtly. "Now, where's the djinn?"

"Gin? Look around, man. This isn't a bar."

"Not gin. Djinn!"

He had a strange way of pronouncing gin. Ketchum gets a lot of tourists, and they're mostly great, but some of them . . . well, sheesh.

"Listen," I said, putting on my business face. "I don't know if you're wearing a hidden camera to punk me, or you're just killing time before the bars open, but this is an antique store. We ain't got gin, or rye, or whiskey or even beer. You're welcome to look around, but I close in an hour and I've got this case to stock and some invoices to mail out before then."

Zabbar the Brightly Costumed gave me the evilest evil-eye I'd ever seen.

"You, sir, are in no position to dictate terms to me! You are the one in violation of HC 45-27-19B. And yes, I said nineteen-bee. I don't think I need to tell you how serious that is."

"HC? Is that a Health Code? We don't serve anything here that could be in violation of a health code. No food, no drinks, and definitely no gin."

At that, the impetuous little twerp looked like he was going to explode. His mustache began to twitch, and his face reddened from his neck up to his bushy eyebrows like a cartoon thermometer. I imagined his turban popping off, champagne-cork style.

"Not Health Code! Hammurabic Code!"

"What? You mean the Code of Hammurabi?" Vague details of that ancient set of Mesopotamian laws percolated up from the depths of my memory, where I stored what little remained from my undergrad history classes. "The Babylonian legal system?"

"The very same," he nodded smugly. "And you, sir, are in violation! Improper storage of a djinn."

I sighed. "I. Don't. Sell. Gin. Or store it. Or even like it very much."

"Djinn!" he yelled. "Djinn! Djinn! Djinn! Say it with me . . . da-zhin!"

"Okaaaay," I said, holding up my hands in mock defeat. "Da-zhin." Must be some fancy French brand or something.

"Better."

At that point, I realized I was just going to have to humor him until the bars opened. So, I figured I may as well have a little fun.

"Wasn't the Code of Hammurabi written on stone tablets, like, uh, four thousand years ago?"

Instead of being insulted, his broad smile indicated that he considered this a point of pride rather than irrelevancy. "It's ancient indeed, so I am glad you are beginning to understand the severity of your situation."

"Yeah," I said, resting my elbows on the glass counter. "And I'm real broken up about it. But wasn't the Code of Hammurabi the first legal system to include a presumption of innocence? Didn't the accuser have to provide evidence against the accused?"

Take that.

"Thank you," he said. "For admitting your culpability. That makes it easier on both of us."

"I did no such thing!"

"Yet you just agreed to let me present the evidence against you, did you not?"

I shrugged. "By all means, go ahead."

Zonkko the Smug reached once more into the folds of his silken outfit and pulled out what looked like an astrolabe: an ancient navigation device of joined metal disks, all grooved and numbered, that helped travelers find their way by the position of the stars. I've sold one or two of them in the store over the years.

His device, however, seemed to have more attachments than the astrolabes I was familiar with: at the bottom dangled a tiny anchor on a silver chain, at the top was a pair of pentagonal rubies, and smack in the middle was a glass bubble containing the desiccated body of a very wicked-looking scorpion.

"Now that I have your permission," he said, "kindly direct me to your phials."

"Files?"

"Phials!" he stamped his foot. "Vials and vessels! Flasks and flagons! Decanters and demijohns. Don't get cheeky. This is an antique store, is it not? Where are your antique bottles, sir?"

Bottles, eh? He was a drunkard. "Why didn't you just say that in the first place? Old bottles: back room, third aisle, bottom shelf. Don't break any."

"You insult me," he snapped, turning on his little slippered heel. As he walked away, he held the astrolabe out in front of him, like a boy scout following a compass. I saw him fiddle with a knob on the device, and a second later the two rubies began to glow with an inner light. I swear I saw the scorpion twitch inside its glass cage.

Then he was gone, disappearing into the back of the store.

Weirdo. Now *I* needed a drink.

Five minutes later I was nearly finished with the cologne bottles, my mind already turning to the stack of invoices by the cash register, when I saw a feather bobbing along behind the far edge of the counter, like a shark fin slicing the surface of the water.

Heading my way.

The feather stopped right in front of me, and two little hands reached up and placed a bottle on the countertop. Then Zeezoh the Minuscule stepped back, and we faced each other once again.

"Excellent choice," I said, picking up the bottle to check the price. As I went to ring it up, however, I noticed his face was even redder than before. He was shaking with rage, and trying to speak.

Finally he managed to stammer, "I . . . suppose . . . you . . . think . . . this . . . is . . . some . . . kind . . . of . . . joke?"

"What?"

"Tonic? A bottle of tonic?"

I looked more closely at the bottle. It was green glass and stopped with what looked like the original cork. The ornate but faded label read:

> Himmelmann's Tonic
> A Remedy for Any Conditions of the System,
> Including Fatigue, Bowel Discomfort,
> and General Nervousness and Anxiety.
> Made from an Old-World Recipe
> by Himmelmann's Apothecary
> 200 Drumm Street, San Francisco

General nervousness and anxiety—heh. Zoltar the Enraged here could do with a little of this stuff. I shook the bottle, hoping against hope that there was some left.

"Yes," I said. "This is—was—tonic."

"1906?" He was spitting with rage. "1906? Do you know how long ago that was?"

"I'm sure I could do the math."

I remembered the bottle. The label was slightly singed, as if it had sat too near a candle. I'd found it on a picking trip to Salt Lake City some years ago, at an auction of lost Union Pacific luggage that had never been claimed and was forgotten in an old warehouse. Nice stuff from turn-of-the-century travelers who rode the trains between California and New York, long before planes or the interstate highway system.

Most of what I bought at that auction sold quickly. This bottle, however, just sat on the shelf. Until today.

I set it down hard on the counter.

"Twenty dollars."

"Twen . . . twenty!" Zantak stammered, picking up the bottle and cradling it like a newborn. "And this is how you treat it?"

"Look, man. It's just an old bottle. You saw the shelf, I have tons of 'em. But don't freak out. For you, I can go to fifteen. Fair?"

"Djinn in tonic," the little man muttered. "Think you're some kind of comedian, don't you?"

I noticed he didn't reach for his wallet. Dammit. I hate haggling, but I wanted him out of my store.

"Ten dollars. That's my bottom line. And I think it's called a gin and tonic."

"Dji—forget it," he spat. "You infidels never learn."

Ouch.

"Well, whatever I am, I think it's clear I'm not a bartender. You want a gin and tonic, you can go down the street to McWilliams Pub, or the Flying Dutchman. Both are open soon. But if you want this bottle, it's ten bucks."

He didn't hear me. He was eyeing the bottle closely now, peering through the thick, bubbled glass, looking for something . . .

"This has gone on long enough!" he said finally, reaching deep into his robes and fishing around.

"I agree," I said, relieved. "Ten it is. Cash or credit?"

I started tapping at the register.

"You will pay for your wanton neglect," he said, still fishing. "But I can lessen the penalty if you assist me."

"Buddy, the only one paying for anything is—"

My heart raced when I saw him remove some kind of weird

metal object. A gun? The little bugger was going to rob me now, and over a freakin' bottle?

No, not a gun. A long, slightly curved ... oil lamp? It was old metal, decorated with impressively intricate scroll work, and in need of a good polish, but even from the other side of the counter I could tell it was a very, very nice piece.

"You want to trade?" I asked, hopefully.

"Not a trade. A transfer." He handed me the tonic bottle, which I set on the counter.

"What's the difference?" I said, reaching for the lamp, a little too eagerly. "I'll need to inspect it first."

Zippy the High Strung recoiled like I was a leper.

"Hands off!" he screeched. "Nobody touches the vessel but me! The ceremony will require our utmost concentration. You shall have but two simple tasks: to unseal that"—he indicated the tonic bottle—"and hold it near this." He jiggled his lamp. "And then—and this is the most important part of all—you must speak the true name to bind the djinn."

"Don't you mean tonic?"

"The djinn! You must speak its name. Are you dense?"

"No," I said, perhaps a little too petulantly. The guy was really getting under my skin. "No, I'm not. So what's this name I'm supposed to speak, anyway?"

"Samsama'il Al-Abyadd. Got it?"

"Sam . . . yeah. Got it."

"I cannot overemphasize the precariousness of this situation," he said. "The state of this djinn is unknown, being bound to this bottle for over one hundred years. It could be quite volatile."

I shook the bottle. "Looks empty to me. And I still say it's tonic."

"Our only hope is to make this transfer as quick as possible. Djinn interactions with mortals can be exceedingly dangerous. Do not bow, do not negotiate, and above all, do not apologize. They can sense weakness. And if they do, well . . ."

"Sounds like an AA meeting," I said. "I guess gin can bring

out the worst in folks, and believe me, I know from recent experience the futility of negotiating with drunks."

I thought that last bit rather clever, but Zarnac was too focused on his lamp and failed to appreciate my sarcasm.

"Remember," he said solemnly. "The price of failure is incalculable. Only by uttering the true name can we bind this djinn to the proper vessel. Ready?"

"Bind gin. Don't fail. Ready, boss."

Zakjak the Serious began to chant. He began to hop. He spun and whirled, and flung colored powder from pouches at his belt. There were scents and smoke, a fistful of feathers, and flashes of light. Up and down switched places, and day became night which became day again. The tonic bottle began to shudder and shake.

"Now!" Zilfin shouted. "Open the bottle and speak the name!"

With the old bottle in one hand, I pried out the cork with the other. It was wedged in tighter than I expected, and it took some effort. Finally, the cork popped free and rolled away behind the counter.

Zoglin was spinning like a dervish, the lamp held high above him. "Now! The name. Say it!"

That's when I totally blanked. Sam ... something. Samuel Albacore? Samantha Albuquerque? Like I said . . . I'm not that great with names.

"Uh . . ."

The tonic bottle jerked wildly, and I had to use both hands to keep it steady. Something green—deep, misty, almost neon—began to pour out like smoke from a chimney.

"Hurry! The name!"

"Er, Samwise . . . ?"

From the green smoke a shape formed. A finger. The finger grew a hand, the hand developed an arm, and then there was a shoulder, impossibly broad and muscular. The tonic bottle began to crack.

"Damn you, now!"

"Salami Alabaster," I muttered. *No, that's not right...*

A head formed above the neon-green shoulder. It was not quite human, but also not quite not human. Long dark hair, thick and curly; eyes like embers; a body both solid and smokey and transparent as jade. Gold rings, gold bracelets, and gold earrings encircled and pierced every inch of its body, except the lower half, which was swathed in billowing red silk.

"It's Samsama'il Al-Abyadd!" Zoofoo shrieked. "Quickly, before—"

The green giant was out of the bottle now, rising and expanding until his head hit the ceiling. But he seemed tethered somehow, as if he were a balloon on a string, and the string was tied to the tonic bottle.

Zolmec was furious. "THE NAME! NOW!"

"Samsonite Alibaba!" I yelled at the top of my voice. That was close, right? In the ballpark?

Apparently not. The creature hovered above us, arms folded across his chest. His grin was imperious, but not quite evil. At least, not yet.

Zanax quivered, dropping to his knees. "Oh Great and Powerful One . . ."

Suddenly, I understood.

"Oh, hey! You meant djinn. As in genie. Not gin. Duh. Well, now it all makes sense. Look guys, I'm really sorry . . ."

Zolfar stared at me, eyes wide in horror, as if I had just cursed his mother and spat on his father's grave.

"You fool! No!"

"What'd I do? Oh, riiiight . . . I'm not supposed to apologize. Sorry." I grinned sheepishly.

The genie spoke, a sound like thunder forming words.

"Your contrition is noted," he said, staring down at us. "And now, I shall exact the price of my long containment. But first, mind if I stretch?"

That was when he showed us his evil smile.

"Run!" Zamsam shrieked.

The tonic bottle shattered in my hands.

The metaphorical balloon string had broken, and the genie was loose in my store. With a clap of his hand, he created a shockwave, and two dozen vintage road signs were flung from the walls. Another clap, and an Edwardian dressing table became highly-polished kindling.

Then, before I could say "abracadabra," the genie was whirling its arms like a windmill. Soon, tiny tornados were dancing down the aisles, smashing knickknacks and winging washboards like, well, tiny tornados in an antique store.

It was pretty much duck-and-cover from that point on. I made it behind a bunker of old sofas, but a flying table lamp (Tiffany) followed by a taxidermied bear (Grizzly) sent me scrambling elsewhere.

I sprinted for the safety of two old pinball machines. But before I could reach them, an incoming barrage of ceramic vases, copper pots, and a devastatingly accurate dime-store Indian blew the machines to bits. I hit the floor to avoid shrapnel from flippers, bumpers, and silver balls.

Behind an old Coke cooler I caught a glimpse of curled slippers. I lunged and grabbed, and Zuntan whimpered as I dragged us both back behind the glass counter.

"What do we do?" I asked desperately.

"There's nothing we can do. An unbound djinn is like a hurricane: it must wear itself out."

"How long?"

"Hours? Days?"

"Ugh."

"It's your fault, you know." He glared at me with one beady eye (the other was covered by his lopsided turban). "How difficult is it to say Samsama'il Al-Abyadd? The D.A.S. will be hearing of this. You'll probably be audited."

"And I eagerly await their call. In the meantime . . . do you hear that?"

"What?"

"Listen."

We listened. The sounds of wanton destruction had stopped. From the front of the store came a faint blubbering.

Carefully, inch by slow inch, I raised my head above the counter. The djinn was cowering before my pictures of the 1910 forest fires. In the afternoon sunlight, those black and white images took on the appearance of real flame, towering and insatiable. The djinn seemed terrified by them. His size had diminished to that of a small boy, and it was crying soft, whimpering sobs.

"So like San Francisco..." it was moaning, over and over again.

"What's happening?" Zxyzzy looked at me, confused.

"How am I supposed to know? You're the djinn guy. Wait... wait a second..."

I remembered the tonic bottle, dated San Francisco, 1906.

Of course! That was the year of the great San Francisco earthquake, which was followed by a terrible fire. What the quake didn't destroy of the city, the fire did.

Slowly, carefully, I made my way to the djinn and gently put my hand on his heaving shoulder. It was like touching lime jello.

"There, there," I said. "Want to tell me about it?"

"The last time I was free was 1906," he began, after running his forearm under his nose. "Was my first time in the States, you know. Very exciting for me, seeing the New World and all that. All the other djinns were raving about it. I found the San Francisco Bay particularly attractive. All those breezes blowing in from the sea... a wonderful way to hover along, over the water, above the city. I highly recommend it, if you're ever disembodied. It was the best few weeks of my many thousand years of life."

"And then?"

"The earthquake! One day, I'm just levitating over a dock in the bay, killing time. The next, everything's shaking violently.

Buildings dropping like a caravan of tired camels. But the worst was the fires—flames everywhere! I was lost in the heat and smoke. I found a man, a seller of tonic. One of his bottles lay open, and I whooshed myself inside. It smelled terrible, but I only intended to hide there for a moment, while I gathered my wits.

"Then there came a cork, and someone gave the man some coins, and before I knew it I was on a train to Ogden, fleeing San Francisco with everyone else. I think you know the rest."

He broke down again, weeping. I tousled his airy, gelatinous hair.

"It's scary here in the New World, you know that?" he said when he collected himself again. "These fires of yours, do they happen frequently?"

"Afraid so. At least, around here. Where you from?"

"Persia, originally. But I've moved around a lot. It's an occupational hazard that comes with living in bottles and lamps."

"Was Persia nice?"

"Lovely, if you don't mind sand in your silk trousers. But oh, the oases. Date palms, burbling pools . . . sheer paradise."

"So I hear. Say, what if we could get you back there? Would you like that? And in comfort, too. No more tonic bottles."

He stopped sniffling. "How?"

"See him?" I pointed to the glass counter, where we could see two eyes and a feathered turban peering back at us. "He says he can offer assistance. He's part of some society."

He perked up. "The Djinn Assistance Society? I've heard good things about them."

Good things?

"Well, he's got a nice lamp for you, anyway. Looks real luxurious. I didn't exactly catch his name, but—"

"It's Abu Jabir ibn Padishah," Abu Jabir ibn Padishah said, coming around from behind the counter and bowing dramatically.

"Yeah, that," I said.

The djinn floated over and stroked one appreciative finger across the lamp. "Oooh, Damascus steel?"

"Fourth-century Syrian." Zoltan Abu ibn Whatever beamed proudly. "You should see the inside. Velvet lined, with Moroccan leather trim."

"Really?" said the djinn. "Any cushions?"

"Egyptian cotton. Silk tassels. Stuffed with extinct Arabian ostrich feathers."

And that was that. Before you could say "forty thieves," the djinn was inside the lamp, and Zoltan the Magnificent was out the door.

"Hey! Abdul Jabbar!" I said, chasing him outside. The sun was setting behind the mountains, and evening was coming on. "That's it?"

"What's it?"

"All of it," I said, pointing back toward my store. "After all that, you just up and leave my store in shambles? Didn't I help you recover your djinn?"

"I'm only authorized for search and recovery. Cleanup is someone else's job. D.A.S. regulations. Sorry."

As he walked away, I thought of something else.

"Wait! Don't I get my three wishes?"

This made him stop. He turned, pointing an accusing finger. "Three wishes?"

"Yeah. Genie, bottle . . . you know the drill."

"You want three wishes? How about this? Wish you had never violated HC 45-27-19B! Wish that you never, ever see me again! And if you do, wish that you had never been born in the first place!"

Then, in a puff of red smoke, he was gone. I was alone on the sidewalk in downtown Ketchum. Jeeps and Range Rovers cruised the street, while hipsters on mountain bikes pedaled by.

"I just wish my antique store was back in order," I muttered, heading inside.

The last rays of sunlight reflected off the windows as I

headed to the back for a broom and dustpan. That's when I noticed everything in the Ketchum Antique Emporium was intact, upright, and in just the right place.

Every road sign. Every washboard. Every teacup.

On the glass counter stood the tonic bottle, corked and whole again, right down to the singed label.

Next to it lay a note, penned in the most beautiful script I'd ever seen.

I.O.U., it said.

Sincerely,

Samsonite Alibaba

Steve Ruskin's stories have appeared in the anthologies *Temporally out of Order*; *Avast, Ye Airships!*; and the *Martian Anthology*, as well as AntipodeanSF; Mad Scientist Journal; and Story Emporium. He is an historian of science and technology, focusing on the Victorian period. He has been a university professor, a mountain-bike guide, and a number of things in between. Visit him online at www.steveruskin.com.

THIS ONE IS SPECIAL

TANYA HALES

THIS ONE IS SPECIAL

My mom only visited me once during summer break, to drop off a present for my nineteenth birthday. I was completely unsurprised when it was something from the antique shop down the block from the grocery store where I worked.

"There's something special about this one," she told me, leaning against the counter in my apartment's kitchen. She had that manic gleam in her eyes that only thrift stores, yard sales, and antique shops inspired. "Even your inexperienced eyes should be able to see it."

I unwrapped the package. Inside was a long box covered in embossed leather. When I slid the lid off, I found a pad of paper with delicate, faded, floral designs lying next to a funky-looking ballpoint pen. I picked up the pen to try to write my name on the top sheet of paper, but no matter how I scribbled, the ink wouldn't flow.

"Don't waste it," my mother warned. "I obviously won't tell you what I spent on it, but this stationary set is quite old. It's from the fifties. But its real value lies in what you can't see. I'm telling you, Felicia, I know it's lucky."

These words from my mom were nothing new. I'd been told

all my life about lucky keys, bracelets that cured arthritis, earrings that made you appear more beautiful, and music boxes that would attract money. It was only in recent years that I had rebelled against all the nonsense.

I sighed, because how do you argue about such things with the person who raised you? Instead, I said, "The pen doesn't even work."

"It's the stationery that's lucky. You can use a different pen."

"And I'm pretty sure the leather on the box is fake."

"Felicia!" My mom insisted. "Just try it out! I know you haven't gone on a date since last semester, so I suggest starting with a few love notes."

"Love notes?" I demanded, appalled. "To whom?"

"This is a college town, Felica!" She was clearly exasperated with my obtuseness. "There are eligible boys your age everywhere. Find one you like and write a sweet note. Boys love that!"

I snorted and said under my breath, "Yeah, maybe back in the fifties." But I assured her I would at least try.

And that was that. She made the two-hour drive back to my hometown, and I went back to my days of working as a checker at the local grocery store and evenings of pouring over catalogs and online articles to help me finally decide on a major.

The ancient stationery set sat untouched on my bedside table until, weeks later, my mom called to ask if I'd done anything with it. I assured her I had great plans for it, and, with a smirk, I pulled the pad of paper out of the box and jotted down my shopping list for the next day. Love notes weren't my style, but lists I could get behind.

That's when things started to get interesting.

Work at the friendly neighborhood grocer started in a typical way the next afternoon. The familiar motions of scanning items and entering codes, of standing and waiting, of smiling and bobbing my head. The repeated, "Hello, did you find everything you need?" and, "Have a nice day!" I'll admit it wasn't my favorite job. I hated the repetition, the meaningless small talk and the fake pleasantries. The other students were the worst, always rushing, barely meeting my eyes over the tops of their phones or wallets. The only relief was when some of the locals who were starting to recognize me would chat a bit more genuinely.

And that's why what happened that evening was such a surprise.

I had just finished ringing up a crabby college kid and then a mother and her three squabbling children, all after a series of card reader problems. I could practically feel my brain brimming with cortisol. There was a lull for the first time in ages, and I calmed myself with some deep breaths until another customer appeared. I greeted him and gave him a glance only long enough to reveal that he was a good-looking, brown-eyed guy around my age. Probably another person awash with righteous indignation about how the prices were more expensive than Walmart's.

I forced a smile and began ringing up his small line of items, most of them odd brands of snacks that I didn't even recognize. I glanced back up at him when he said, "Felicia, is it? Can I ask you a question?"

I almost made a self-pitying remark about how the name pinned to my shirt was actually a new slave name the store had given me, but instead I said cheerfully, "Sure! How can I help you?"

The young man smiled, revealing dimples and a mischievous sparkle in his eyes. "I just wanted your opinion." He held up two bags of fruit. One held a single lemon and the other held an apple. "I've just become aware of a bad habit of mine. See, I bag fruits and vegetables even if I'm only getting one. Seems like a waste, eh?"

I shrugged one shoulder and gave him an amused smile. "That's pretty common. Most people bag single fruits and veggies."

"That's what I was wondering," he said, nodding. "Which

leads me to my question. Is it even a bag anymore if it's not being used as a container? Or is it just a protective barrier?"

My smile widened. "I think you could make a valid argument that it's just a shield against germs. I'd buy that theory. Especially because I know how grimy the conveyor belt can get."

The boy sighed. "Well, in that case, I'll have to continue wasting bags wantonly."

I finished ringing him up. He paid with exact cash and change, then thanked me for chatting. And that was it.

But, for some reason, that unusual conversation had me still smiling as I got off work and did my own quick grocery shopping. As I moved around the store, I tried and failed to shake the young man from my mind. But then I noticed something odd. Everything on my list was on sale. Every single thing. As I went through the self-checkout, I grinned. I had never spent so little money on so much stuff.

Well, maybe my mom was right about the stationery being lucky. At the very least, I could call her and make her feel good about herself by telling her as much.

Work the next day looked almost exactly the same. The same tiring routine, the same aching feet from standing so long.

And then, suddenly, he appeared again. The same boy. The same smile. This time, along with his small pile of groceries, he was holding up a small packet of seasoning. Without introduction, he said, "I have another question for you."

I smiled back. "Fire away."

"Well, there was this display stand with these free seasoning packets to flavor the party snack mixes they want you to make. Typical commercialistic gimmick. But here's the thing. The sign said: 'Free. Please take one.'" He made air quotes with his fingers as he said "free." "You seem like an educated person, Felicia. Why do you think they'd put quotes around the word 'free'? Is it a misuse of punctuation, or were they actually trying to tell us something?"

I couldn't help but grin as I said, "I noticed that stand

yesterday too. It did make me feel like I was getting tricked into something. You know. Because it's 'free-ee-ee.'" I made the air quotes too as I drew out the word. "So I couldn't bring myself to take one."

He laughed. "Well, if an evil genie appears to me saying that I've unwittingly entered into a contract by taking the seasoning, I'll let you know. Or maybe it would be the spiteful ghost of the store's founder."

"Probably coming to haunt you because you took the seasoning without also buying the pretzels, Chex cereal, and peanuts that it's supposed to go so perfectly with," I chimed in.

I scanned his items, picking up the jug of orange juice to examine a brand name I didn't recognize. He also had some old-fashioned-looking packs of gum that I'd never seen before, but I shrugged it off since they scanned in just fine. Then I grimaced as my foot lit up with pain. I bent to adjust my sock. The padding on the bottom of my worn shoes was all but gone now.

While the boy counted out bills, I discreetly pulled out my stationery pad, jotting down a reminder to buy better tennis shoes.

The boy glanced over, noticing the aged stationery. "Wow. That paper looks old."

I hurried to put it away, kicking myself for getting distracted on the job. "It is. And my mom seems to think it's magical."

"Not a bad find, then." He gave a sideways smile. "Magic aside, someone might pay good money for antique stationery like that."

I grinned, pulling it back out to extend it toward him. "Ok. How much are you offering?"

He took a step back, raising his hands defensively. "Sorry, but I'm pretty sure those are roses along the border. It's not really my thing. My taste is a bit more in the direction of lilacs." I laughed, and he added, "You could try selling it to the antique shop down the street. It's the kind of thing they'd go for."

I smiled, trying not to look bitter. "That's where my mom got it. Birthday present. Even though all I'd asked for was help with tuition."

He gave me a knowing look. "Well, if you need help with tuition then that's an even better reason to sell it back. You should at least see what they think it's worth. Not to mention that the shop itself is really cool. Totally worth checking out."

I promised him that I'd think about it, but what I didn't say was that, because of my mom, I'd seen enough antiques shops to fill several lifetimes. Before he could finish walking off, I called out to him, "By the way, what's your name?"

He smiled. "Terrence."

And then he was gone and my shift was over.

Terrence. This time, I let myself think about him that evening. Just a little bit.

Things continued in this way for more than a week. Every day I worked, Terrence showed up just before my shift ended. We would banter about funny store policies and displays, or about my "magic" stationery pad, which I was wasting away by using it for my shopping lists.

Every time he saw it sitting out near the register so that I could jot down reminders of things I needed to get, he'd shake his head and say that I should take it over to the antique store. "It's closing permanently in a week, but the owner is a real collector. He may be willing to buy it back from you anyway." He shrugged, then winked. "Maybe the magic of it is that it can get you some more college money in a pinch."

I wasn't sure why I didn't do it. Maybe it was because I wanted to get back at my mom for getting me something so useless and expensive by writing equally useless notes on it. Or maybe it was because it felt kind of scummy to sell it behind her back.

But there was one thing I was sure of. I really liked Terrence. A lot.

And he just kept showing up. I waited expectantly each day as he brought his small assortment of odd groceries through the line. He was always dressed up in a white, button-up shirt that was tucked into his slacks, and hair that was combed back from his forehead in an old-fashioned, charming way. And he always paid for everything in exact cash, usually in old bills and coins which, combined with his frequent talk of the neighboring antique shop, made me realize that he was a collector like my mom. This gave us another thing in common to talk about.

But each day, after an amusing few minutes of banter, he walked away.

And that was it.

So, I decided to take things into my own hands. If he wouldn't ask me on a date, then I'd have to ask him.

Late one night, I pulled out my trusty stationery and made lists. Lists of things I knew about Terrence. Lists of things I liked about him. Lists of things we could do around here together. Lists of which things were actually good options for a first date.

I found lists comforting. Creating them felt like exploring every option, like accomplishing something through words and paper alone. If nothing else, my mom's gift of rare fifties stationery had given me that comfort.

I lay on my bed with only a dim lamp for light and wrote down every thought and idea. I wrote late into the night until, with shock, I saw that I had filled and torn out every page in the stationery pad except two. I shook my head. Well, it wasn't like I was ever going to sell it back anyway.

I stared at that top piece of paper, thinking of the unusual boy I'd grown such a crush on. He'd transformed my hours of monotony by giving me interesting conversations to look forward to each day. His smiles and unexpected jokes had lifted my spirits this summer break like nothing else had. I let out a satisfied sigh, then wrote down the culmination of my thoughts on the top of the page.

Antique shop, I wrote, circling it. That's where we'd go. Even if old, dusty, pretentious shops like that were a tiresome scene for me, I could tell by the way he talked about it so much that it was a store that he was genuinely fond of. Maybe it was weird, but it also seemed inevitable and perfect.

My thoughts lingered again on his easy smile and witty comments and how I'd never met anyone like him before. My pen hovered over the page again for a moment before I wrote, *You're too good to be true.*

And with that, I rolled over in bed, clicked off the light, and smiled myself to sleep.

The next day, I waited all morning, then all afternoon, then all evening. I glanced at the clock as the end of my shift drew nearer. Terrence would be here any minute with his specialty selection of candies and crackers. But the end of my shift rolled around. Then went by.

Terrence never came.

I shopped for my groceries, going slowly for the first time in ages because I'd forgotten the last page of stationery at home and hadn't made a list that day. The sales I'd gotten so used to seemed to have vanished, so I spent a lot of time walking around hunting for them. Or was I just going slowly on purpose in the hopes that Terrence would show up suddenly?

I drove home.

I walked into my apartment in a haze of disappointment. It was a Friday evening, so my roommates were all out on dates or at parties. I moved down the dark hall, clicking on the lamp in my bedroom to shine a low light on all the pages of stationery I'd left scattered on the floor. My eyes glanced over all the lists, and I shook my head at my own foolishness. My luck with boys had always been bad. Maybe I should quit while I was still ahead.

I swept all the lists aside with my foot, sinking down onto my bed. My eyes landed on the two papers still sitting on my bedside table. One was the last page still attached to the stationary pad, and the other was the note I'd written last night. At the top were still the words *Antique store*, and beneath that was my silly, late-night thought: *You're too good to be true.*

But was it just me, or was something new written beneath

that? I leaned forward, squinting. My eyebrows came together. Written under my words in very different handwriting than my own were the words, *You're right.*

Behind me, my bedroom door slowly creaked closed and I whirled around. Previously hidden behind the door, but now revealed, was a figure. I shrieked as he stepped into the light.

It was Terrence.

"What are you doing here?!" I demanded, heart in my throat. My shaking hands scrabbled at the drawer of my bedside table until I could yank out a heavy metal flashlight and raise it like a weapon.

"Jeez," Terrence said, raising his hands to show that he meant no harm. "I'm not here to hurt you."

My voice trembled as I said, "Oh yeah?" The young man standing near my bedroom wall looked just like Terrence, the same buttoned shirt and slacks, the same brown hair, but something was different. His eyes. They looked dark. Like storm clouds.

Terrence folded his arms, leaning back against the wall with a forced air of casualness. "Well, I won't pretend that I'm not a little bit angry." He gestured to my floor. "In just one night you wasted the entire stationery pad. All but one page. Did you really never figure it out?"

My eyes kept darting between him and the door. I didn't let my makeshift weapon drop an inch as my mind raced in circles around the same panicked objective. *Get out, get out, get out.* "Figure out what?"

He sighed. "Apparently not." He stepped closer, and I stiffened, hefting my weapon higher. Undeterred, he pointed at my stationery pad. "Your mom was right about it, you know. Except it isn't magical. It's cursed. At least for me. But if you had figured it out before wasting it, it would have been like genie's lamp for you. You could have gotten whatever you wanted from that stationary if you'd have written the right things before tearing the pages out."

"You're crazy," I told him, trying to keep the tremulous note out of my voice. "Get out, now."

"I can't. Not really. I can become invisible again, if you'd like. But I can't ever truly leave that stationery pad until all the pages are used up."

He stepped closer, and I leapt back, actually climbing onto my bed to give myself the advantage of higher ground. I cursed myself for leaving my phone in my purse on the couch.

Terrence halted, eying me. We stared at each other for several silent seconds before I whispered, "Get out, or I'll scream."

Equally quietly, he told me, "If anyone comes, they'll just think you're crazy."

My arms holding up the metal flashlight were shaking. "Oh yeah? Why's that?"

He gave me his familiar smile. "The only person who can see me is the last person who wrote in the stationery pad." He stepped even closer, until he was just feet away. "Have you really not noticed it yet? I'm not here to anyone but you. It's why I only showed up at the end of your shift when no one was around."

A shrill, skeptical laugh escaped me. "So, what are you, a ghost?"

His smile widened. "What if I am?" He took another step closer.

"Get back!" I yelled, swinging the flashlight with all the force I could muster. It made an arc into his shoulder.

And went right through it.

I was so surprised that the flashlight went flying from my fingers. My mouth hung open, and I backed against the wall. I had to be going loopy. This wasn't real. Reality didn't work this way.

"But you bought groceries from me." I squeaked. "Nearly every day for two weeks!"

He shrugged. "It was all part of the vision that accompanies me. Just look in your computer's history of purchases. None of mine were real. Not even the money or groceries were real. They don't sell Turkish Taffy like that anymore."

I shook my head, mind spinning, and whispered, "What do you want from me?"

He smiled placatingly. "I just want to go home. And I need you to help me get there by taking that," he pointed at the stationery pad, "back to the antique shop."

I clenched my fists. "Why don't you do it yourself?"

He ran his hands through his hair, frustrated. "I would, but I can't. While I can interact with some objects in a limited way, I can't directly touch the stationery pad because my soul is attached to it. That's why I've been trying to convince you to go sell it back." His gaze fell to the ground. "Especially now that my brother has lost so much money that he has to close the shop."

"Your brother?" The cogs of my brain clicked in circles for a few unsuccessful seconds. "But isn't the owner of that antique shop an old man?"

He raised an eyebrow like I was being a little dense and said, "Yeah?"

I blinked. Oh yeah. The stationery was old.

"That store has been in my family for ages." Terrence's voice was quiet, his gaze on the floor again. "It breaks my heart that it's shutting down. My family put everything they had into that store, but now my brother, William, is the only one still interested in keeping it around." He let out a self-depreciating laugh. "Maybe it makes sense. It's a dangerous business, what with so many antique objects being cursed or haunted. But as far as I know, I was the only casualty in my family in several generations. I discovered that paper could grant wishes. But what I didn't know was that it needed a human soul inside to fuel it, and that position was open." His voice dripped with bitterness as he said, "So here I am."

I swallowed. My mom had always talked about lucky objects. And cursed ones too. The rational part of my brain wanted to reject all of it, but my hand still seemed to be reverberating from the impact with Terrence's shoulder that had never come.

"No one in your family knew you were stuck inside the stationary?" I asked quietly.

He shook his head. "I could see them, but not the other way around. They would have had to write on the paper in order for me to appear and talk to them. And that never happened. Not in fifty years."

Terrence suddenly looked so small and vulnerable that I found myself slowly sinking down to sit on the bed to be more on his level. I wrapped my arms around my knees. "Then tell me again. What exactly do you want?"

He stood for several moments, as stony as a statue and eyes just as hard. He finally told me. "My brother is in the hole. The store is done for. It's closing, and it will never be back." He exhaled slowly. "And if the antique store has to die, I just want to die along with it."

I bit my lip, breath catching. I couldn't think of anything to say.

Terrence sighed. "I didn't want to come here and threaten you, but I didn't know what else to do. I had to make you give the stationery pad back somehow."

My face tightened. "Do you really think so little of me? Like I couldn't be reasoned with without you breaking into my bedroom and freaking me out?"

Terrence looked away. "Listen, if you'll just take me back, you can use that last page for your own personal wish. I'll teach you how."

I licked my lips. "And what will happen when the last page is used?"

His eyes lifted to the ceiling and he said frankly, "I'll finally finish dying. But at least I'll die at home. That's all I want now." His brown eyes flicked to my face, searching my features. "Please," he said softly. "Just do this for me."

I stared back into his young, handsome face, then turned my

gaze on the last remaining page on the stationary pad. I let out a breath. "Ok. Just tell me what I need to do."

⸻

The next morning, I walked into the antique shop just two minutes after it opened. A bell on the door jingled as I entered. In spite of the warm, yellow light shining through the shop windows, the store was surprisingly cold. My eyes fell across the familiar antique store sights: a cluttered layout, mismatched items stacked one on top of the other on shelves and tables made of dark wood, clocks and framed vintage posters covering the walls, and priceless, burnished jewelry gleaming in glass cases. The store was quiet. All antique stores had a mysterious hush about them.

"I'll be right out," a man's voice called from another room.

Behind me, Terrence inhaled slowly. "That's him."

I glanced over my shoulder at him and said quietly, "But he won't be able to see you?"

Terrence shook his head wordlessly. He'd been quiet all morning. I suppose I would have been quiet too if I'd been willingly walking toward my own death.

I pulled the stationery box out of my purse and removed the lid to look at the last page. The delicate floral print gazed back at me invitingly.

"Have you decided on your wish?" Terrence asked.

I paused, then nodded. I had thought about wishes well into the night. How could I not? Even if this was all in my crazy little head, my mind couldn't help but run rampant, thinking about all the things I wanted. "Yeah. I've decided."

"Then this is it," he told me. "You remember my instructions?"

I nodded and pulled out a pen. The tip of the pen hovered over the page like an arrow pointing into the future. I looked up at Terrence. He gazed back somberly.

"Thanks for doing this." He gave me his familiar, crooked smile. "For a minute last night, I thought you might tear out the last page out of spite. I'm glad you're letting me die here like I wanted. And that you get your wish."

For a moment, his eyes held me captive. I wanted to reach out and feel his face, to reaffirm that he really was there. That he really wasn't.

But then I pulled my gaze away, put pen to paper, and wrote down my wish.

"Ready?" I asked Terrence.

He nodded.

I raised the stationery pad to where he could see my wish. His face went slack. His brown eyes lit up with genuine surprise, then contentment.

I tore the page free.

Like a sigh released from a child falling into slumber, Terrence faded and vanished.

I was alone.

There was shuffling as William, the aged store owner, entered the room. "Can I help you with anything?" he asked me. "We're having a closing sale, so now is a good time to buy."

I stepped up to him as I slipped the page with my wish into a large manila envelope. Then I held it out to him. "I don't really know you, but I have a gift from someone who does."

The man looked puzzled, taking the big envelope. He slipped on his glasses and peered inside. His jaw dropped. "I'm sorry, but what…?"

"It's a donation," I told him as he pulled out one of the bills that made the envelope bulge. "It should keep your store running for many years to come."

"Miss!" He insisted, eyes still wide. "I can't take this! It's too much!"

I stepped back. "I insist. It's from someone who cares about you very much."

I turned to leave as he protested further. "Please! Won't you at least tell me this person's name?"

I paused briefly, my hand on the door. "Terrence."

His expression grew reverent, and I saw him glance down at the empty stationary box I was still holding. Before I could open the door, he said, "Wait. I have a gift for you."

He opened a drawer behind the front desk, then walked over to hand me an elegant black pen. "This went with a stationery set I recently sold." He glanced meaningfully down at my box. "But I kept it for sentimental reason. It's now yours." He pressed it into my hand. "There's something special about it." His eyes twinkled knowingly. "I think your eyes are experienced enough to see it."

Later that day, I called my mom. We chatted about this and that before the topic of the stationery inevitably came up.

"So?" she asked. "Has it helped you meet anyone yet?"

I lay back on my bad, smiling in order to cover the ache in my heart. "Yeah, I met a guy."

I could hear the satisfaction in her voice as she asked, "How did it go?"

I shrugged. "He was too old for me."

"Well, darn," she said. "And you used all the pages up? I guess it was a waste of a birthday present, then, huh."

My mind traced over the memories of the past few weeks, of Terrence's infectious laugh, of his happy surprise as he'd seen my wish, of walking out the antique shop's door, leaving the full envelope in the hands of a stranger. I had lost my chance to gain unimaginable riches of my own. But the wish had never really belonged to me anyway.

"It wasn't a waste," I said softly. "Not even a little bit."

I looked at the aged, black pen resting on my bedside table and wondered.

. . .

When Tanya Hales was a baby, she enjoyed books by chewing them to pieces before eventually moving on to the higher art of reading. Tanya splits her time between her writing projects, her work as an illustrator, and her role as a mother, all of which she loves intensely. She now lives in the Utah Valley with her husband and two creative kids. This is her first published story. For more information visit https://tanyahales.com.

MORE THAN YOU BARGAINED FOR

LAUREN LANG

MORE THAN YOU BARGAINED FOR

The door to New World Rarities opens with its characteristic chime, the antique bell announcing my arrival. The smell of mothballs, dust, and stale air washes over me. Andy, the ancient proprietor, only briefly glances up from his novel before turning back to whatever popular garbage he's picked up this week. He squints at it pointlessly. His eyesight is so bad and his hands shake so hard I'm not sure he's even able to read the thing. Like his shop, he reeks of old age and neglect.

"Andy! Good afternoon. Got anything new in this week?"

He gives me a sidelong glance and grunts as I walk past him, threading through the maze of unwanted antiques and signs warning of dire consequences for thieves, on my way toward the two dusty cases in the back of the store. What kind of a person would want to steal any of this junk anyway?

"Never mind, Andy. I'll just take a look for myself."

The two coin cases are the only clean part of the store. I demanded Andy start wiping them down at least once a week after a swarm of miller moths descended on the area last year and dead insect carcasses laid around inside the cases for months. I was so disgusted with the lack of pride in the ownership of such a historic establishment that I swore off coming in for a full two weeks.

The familiar collection of coins greets me, oxidized wheat pennies and tarnished half dollars laid out like treasures meant to goad the ignorant into parting with currency of actual value. There's little point to coming here for a numismatic, but I find myself wandering in like clockwork every Saturday on the off chance someone's dead grandfather was a collector and their surviving relatives didn't know what they had. No such luck this week.

As I turn to leave, the light catches something in between the cases. I squint at it, eventually making out a distinctive lack of an edge on a silver coin. It must have fallen when Andy was wiping down the case.

I take a quick glance over my shoulder. Andy is engrossed in his novel. I bend down silently and snatch the coin, pocketing it in one smooth motion before heading toward the door.

"Thanks, Andy. Good to see you, as always. You're looking great today, by the way!"

Andy grunts something unintelligible as I make my way out of the shop and into the summer heat. The store is only blocks from home, and in just a few minutes I'm through the front door, studying the coin under the magnifying lamp in my office.

The coin is easy to identify under the right light. It's a 1943 Steel Penny, conceptualized and produced during WWII when copper was more important to the war effort. Satisfied with my ill-gotten gains, I gently lay it on the desk and head for the shower. I have a date to get ready for.

Forty-five minutes later I'm washed, shaved, dressed, and have dabbed on just a bit of the cologne women tend to find irresistible. My date for the evening is meeting me at the hottest little spot in town: the brand new Asian fusion joint that opened a few weeks ago. I had to pull some strings; I know the owner and got a reservation on short notice. It's sure to impress her.

Pulling up in a panty-dropper doesn't hurt either. I'm 100%

Classic American muscle with a red 1967 Mustang Shelby GT500 Super Snake. If online dating is a meat market, this car makes me prime rib. I jump in and start it up, savoring the hum of $250,000.

It's a quick trip over to the restaurant, and I don't see my date's car. When I pull in the parking lot, it's hard not to notice the appreciative glances the car gets from the younger women walking in with their boyfriends. I take my time parking, making sure my baby is safe in the back of the lot before heading inside. My phone buzzes with a text. Great. My date is running late. I check in with the maître d', who seats me, and I settle in to wait. She shows up about ten minutes later wearing a black dress that's slightly too tight with a scuffed pair of high heels. She looks older in person than she does in her pictures.

"Clarence, hi! I'm so sorry I'm running late. I was so close to finish painting the dining room that I just couldn't stop with so little left to go. I hope you'll forgive me."

I rise and give her a quick peck on the cheek. "It's totally understandable. Don't worry about it a bit," I tell her, but I'm slightly annoyed with such a lame excuse. "You must be starving after slaving away all afternoon. Sit down. Let's eat."

The meal is a traditional mix of boring get-to-know-you conversation punctuated by semi-awkward silence as we consume overpriced appetizers. By the time entrées arrive she's told me all about her home renovations and her job as a reporter at a local television station. Over a plate of sesame chicken, she waxes on about the health benefits of yoga and juicing. It's mind-numbing.

Finally, as we're finishing our food, she asks, "So, do you have any hobbies?"

"Well actually, I'm a coin collector. In fact, I picked up an extremely interesting piece just this afternoon. Have you ever heard of a steel penny?"

She confirms she has not, and just as I'm about to offer her a unique window into this fascinating part of American history, the waiter appears with a dessert menu.

"Can I offer you some green tea ice cream?" he asks slyly.

She looks to me, hemming and hawing. "Oh, I really shouldn't. . ." But she does.

I eye her dress again and the strain the meal has put on the seams but say nothing. "Nothing for me, thanks," I reply. But before I can pick up where we've left off in the conversation she's delving into the anti-aging properties of green tea. I want to run from the restaurant screaming.

Finally, she finishes and the check arrives. I am definitely not paying for this torturous experience. "So, this is awkward," I begin, fake patting down the back of my pants, "but I was so excited to meet the famous new reporter this evening that I wasn't thinking straight and left my wallet on my nightstand. Can you get this? I'll get you next time."

She makes a disappointed expression but agrees. Hey, if she wants to be wined and dined she has to be worth wining and dining, and this is not a woman I intend to see again.

We exchange the typical awkward end-of-date pleasantries as we walk out of the restaurant, culminating in the oh so cliché, "I'll call you."

She'd better not wait by the phone.

The ride home is blessedly silent, punctuated only by the hum of the motor. I pull into the garage and savor the sound of nothing. What a waste of an evening. It wasn't even worth taking the car out.

I wander inside the house and pause as I pass my office. For the second time today, a slight glint has caught my eye. I remember the steel penny I left on the desk, but the whole area seems significantly shinier. Wandering over, to my amazement, I find not one but multiple coins sitting on the desktop.

"What the . . ." I pick up the newly appeared coins. "Where did these come from?"

There's a small pile of steel pennies. This isn't right. Confused and somewhat fearful, I pick up the top coin and inspect it under the light. It's an identical copy of the first. Slowly, I inspect each coin and find they are all the same, right down to the pits that are only visible under magnification. It's as if the coin copied itself.

My hands shake, picking through the pile, which seems slightly larger, and I drop one somewhere under the desk. I fall to the floor, desperate the find it, but to no avail. It's made its way into one of the crannies under the heavy furniture, and I can't reach it.

More worried about the seemingly larger-still pile on the desk, I stand and open the lap drawer and shove the coins inside quickly, slamming the drawer shut once they're gone. Frantically I search for the key on top of the desk and lock the drawer when I find it, deeply disturbed by the jingle of change as I do. A million questions cross my mind. Is this someone's idea of a sick joke? Where did those coins come from? I have no plausible explanation, and this only frightens me more. I need to lie down.

I walk toward the bedroom and toss my keys and wallet on the nightstand. The keys skid across the surface and fall behind the furniture, but I'm too sick with terror to find them now. I swear I can still hear the coins jingling. I don't even bother to take off my clothes or turn off the light, I'm so desperate to get my head onto my pillow. I think I might puke, and the thought of facing whatever that is in my office in the dark makes me panic. Cold terror grips my gut as the sound of jingling coins continues to ring in my ears. It's hard to tell if it's real or just my anxiety, but I'm desperately trying to convince myself it's all in my head. The signs in the shop promising dire consequences for thieves. The more I listen the more convinced I am that the sound is growing louder.

"But it was only a penny!" I think.

My fears are confirmed when a terrifying bang, followed by clinking, erupts from the direction of my office.

In full-blown panic mode, I leap off the bed and run toward

the source of the noise. The desk drawer has literally exploded, and coins are erupting from the space and spilling onto the floor.

"No!" I scream as I frantically run to the window, careful not to trip over the ever-growing mound.

The coins multiply even as I throw open the bottom pane of glass and knock out the screen.

"Get out of here! Get out!" I yell as I grab handfuls of steel pennies and hurl them out the window.

For every handful I grab, double appear on the floor. The mass is oozing toward me now like some kind of a numismatic monster. It's obvious that there are too many to get out by hand, so I abandon my plan, running instead toward the garage.

There! I spot a five-gallon bucket just inside the door. I grab it and run back to the office, hurling it under the veritable waterfall of pennies coming out of the desk drawer.

With the bucket now slowing the growth of the pile on the floor, I resume trying to hurl as many pennies as I can out the window, and for a few moments, I seem to be making progress. The entire floor around me is now covered with dropped coins, but the overall accumulation seems to be slowing.

Heartened by my progress and still in shock, I pause to catch my breath. None of this makes any sense, but my panic is making it hard to think straight. That's when I hear a sickening crack. The desk! Each penny only weighs a few ounces, but the combined weight of them all is too much for the drawer to bear. Terrified, I watch as the wood begins to split. The bottom of the drawer rips itself apart with a final sickening crunch, and the pennies that were inside hit the floor.

I lose all hope as the rate at which the pennies are multiplying triples. Suddenly, smaller but quickly growing piles spring up everywhere the pennies touch. Within seconds I'm up to my ankles.

I do the only thing I can think of and begin wading toward the door. The entire floor is now completely covered, and I almost lose my footing trying to make it into the hall. I begin pulling as hard as I can, attempting to get the door to shut despite the coins in the way. A small avalanche makes its way into the hall as I finally drag the door closed in an adrenalin-fueled rush to contain the disaster.

But I can still hear the telltale clink of falling coins as the number within the room continues to grow. The coins in the hallway aren't stopping, either, and those that escaped with me are now multiplying as well.

Calling for help seems like the only option. I whip out my phone ready to dial 911. Just as I go to unlock the screen the phone begins to ring and my finger accepts the call.

"Hey, Clarence, I had such a wonderful time tonight that I didn't want to wait to call —" is all I hear before I manage to find the end button and hang up.

It's only been a matter of seconds, but the noise from inside my office has grown significantly louder, and I'm being forced to slowly back away from the door as the pennies outside spill toward my feet.

My hands are shaking so hard it's almost impossible to use the phone, but I manage to hit the emergency button after a few attempts.

"9-1-1. What's your emergency?"

"Hello, operator? My house is filling with pennies. Send help!"

"I'm sorry, sir, could you repeat that?" says the voice on the other end of the line.

"I can't explain. 3200 Central Ave. Send someone quickly!" I scream before cutting the call.

They immediately call me back, but I'm too busy running toward the kitchen to grab pots and pans to answer. I can swear the office door is starting to bend as I arrive, soup pot in hand. I start shoveling coins in the hallway.

Running to the front door, I throw the pot filled with pennies out of the house and into the yard, only to see coins spilling out of the open window in the office and mounding around the side of the house. To my absolute horror, they're multiplying as well and beginning to pile up along the side of the house. As I stand, slack-jawed, the porch light catches a slight glint from the direction I tossed the pot of coins. Small piles are beginning to form in the grass.

It seems there's nothing I can do. There's no way to contain the pennies inside the house with how fast they're spreading, and the yard is quickly beginning to fill as well. I need help. Not knowing what else to do, I wander to the street, dazed and in shock, to wait for the police.

A cruiser pulls up a few minutes later. I'm standing on the sidewalk as the officer hauls himself out of the car.

A large crash emanates from inside the house. The officer instinctively reaches for his gun but doesn't draw the weapon. "What was that?" he demands.

"Oh, if I had to take a guess I would say it's the door to my office giving way under the weight of millions of pennies," I reply.

"Pennies?" he says incredulously. "They're silver. They look like dimes."

"Trust me. I'm a coin collector. They're pennies. And are you really going to argue semantics with me right now? Shine your flashlight into the yard. It's filling with them as well. There are bigger problems here," I say, beginning to become angry at the entire situation. "The inside of the house is full of them too."

"I'm calling for back up," he states, as wide-eyed as I was a mere half hour ago. He jumps on the radio to request additional units.

My anger is growing as fast as the piles of pennies now. How dare he? That Andy, stupid old man, he's somehow responsible for this. He made this mess. It's all his fault!

The officer is still trying to convince dispatch that the call is for real when I suddenly remember my car. My baby is still in there! The house I can fix—I'll certainly have the money to do it—but the car is priceless to me.

Taking a long glance at the front door, I make my decision. I must save it.

Without warning, I sprint toward the still-open entry, only faintly hearing a surprised, "Hey, stop!" from the officer still standing on the sidewalk.

The coins haven't made it all the way into the foyer yet, and entering is relatively easy. But something about my presence seems to spur the pennies on, and the clinking grows noticeably louder when I enter.

My office is on the opposite side of the house from the bedroom, so my idea is to quickly make my way to the nightstand, grab the keys, run back out the still-open front entryway, open the garage door and pull the car out of the still-relatively-clear driveway. It seems like a solid plan, but I run into complications almost immediately. My keys fell behind the nightstand earlier, and they aren't immediately visible.

I hurl the nightstand sideways, knocking it over onto the floor. The keys are lying against the baseboard, but in the precious seconds I've wasted looking for them the noise from the other room becomes deafening.

Running full tilt from the room, I find the hallway filling quickly. The coins have made their way to this half of the house just since I came in. Desperately, I start trying to wade through them, but it's like walking through mud. My footing is uneven, and I'm slipping while my shoes and socks fill with pennies.

"Hey, help! Help me!" I scream to the officer outside.

New voices answer me. "Sir, where are you? We can't see you!" The backup must have arrived. Help is here. I redouble my efforts, but the coins seem to respond in kind, seemingly shifting and moving to block my escape.

"I'm here!" I try to scream over the noise. "I'm back here!"

Unsure if they can hear me, I keep wading forward. The house is almost unrecognizable amidst the sea of pennies, but I just keep pressing forward one slogging step at a time. About halfway down the hallway, I'm up to mid-calf in pennies, and my legs are starting to tire. They're burning with exhaustion, but I have no choice but to press on as quickly as possible. After a few more stuttering steps I'm up to my knees, but I keep pushing until finally, buried up to my mid-thighs, I can see the door.

A bewildered firefighter stands there, staring in disbelief at what's happening.

"Hey! Here! I'm right here!" I scream to him.

He hears something and cocks his head but doesn't look at me, so I start waving my arms.

"Here! Help me!"

Finally, he catches a glimpse of my arms and yells something over his shoulder out the door. Working my direction, he shoves coins aside with his hands in an attempt to clear a way out.

I take one more step forward . . . and the ground shifts dramatically underneath my shoes. Without warning, I plunge into the pile of coins. My fall triggers a veritable avalanche from the deeper part of the pile in front of me, and pennies wash over me as I struggle to orient myself.

I can no longer hear anything but the sound of falling change. It's dark in the pile and strangely cold. I thrash my arms, trying to find anything resembling the top but despite the adrenaline coursing through my veins my limbs feel weak and limp. Where I was determinedly shoving through the pile just moments ago I now feel tired and unable to move. No, not unable, unwilling

What? No! I must keep fighting. I have to get out. My car! I have to save my baby.

I try to open my mouth to call out to the firefighters who are looking for me ,but my mouth fills with coins. I panic and try to spit them out, but I can feel them multiplying inside me. I can't scream, I can't breathe, I can't move, and the world is starting to go dark.

"But it was only a penny!" I think to myself as I descend into blackness.

MORE THAN YOU BARGAINED FOR

"You know, Rick, I swear this is the guy I went out with last night."

"Angela! You're live in five, four . . ." I snap to attention as my photographer, Rick, counts down the rest of the numbers silently so that his voice doesn't go on television. I take a quick glance over to my right before he cues me to make sure that our guest is ready for primetime.

Lead anchor Marcela Anthony's voice fills my earpiece, tossing to me at what we've dubbed the "Penny House."

"Reporter Angela Ioane is live at the scene of an event authorities are struggling to describe. Angela, what can you tell us?"

"Good evening, Marcela," I say into the microphone. "Police and fire officials don't know what to make of the bizarre situation at 3200 Central Ave that took the life of a man late last night.

"Police tell us Clarence Jones called around midnight to report his home was filling with pennies. After they arrived, they say the man ran back into the house for an unknown reason and died after he slipped and fell into a pile of the coins and suffocated. Police say the pennies were seemingly multiplying on their own but appear to have stopped sometime after they believe the man died.

"Now as you can see here, these aren't normal pennies. They look more like dimes. But experts tell us they are really 1943 steel pennies. Here to tell us more about this unique coin is Andy Plutus, owner of a local coin and antique shop." I turn to the shop owner. "Andy, why are these pennies silver?"

The old man wheezes into the microphone before whispering, "I recognize this coin. I had one for sale in my shop once, but someone stole it. You shouldn't take what doesn't belong to you."

Pulling the microphone back, I attempt to end the disastrous interview, "Thank you for your insight, Andy."

But the old man, doesn't let go of the mic. "You just might get more than you bargained for!"

Rick begins to pan the camera back over to me to get our guest out of the shot. "As for what will happen to the money, authorities tell us they've contacted the US Bureau of Engraving and Printing, who will collect the coins and destroy them. This is Angela Ioane reporting for KWQB. Back to you, Marcela."

Lauren Lang is a freelance photographer and videographer living and working in Denver, CO. She has had the urge tell stories since a young age, dictating her first piece of fiction to her mother before she was old enough to write. As she grew she continued to be attracted to storytelling—eventually becoming a broadcast journalist in her quest to tell compelling, true narratives. She crossed three states in seven years working as a video editor, producer, and writer at several local television stations. "More Than You Bargained For" is loosely based on her professional experience in the industry.

THE SEVENTH STRIKE

FRANK MORIN

THE SEVENTH STRIKE

Inetto Manichino floated high above Silicon Valley as dawn crept slowly across the land. He might be the invisible spirit of a man who died in 1372, but he still loved a good sunrise. It helped take his mind off the delicate, deadly game he was preparing to play for the seventh time.

Just to his left, a point of absolute darkness formed in the air and began to grow, swelling into a sphere over ten feet across. No light penetrated that area, and a chill wind whistled out of it. With a thunderclap and spray of liquid fire, Kako the demon stepped out of the darkness.

After six and a half centuries, Inetto was used to Kako's dramatic flair. The demon's presence always made him nervous, but it wasn't like he could sweat. His voice didn't even shake. He'd found few advantages of his spirit form over a physical body, and he needed every single one.

So he said in a deadpan voice, "Speak of the devil. I was just thinking of you."

"You've never been funny. Don't try to start now," Kako growled. He seemed to be in a fouler mood than normal. For him, that took real effort.

Kako Epitiritis perfectly fit the image of a demon that Inetto had formed in his youth while listening to his devout mother's descriptions of hellfire and damnation that would strike down the unrepentant sinner. He was roughly man-shaped, with a red hide that smelled of brimstone, a pointed tail, batlike ears, and a forked tongue that regularly tasted the air as it flitted between his sharp teeth. Kako's monstrous form perfectly reflected his inner ugliness.

The demon's sphere of blackness dissipated as he paced the air around Inetto and swept one clawed hand across the beautiful morning vista. "Well? Who is your new target?"

"I'm still looking."

"To heaven you are," Kako growled, and his small, batlike ears flapped against his hard skull, a sure sign of his dark mood.

"I'm trying. It's just, there are so many inventions. The world is making progress on every front, and I've only got one curse."

Kako scraped a dark claw across one of his curving horns and snapped his fingers. A long scroll appeared in the air beside them, rimmed in crimson fire. If only those flames could actually consume the foul contract.

"You're running out of time, Inetto. You've failed me six times. Six! Bungle your curse again, and I'll exercise the failure-to-perform clause."

Inetto bit back a fourteenth-century Venetian swear. If he could sweat, he'd be dripping with it. Even though he lacked physical form, his breathing quickened. "I'm doing everything I agreed to. That's not fair."

"To heaven with fair. The contract is clear. You're supposed to win souls to gift to me, and I need a soul."

"I'll find someone. This week," Inetto promised quickly, but his thoughts were racing.

Kako seemed almost desperate. His eagerness to get his claws on fresh souls had grown each century, but this was different. Anything different was worth paying close attention to. It might offer the chance Inetto had sought for centuries to slip out from under the demon's burning claws.

On the surface, the contract seemed simple. Inetto received one curse every century, one curse to cast upon an unsuspecting mortal. His mission was to push desperate people to sell him their souls, which he would in turn gift to Kako for whatever vile purposes the demon had in mind. Inetto had never ferreted out what those might be, but he was starting to wonder if Kako had debts of his own to pay.

That meant the demon needed him.

Kako barked a laugh. "I will not waste another century on another failure. The world advances too quickly, and you only seem to encourage it."

If only he knew.

"Edison wasn't my fault. Cursing him with repetitive failure seemed perfect."

"And yet he still invented the light bulb!" Kako gestured at the cities sprawling north and south along the coastline and the millions of lights glittering like diamonds in the early morning light. "With his cursed bulb, Edison pushed back more darkness than anyone in the history of the world."

Which was exactly why Inetto had chosen him. He'd sensed greatness in Edison's work, but couldn't risk allowing the man to settle for partial progress. Through his curse, Inetto had guaranteed Edison must push on until he achieved unparalleled success.

Even more perfect, he'd used the light bulb as the vessel to deliver the curse. Every curse needed a vehicle, and picking the right one was as important to Inetto as picking the right target.

Grumbling about Inetto's failures was one of Kako's favorite pastimes. "No one fears the night any more. Your bumbling made the man an inspiration to other stupid mortals to keep trying. That fiasco was even worse than Columbus."

"You're the one who insisted the world was flat and he'd sail right off," Inetto pointed out, loving how that reminder made the demon fume.

Cursing the helm of the Santa Maria had been a stroke of genius. Inetto had secretly floated across the ocean long before

Columbus made his famous journey. It still seemed remarkable that Kako never had. It was almost as if the demon feared the deep, although it posed no real threat to him.

"I might have believed that was simple bad luck, but not after Shakespeare and Beethoven," Kako fumed.

"You don't have to remind me about those," Inetto said, assuming an embarrassed expression.

Actually, he loved it when Kako threw his so-called failures back into his face. It was the only victory he'd ever gained over the foul creature, and those two had been particularly brilliant.

How had he ever thought signing that contract was a good idea?

Well, he'd been a second-rate painter, convinced he was really a world-class artist who just needed a break. Only with the demon's help had he painted a real masterpiece. Selling his soul had seemed a small price to pay until Poitiers was invaded and he died defending his life's work.

He'd lost more than everything, and after finding himself chained to the demon's will, shackled by the terms of the contract, his anger had instead focused on Kako. He'd dedicated himself to finding ways to undermine the demon using the very curse he was supposed to use to win new captive souls. It was a dangerous game, and if Kako ever found out, he'd cast Inetto into eternal suffering.

But now it appeared Kako might be vulnerable. The only way Inetto could escape the demon was if Kako broke his part of the contract.

He assured the demon, "I'll find a good target. I know what I'm doing."

"Heavens you do," Kako snarled.

"I still have a couple more decades to decide."

"Oh, no. I'm going to personally oversee your choice, and you'll make it today."

"That's not part of our deal," Inetto objected, but he secretly exulted.

He glanced at the contract still hanging in the air nearby. Kako always insisted on strict adherence to the terms and loved reminding Inetto of the never-ending torment he'd suffer should he stray beyond the agreement even a tiny bit.

"It's not expressly prohibited, either," Kako said.

"It sounds like you have a target already in mind."

"I do. I've found a desperate woman who will gladly sell her soul to you with a little push. Follow me."

Kako plummeted down toward the ground. Inetto followed, worried. It usually took a lot of time and careful planning to prepare an effective curse that looked properly devilish on the surface but accomplished the opposite result.

On the other hand, Kako was clearly desperate. He needed a soul. Inetto wasn't sure why, but would his desperation push him to make a critical mistake?

The invisible pair descended to a poor neighborhood and floated into a tiny, one-bedroom apartment on the fourth floor of a shabby building. It might have been considered hip twenty years ago, but poor maintenance had aged it prematurely.

A woman sat in the living room rocking her young child. Despair rose from the woman like steam, although she looked young to feel so hopeless. Maybe thirty years old, still trim and pretty, with her dark brown hair styled in current fashion. Her clothes might be a bit worn, but she didn't look impoverished.

Her little girl was very cute, but obviously sickly. At most a year old, she clutched at her mother with scrawny little arms, and her lungs sounded weak, even though she cried constantly.

Happy, established households provided a real defense from demons, but the apartment's threshold barely resisted Inetto as he followed Kako inside. The apartment was dingy, but clean. Every surface in the kitchen gleamed, and a fresh sheet covered the ratty old couch.

Kako waved one clawed hand over the woman's head, and her history appeared above her, like a silent movie playing for Inetto.

Dyani Oxendine was a twenty-eight year old widow who struggled to keep a job and was late on the rent. Her eleven-month-old baby girl, Aiyana, had suffered severe pneumonia and was struggling to recover.

That explained the desperation, but why had Kako targeted her?

The demon grinned and his long tongue flickered out between his pointed teeth. "This is the one. She has already vowed to sell her soul to save her child, if it came to that. You're going to make sure it does."

Inetto cringed inwardly. Those words attracted demons faster than dung attracted flies.

As the woman soothed her child, Inetto shook his head. "My contract clearly states I must give priority to artists and inventors. Her child is neither. I can't risk it."

Kako drifted closer and growled, "Don't quote terms to me. A baby is not a preferred target, but her mother is ripe for the plucking, and I'm ordering you to use your curse on the child."

If Kako could wield the curse, he would unleash it upon the poor child in a heartbeat, but he couldn't. Inetto must give life to the curse, choosing the words and the conditions of the affliction the targeted soul would suffer.

Dyani was one woman who didn't need any more curses, and if Inetto ever cursed a baby, he'd deserve eternal punishment. "She doesn't feel right."

"To heaven with your feelings, fool. You haven't picked a good target in five hundred years. I'm choosing this time."

"That isn't part of our arrangement."

"Nor is your ineptitude," Kako hissed, leaning threateningly close. "Do you object?"

Inetto shook his head quickly, not having to pretend his fear, but it wasn't the fear Kako would assume. This really was his long-awaited opportunity. It would require delicate handling, but the demon was really going to step over a critical line.

"It's just . . ."

"Just nothing! She is the target. Curse that child and I will own Dyani's soul."

"I really think that if I wait another decade or two—"

Kako hissed, and actual flames burst from his mouth. "No! I can't wait decades. If I don't deliver a soul . . ."

He bit off the rest of the sentence, but he'd said enough. Inetto had assumed correctly. Kako had his own debts. Inetto understood the desperation those kinds of debts carried. For the first time in centuries, he felt a flicker of real hope. It warmed his soul and reinforced his courage for what he had to do.

He pretended not to have noticed the important slip. "All right, but I'll need time to figure out how to arrange it." Finding the right object to act as the vessel for the curse would be more critical than ever.

"We have time," Kako said, looking content to wait however long for the right moment to strike now that Inetto had submitted to his choice of target.

Inetto followed Dyani all the next day, watching, studying, considering possible vehicles for the curse and how to use it to break free of Kako's hold. Kako hovered close, an annoying presence, clearly not trusting Inetto to finish the job properly.

That was probably for the best. Focusing on the target kept Kako distracted from the breach he was making in their arrangement. Kako was not the source of the power that infused the curse, so if he stepped outside of the bounds of the contract, did that free Inetto to use the curse in ways that would have been prohibited in the past?

"There!" Kako cried that afternoon, drawing Inetto from his deep thoughts. The hated demon laughed evilly and pointed at a little antique store that Dyani had paused in front of.

Kako floated close behind her. His soothing voice would sound like the whisper of her own thoughts. "Go on in. Perhaps you'll find something on sale, something that will comfort Aiyana. She's worth it."

Inetto was supposed to do the whispering, position the target for cursing. One more mistake.

Dyani hesitated, but with another word of encouragement from Kako, she strode up the stairs and pushed open the door.

Kako cackled. "So easy. Oh, this is delicious. She will be my easiest conquest of all times."

"My conquest, you mean."

Kako glared, points of fire in his black eyes. "You will hold her contract temporarily, but you must gift her to me immediately."

The two invisible beings followed Dyani into the store and ghosted after her, hovering over her shoulders like very real shoulder devils. She browsed for a few minutes, but always the price tag made her shudder and move along. She was desperately poor, but Inetto was starting to hope she might indeed find a suitable item he could curse.

She eventually stopped in front of a display of Native American dream catchers. She fingered the soft feathers of a large, ornate one that she could never hope to afford.

She even dared ask the nearby shopkeeper, "Are these prices negotiable?"

The old lady had noted her journey through the store and clearly read her financial condition. "For that one, I couldn't let it go for less than ninety."

Dyani gasped and the old lady nodded to herself, as if confirming her suspicions.

Kako cursed, "Heaven take that greedy old fool. A dream catcher would be perfect! What better target for our curse than an item supposedly blessed to protect her precious little baby?"

He cackled at the idea and glided over to the shopkeeper, whispering suggestions in an urgent, near-silent stream.

That was it, then. Kako was a champion whisperer, although he rarely pushed his influence so hard. Doing so would leave him exhausted. And possibly slower to react to the unexpected?

Inetto didn't pretend he was a clever man, but he'd hungered for this moment for centuries. Even he could come up with a good idea or two over that much time.

Dyani began to turn away, looking dejected but not surprised by her failure to procure any little treasure for her beloved daughter. The old woman cracked under Kako's constant barrage of whispered urgings.

"Who are you shopping for, dear?"

Dyani's face lit with the smile of a devoted mother. "My little girl, Aiyana. She's so sick. I had hoped to find her something that might help."

The old woman beckoned her back to the display of dream catchers. "Well, if she's a young one, she doesn't need a great big dream catcher, does she?"

"No." Dyani returned, clearly surprised by the woman's warmer tone.

The old lady chuckled to herself and opened a drawer of a nearby cabinet and extracted a tiny dream catcher, barely larger than her wrinkled palms. The small hoop was made of rainbow-colored plastic, the spider-web filling simple string, but the three feathers hanging on beaded leather cords looked real.

She held it out to Dyani. "For you and your little girl. How about ten dollars?"

Dyani hesitated and Kako flicked over to her, whispering quickly. Then he glanced back at Inetto. "This is the vehicle."

"But I'm supposed to—"

"Stop resisting. This curse is mine, and I'm ordering you to target this object," Kako hissed, drifting closer, his eyes filling with crimson fire and the smell of brimstone wafting from his red leather hide.

And with those words, Kako formally overstepped the bounds of his contract. Inetto shook with the realization, with the new possibility that illuminated his mind with unfamiliar cleverness.

Did he dare take the chance?

"Very well." He spoke softly, barely able to get the words out.

Kako sneered and gestured toward Dyani. "Get on with it, oaf."

Inetto floated over to the dream catcher. Dyani was holding it, fingering the feathers. Inetto had seen enough human interactions over the past few centuries to clearly read her growing intention to buy. This was indeed the perfect time to set his best-ever curse.

So he touched the dream catcher. Neither woman noticed the slight flexing of the central threads, as if from an invisible breeze.

Wording of each curse needed to be specific and carefully crafted. Inetto usually spent days perfecting each one. This time they came to him in a rush. As he spoke the words, he committed the entire force of his will into activating the curse. Power flowed through his ethereal fingers, shaking his spirit frame with its intensity. This curse seemed especially powerful. It would not fail him.

"I'll take it," Dyani said.

"Done."

As the two women headed toward the cash register, Kako frowned. "What happened? I don't feel the curse activated yet. There's no connection to her soul."

"I don't . . ." Inetto retreated, stammering with fear and self-doubt.

"You fool! I will not allow you to fail me again!"

"Maybe if you double-check it," Inetto suggested.

"How the heaven did I end up with such an idiot?" Kako growled, rushing to the dream catcher and grasping it with one clawed hand.

The dream catcher burst into blinding white light. Kako screamed, covering his face with his free hand and trying to retreat.

He couldn't pull away.

The demon tugged at the little object with frantic strength, but it held him as securely as if he'd shackled his soul to a mountain. After trapping so many other souls, he shouldn't look so surprised now that he got to experience it himself.

The women chatted about Aiyana as the shopkeeper rang up the sale and Dyani dug out several small bills and a pile of coins. Neither of them noticed the supernatural events unfolding right beside them.

"What did you do?" Kako shrieked as thick, oily smoke began billowing off his leathery skin.

Inetto barely believed his own eyes. "You broke our contract."

Kako gasped as the awful truth struck. He met Inetto's gaze and asked again in a fearful whisper, "What did you do?"

"You're the target."

"You can't do that!" Kako shrieked, tugging uselessly against the dream catcher.

"Not in the past, but you said the words yourself. This curse is yours. I obeyed your command and gave it to you."

Kako shrieked again, the dark smoke growing so thick that it totally obscured him. His voice cracked with the anguish of a condemned soul.

"To heaven with you!"

Inetto grinned. "No. You're actually the one who has to worry about that trip."

"What?"

The smoke cleared, and Kako hung from the dream catcher, hand still sealed to its ring. He panted, every breath labored, his strength gone.

So too was his red skin, forked tail, and claws.

Kako now looked like a very frightened, rather pudgy fellow with bad teeth.

"Heaven," Inetto said, drifting closer. "You curse me with heaven all the time. That's what gave me the idea. I don't think you're going to enjoy stepping into the light up there. Good bye, Kako."

A piercing column of light suddenly split open the ceiling and plunged down over Kako. He screamed, long and loud and panicked, the sound of a damned soul about to meet his maker.

Dyani and the shopkeeper paused in their conversation and glanced down at the dream catcher. The feathers were stirring, the little string web fluttering in the still air.

The old shopkeeper said, "Looks like this one works. I could have sworn I felt a nightmare get caught."

"Me too," Dyani said, rubbing at goose bumps that rose along her arms.

Inetto laughed, exulting in the first feeling of real joy in centuries. Shackles of blinding light wrapped Kako's arms, and he screamed at their touch, then began slowly ascending the imprisoning column of light. He writhed in his bonds, screaming and beating his head against the barrier to no avail. Once he reached the ceiling, he suddenly shot upward and out of sight. The light snuffed out a second later.

Inetto was still laughing, quicksilver tears streaming down his cheeks, when a second column of light burst into the room and settled over him. The warm light felt like his long-forgotten mother's hug, and it sounded like her voice. As he rose toward the ceiling, he felt hope for the first time since he was a little boy.

Whatever came next, he was ready.

Frank Morin lives in Oregon with his wife, Jenny, and his four children. In their home, storytelling is a cherished family tradition that keeps magic alive. When not working or spending time with his family, Frank is an avid outdoors enthusiast and can often be found hiking, camping, scuba diving, or otherwise exploring the great outdoors. For more about Frank and his writing visit www.frankmorin.org.

HAUNTING AT HIGH NOON

MIKE JACK STOUMBOS

HAUNTING AT HIGH NOON

Don't ever let folks tell you the scariest things only happen after dark. If that's all you've ever known, then you, my friend, should count yourself fortunate, because there's nothing more chilling than seeing the thing you most fear in the searing light of day and being powerless to stop it.

For out-of-work actor Don Driscol, that moment came the first time he found himself in a real, live fistfight. His opponent used a mean left hook, and Don had no choice but to block it with his nose. One loud crunch and two low-rent doctors later, Don Driscol had himself a souvenir hooked nose, which turned out to be the perfect asset for his next audition. Armed with a new nose, he looked just gritty enough to land the headlining role in the reenacting cowboy town of Greeley, Nevada.

And the next time someone threw a punch at him, Don Driscol ducked.

"Gather round! Gather round, folks!" Big Sam would call to the sparse clusters of spectators. "And witness the greatest showdown in American history—the fateful day when Greeley's own sheriff, Walter P. Millstone, confronted and shot down the Three-Knot Killer!"

As always, Big Sam paused for applause, but the audience must have missed their cue. In an attempt to rebuild momentum, he pointed at the nearest person and said, "Now, I see y'all shakin' in your boots at the mere mention of such a feared outlaw, a man who murdered not one, not two, but three God-fearin' folk by means of rope!" He counted off the victims on his sausage fingers. Then Big Sam pointed emphatically at the doors of Stacey's Saloon.

A hand shot out of the dark of the saloon, thrusting forward both doors at once, cuing a loud squeak from the left one—they would have to get some WD-40 on that before the evening show. The "Three-Knot Killer" was dressed all in black, as every good outlaw should be; he was tall and slender and had a habanero kick of crazy in his eyes; he wore a hat with a bent brim and boots with prop spurs whose rowels were welded so securely, they did not clink even once. The only thing bright about his appearance was his gun handles, which caught and reflected every drop of sunlight.

Someone in the crowd checked his watch; another didn't bother to stifle a yawn.

As Three-Knot slinked across the porch and down into the road, Big Sam continued his speech. "Now, the dreaded Three-Knot Killer thought he could go anywhere without fear of the law, for he was not only a bona-fide murderer but a terrifyingly quick gunslinger, such that no one would dare challenge him— no one but Sheriff Walter P. Millstone." Taking wide strides under his immense weight, Big Sam stepped to the side, clearing the way for Millstone himself.

Don Driscol, his hooked nose shadowed by a wide-brim hat,

sauntered out into the middle of the street, his trigger fingers twitching. He wore a light-blue shirt and a bright-red neckerchief, and he had the big polished sheriff badge right next to his heart. After nearly ten years as the headliner in Greeley's Wild West Show, Don had learned all the right moves to sell the part completely. Sure, it was a rather puny audience, but he was determined to do his final scene of the morning tour with all the drama it deserved—in other words, with more poetic license than historical accuracy.

Don planted his feet so the toes pointed straight at his quarry, and, in his best Sheriff-Walter-P.-Millstone, he called out, "It's over, Three-Knot! You'll never hurt another living soul."

The Three-Knot Killer sneered his meanest sneer and snarled back, "You'll never take me alive!"

But before Don could reply, they were interrupted by the loud electronic medley that could only be produced by a cellular device. There were a couple of amused giggles, and someone in the crowd fished in her purse for the still ringing phone. "Hello?" she half whispered, but the damage was done.

Three-Knot dropped his gunslinger stance, turned toward the patron and said, "Dude, don't be a jackass! Turn off the phone."

A few more giggles sounded as the woman, mildly embarrassed and apparently a jackass, ended the call.

As the final cherry on the sundae, Three-Knot actually asked, "Where were we?" before resuming the scene. He got back into his bowlegged stance and repeated, "You'll never take me alive!"

Now, most men might have been a bit rattled by such a snafu, but not Don. Ever the professional, he channeled his frustration into the gritty reply: "That's the idea."

Three-Knot drew, but Sheriff Millstone was faster. There was a bang, a burst of smoke and powder, and Three-Knot fell dead.

Don Driscol spun his Sheriff-Millstone pistol and then reholstered it. It wasn't until he had started to walk away that people realized they were supposed to applaud.

Don was already opening the break room door by the time Big Sam started his wrap-up speech to conclude the morning tour. Soon, all the guests would be in the saloon, "Three-Knot" would be picking himself up off the ground, and the employees would reset for the afternoon show—and the fast-fading dream of a bigger audience.

Yes indeed: after almost ten years in Greeley, Don Driscol was still the headliner in the world's worst Wild West show.

◆

Though they didn't talk about it directly, everyone involved in Greeley's Western Experience knew that the tourist center, and therefore the town of Greeley, Nevada, was nearing the end of its frail rope. At one time, it had been a whole grand experience with dozens of employees and volunteers and folks coming in by the busload—but then a thing called Google led people to Greeley's secret: that the great big showdown between Millstone and Three-Knot was a great big lie. No matter how much the reenactors insisted that a good story was better than historical accuracy, patrons were getting harder and harder to come by.

But on that day, Big Sam had got his hand on something that he just knew would turn it all around. And when he came into the break room with the box under his arm, he was brimming with genuine excitement that set smile lines beyond even the reach of his mustache.

"Fellas!" he said, his voice a little higher pitched and a lot less gravelly—(he tended to drop the old-timey prospector bit when not in public), "We've got ourselves an antique acquisition." All of the reenactors present gathered around to see just what it was that had so lifted his spirits. And when Big Sam giddily unwrapped and opened it, Don and the others leaned in to see.

Under the lid, nested in packing foam, lay an antique six-shooter, a colt, "the gun that tamed the west." It didn't look like anything special: just another half-rusted, half-busted pistol.

Big Sam beamed. The others just stared and wondered, "Why'd you pick up a rusty gun?" and "Why, it don't even shoot!"

"Fellas, fellas, don't you see?" Big Sam went on, trying to rally some enthusiasm, "This is the very gun used by Sheriff Walter P. Millstone! This is a piece of history! And now, it's owned by Greeley's Western Experience!"

This generated a few murmurs. Most of the weapons they carried around were cheap facsimiles that held one cap at a time. Only Don and 'Three-Knot' had six-shooter cap guns, and even those were more than a little chintzy. But this was an actual gun, and maybe that did mean something. For a troupe of actors made up of summer jobs and showmen who couldn't cut it in Vegas, any prop with actual value was a change of pace.

But Don, his arms folded across his chest, asked, "So why isn't it in the museum? It is a piece of the 'town's history' after all."

"True, true," Big Sam nodded, "but the Greeley Historical Society don't need it anymore on account of they're closing."

A few groans issued in response. One person asked why, even though they ought to have known the answer:

"Not enough patrons to pay for the air conditioning and preserving the antiques. So, other than a few choice parting gifts," Big Sam explained, proudly displaying the pistol, "they're selling stock and reinvesting all proceeds back into the town," which actually meant Greeley's Western Experience and Stacey's Saloon, the only tourist businesses still making any money. Not profit, mind you, but unlike the rest of Greeley they weren't losing money. Yep, a drought had settled on Greeley, and folks in Nevada knew that droughts could last a mighty long time.

Big Sam parted the foam and lifted the old weapon with two careful hands. "See, I was thinkin' that you'd carry it in some of the in-between scenes," he said, handing it to Don. "You know, the ones where you don't have to shoot no one."

Don didn't refuse, but he still didn't find it very glamorous. The gun looked old and real and heavy, but it mostly felt like another hunk of loose hardware. He proceeded to spin it about, showing none of the delicacy and reverence that Big Sam had. He assumed his gunslinger stance and aimed the weapon, trying to picture how the real Sheriff Millstone might have looked and what he might have seen—actively ignoring how the real Sheriff Millstone had actually handled that duel.

Don knew how to focus out distracting environments like modern break rooms, and so he placed his mind back in the open street, starting to visualize old Three-Knot—and his heart leapt into his throat for what he saw!

Don nearly dropped the gun, but when he opened his eyes and found himself still in the break room surrounded by coworkers, he tried to play off the gasp as a hiccup. See, somewhere between boredom and daydreaming, Don figured he must have cooked up a specter in his mind: an evil, ghostly gunslinger who bore only passing resemblance to the actor who played the Three-Knot Killer; Don had distinctly envisioned a faded grey nightmare who would have stood a head taller than himself, with fire in his eye sockets, and who'd thrust into Don's own mental image like a red-hot poker. Maybe it was the heat getting to him. He shoved the gun back into the box without bothering to position it within the foam.

"Careful!" Big Sam exclaimed, rushing to right the antique in its protective packaging. He made sure that the chambers and trigger were set just so, even though the mechanisms that had moved them were long since broken. "Jeez, Don! You look like you saw a ghost."

One of the reenactors was ready with a retort: "Nah, just a vision of his next paycheck."

As the group laughed and Big Sam flushed, the break room door opened. TK let himself in, his face cleaned off and the rag in his hand full of dirt. The actor who played the Three-Knot Killer always went by TK when on set, and had for so long that most of the employees still didn't know his given name. TK was long and lean like the original Three-Knot Killer had been, but he was more prone to sarcasm than violence; in truth, his bite was milder than the fake spurs on his boots.

TK must have caught a comment or rumor, for he went straight to the antique pistol and let out an amused whistle. "This the new piece? Longer than ours," he observed. "Looks more like a villain gun if you ask me. Maybe give my character some spice." And he laughed at his own suggestion, to play it off as mere jest. Don knew that TK would gladly take anything to amp up his character, especially since he only got a few lines and almost no audience interaction.

"No, it's for the sheriff!" Big Sam declared, closing the lid over the gun before TK could touch it. Then, with none of the same fervor and his best stab at enthusiasm, he added, "We'll work it into your prop rotation tomorrow, Don."

Don, having already shrugged off the horror as overactive imagination, gave a smile and a nod. He was glad he didn't have to fold a new item into the afternoon tour, especially something as old as this piece. Of course, after so many fully committed performances, Don could handle a lightning quick draw and all manner of flourish with any pistol, but he'd prefer to practice first to make sure all of the spinning didn't just break the darn thing.

Big Sam checked his pocket watch and reminded everyone that the midday tour bus was scheduled to arrive soon. It would pick up the morning folks from the saloon and drop off the afternooners—if there were any today.

The reenactors took a last bite of lunch or a last sip of soda and began to disperse, some to the saloon and others to the front gate. On his way out, Don clapped a hand on Big Sam's shoulder and gave the man his most reassuring nod; luckily, Don was a pretty decent actor.

Big Sam stepped out into the hot sun and drew a gallon-sized gulp from his water bottle. He placed his fists on his sizable hips and looked around at the rustic storefronts, most of which were plywood sets, losing character with each passing year.

Big Sam, owner and founder of Greeley's Western Experience, tried to smile at the historical town he had brought back to life, tried to picture the crowds of cowfolk and outlaws and wide-eyed spectators that might have been. He imagined the silence of a hundred people holding their breath in the seconds before a real gunslinger drew and the tell-tale tumbleweed that might drift across the road. But when an empty paper bag, stained with fast-food grease, blew past him instead, Big Sam couldn't help but sigh.

The bag ran into the steps of the hangman's platform at the end of the street, and there it rested—a pair of golden arches blatantly reminding people that they hadn't really stepped back in time.

Big Sam walked to the platform to collect the trash, but he paused when he heard the shhnk-shhnk-shhnk of spurs behind him. He looked around, the sweat on his brow growing colder—and then he laughed at himself when he saw an empty street. He could hear faint music from the saloon, the distant rumble of the incoming bus, but no one else was on the street.

But when Big Sam stooped forward to collect the brown bag, he heard the shhnk again, louder and closer. The hair stood up on the back of his neck for hardly a second before a thick rope pressed those hairs flat again, and yanked!

Big Sam tried to scream, but his throat was closed tight, and the rough twines burned and scraped the flesh of his neck. His body banged against the platform as he was hauled up, but at the same time, the town's clock tower struck noon, loudly enough to drown out the knocking wooden planks and the desperate gurgles.

Big Sam was stone dead by the time the twelfth toll sounded.

❖

Since the beginning of Greeley, there had always been a Stacey's Saloon, which meant that the reenacting town had to have a Stacey. Even though the original Stacey had been a giant, bearded man, the current owner and operator was a feisty, wizened cowgirl who had been in Greeley almost as long as Big Sam and dyed her hair red every two weeks to keep from looking too old. And, as far as anyone knew, her honest-to-goodness name was Stacey.

Every Greeley tour concluded in that saloon, which still had a fair amount of the old-world charm the public expected, and it was probably responsible for keeping the town afloat. It was the first thing to open every morning and the last to close, and many of its best after-hours patrons were the reenactors themselves.

Whenever a bus arrived to swap out the audience, Stacey would excuse herself from the saloon to have a smoke. But on that day, as she stepped out and took a look toward the hangman's platform, she dropped the cigarette and might well have quit smoking altogether.

Unfortunately, in the time it took Stacey to find her voice and her balance again, the morning tour was gone, and the afternoon patrons were taking the short walk in. And their first sight coming into Greeley's Western Experience was Big Sam swinging.

At first, the tourists had thought the hanged emcee was a gruesome decoration, and snapped several morbid selfies before they were robbed of that illusion.

Don was called to the scene, and no amount of training could have masked his initial reaction. He gawked, he sputtered, he flailed in confusion and horror and whatever lay in between. And then he set his face straight because he'd have to handle the questions about what to do next. See, with Big Sam croaked and

Stacey ready to faint, Don Driscol was pretty much the senior member of the company.

It probably took them longer than it should have to sort through the necessaries. They called 911 and—through spotty reception—reported a suicide. They took the body down and brought it to the break room where there was air conditioning; that seemed important at the time. When they went to lay Big Sam on the table, they knocked off the wooden box, out of which tumbled the rusty antique pistol.

Stacey picked up that pistol in shaking hands, mumbling about how she had seen the prince of hell at Big Sam's dangling feet. She put the gun back into the box and handed it to Don, continuing to ramble about the devil.

By the time he'd finished soothing Stacey out of a panic attack, it was nearly one o'clock, and Don knew that they had a crop of tourists somewhere between traumatized and bored. Shocked though he was by Big Sam's sudden departure, Don knew that neither the Experience nor even Stacey's Saloon could stand up to more negative reviews online.

He told himself, "the show must go on," and decided to find it more inspiring than clichéd as he tromped back toward the saloon, absently carrying the pistol box under his arm.

Don arrived to find that, sure enough, audience and employees alike were self-medicating with alcohol and vying for cell phone reception. At least they still seemed civil, and even the youngest tourist appeared relatively unfazed as he flicked his thumbs on whatever time waster he was playing.

TK pulled a chair out for Don and asked him, "What's the verdict?"

Don sighed and put the box on the table, the antique pistol still safely inside. He sat down among the other reenactors, who, despite some midday alcohol intake, had been startled sober upon discovering Big Sam's swinging corpse less than an hour before. "Well, the county sheriff's on her way. She and Sam are friends—" Don grimaced and wondered if that should've been past tense. "Um . . . but yeah, they're coming out to confirm the suicide. But it looks like he hung himself between shows, on his own set piece, the poor guy."

"No, not that," TK said quietly. Even though they hadn't thought Big Sam depressed enough to go through with it, everyone figured it was suicide—but they still had another pressing question: "What's happening with the afternoon tour?"

Don stared hard at TK and then between the other faces at the table, and apparently they all wondered the same. "Um . . . we have to refund the tickets, obviously," he said, and was met with groans. "But we've got an audience, and they've got another couple hours before the bus gets back, so . . . entertain them here at Stacey's, I guess."

The audience for the afternoon tour was only seven strong. Six of them had drinks in hand, and one was a minor. So, with little else to do, TK decided to engage the patrons (and their approval ratings) before they found enough signal to leave a one-star review.

He sprang to his feet and called out, "Hey, y'all wanna see something cool?" And without waiting to gauge their reaction, he continued with, "We got ourselves a genuine piece of history right here!" He flipped the lid off of the box, drew out the antique pistol, and pointed it toward the sky.

"Now, I know we're off to a rocky start," he went on, careful to make meaningful eye contact with everyone he could, "but you are in the heart of the historical Wild West, and every one of us here has wonderful things to show and tell you. Starting with this here pistol: this was the weapon carried by Walter P. Millstone, and it was the gun that shot down the Three-Knot Killer."

TK was about to ramp into a real gem of a tale, for he could stretch them to the ends of the earth given half a chance, but a smarmy voice cut him off cold. This little snot, a kid too old to be excited about cowboys but too young to sit at the bar, held up his cellular device and announced, "That's a lie."

"Dude!" TK balked, more shocked than immediately angry. "Don't be a jackass."

But the snot would not be silenced. He jabbed a finger at the screen as if to cite his source. "It says here that the Three-Knot Killer wasn't shot; he was hanged, and 'Millstone tricked him with a fake duel—'"

"Hey! Who is telling the story?" TK demanded, gesturing with the pistol itself.

Evidently, the boy did not find this threatening, for he read on, "'The alleged killer was not even given a trial by jury before he—'"

TK took a bold step forward and looked about to pop the kid, when a sudden rush of wind shoved the saloon doors open and startled both into silence.

Everyone paused to listen to the shhhnk-shhhnk-shhhnk of real-sounding spurs on approach; they were joined by the steady tuhkk-tuhkk-tukk of boots on the wooden porch as a stranger approached Stacey's Saloon.

The figure outside was nearly as tall as the entryway and seemed to block out the sunlight without casting a shadow on the floor. When he reached out his right hand to push open the door, it simply passed through.

A long leg emerged, knee-first, through the slatted wood. With one more step, the ghostly gunslinger was in plain view, all six feet, two inches of pure malice. He was dressed not all in black, but in faded grey denim that was now dripping with rot. In fact, everything from hat to boot was a pale waning color that looked like it might disappear after one more trip through the wash—everything except for his eyes, whose centers burned with a blood-red flame.

Witnesses to the phenomenon wouldn't be able to agree if the air became cold as death or hot as hell, but one thing was sure: not a soul dared utter sound, and the ghost strolled slowly enough that two of the guests passed out from holding their breath.

TK stood paralyzed in the middle of the room, slack-jawed with hands raised to the sky, the antique pistol hanging uselessly from his thumb. And as the ghost moved from the door to the bar, TK found himself squarely in its path.

Don Driscol was on his knees behind the table, ducking under cover, frozen in fear. It seemed the only sensible thing to do, and most of the other reenactors had taken a similar course of action, but that meant leaving TK alone to face down the horror.

As the ghost drew closer, TK managed to get out a small whimper, and his eyes frantically darted about to see who—if anyone—might help. His gaze met Don's, and his lips started to form a plea—

But without warning, TK was gripped around the waist by an invisible rope, and as it pulled him out through the front door, the man found his voice. "Holy sheeeah—" trailed TK as he was whisked out of sight, the saloon doors swinging wildly in his wake. The antique pistol had fallen from his fingers and clattered to the ground.

Some continued to cower, but a couple others found their feet and tore off after TK. Don wasn't leading the charge, but at least he had the courage to join it. Don burst out the doors and into the dirt road, where the kicking, dragging trail of TK was obvious. Because he kept himself in great shape (just in case a Hollywood scout stopped by), Don quickly overtook the other sprinters in chasing the ghost. Of course, he didn't have a clue what he should do when he caught up, but actors like Don were pretty experienced at improvising.

Though they quickly lost sight of TK, the impromptu posse followed his drag marks until they hooked down a narrow street near the edge of Greeley, and there they spied TK, or what was left of him.

TK had been tied to a boulder by a mass of interwoven ropes and strapped by the wrists and ankles so he couldn't free himself. Anyone who might've stumbled upon him would think he'd been there for days. His skin was sunburnt and getting worse, his lips were cracked, and his breath came out in rasps. Confusion and desperation shown on his face, but not the wherewithal to call for help.

The once-invisible lasso that had snared him was now real enough to touch—old and gnarled and spun by hand instead of modern machine real. So, while TK withered and dried out before their eyes, Don got to work on the rope. He didn't have more than a pocketknife, but it would have to do.

As he sawed through the strands, he had the sinking feeling that he was not working fast enough—not as quickly as some devilish magic was sucking the life out of TK.

"Help me!" he called to the people behind him, who all stood too stunned to work out a course of action. To them, it was still impossible, and, therefore, there was nothing to be done to stop it.

Don didn't have time to convince anyone, so he kept working at the rope, finally freeing TK's right wrist.

But Don was surprised as any of them when Stacey came rushing out, hollering something unintelligible and armed with a hatchet. Don jumped out of the way as Stacey brought the hatchet down with sickening, scraping clang and a fountain of sparks. One, two, three solid whacks through the ropes, the last of which seemed to ruin the blade beyond repair. After all, hatchets don't do well on stone.

Don heard a screech that came from neither steel on stone nor a human throat, and he turned to see the ghost, once more on approach, walking with deliberate swagger toward them while Stacey continued to slice and slash at the ropes.

On instinct, Don's hand flashed down to his hip and back up, a click emanating from the toy gun, which was now out of caps.

Still, the ghost tried to jerk away, as if hoping to dodge an oncoming bullet, and in that moment, Stacey managed to wrench apart the last strands binding TK.

And before the ghost could start toward Don again, it whisked away in a billow of dust, just as the clock tolled one.

Don blinked several times, trying to make sense of what he'd seen, until Stacey asked for his help in carrying TK. As they hauled their emaciated coworker off of the boulder, Don told someone to dial 911.

"I did," came the reply of one of the patrons, "but there's no signal . . ."

They could hear a hideous cackling in the air around them, and somehow Don knew that their ordeal with the ghost wasn't over.

⁂

Several minutes and many failed calls later, everyone begrudgingly came to the same conclusion as Don: there was a ghost in Greeley's now haunted Western Experience, and he had struck twice — once with full effect on Big Sam, and once a little less successfully on TK, who lay wheezing on the bar with a cool cloth over his forehead.

Some of the reenactors declared that they were leaving, but the weather was suddenly bent on blocking their escape. Don stepped outside to see for himself and discovered that he couldn't even see the bus turnaround through a wall of blowing dust, which seemed to stop just before the hangman's platform. Two of the new tourists set out on a restless walk around the little reenactment town and confirmed that they couldn't set foot beyond the fences and gates without being pelted by flying debris that stung at the eyes and throat.

Someone tried to remind the group that the authorities were already on their way to pick up Sam, who was still in the air-conditioned break room. But someone else pointed out that no one in their right mind would be able to get through this storm. The sound of wind and the distinct absence of sirens seemed to confirm that they were alone.

So, with no way out, no way to call for help, and no ideas of how to fight a ghost, they all huddled in fear in the saloon, wondering who would be the next target. Although they didn't talk about it directly, nobody had dared to move the antique pistol, so it lay on the floor where TK had dropped it, reminding them that the original Walter P. Millstone hadn't put the Three-Knot Killer down well enough.

They had been sitting in silence for a darn long time before one of the patrons, a mousy middle-aged woman, finally asked the boy, "What did you mean when you said it was a lie? What really happened to the Three-Knot Killer?"

Don looked to Stacey, who raised her eyebrows in a shrug. If this smidgen of audience survived the next few hours, it wasn't as if the real story could damage their reputation any further.

So Don took a last swig of the bourbon-to-pass, and settled in to tell the shameful truth. "The Three-Knot Killer—the real Three-Knot," Don clarified, with a glance toward TK, "was an actual American outlaw, and he was most famous for the three murders he committed with rope." Don held up three fingers and counted each one down as he went. "First, he killed a man by hanging him—tied him at the neck and kicked him through a second-story window. Next, he left some poor soul strapped to a rock in the desert, where he died of heat and thirst. Finally, Three-Knot horse-dragged a fellow tied by the ankles; pulled him so long after he was dead that one of the feet came off. Then Three-Knot brought the corpse, the rope, and the foot to the man's widow." Someone winced, but most were staring wide eyed.

Don scratched his head, letting himself recall all of the terrible things he had heard about the original Three-Knot Killer, the one whose dossier they'd adjusted for the sake of entertainment. But now he announced without reserve, "There were reports of a dozen other victims, most of whom he shot, some in duels, some not, and though it was never proven, some say he set a town on fire. I don't think anyone knows the body count—

heck, even his ghost might not be sure of it. But he's famous for the three murders with rope."

A shaky voice ventured, "Yeah, but . . . but they got him in the end, right?"

"Sure, but not the way we tell it." Don sighed. He'd known about the lie since his first year in Greeley, knew it was part of the tourist draw, and—until now—he'd never really minded the minor mislead. After all, a good story was usually better than the truth. "Truth is, Three-Knot was a quick draw. Quick enough that most wouldn't face him. But Sheriff Walter P. Millstone of Greeley, Nevada, called him out, said he'd stand against him. Apparently with that pistol." He nodded toward the gun on the floor. "Seemed really brave. But Millstone didn't intend for there to be a gunfight. No, when they walked out onto the street, Millstone used the duel as a distraction. Got some folks to jump Three-Knot, disarm him, and haul him into the jail for the shortest trial ever in the history of Greeley. Reports say it was daylight that same day when they hanged him."

There were a few murmurs that Millstone had done the right thing.

"Well, sure," Don agreed. "It made all kinds of sense at the time, but imagine a guy like Three-Knot being hanged instead of killed in a duel. Imagine the anger of his soul over something like that." Don wouldn't say that he sympathized with the Three-Knot Killer, but as he retold the story, the actor felt like he had a much better understanding of the outlaw.

He would have conferred with TK, who'd been playing the role for a while now, but the man was still mostly nonresponsive.

The other big question that lingered in the air was what now. As their only expertise came from one former Catholic and one die-hard *Supernatural* fan, each theory seemed about as legitimate as the last—and not a one was positive.

By anyone's guess, the ghost had won: he had them trapped, powerless, and ready to pick off until he had finished whatever he had come there to do.

Perhaps, if they were lucky, there would only be one more attack before the Three-Knot Ghost was satisfied. After all, the ghost had struck twice, each time on the hour, and in the style of a Three-Knot killing, only one of which remained. And each time, Don was pretty sure the ghost had gone after the last person who held the gun: first Big Sam and then TK. Maybe if no one else touched it, not even through a glove or handkerchief, then no one would get dragged away by an invisible horse.

But Don had handled the Sheriff's weapon, and—Don looked over to Stacey, and, from what he could read of her drawn expression, she too expected the axe to fall on her.

And yet . . .

Don closed his eyes. He visualized himself next to that boulder, drew up the sounds and smells of steel on stone, witnessed his own last encounter with the ghost. He had been glued to the floor in terror when it first came through the saloon door, but within a minute, Don had gone and faced the ghost, seen even a red-eyed nightmare flinch away from a toy pistol drawn by a practiced showman.

And Don had an idea, one that would live up to the fictional legacy of Walter P. Millstone and that rusted pistol.

❖

Don Driscol, a line of sweat following the hook of his nose, sauntered out into the middle of the street, his hands pale and shaking. And, in his best Sheriff-Walter-P.-Millstone, he rasped, "It's over Three-Knot!" And then a little louder, "You'll never hurt another living soul."

From inside the saloon, hiding behind windows and the edges of the door, a small collection of reenactors and tourists continued to stare at the lone actor in the street—unwilling to look away as the shhnk-shhnk-shhnk of spurs preceded the appearance of the Three-Knot Killer. And there, they stared at each other, fingers barely willing to twitch.

For a time, no one spoke; hardly a soul breathed, and no wind blew; but the second-hand ticks brought them incrementally closer to two o'clock.

The ghost of the Three-Knot Killer drew up one corner of his poisonous lips, exposing moon-white teeth, and the long-dead murderer let out a hissing wail, as if to say, "You'll never take me alive!"

As the ghost readied to draw, Don whispered, "That's the idea."

The ghost drew his pistol and was starting to pull the trigger even before it was fully out of the holster. But Don was smarter.

Don let his legs go limp and felt the jet of air above him as if a bullet shrieked by, missing his head by inches. And as he fell, Don pulled the trigger of the old, rusty, long-barrel pistol, almost as quickly as the ghost had. After years of practice, he knew just the angle to shoot a long, lean gunslinger in the heart, and this time, even though the weapon had no bullets or powder, Don would have sworn he felt the Millstone pistol kick with authority as it sent one last honorable slug at the devilish outlaw.

The ghost staggered back, one hand going to his abdomen. He dropped his gun, which faded into nothing more than ash. Then the feet started to crumble, and then one hand, starting with the trigger finger. As his body became charred-white dust dispersing on the breeze, the wicked light seemed to drain out of his eyes. And in the last moments, Don Driscol would have sworn the ghost mouthed the words "Thanks, partner," before disappearing entirely.

Silence hung for maybe a minute more, and then the clock struck two with such fervor that Don nearly collapsed on the spot. But with that tolling bell came something that he hadn't heard in Greeley in a long time: applause.

Don Driscol, as the better version of Sheriff Walter P. Millstone, faced his audience and took a deep bow.

Hard though it was for the authorities to believe, the meager crowd of attendees all gave the same testimony about Three-Knot's ghost and the actor who was brave enough to end him. And thanks to a thing called Google, the story spread to believers and skeptics alike. So, the next time Greeley opened for tourism, they received full busloads and several eager drive-ins.

On reopening day, many of the reenactors, including Stacey and TK, were nervous, but Don Driscol, the owner and star of Greeley's Ghost Town, had already faced his worst fear: the very real threat of an empty audience. Now, nothing could possibly scare him.

Mike Jack Stoumbos is a high-school teacher and test-prep tutor who lives in Washington State with his wife and their parrot. Between classes and grading, Mike Jack devotes his creative energies to partner dance, karaoke, and—of course—writing. In recent years, he has written and produced several original plays in the Seattle area and self-published his first novel, *The Baron Would Be Proud*. This marks his second appearance in an anthology, following his contribution to *Dragon Writers* in 2016. For more about Mike and his writing visit www.mikejackwrites.wordpress.com.

THE EMPATH

KELLY LYNN COLBY

THE EMPATH

Gina and Amelia called it "antique shopping." I hadn't seen anything I'd put that label on yet. The repurposed, turn-of-the-century homes peddled little more than trinkets and handmade jewelry. The attempt at pulling off a quaint center of town, circa *Little House on the Prairie*, fell apart when you crossed the heavily trafficked road of cars coming home from work in Houston.

Don't get me wrong. I was glad most of these stores were full of innocuous junk, not old possessions. You never knew what was left behind on a true family keepsake, on something of value to the person who held it. I tucked my gloved hands deeper into my crossed arms. Still, I hadn't touched anything all day. Just in case.

Gina waved at me from the porch of another shop. "Fauna, come on. This one is my favorite." Her ponytail bounced as she stepped over the threshold, the tiny bell announcing her arrival.

"I'm coming." I wasn't thrilled about it, but anything was better than the crowded mall or the close quarters of a movie theater. My skin crawled at the thought of all those emotions shoved into touching range.

I wiped my feet at the crooked steps to the old home with

freshly painted green siding and a newly repaired stair railing. The words Finishing Touches swung from the door on a carved wooden sign. At least the owner maintained this place. A quick glance in the window showed eclectic, but obviously new, Halloween decorations next to stylized jack-o'-lanterns. This store should be safe. They seemed to be imitating the holiday section of a craft store, only with a funkier selection. It could even be fun. Maybe I'd find something unique to display at the bookstore on Monday.

I caught the door as it swung toward me. The store smelled of mildew and retirement savings.

Gina pushed her sunglasses through her tied-back hair to sit on her head like an extra set of eyes. She rocked back and forth from heel to toe as if we didn't move fast enough for her. Well, if she would quit running marathons, she wouldn't have all that extra energy when we wanted to take it easy. She pointed at my hands. "I don't know how you stand those things when it's ninety degrees outside?"

I displayed the soft brown leather like a surgeon with freshly scrubbed hands. "Better safe than sorry."

My friends thought I was some sort of germaphobe since I never went without my layer of protective wear. Bacteria had no emotions; at least, none that I could feel. I had no fear of them whatsoever, but I let everyone believe as they wished. The truth was so much harder to explain. Since I'd never met anyone else like me, I'd decided long ago it was better to be seen as neurotic than full-on crazy.

Amelia followed me in. She gave Gina a leave-her-alone look. "This is where I bought those cute snowmen last year. Remember?" The splatter of freckles still looked weird to me. She used to cover her fair face with foundation, before she went on a natural beauty kick. The speckles matched her auburn hair, and I hoped she'd keep them on display.

"The little ceramic snowmen dressed up like the three bears with Goldilocks trying on their noses, right?"

"Yes. I love them so much. Dorian, the owner, gave me the artist's name, and he just sent a newsletter announcing his new shipment. I must add to my collection." Amelia vibrated with excitement. She knew I didn't like to be hugged. So, she patted me on the shoulder as she walked past.

I could sense her joy, but it didn't penetrate. The feeling floated on the surface of my jacket and fell off like a light snow. A deep breath of relief caused me to cough as I was assaulted by the smell of mildew. Again. Dorian was trying, but she couldn't shake the age of the building without replacing it board by board.

A tingle touched the back of my neck. Someone in this store exuded a strong emotion. I typically couldn't read people unless I had skin-to-skin contact. Whatever this person felt had to be so overwhelming that it leaked from their pores and filled the air like rolling fog.

I closed my eyes and rubbed my arms, trying to calm my nerves. The feelings weren't mine. I was out having a good time with my friends. Well, with a couple of people I kind of knew, who had no idea what I struggled with every time I left my home.

My own fear at always being alone mixed with the confusing onslaught of the other source to the point that I couldn't turn it off. My lungs tightened, and red spots impaired my vision.

I had to escape. Right now.

I turned and reached for the doorknob.

"Wait, Fauna." Gina bounced around the corner. Her flip-flops smacked her feet in an eager rhythm. "You've got to see this old furniture. Apparently, it belonged to the original owner. They use them to display the art now."

I flinched as she grabbed my elbow. Somehow, though nothing bled through my jacket, her presence calmed my panic. Gina's emotions were usually pretty in check, which made her a bearable companion. Maybe something about her natural calm cut through the emotional turmoil swirling in the air. Plus, she certainly wasn't panicked about some sort of emergency around the corner. What did I have to be so scared of?

As Gina guided me around the corner, still holding my elbow, a turbulent wall of unbound emotion stopped me cold.

Gina fell forward. "What are you doing?"

"I . . ." A probing tendril of humanity invaded my thoughts. "I don't feel so good."

"Sit." Gina tossed off a Do Not Sit on the Furniture sign and guided me toward the seat.

I fought her until the first touch told me it wasn't the chair. It was clean. I fell into the cushion, sending a cloud of dust into the air. Gina coughed, but it didn't bother me. I was hardly breathing as it was.

My hands covered my head as I tried to block the onslaught of energy. My mood swung uncontrollably from elation to devastation to sorrow. I'd never felt anything so intense. I received no images or specifics, just an overwhelming surge of others' memories bleeding into the air around me.

I had to get it under control before I passed out. I focused on my own grounding memory of my mother singing her favorite hymns and focused on the texture of sound. Her angelic voice filled my mind and drove back the attack to a slight humming in the back of my head.

Gina squatted in front of me until my eyes met hers. One deep breath later, I nodded that I was okay. She didn't understand. No one ever did. At least, she didn't roll her eyes at me.

"Excuse me, ma'am. You can't sit on that. It's an antique." An older woman crossed her arms and stared down at us over the frames of her reading glasses stuck on the end of her nose. Her white permed hair and big red apron tied around a big round body reminded me of Mrs. Claus. Her stern expression reminded me of my college librarian.

Gina sprang to her feet, standing in between me and her.

Amelia tapped the disapproving woman on the shoulder. "Dorian, I'm really interested in these ceramic pumpkins reenacting little red riding hood. Do you have a box for them?" She held up the ceramic piece.

Dorian's face lightened as she turned to her potential customer. "Of course, my dear. I'll go fetch it for you." She gestured to a display around the corner, but kept her feet firmly planted. "Did you see the scarecrows in a Rapunzel pose? The details of the straw hair are brilliant."

I leaned forward and accepted Gina's help to stand. That seemed to satisfy Dorian. She pivoted on her Skechers and headed to the back. Amelia winked at me as she followed. I would have winked back but my head swirled with cloudy voices, a deep baritone, a screaming child, a pathetic moaning.

I had to get out of there. Rushed and disoriented, I went the wrong way and headed deeper into the store.

Gina stepped around a display case to keep up with my pace. "Fauna? Are you sure you're okay?"

As much as I wanted to explain what was happening to me, where would I even start? Normal people don't sense others' emotions. They certainly don't see memories left behind on objects. And I'm not talking about loving events like birthday parties or family dinners. No. For a memory to stick around, it had to be strong, like on the life-changing level. Those kinds of remnants were rarely pleasant.

My skin tingled with the tiny pressure of hundreds of crawling ants. I resisted the urge to itch. I'd never experienced anything so dramatic without having touched the source.

A strong voice rose above the rest. "Don't fight it. Embrace your gift and come find me."

I turned in a circle trying to see all around me at once. "Who was that?"

Gina shrugged. "Just Dorian, the owner. Apparently, she's a bit protective of her inventory."

I shook my head. "No, I mean the man's voice."

Gina's carefully groomed eyebrows rose and her head cocked

in a perfect reflection of my own confusion. She didn't hear anything.

What I heard wasn't a living voice. But it had been so strong. "Don't fight it. Embrace your gift and come find me." The message repeated, more like a recording than a trapped memory.

My fear subsided as curiosity took over. Where is that coming from?

Amelia's delighted giggle ahead warned me of Dorian's presence. "These are adorable!"

I didn't want to run into the stuffy owner. Turning the other direction, with Gina at my heels, I pushed past an awkwardly placed faux fireplace to a wall of overstuffed curio cabinets. In the corner, between displays crammed with inventory, stood the torso of a wooden man on a thigh-high pedestal, his piecemealed face level with my own. The impressions radiated from him, warping the surrounding air like heat waves.

All my life, I'd never encountered anything this intense.

I've had this ability as far back as I can remember. Before I could identify emotions as happy or sad, intense feelings invaded my every interaction. When I was six, I snuck Grandma's wedding ring from my mom's jewelry box. The room around me disappeared and I found myself sitting on a quilted bed starring at my hands. But they didn't look like the plump, pink fingers I was familiar with. The wrinkled and spotted skin surrounded by meticulously manicured fingernails were completely foreign to me. In my grip, I clutched the wedding ring. My warm tears dripped onto my cold hands while emptiness and loss flooded the rest of me.

In retrospect, I knew I had read the strong emotion my grandma left on her fifty-year-old wedding ring when my grandpa died. At the time, it was difficult to separate what was me and what was her. I had gained some control as I dealt with other impressions, but it was rarely a pleasant experience, and I tried to avoid all such contact.

But this. I had never felt anything like it. And I had certainly never seen waves of memories vibrating around an object.

I swallowed my fear as I drew near the statue. Like one of those old Hitchcock movies, it seemed like the rest of the room turned into a tunnel and the statue moved toward me instead. Up close, I could tell it was not one piece of carved wood. Many different wooden and metallic objects had been melded together in such a way to create the upper body of an automaton. I wasn't sure if the thing moved physically, but its energy was certainly powerful enough to attract my attention all the way from the door.

Who could put together such a piece? And why? Maybe there was someone else like me, another empath. How else could they gather so many items impressed with memories? I had never met anyone like me. I had been positive I was the only empath. Maybe I wasn't alone in this isolating quirk. I had to find the artist. I had to know this impossible collection wasn't just a coincidence.

His voice repeated the invitation. "Don't fight it. Embrace your gift and come find me."

There had to be a clue on the statue itself. My gloved hand hovered a breath away from an arm that looked like half a child's baseball bat. A blur of a swing followed by triumphant joy prickled in the back of my mind. Too old. The guts of a music box stood in for the vocal cords. I got as close as I could without touching the pieces surrounding it.

Four or five images swirled in my head, followed by a bout of dizziness. I puffed out a breath of air with my eyes closed. Too many impressions fought for attention. I'd have to touch a piece to drive the rest away.

Too close to block completely, Gina's worry added to the chaos. "Are you okay?"

I had to get her to back off. Her fresh and vibrant fear for me rippled through the summoning voice. "Just a little dehydrated. Do you think Amelia has a water bottle?" She always carried a Mary Poppins bag that seemed to magically hold whatever we needed. Hopefully, searching Amelia out would distract Gina long enough for me to interpret the message in the statue.

"Probably. I'll go check." Gina's ponytail swished through the air as she quickly turned back to me. "Are you sure you'll be all right?"

"Yeah, I just need some water." I smiled in what I hoped wasn't a grimace, as I fought the tears threatening to pour down my face from the throbbing pain in my head.

Her forehead crinkled, but she left to find Amelia anyway. Her bobbing hair left a wake in the emotional waves from the statue. This was why I rarely left the house. I never knew what I would encounter.

Despite my fear, impressions were rare. This conglomeration of memories from different times and places had to mean I wasn't alone. My fingers closed into fists as I realized what I had to do. Either I take a chance, or I remain alone forever.

Though my hands shook, I slipped a leather glove off and plunged my finger against the cylinder of the music box. My body dunked into cold water as every pore shook with grief. My baby girl was gone. I'd never see her again. I rocked on the pink carpet, as "Send in the Clowns" tinned from the slowly turning ballerina.

I yanked my finger off and blinked away tears that shouldn't be mine. I don't have a daughter. This isn't my grief. I shook my hand as if I could shake away the memories. The nose of the wooden man, embedded in the center of the ball-shaped head, looked like the handle of something. Maybe an artist's tool? That could be the item.

As soon as the tip of my finger touched, agony tore through my gut. The face of my murderer was shadowed by the light of the dining room chandelier. I coughed, unable to breathe as he yanked the knife out of me. My own steaming blood dripped on my face before he plunged the blade into my chest. I grabbed at the weapon. He leaned close to me, his teeth shining bright against his olive skin. He looked human, normal, maybe even handsome. Then his lips curled and his eyes widened in satisfaction as he pushed the blade all the way through to the floor. I screamed, but nothing came out. I couldn't breathe. I couldn't . .

My shoulders vibrated as my head rocked side to side on a squeaky wooden floor. A shadow leaned over me, shaking me. I threw my arms up to deflect another blow.

Gina's voice broke through the vision. "Fauna, are you alright?" She turned her head to Amelia on my other side. "We might need to call 911."

I waved her off with my tingling arm. "I'm fine. I'm fine. I don't need an ambulance." The agonizing pain and rush of adrenaline faded, leaving me shivering and achy. I had to find this artist, this person who had the same curse. And when I did, I was going to punch him in the nose for tormenting me like this.

Sucking in air delicately, grateful to be able to breathe again, I pushed up from the floor to prove I could. My numb lower body threatened my balance. I was sure I'd end up back on the ground.

Dorian sidled over and placed a wood stool behind me. "Are you sure you're okay?"

"Yes. I'm good." I hoped my voice didn't give away the terror that still lurked in my mind. I tried to sound casual. "I do love that piece there, though. I wonder if I could have the name of the artist?" The powerful memory short circuited whatever mechanism made me empathic. I could still see the waves radiating from the wooden man, but none of it internalized.

Dorian crossed her arms; her forehead grew extra wrinkles. I didn't have to sense her emotions to know she was annoyed. "That's Julian Mendoza's work. It gives me the creeps."

Amelia leaned close to the statue's face. "It's amazing, all the pieces put together to make this tin man-looking thing."

I put my glove back on and bit my tongue to resist the urge to scream at her not to touch it. But it wouldn't matter. The impressions couldn't hurt her.

I turned to Dorian. "Do you happen to have his contact information? I'd love to get a custom piece for my book store."

The store owner dropped her hands and cocked her hip. "I'm sure I can dig up all of that information when I write up the bill of sale."

That's great. She wanted to take my money along with my dignity. I sighed deeply as exhaustion set in. "I'll take it."

Amelia shook her head at me and pointed at a tiny yellow sticker stuck to the pedestal. "Are you sure, Fauna?"

I wasn't going to get close again. I couldn't risk touching it and passing out from another strong impression. "I'm sure." I'll save the embarrassment for my own kitchen floor.

"Wonderful. It's a unique piece that will immediately draw in your guests." Dorian clapped her hands like a gavel proclaiming the final verdict.

Not that I have any people over. Ever. Besides, what would the entertainment value be? Watch our hostess pass out in front of this inert statue for no apparent reason?

Gina glanced over Amelia's shoulder and whistled. "Ouch. That artist is proud of his work."

"I don't care how much it is. It's coming home with me." I followed Dorian to the register and pulled out my emergency credit card. This qualified as an emergency. I was not the only empath. Someone else had been dealing with this curse and was comfortable enough with it to call out more like him. Nothing could possibly be more important than that.

"That'll be $3,000 even." Dorian pointed to the scanner where I swallowed heavily as I inserted the plastic.

❖

I closed the door on my friends after assuring them again that I was okay and just needed to lie down. Alone. They'd helped me carry the still-wrapped automaton to the corner of my dining room. Despite the layers of packing material and my gloves, I still caught sharp rays of scarring memories. There was no way that thing could stay here with me. The voices would keep me up all night. I still couldn't scrub the memory of the murdered woman. I prayed they caught the guy.

From my purse, I took out the receipt with the information that was supposed to answer all of my questions. The PO Box number stared up at me, completely useless. What was I supposed to do now? Track down the location and wait for someone wearing gloves in the middle of summer to check his mail? Angry, I tossed the slip on the table with the rest of the bills.

I used my phone to search on the drive home and couldn't find any mention of him outside of a small show in Austin a decade ago. Where was this guy? Why would he leave a beacon for an empath in the corner of an unremarkable store and then make it impossible to unite?

Now I was stuck with this thing that would torment me every moment I was home, the only place where I could relax. Maybe I should have had Amelia and Gina leave it on the lawn for the garbage man. That would have been fun to explain. I'm so pathetically lonely that I spent three months' rent on a nightmare just for the minuscule chance that I could find someone, just one more person, who understood.

But he said to find him. There was no way he went through all this trouble and then made it impossible. I grabbed scissors out of the junk drawer in the kitchen and marched to the statue. I sang my mother's favorite hymn, "Be Still My Soul," in preparation to block the flood of impressions. Before fear froze my actions, I cut through the thick tape and ripped the brown paper from around him.

The waves beat over me like an icy tide. My anger and my mother's voice in my head strengthened my own identity, building a barrier between me and the onslaught of foreign emotions. Dropping the scissors in the mess on the floor, I flung both of my gloves off at the same time.

Alright, Julian Mendoza, tell me how to find you.

"Don't fight it. Embrace your gift and come find me."

I focused on his voice, driving every competing impression back into its object. The artist's message tingled through me as I gave it control. My hands flared like they were holding a ball. No, not a ball, a globe. The head! I felt Julian cradling the automaton's head in his hands.

I blinked to bring the statue back into focus. The round head had continents carved into its surface. The dull sepias of the antique piece contrasted so drastically with the blues and greens of modern globes, I hadn't noticed what it was at first. Careful to avoid the nose, I placed my fingertips only on the sphere. As soon as I made contact, all tension left my body.

Julian was calm. More than calm—comforting. I'd never felt such an impression before. I'd always believed that peaceful feelings lacked the intense energy needed for a remnant memory. Somehow, Julian had managed.

I closed my eyes to focus on the message playing in my head. Through Julian's eyes, I saw a street sign swaying beside a traffic light: Bagby. I knew that Houston street well. I wonder how many times I had walked by the artist and never knew he was there.

Acid sloshed in my stomach as the image jumped ahead to an apartment building. No, that wasn't quite right. They were condos with wrought-iron balconies and HardiePlank siding that began light blue close to the street and darkened to deep navy at the top floor. I thought I recognized that building across the street from my favorite Mexican restaurant.

The image jumped again, and I wondered how many more leaps my stomach could tolerate. Julian showed me the front of a bright red door with curly numbers affixed above the peephole: 413.

Then I heard the words as the door opened: "Don't fight it. Embrace your gift and come find me." The vision popped back to the beginning and the Bagby street sign. I blinked my eyes open as I released the automaton. Like before, the intensity of the image dulled my senses, quieting any other impression that wanted to impose. Midtown. I had to go to Midtown Houston. It was only a fifteen-minute drive, but it was Saturday at dinner time. I should call first. But I don't have his number.

I shook my head as I bent to the floor and retrieved my gloves. He assaulted me with these images and this emotional roller coaster and didn't give me a warning. Why should he have the advantage?

Alright, Mr. Mendoza. I hope you're ready for a visitor. I've been the only empath my entire life. If there was the possibility of another one out there, I had to know. Tonight.

W hat do I say? What do I say? I hovered in front of the elevator for ten minutes and starred at the red door at the other end of the hallway. My heart raced as if I'd just finished a marathon.

Nope. I can't do this. I pressed the elevator button. What was I thinking driving into the city to bang on the door of a complete stranger and demand answers for questions I didn't know how to ask? The elevator doors slid open and I took one step over the threshold.

If I left, I might never know. I could be alone forever, stuck in this not-life. I had to take the chance. I pivoted on my heels, marched down the hall, and knocked on the door of 413 in one determined movement. It swung open before I had a chance to drop my fist.

A middle-aged man with large brown, friendly eyes and dark curly hair smiled the most welcoming smile I'd ever seen. "There you are. When Dorian called and told me Jonathon had sold, I knew you would find me."

"Jonathon?"

"My sculpture you bought. You must realize he has a name;

all great works do, and Jonathon's one of my finest." He tapped on the red door frame with his gloved hands.

I raised my leather-covered hands. "Then you are . . .?" I stood there staring at another human being who might be like me. Yet, I couldn't bring myself to ask. What if the answer was no?

"An empath?" The hinges squeaked as he opened the red door all the way, revealing half a dozen people waving from his living room. Everyone wore leather gloves. "We all are."

Tears trailed down my cheeks before I knew I was crying. Julian ushered me into his home, careful not to touch me. "You are not alone."

And I wasn't. I was not the only empath. I sat down in the folding chair he offered me. Everyone else sat on various pieces of furniture forming a rough circle, like a support group meeting. They left a respectable amount of space between one another. I recognized and understood that precaution. I felt like a spy when I accidentally invaded another's emotional state, even though they never knew I did it. To watch an entire group of people move as I did was shocking, and oddly comforting.

Julian sat across from me. "Now. What questions do you have for us?"

Who knew that forcing myself to go "antique shopping" with a couple of friends would lead to this revelation? Among these empaths, I knew, I had finally found my people, my tribe.

Kelly Lynn Colby is a professional volunteer who lives in the suburbs of Houston with a menagerie of two-legged and four-legged family members. She's an avid believer in community and promotes the writing one wherever she goes. Her BS in biology hangs above her desk looking important while she writes about magic and dragons. To find out more about her and her other publications, visit her website at www.KellyLynnColby.com.

TRUE REFLECTION

JACE KILLAN

*Mike,
Thanks for all your help w/ this & sorry about the mispell*

Sorry about the writing
Kinda in a hurry
Thanks for the

TRUE REFLECTION

With the full moon tonight, Betty would see her daughter again. How she yearned for these monthly sessions. In preparation she pulled the antique hand mirror from the vanity and removed the black silk swaddle, revealing its simple silver frame. As usual, it had tarnished since the previous session. Taking it by the bone handle, she carefully applied polish to the frame and rubbed it in, bringing it back to life.

When finished, she held the mirror out, affording a good look at her pale black face with blotchy cheeks and drooping dark sacks below the eyes. She hated looking at herself. Her daughter had been her true reflection—bright and brilliant, with a smile on her face. Tonight Betty hoped to finally see that smile again. The prior sessions had progressively improved with the medium. At first, Jenn's image was not much more than a shadow on the face of the mirror, but over the year it had gradually formed the image of Betty's daughter, though still slightly out of focus.

When night fell and the moon appeared, the mirror darkened at first, followed by Jenn's fuzzy apparition.

"Oh, my baby," Betty cried. "I'm here, honey."

The image spun around several times as it came into focus.

Tonight her daughter wore a red strapless gown, like the one she would have worn to prom her senior year in high school, had she been allowed to go.

"Mama?" Betty thought she heard, though the whisper was so soft, she didn't know if she'd imagined it. She'd never communicated through the mirror herself before, though the medium promised it would be possible, eventually. Up until now, she had needed to use the medium as an intermediary.

Jenn's image grew as she approached from inside the mirror, functioning more like a window into the afterlife. "Mama, is that you?"

"I'm here, Jenn. It's me. I'm here."

"Where?" Jenn whispered. "I don't see anything. Only darkness."

"Keep walking toward my voice, baby."

"Is this a dream? Where am I? Where did everyone go? Did I do it again?"

Hearing her daughter caused Betty to cry. "Oh, child. Mama's here. I've missed you. Come closer; I want to see you."

"Missed me? Why, Mama?"

Why? Did her daughter not know she'd died? Such wasn't the case the other times she'd communicated with Jenn through the medium. Her daughter had acknowledged the car accident. And knew she was in another place, one she disliked very much. And she missed her mama. That was understandable.

"Mama?" Jenn said.

"I'm here, child. It's me."

Jenn's face grew close now, finally in full focus, just like Betty remembered when her daughter was alive. Jenn had high cheeks that would ball up when she smiled. She wore her black hair buzzed short.

"Can you hear me?" Betty said. "Can you see me?"

"I hear you, but I only see blackness. You can see me?"

"Yes, dear."

"Are you dead too?" Jenn asked.

"No, baby. I'm sitting in my kitchen."

"Oh. Then how did I get here? I don't like it. Everything is dark."

"I wanted to see you." Betty cocked her head. "And before I forget, happy birthday. You turned thirty-five last week."

Jenn laughed at that. "Oh, Mama. I'm much older than thirty-five."

"Do you feel okay? Haven't you missed me?"

"I am wonderful. You'll love it here. Well, not here . . ." she glanced to her side. "I don't know where here is. Why am I here, Mama?"

She'd asked that before. Betty tried her best to answer this time. "You were killed by a drunk driver, honey."

"I know that, Mama. But why am I here? I was with Grandpa, and Aunty Gene, and Marvin. Oh, you should meet Marvin. He tells the silliest stories. Yes, you must meet him. But I don't know where he's gone. He was here, just a moment ago." Jenn spun around and backed away in the mirror. "Marvin? Are you hiding? Come meet my mama."

"Baby," Betty said, "there's only you and me here. Just as it should be. Come back closer. Let me see you. Let me talk to you. I've missed you so much."

Jenn's posture slumped, showing a bit of cleavage in her red gown. Betty fought the urge to reprimand her for the inappropriate attire. Now wasn't the time. Maybe later.

"Go ahead and talk, Mama." Jenn's face darkened, triggering a flood of memories. The smirk Jenn would make before she would kiss Betty goodnight. The resentment she bore in her eyes. The disrespect. Betty had tried to slap it out of her only child more than once, but it always seemed to return, and it was there now.

"Jennifer. You are my daughter. I am your mother. You'll give me the respect I deserve."

Jenn nodded though her face was void of any emotion.

"Now, apologize."

"I'm sorry, Mother."

"That's better, dear. I forgive you. You don't understand that I'm trying to help you."

Her eyes lifted to meet Betty's. "Help me?"

"Yes, baby. I can't imagine how lonely you must feel. You must miss me. Don't you?" Jenn didn't answer, so Betty persisted. "Don't you? Don't you miss your mama?"

Jenn affirmed with a nod.

"Now, I paid good money so that you and I could have these chats once a month. I know it should be more often, but this is all the mirror allows for. So let's not waste it."

Jenn's eyes grew wide. "You've done this to me before?"

Betty didn't appreciate Jenn's tone, but she forgave it anyway. "I've seen you on every full moon over the last year."

"Oh, Mama." Jenn began to pace back and forth. "That makes sense now. We thought I was sick. I'd disappear. Yes, twelve times I've disappeared. That makes sense. This mirror must bring me here, to this dark place. It was you."

"Yes, child. I've brought you here to be with me. We deserve to be together, don't we?"

"Mama, please listen. I love you, and I'll see you soon. In just a moment, you'll be with me. And it's lovely. It's everything the Bible says it will be. But this here, this darkness, this place you've brought me to, I don't like it. I think this is hell."

Betty fought back the rage. After all she'd gone through. After all she'd suffered and waited. This wasn't hell. This was heaven. They were together. That's what heaven meant, right? To be with those you love? Forever?

"You're confused, baby. Now come closer so I can see you."

"I'm not confused, Mama. You just don't remember. I don't blame you, for any of it. You just don't understand. But how could you?"

"What's that supposed to mean?" Betty fought raising her voice.

"To know heaven, you have to love."

"I love you!"

"No. You think you do, but you don't love me. You've summoned me here for you, not me, Mama."

"How can you even say that?" Betty's eyes blurred with tears, and she didn't hold them back. She sobbed, monstrous cries. She wailed, seeking relief from the pain in her heart, just as she'd cried over Jenn's grave. Such relief had come then, when she met the medium.

"Don't cry, Mama. I'm sorry you're upset."

"Upset? Why do you think I'm upset?" Betty's pain turned to anger. "I wait all month to see you. This time we finally get to talk, just the two of us, and you don't want to even spend a moment with me. And you accuse me of being selfish? I died that day with you. I've been in hell since. Don't you understand? Why can't you understand?"

"I do understand, Mama. But this . . ." Jenn spun around slowly with her hands held out. "This isn't right. This isn't how it is meant to be. We'll be together soon enough, but not like this."

The image on the mirror began to fade as dawn's early light filtered into the home. Had they really spoken all night? It felt like only an hour, maybe less. But it was just as before. Time seemed to speed up while she stared into the afterlife through the mirror.

Still, this experience hadn't been like the others. While it should have been more glorious, she didn't once remember feeling so angry and depressed afterward. How could her daughter be so ungrateful? Betty would have to make more of an emphasis on the sacrifices she'd made on Jenn's behalf at their next session. Perhaps Jenn had been ill. Not herself.

※

After a week, still upset with how she'd left things with Jenn, Betty made a special visit to Laura, the medium.

She entered the adobe-style building, the word PSYCHIC

hand painted on front in big blue letters. Inside she touched the bell several times before the medium arrived.

"Ah, Bethanne, I've been expecting you," the short white woman with a large backside said in her usual Southern drawl.

"You have?" Betty asked. "Well, then you must know what happened with Jenn and the mirror."

Her eyes narrowed. "Of course I do, dear. But why don't you tell me what you think happened."

Betty took a seat in the wicker chair opposite a glass table where Laura sat dressed in a grey pantsuit.

After catching her breath, Betty explained how, this time, she'd been able to speak with her daughter.

"That's wonderful," Laura said. "Soon the bond will be complete and you won't need to wait until the full moon to communicate. You'll be able to see her always, in the mirror."

"But Jenn was acting . . ." she considered how to describe her daughter's behavior. ". . . crazy."

"Oh my." Laura leaned forward and held out her hands. "Let's speak with her now and find out what was wrong?"

Betty took Laura's hands. In initial meetings the medium would create the ambiance Betty had expected. She would dim the lights, light candles, and chant a while before beginning a séance. But eventually the sessions grew less formal. Betty had asked about it once, but Laura explained that such pomp had become unnecessary because their bond to the deceased had deepened.

"Jennifer, are you there?" asked Laura. "Your mother is worried about you."

A moment of silence followed until Laura's chubby face contorted and her eyes blinked in rapid succession. Some variation of this happened each time they contacted Jenn.

When Laura opened her eyes, she looked around frantically until she settled on Betty. "Mom?"

"It's me, child."

"Mom, oh, I've missed you."

Betty started to cry. Even though she stared into this woman's green eyes, she saw beyond that, to the eyes of her daughter. What gave her more comfort was the knowledge that her daughter could see Betty too. Not like the mirror. Perhaps that is why Jenn was so distraught. She couldn't see. She did mention that.

"Honey, I was worried about our meeting the other night. You seemed . . . out of sorts."

"I wasn't well," Jenn said vicariously. "I couldn't see you. Not like now."

Betty nodded. That made sense. Perhaps, just as over time Betty was able to see Jenn more fully, and now communicate with her, Jenn would eventually see Betty also. "Someday," Betty said.

"Yes, someday. At the next full moon. It is time for you to join me."

"Join you? You mean die?"

The medium's laughter, her daughter's laughter, surprised Betty.

"No, silly. You don't need to die for you to be with me forever. You should come into the mirror with me. It is glorious. You'll love it here."

Betty relaxed, unaware at how tense she'd been. She hadn't been aware she could go into the mirror with her daughter. Then they could be together forever. "How do I do it?"

"Speak the words, Mom." Laura's head dipped. "Speak the words," she whispered. "Speak the . . ."

A second later Laura glanced up, blinking as if waking from a dream. "What happened? Did you speak to her?"

"Yes," Betty nodded. "She wants me to visit her in the mirror. She said I should speak the words."

Laura's eyes widened. "She said that? Then you should do it. I can show you. But . . ."

"But what?" Betty asked.

"It isn't cheap."

Betty frowned. "I've already given you everything I own."

"Everything?" Laura shook her head.

"Well, not my house. But where would I live?"

"With your daughter, of course. You'll have no need of a house. That's just a material thing anyway. Where your daughter is, you will want for nothing."

"If I can go there, then why can't she come here?"

"My dear Bethanne, your daughter is the happiest she has ever been. You wouldn't want to take that away from her, would you?"

The more Betty thought about it, the more her excitement grew. No more bills, no more wondering what to eat for dinner, no more telemarketing phone calls. Just her daughter by her side, as it should be. She'd find happiness. She needed to have faith; that's what the medium had told her. And she would. She'd have faith.

After signing over the deed to her house, Laura gave Betty a list of arrangements she'd need to make before returning on the night of the next full moon.

Betty complied with the list, precisely as written. She left a note that she'd gone to live with her daughter. She completed her tax returns. She willed all her assets to Laura. She held a series of yard sales where she sold every piece of jewelry, every book, everything belonging to this world, except the mirror and a change of clothes. She didn't need any of it anymore, not where she was going. She even sold her daughter's things, down to the red prom dress her daughter had never used.

With all the cash she'd acquired, Betty purchased and delivered a cashier's check to Laura's office. The thought of giving it all away didn't bother her in the least. It was worth it to be with her daughter again.

She could hardly contain herself when the day that preceded the full moon arrived. She took time bathing one last time. Her neck ached from sleeping on the bare floor. She only had to put up with the stiff neck for a few more hours.

She ate Taco Bell burritos for her last meal on earth, though Laura assured her she could eat whatever she wanted when in heaven with her daughter.

The sun was setting when she arrived at Laura's office with the antique hand mirror secured under her arm. When she entered, she didn't find the quaint entry and worn furniture. The place had been cleared, except for a symbol involving a circle and several skewed lines made from white sand on the shag carpet.

In the center sat the robust medium, her hands raised to the sky as if in supplication. Her multiple shadows danced about the room from the dozens of lit candles round about.

"You're late," Laura said.

"It isn't dark yet," Betty said.

"Tonight the full moon is fully visible at dusk. Sit. We haven't much time." The medium pointed at a part of the circle sectioned off by one of the sand lines.

Betty did, though she felt cramped in the allotted space, so close to the hefty medium.

"Give us the mirror." Laura reached for the bundle under Betty's arm.

Betty removed the silk cloth and stole a glance in the mirror. It bore no reflection. Excitedly, she held it up. "Jenn? Are you there?"

"Give it here," Laura snapped, making an exerted effort to reach the mirror.

Betty didn't usually respond well to harsh demands, and she could see Jenn in the distance, still dressed in the red prom gown, though it looked soiled and torn. "I'm here, baby."

"Mama," Jenn raced toward her; the image in the mirror grew. "Mama, you have to let me go. I've been trapped in there for..."

"Dammit, Bethanne! We're running out of time." Laura took the mirror and set it at her side, face down. "Look into my eyes. We have to speak the words, remember?"

Betty did as instructed, but Jenn's distant voice seemed distraught. "What is she saying?"

"She wants to see you. She wants you to speak the words." Laura held out her hands, inviting Betty to place hers on top.

She did.

"Now repeat after me," Laura said. She muttered something tribal and Betty did her best to match the tones. Distant screeches came from the mirror. What was Jenn doing? Halfway through the next phrase, Betty broke the connection and snatched up the mirror. "She's trying to tell me something."

"How dare you!" Laura slammed the table with both hands.

"I'm sorry, but I need to speak to my daughter." Betty stood and held out the mirror.

"Mama. I can see you. What are you doing?"

"I'm coming to visit you, baby. To be with you. As it should be."

"No, Mama. You don't want to come here. This is hell. This isn't right. You've trapped me here."

Betty only half paid attention. She had to turn her back to Laura, who struggled to take the mirror. But if the medium was trying to reunite Betty with her daughter, why would she care if they spoke? Something wasn't right.

"Mama, you've got to let me go. You've trapped me in hell. I've been here since I last heard your voice. All the other times I went back to heaven, but now, I'm afraid I won't be able to. Not ever again," Jenn sobbed.

"I don't understand," Betty said to the mirror. Then to Laura, "What does she mean? What is she saying?"

"Nothing, Bethanne. She's not herself. Let's speak the words, then you'll be with her."

Betty spun and grabbed the chubby woman by the neck. "I'll be with her, like trapped in the mirror? Trapped in hell?"

Laura fought the grip with both hands, struggling for relief. "No, in heaven. Just speak the words and you will see."

"Please, Mama. Let me go," Jenn cried.

"How? How do I let her go?" Betty squeezed tight, forcing the medium to cough.

"It's too late for that. She's in the mirror." Laura wheezed. "You should join her."

Betty looked at the mirror she'd paid so much for, then into her daughter's frantic eyes. The medium had taken everything from her with the promise of giving her back her daughter. But her daughter wasn't happy. Jenn had been right. Betty was selfish. She'd given up everything she owned for what she wanted, but for Jenn to be at peace, Betty needed to give her up too.

"Break the mirror, Mama," Jenn screamed.

In an instant, Betty saw all of her faults. Her neediness. She hadn't let Jenn live. She'd kept her caged like a trapped bird, no different than now, damned to the mirror. Jenn had gone to get a gallon of milk because Betty had demanded it of her—and that had ended her life on earth. Had Betty let her caged bird fly, maybe Jenn would still be alive. Betty could have gotten her own damn milk.

Laura throat punched Betty, causing her to release her grip and double over. While Laura reached for the mirror, Betty turned her backside into the chubby medium, pinning her against the wall.

Betty stared into the mirror. "I love you, Jenn. I'll see you in heaven." Betty spun and smashed the mirror over Laura's head, knocking her out cold.

Betty slumped to the floor and took up a shard from the mirror. In it, she saw her reflection. It smiled back with sad eyes. Sad that she'd have to wait to see her daughter again. Sad that she'd been played. And sad that she'd been a fool of a mother while Jenn was alive. But there were no tears now. She'd done what she never could do in Jenn's life. She'd let go. And for that reason, she smiled.

. . .

Jace Killan lives in Arizona with his family, wife, and five kids, and a little dog. He writes fiction, thrillers, and soft sci-fi with a little short horror on the side. He has an MBA and works in finance for a biotechnology firm. Jace plays and writes music and enjoys everything outdoors. He's also a novice photographer. For more information about Jace Killan and his writing visit www.jacekillan.com.

CHASTENING

JO SCHNEIDER

CHASTENING

I've sat in palaces. I've sat in estates. I sat on the edge of the discovery of the new world, and now I sit atop cracking tile in a bleak entryway covered in blotches of color. What kind of *stronzo* paints a sixteenth-century Italian sgabello chair with garish flowers and butterflies?

The front door opens. Sunshine hits me, and the *stronzo*'s voice floats in. Her attention is on the device held up to her ear.

"Janice, he's a married man."

My newest owner dumps her battered purse on my seat.

"Anyone can see he's not happy, but I would never—"

I feel a rush of lust as my owner thinks about the man next door. Oh, but she would if given the chance. Her unrighteous desire prickles inside of me.

My profession in life had forced me to deny the existence of magic, but my curse for following the carnal desires of my own flesh sent me down a path that ended here—trapped for centuries in a chair stained by my own blood, with my soul bound to the fibers of wood until I had either performed enough righteous vengeance on those who gave in to their lust, or I faded away. One path led to redemption, the other to eternal burning.

She giggles. "Janice, stop. You're making me blush."

I draw on her desire, and it fills me. If I still had a body, I would shiver in delight. The power washes over me like a wave from the ocean. I soak it in, each fiber of my wood warming.

She walks into the other room. "Of course I'll call you if anything happens."

It isn't often that a person gives me this much magic. Like breathing, I gather it, hold it, and then let it out. I move a few inches, my legs chittering across the floor, and then stop.

Not far enough for her to notice. I hope.

With any luck, she will give me more in a few hours. My optimism increases as she begins to bake.

The man, who is no innocent player in this game, follows a schedule that the sun could use as a clock. He arises early, exercises, and leaves for work before most of the neighborhood is awake. He arrives home in the middle of the day. Alone.

This time, she is ready.

With the innocence of a devious small child, she waits until the appointed hour, then changes into clothing that reveals most of her skin and saunters out to the mailbox just as he arrives home.

She leaves puddles of yearning in her wake, and I gather them to me. I think about moving again, but I decide to wait. There will be more. Perhaps much more.

The door remains ajar, and their voices float in.

"How was the radio station?"

"Fine. How was yoga class?"

"Great. You need to come sometime!"

"I'm not sure I'm cut out for yoga. All those crazy poses."

"I can help you learn."

"Oh yeah? When are you going to come jogging with me?"

"When you don't do it at three in the morning."

"Is there something else I should be doing at three in the morning?"

She giggles. "Listen, I baked some scones. You should come try one."

"Should I?"

"Why don't you come in through the side door?"

"Mmm. What's in it for me besides scones?"

"You'll have to come and find out."

She runs back in through the front door, leaving a stream of desire in her wake—so much that I can barely hold it all. She goes by so fast that I don't have a chance to move.

I'm not concerned. This is better. My chain shortens each time I punish the sinful. The more sinful, the more links are removed.

He comes. They eat. They drink. They pass me as they go upstairs to her room.

When they come back down, hours later, they are deliriously happy. I am overflowing.

They stop in the entryway for one last passionate kiss, and I use the power that I'm now swimming in to move. My back leg swings. My front leg stays in place and I pivot, coming to a stop with a soft thump.

They don't notice. They are focused only on one another, and they are coming my way.

Their continued passion allows me to move again—right into their path.

He continues to kiss her, and she retreats, pulling him toward the living room.

Neither of them knows I'm there until it's too late.

They take one step. Then another. The back of her knee hits my seat. His feet keep hers from moving. Muscles wail. Tendons pop. Bones groan. She cries out, but he is too distracted by other things to notice that something is wrong.

Her purse slips off my seat and spills its contents onto the tile. She arches her back, trying to stay upright, and for a moment I am afraid that it will work, but it does not. She falls.

The crack of her skull on the tile makes me excited in a way I haven't felt since my first lover. Blood flows. Life ebbs.

"No!" he cries.

I continue to gather power. The ridiculous paint on me begins to blister and peel.

He falls to his knees next to her. He blubbers, begs, wails—but she is gone. Punished for her sins.

With shaking hands, he uses me to stand, then sits on my seat.

He pulls out his phone and stares at it.

I consider throwing him off. I could, but I wait. How will he cover this up? What lies will he tell? How many more links could I remove with just this one man?

I push power into him, and suddenly he can't live without me. He'll take me to his house—a present for his wife. I will wait.

And then he will die.

Jo Schneider grew up in the Wild West and finds mountains helpful in telling which direction she is going. Her lifelong goals include: travel to all seven continents, become a Jedi Knight, and receive a death threat from a fan. So far she's been to five continents and has a black belt in Kempo, but she is still working on the death threat. Being a geek at heart, Jo has always been drawn to science fiction and fantasy. She writes both and hopes to introduce readers to worlds that wow them and characters they can cheer for. Visit her at her website www.joannschneider.com.

DIAMOND IN THE GRAVE: A GOBLIN STAR STORY

GAMA RAY MARTINEZ

DIAMOND IN THE GRAVE: A GOBLIN STAR STORY

The whiteness of hyperspace peeled away as the elven transport ship *Lenari* dropped to sublight speed. They were on the outskirts of the star system, so far from the system's white dwarf that it hardly seemed bigger than the rest of the stars in the sky. Before them, a large ship, looking like a half-mile-long box, floated in space. The hull was a patchwork of metal Yevul suspected would be strong in spite of coming from half a dozen worlds. It was hard to believe that this seemingly thrown-together vessel, so unlike the elven vessels Yevul was accustomed to piloting, could hold the jewel he had been seeking for decades.

"Status?" he asked.

Elina tapped her screen. "The hyperdrive is offline, Master Yevul. It looks like there's been an accident."

"Life signs?"

She paled, and her eyes went wide. "Nothing."

He gave her a small smile. "Did you remember to increase the resolution so that it would detect rodents?"

"Oh, right. I'm sorry." She started making the adjustments, though she had to start over twice because of mistakes.

"There's no need to worry. The Shades wouldn't have recruited you if you weren't qualified."

She nodded, but he could tell she didn't believe him. The elven spy network, the Shades, operated on the edge of what was legal and what wasn't. Newcomers often had a rough transition, but Elina was one of the most skilled mental mages to be recruited in five generations. Their leadership had thought she would be best apprenticed to one who often masqueraded as a trader, and Yevul had no doubt she would be a valuable addition to the organization once she grew into her role.

"Two thousand life signs."

"Good. Hail them."

She tapped the screen but shook her head after a few seconds. "Nothing."

"Give it a second."

She nodded. It was nearly a minute, which admittedly was longer than Yevul expected, before Elina looked up.

"There's one humanoid life sign. We're receiving docking instructions, but there's not an active communication channel."

Yevul glanced up. "That system could be offline as well."

"Doesn't that worry you?"

"Not particularly," he said as he directed Lenari toward the open docking-bay door. "It's a wererat vessel. At any given time, half the systems are inoperational."

"You really think they could have the gem?"

"Grevior said he did, and his pack are some of the best scavengers in the galaxy."

"Is that why their ship looks so . . ."

She indicated the cobbled-together vessel, and Yevul nodded. "Wait until you see the inside."

Fortunately, the docking-bay shield, which kept in the atmosphere but allowed friendly ships to enter, was still online, and they passed through without incident. The docking bay was poorly lit. Most of the lights were little more than pinpricks in the darkness, except for one that gave a soft glow. The whole thing made the ceiling look like it was a night sky illuminated by a full moon. Yevul activated the ship's exterior lights and searched for a place to land. The docking-bay floor was covered in pieces of starships, everything from capital vessels to small drone ships used for asteroid mining. Yevul saw ships built by humans, dwarves, goblins, and even a couple by the elves, though those were illegal for a nonelven person to possess.

He set down in the one spot big enough to fit their ship, killing the engines and the lights. At his command, the back hatch opened, forming a ramp down, and the two elves stepped out. Something skittered in the shadows. Elina's eyes went wide, but she didn't react otherwise. Yevul gave her a nod of encouragement and waited.

A few seconds later, a tall man stepped out of the darkness. In spite of his ramshackle surroundings, he wore a tailored suit in the human fashion. In fact, Grevior looked human, and it was only the twitching of his nose and the way his eyes darted around that gave any indication that he spent much of his time in the form of a rat.

"What are you doing here?" His voice had an odd cadence and an unfamiliar lisp Yevul hadn't noticed before.

"What do you mean, what am I doing here, Grevior? I'm here for the gem you told me about."

Grevior blinked at him and stared for several seconds. "Oh yes. The gem. You want to take that."

Yevul glanced at Elina before returning his attention to the wererat. "Yes, I want to take it. I have half a ton of refined silver in my ship to trade for it."

"Silver." Grevior's nose twitched. "Silver is bad for us."

Yevul spoke slowly. "It's also what your star drive runs off of. If our scans are any indication, you need more of it right now."

"We do?" Grevior took a breath. "Yes, silver. Like crystals."

A chill ran down Yevul's back. He reached for his blaster. "Elina, get back to the ship."

"What?"

"The ship. Now."

She nodded and backed up, but before she had gone, a shadow rose up behind her, shedding its rat-like features and taking the form of a dwarven woman carrying a long knife. She put the point to Elina's back. The elf froze. Yevul glared at the man who had first addressed him.

"Who are you?"

"I am Grevior."

"No," Yevul asked. "Who are you?"

The wererat's eyes stared at him, but the thing that was behind them didn't answer.

"Master Yevul," Elina was on the verge of panic. "What's happening?"

"How are you at exorcisms?"

"What?"

Chitters and squeaks erupted from all around. Elina let out a short gasp and moved closer to Yevul, though her wererat captor kept the knife at her back.

"How did you know?" the thing controlling Grevior asked.

"A wererat trader who doesn't know about the deal he made and doesn't recognize the use of silver in shapeshifter magic? What else could it be? Who are you?"

He gave Yevul a toothy grin. "Lavencior."

Yevul let out a long breath. "I was really hoping you wouldn't say that."

Beside him, Elina had gone pale. Lavencior, the Black Wind, an elven general from the depths of antiquity who had rebelled against the rule of the council—his atrocities such that even now, thousands of years later, parents used stories of the Black Wind to scare their children. Most histories said he and his army had been killed, but there had always been stories that their souls had been imprisoned in an ancient gemstone, apparently the same one that had been found by the wererats.

"What do you want from us?"

Lavencior waved his hand at the surrounding rats. "These

individuals disabled this vessel before we had full control. We tried to repair it, but while we have access to their knowledge, their magic is beyond us."

"You couldn't fix it."

"Your vessel, on the other hand, provides us with other options."

"You can't fly that without my security codes, and I'm not about to give those to you."

"I still have soldiers who need hosts." As if on cue, a dozen bluish figures rose from the scattered piles of ship parts. Yevul could feel the cold energy emanating from them. Grevior took a step forward. "You won't have a ch—"

Yevul drew his blaster and fired into Lavencior's face. The wererat cried out and drew back. Yevul spun around and shot the one holding Elina. She pulled away, drawing her own blaster so quickly it couldn't be anything but instinctual. Yevul almost smiled. No doubt she was still frightened, but nearly a decade of training had drilled certain instincts into her, though you could never tell how someone would react to danger until they faced it for the first time. For her, the training had taken over. Together, they headed for their ship but stopped when they had gone a dozen steps. The ship was crawling with rats, far too many for the two of them to deal with.

"There!" Elina pointed at an open door on the other side of the docking bay.

Yevul didn't take the time to answer. He just took off in a dead run. Some of the rats between them and the door started to change shape, but Elina's clear voice rang out in a song, infusing the air with power. Yevul stumbled and for a moment didn't know where he was. A young woman he didn't recognize grabbed his wrist and pulled him forward. The befuddlement only lasted a few seconds, and as the power of Elina's confusion spell wore off, he saw the rats returning to their senses. The two elves ran through the open door, Elina slamming her hand on the door panel, which slid shut.

"Cleverly done," Yevul said.

She tapped the control panel but shook her head. "There's no locking mechanism."

Yevul pointed his blaster at the panel and fired. It sparked, the air filling with an acrid scent.

"That won't hold them for long," he said. "If I recall, there is a lift just down the hall."

"But our ship?"

"There are two other docking bays on this vessel. With luck, we can find another ship."

"How did Laverncior's army possess a pack of wererats?"

They entered the lift, and Yevul tapped a button. "How much do you know about the gem's history?"

"It was crafted by a contingent of powerful mages on Earth, but when our people abandoned the planet, it got left behind."

He nodded. "I mean more recent than that. What did the humans do with it?"

She stared at him blankly. "I haven't the slightest idea."

"It passed from owner to owner, many of whom died under mysterious circumstances. It was lost when the goblins attacked Earth during the war. The gem became rather famous and was reputed to be cursed."

"Cursed?"

"I suspect that after a thousand years, the workings of the spell inside started to decay."

It only took a second for Elina to understand the implications. "They were trapped in the gem?"

Yevul nodded. "The breakdown of the imprisonment spell caused a leak of magic. Tinged by the malevolent energy of the spirits . . ." He waved a hand. "It's not technically a curse."

"But it would be close enough."

The lift door opened. Yevul lifted his weapon, but there was no one there, and they stepped into the empty hall. The lights flickered above as the elves moved through the hall on silent feet. Creaks and groans echoed through passageway, as if the ship were some ancient building settling upon its own weight. The fact that no object in space should be making those kinds of sounds made a shiver run down Yevul's spine. Even so, his ears picked up the clinking sound the moment they came out of the lift. Elina, who hadn't known to look for it, didn't hear it for another few seconds.

"What's that sound?" she asked.

He waved off her concern. "They're in the vents."

"You mean they're watching us?"

"It's hard to go anywhere on a wererat ship without being seen. They probably enchanted the walls against spirits so the ghosts can't just walk through them, but they know exactly where we are."

"Doesn't that worry you?"

"Of course it does. There's just not a whole lot I can do about it. I think the docking bay is this way."

She stumbled. "You're not sure?"

"Grevior normally had what I was buying ready for me whenever I arrived. I've never actually been to any other part of the ship. I've studied the schematics for this type of vessel, but wererats tend to reconfigure everything to suit their needs."

He tapped a panel, and the door slid upward. The room beyond made the docking bay look like it had been meticulously organized. Almost every inch of the floor was covered in objects, many of which were unlike anything Yevul had ever seen. In addition to spaceship parts, weapons—both ancient swords and modern blasters—lay scattered across the ground. There was a bronze statue that could've been a dwarf if such beings grew to a height of twelve feet. Ingots of various metals sat alongside sealed crates. The smell in the air seemed to be a mix of machine oil and flowers and rotting food.

"I don't think this is the right way," Elina said.

Yevul nodded, but before he could say anything, a glimmer of blue caught his eye, sitting atop what looked to be a merfolk escape pod. He pointed. "The gem."

"Don't you think we should worry about getting out?"

"I think we're on a ship with two thousand possessed wererats and that this is the spell prison that's kept them locked up for millennia. We need every weapon we can get."

He stepped in without waiting for her to respond. It was an effort to force his way through the junk. He had to be careful to avoid triggering some ancient bomb or long-dormant curse, but he made it to the merfolk pod without incident. As soon as he touched the gem, he sensed the lattice of power within. The framework was still in place—that thing which allowed it to affect spirits—but the prison spell itself was completely gone. He shook his head as he explained his findings.

"I was hoping it was just damaged. I might be able to rebuild the spell if I had a few decades. Probably not, but maybe."

"A mind burst," Elina said.

"What?"

"Can I put a mind-burst spell into it?"

He started to shake his head but paused. A mind burst, a strong one, could reduce a person to a gibbering pile of flesh and bones, but ghosts were made of spirit, held together by will. A mind burst designed to affect them . . .

"That might actually work. Can you give it enough power?"

She hesitated. "Not quickly, but the gem should handle more of that."

He thought for a second before nodding. He handed over the gem.

"How many ways can you split your concentration?"

"No more than three, but if I do that, it will slow me down even more."

Across the docking bay, a different door than they had come in through groaned as it slid upward. "Better to finish slowly than not finish at all. Do it."

She vanished before he finished speaking. He summoned his own power. Almost all elves had some magic ability, but their strengths were different. Elina had a remarkable ability for mental magic. She wasn't invisible, not really; she was fooling others' minds into not seeing her. He only hoped it would be enough. Yevul couldn't affect the external like she could. His power had always been focused within.

His sight, his speed, agility all increased a hundredfold. The first rat had just showed its nose before Yevul blasted it. More poured through the door, but Yevul's reflexes were nearly at supersonic speeds. However, his blaster fire wasn't infused with silver, so it would take a great deal of damage to put one down permanently. He could still hurt them, though, and he laid down a veritable wall of blaster fire. The rats squealed in response, but they didn't get more than a few feet into the room. Unfortunately, he couldn't do anything about the ghosts.

A translucent blue form flowed into the chamber. Yevul tried to hit it, but his blasts went right through it. To make matters worse, the diversion of his attention away from the door even for a little while allowed the invaders to come through. They scattered throughout the room and were scuttering closer. One took form right next to him. He shot it, but not before a blue light entered him.

He expected pain. He thought there would be a battle for his mind and body, but there wasn't. He was simply shoved aside, a fog descending over his mind. Though he didn't remember falling, he found himself rising. A joy not his own suffused him, and he felt a smile form on his face. There was a sensation like worms burrowing through his mind as the spirit combed through his thoughts.

"I can do it," his voice said. "I can get us out of here. This one is a wealth of information. He knows secrets that even many elves do not know. There are half a dozen outposts full of supplies we could get to in a few hours." Pain lanced through Yevul's head. "The girl! Find the girl!"

Rats spread out across the floor. A scream penetrated the air as Elina appeared only a few feet from where she had been. She tried to sing out and summon her magic, but they swarmed all over her. After a few seconds, she went still. If Yevul had had control over his body, he would have thrown up.

One of the rats stopped in front of Yevul. Its form writhed for a second before Grevior stood in front of him. The spirit controlling Yevul told him of a nearby weapons depot. They couldn't fit everyone aboard Yevul's ship, but if they took the shape of rats, hundreds could fit inside. An elven ship belonging to one of the Shades wouldn't be questioned as it approached the depot. They would be completely unprepared and would fall easily.

"We should depart immediately. The people of this age are soft. Once our army is outfitted, no one will be able to stop us."

Yevul felt himself nod, and his arm motioned for the others to follow. He tried to resist, but it wasn't even a contest. It was like trying to move a mountain by looking at it. Maybe if he had the gem . . .

The thought rushed through him only to be picked up by the thing controlling him. Its head snapped around to look at Elina's body. The gem was gone.

"Who has it?"

Confusion spread through the crowd. No one had it. A pair of rats went for the body, but as soon as they touched it, they passed right through it. Yevul felt the spirit's surprise. It plunged into his mind. Elina was a powerful mental mage. She had fooled everyone into thinking they couldn't see her, and now she had apparently done the opposite. They had never found her. All this time she had been working her spell.

Elina's clear voice filled the area as she appeared in the center of the room, holding up the gem, which gleamed so brightly it might have been a second sun. This time there was pain. Yevul's vision went red. He cried out before falling into darkness.

He was surprised when he woke up slumped in an old chair that creaked when he moved. All around him, rats were waking up. Elina, who was seated on a crate a few feet away, blinked and leaped onto the ground before running to him.

"Master Yevul, are you okay?"

He nodded. "What happened?"

"The mind blast destroyed the spirits." She looked a little pale. "All of them. I didn't expect it to be so . . ." She let out a breath. "Is it always so hard?"

Yevul pursed his lips and nodded. "It's never easy to destroy. You have the gem?"

She nodded and pulled it out of a belt pouch and held it up to the light. The blue diamond glittered, and Yevul could almost feel the vast well of power inside. It still had the lattice that allowed it to affect spirits, but that could be removed. A gem like this could be enchanted to do almost anything.

"Yes," a gravelly voice said. "The gem." Grevior stepped out of the shadows, no sign that he had just been possessed. "Once we have the silver . . ."

Yevul raised an eyebrow. "We just saved your entire pack. Don't you think that entitles us to anything?"

"Business is business," the wererat said. Yevul leveled his eyes at the man, who cleared his throat. "Perhaps a twenty percent discount is in order."

Yevul threw back his head and laughed. "Done, my old friend."

In less than an hour, they were on their way. Elina held up the gem as they pulled away from the freighter. It practically glimmered with its own inner light and was one of the most beautiful gems Yevul had ever seen."

"The humans really thought this was cursed?" she asked.

"After what just happened, can you truly blame them?"

She smiled. "No, I suppose not. I want to look through their records to see its history."

Yevul nodded. "Probably a good idea. I imagine knowing its name would help with that. They called it the Hope Diamond."

. . .

Gama Ray Martinez lives near Salt Lake City, Utah. He moved there solely because he likes mountains. He collects weapons in case he ever needs to supply a medieval battalion, and he greatly resents when work or other real-life things get in the way of his writing. He secretly hopes to one day singlehandedly slay a dragon and doesn't believe in letting pesky little things like reality stand in the way of dreams. Find him at http://www.gamarayburst.com.

OTHER SIDE OF THE TRACKS

MARTIN GREENING

OTHER SIDE OF THE TRACKS

Alexis tossed the unopened envelope—stamped "Final Notice"—atop the other past-due bills on her kitchen table. The pile held for a moment before sliding, then picking up steam like a train pulling from the station and falling to the aged linoleum. She stood, skirted the new pile, and went to the refrigerator for a Coke—and some rum. Not the El Dorado Three Year White but the Appleton Estates. The bottle had a finger left—a half finger after Alexis filled her mug.

Her iPhone buzzed and skittered on the table, threatening to join the bills. Alexis picked up the phone, sipped her drink, and walked to her desk. No name appeared on the screen, just a number. She ignored it. Probably a spammer or bill collector. Both were as bad as lawyers—maybe worse. Or maybe it was that tall guy she met at Lucky's last Friday. What was his name? She waited until a tiny number one superimposed itself onto the voicemail icon, then opened the app. "This message is for Alexis Freeman," a woman's voice called through the tinny speaker. "If you are not Alexis—"

She hit delete and dialed Mandy.

"Want to go shopping?" Alexis said and waited for Mandy's reply. "Great. Pick me up in ten." She sniffed her hair, then shrugged. Still a hint of lilac from yesterday's shower. Her wardrobe consisted of jeans and a white T-shirt that read "Yes, I Am a Big Deal" in red script across the chest. She slipped on a pair of black, two-inch heels (three inches was far too high for shopping, and one inch was not enough), grabbed her Michael Kors purse and black leather jacket, and headed downstairs.

The early spring clouds pressed low, like steam billowing from a locomotive, and road noise and honking cars drowned out the chirping of finches. The sounds echoed between the block apartment buildings that flanked the busy street.

Mandy's Subaru pulled up to the curb. She honked only once, one minute early. Mandy was good like that. Had a steady job with a law firm ever since they'd both graduated from Green Hills High six years ago—paid her bills as soon as they arrived and bought a used car.

The thoughts brought a grin to Alexis's face.

Alexis opened the passenger door, and Britney Spears's "Hit Me Baby One More Time" blasted from the radio. "Really?" Alexis said.

Mandy turned down the volume as Alexis ducked inside. "You don't like the classics?"

"We can't be friends anymore."

"Whatever."

It was a running gag with them. Mandy loved pop, whether it was from the '90s, the 2000s, or even the recent garbage. Alexis tolerated it, but it didn't get the blood pumping like Metallica or Sevendust.

"Where to?" Mandy said. "Saks?"

"The antique shop," Alexis said. "The one on Fifth."

"Ew. Why?"

"Just humor me."

"More stuff for eBay?"

"Something like that."

Fifth Street was the kind of street a town forgot. Low rent meant the shop had a good selection of underpriced merchandise

Alexis could flip online. She rubbed her hands in anticipation of finding a few good deals.

Two large bay windows flanked the glass door to the shop. Plywood covered the leftmost pane. Alexis opened the door and held it for Mandy. "Age before beauty." Mandy was three days older, after all.

"With age comes great wisdom," Mandy said as she entered.

Alexis followed. "Whatever."

The smell of mothballs and neglect hit them upon entering. Old cabinets filled with china and porcelain figurines spaced themselves around the shop, and several framed landscapes—none of which had monsters or spaceships painted atop the original—adorned the back wall. A woman sat behind a glass counter in a bar chair, her faced stuffed into a book of Sudoku.

Alexis pointed to the plywood. "Trouble?"

The woman looked up. "No trouble. Everything fine. You need help?"

"Just browsing," Alexis said. The woman returned to her puzzles.

Alexis and Mandy took their time strolling between the tables of old clocks, chinaware from the last century, and Coca-Cola memorabilia.

Mandy pointed to a metal Scooby-Doo lunchbox and said, "How about this?"

"The markup is hit or miss," Alexis said. "I need something good. Something that'll sell for a lot." She wandered farther down the aisle toward the toys. People had no control over their wallets when it came to old toys.

An old electric train caught her eye—a black steam locomotive lacking any cars, with two large wheels on each side, several smaller ones, and a thin layer of dust glued tight from years of oil and indifference. It smelled of smoke—both an artificial scent to make the train seem real as well as the pall of a previous owner dragging on a cigarette whenever the train made its rounds on the track. The faded gold letters on its side read "American Flyer No. 290."

Something about it called to her. She pulled her phone from her purse and searched for American Flyer on eBay. Two listings: one Buy It Now for $150 and one auction at $96.15 with twenty-seven bids.

"How much for this?" Alexis held up the train.

"Five dollar," the woman behind the counter replied.

"I'll give you three."

The woman scowled. "Five."

"Four?"

"Five."

Alexis set the train down. "Whatever," she whispered.

"It's only two dollars," Mandy said, then whispered. "How much is it worth online?"

"Doesn't matter."

"I could spot you the two dollars."

"I said it doesn't matter." Alexis left the train and walked down an aisle of glass- and silverware.

The door chimed, and an old man entered. He wore a blue Members Only jacket over a dark sweater-vest and hobbled along with a cane and pair of Velcro shoes. He walked directly to the toy aisle, though he moved like the proverbial tortoise. His eyes appeared fixated on a single spot—the train.

The geezer must have seen this before and saved up his social security, Alexis thought.

Alexis shadowed the old man down the aisle, then snatched the train before his hand could touch it. "This is mine," she said.

The man scoffed.

"Not yours until you pay for it," the clerk said from behind the counter. "Five dollar."

Alexis ignored the old man's protests—something about the rudeness of millennials—and carried the train to the counter. She fished three crumpled one-dollar bills from her purse and placed them next to the train.

"Five," the clerk said.

"I know." Alexis dug through her purse and began to drop coins next to the bills. Two quarters, a dime, three nickels, and a handful of pennies.

"You sell purse?" the clerk asked. "Give you good price."

Alexis continued her search. "No. I just want the train."

Mandy stepped up beside Alexis and opened her purse. "You want—"

"I got it." A few more coins joined the cash before Alexis pulled a small manila envelope from her purse. On it, written in neat blue ink was "Emergency Money—Love, Mom." She dumped its contents onto the counter, coins clinking against the glass, then proceeded to sort them. It was an emergency. Mom would understand.

Alexis counted out five dollars and thirty-six cents, pushed the five toward the clerk, and swept the rest back into her purse. "Thanks." She picked up the train, grabbed Mandy's arm, and the two strode out of the store, leaving the old man behind.

Alexis took two steps from the shop door, then yelped as her left leg buckled beneath her. The heel of her shoe had snapped at the base and now stared at her from the sidewalk. She stomped her foot, the one with the broken shoe. "Ugh! These were $300."

She retrieved the errant heel and took two more steps before stopping. Walking barefoot would be much easier than trying to walk in a broken heel—a feat Alexis had accomplished before, although not while sober—but one look at the patches of gum, goo, and turds speckling the sidewalk and her decision was made. "Get your car."

While Alexis waited for Mandy, she retrieved her phone from her purse to list the train on eBay. The blank screen did not respond to her attempts to wake or start the phone. What the . . . ? *You were just working.* She tossed the ornery device into her purse. Stupid phone.

Mandy arrived curbside in front of the shop, and Alexis made a quick dash to the car.

"Buckle up," Mandy said once Alexis was inside, "or we don't go anywhere."

Alexis stared at the train she held. "What?"

"You know the rule."

"Oh yeah." Alexis strung the seat belt across her lap, then tucked the shoulder belt under her arm.

Satisfied, Mandy checked for traffic, and further satisfied, began driving. "Where to now?"

"Where's your phone?" Alexis asked.

"What for?"

"I need it. That's what for."

"What's the matter with yours?"

"It's not working."

"Alex . . ." Mandy said in a motherly tone. "Not working, or did you forget to pay the bill again?"

"I paid it."

"Last month?"

"I don't know. Maybe. Just give me your phone."

Mandy sighed. "In my purse."

Alexis reached around to dig through Mandy's purse, which sat on the mat behind the driver's seat. She was immediately thrown sideways, her head slamming into the side of Mandy's seat before her body whiplashed the opposite direction. Her head hit the car door, and she lost consciousness.

※

The rhythmic beep of a heart monitor woke Alexis. She lifted a hand to her head and winced. "Where . . . ?"

"You're in the hospital," her mother said as she stood from a chair near the bed and cradled Alexis's hand. Sunlight streaming through the open curtains lit her curly red hair, and she wore her trademark green sweater. "You were in an accident."

"Accident?" Memories rushed back—the antique store, the

train, the crash. She tried to sit up, but a sharp ache in her legs stopped her.

"Lie down," her mother said. "You've broken both legs. The doctor says it will take some time to heal, but you'll walk again." She patted Alexis on the back of the hand, then retrieved her phone from a small table next to the chair. "Mandy asked me to call her as soon as you were up."

"Walk?" A queasiness hit Alexis, and the heart monitor beeped faster.

Her mother smiled and chatted on the phone for a minute. When she hung up, she dragged the chair closer to the bed and told Alexis what the doctor had told her.

Tears quickly blurred Alexis's vision.

A short time later, Mandy entered the room, her arm in a sling, her face drawn in a long frown. "I'm sorry, Alex. I should have seen him."

"It's not your fault," Alexis's mother said, directing Mandy to the chair.

Alexis's jaw tensed. *But she was driving.*

"I've never been in an accident before," Mandy said. "Maybe if I had side airbags . . ."

Visions of wheelchairs flitted about Alexis's mind. "What difference would that have made?"

Mandy looked up, her eyes wide and watery. She stammered, "A-alex—"

"Go away. I'm tired."

Mandy tried again.

"I said go away." Alexis turned her head away and closed her eyes.

Two pairs of feet shuffled from the room. Alexis let out a deep breath and began to sob.

The next few months were consumed by surgery, doctors' visits, more surgery, more doctors' visits, and the unending evil that was physical therapy.

Then came the bills.

They arrived slowly at first but then quickly outpaced Alexis's credit cards and utilities. She sold some of her clothes and best handbags, but it wasn't enough, and Alexis soon found herself on her parents' doorstep, leaning on a pair of crutches and hoping they had not rented out her room.

Her mother had left Alexis's bedroom just as it was the day she'd moved out — posters of movie heartthrobs and heavy metal bands tacked to the walls and part of the ceiling; a surplus clothing rack acquired from a going-out-of-business sale that looked quite the part with its sparse contents; and pictures of Alexis and Mandy covering the perimeter of the vanity mirror. The few remaining boxes of Alexis's belongings barely covered the space between her twin bed and the window.

Alexis shuffled through the stack of bills atop the dresser. Guess I'm going to be here a while. She dropped the pile, moved over to the boxes, and opened the one on top. Under a cushion of folded shirts sat the train, its lone headlight staring at her.

Alexis pulled the train from the box and hurled it against the wall with a satisfying thud. The hole it left in her Flotsam and Jetsam poster — and the drywall behind it — was less desirable. She threw her arms up. "Ugh! You'll be the death of me."

Her mother knocked on the bedroom door, then peeked in. "Everything okay?"

"No. That stupid train — all this started when I bought it."

"Oh, that's nice, dear."

"How did it get here?"

"The train? I think Mandy brought it. Said something about it surviving the wreck and thought you might want—"

"Well, I don't. I'm taking it back to the antique shop tomorrow."

The left bay window of the antique shop now shone plywood-free, but the new glass with fresh gold lettering stood out of place among the grime of Fifth Street. Alexis struggled over the threshold, nearly tripping when it caught one of her crutches.

"You need help?" a woman asked, heading towards Alexis. The same woman who had sold her the train.

She pulled a stray backpack strap into place and righted herself on her crutches. "I got it."

The woman returned to the counter, picked up a book, and resumed reading.

Partway through the door, Alexis was struck by an air of cleanliness. The shop seemed different. More cabinets lined the aisles—some with fresh varnish that tickled her nose; others seemed to have been dusted and polished. A few vacant squares hung between the framed landscapes along the wall, and even the china and porcelain figures seemed to dance as Alexis hobbled up to the counter.

The woman put down her book when Alexis arrived. "You need help now?"

"Yes," Alexis said as she removed her backpack and set it on the counter. "I want to sell this." She unzipped the pack and withdrew the train.

The woman's eyes bulged, and she stepped back, her hands waving in front of her. "No. No. Bad luck. You leave now."

"It's fine. It's just a train."

"Bad luck. You go now. Take with you."

"Look—"

"Go now or I call police."

Alexis huffed. "Fine." She tucked the train back into the backpack before slipping it onto her back and making her way out of the store.

Two buses later, Alexis entered Jackson's Pawn Shop on Eleventh and C Street, which put Fifth Street to shame for the most run-down section of town. An old Camaro sat on bare wheels in the alley next to the shop, grass pushing its way through the ragged asphalt and into the automobile's body.

She entered without tripping. *Ha! Getting better at these crutches.*

A wolflike man called from behind a small barred window set into the wall to her left, "Honey, you lost?"

"No. Have something to pawn," Alexis said as she moved to the window. She drew the train from her pack. "How much for this?"

The man disappeared to her right, and the top half of a Dutch door opened. "Lemme see."

She handed him the train, and he twisted it around in his calloused hands, looking at it closely before saying, "Probably not worth much with this broken linkage." He pointed to a flat piece of metal that normally connected the two large wheels on one side.

"Is it worth five?" Alexis asked, trying not to sound too desperate.

The man looked between her and the train a few times. "Sure."

Alexis accepted the money and left the shop as quickly as her crutches could carry her—as if the weight of an actual train had been lifted from her shoulders.

She took three strides before the sun glinted off an object on the sidewalk. She stopped, placed both crutches in one hand, and leaned on their support. Then she bent over and picked up a Thomas Jefferson nickel—minted in 1943. Alexis shrugged and tucked it into her pocket. Won't pay for everything, but it's a start.

Her phone rang. Mandy's name appeared on the screen. She let it ring three times before answering, "About time you called."

. . .

Martin Greening was corrupted early by his older brother's interests in heavy metal and Dungeons and Dragons and enjoyed reading as a child. Tolkien, Eddings, Salvatore, Weis, and Hickman were some early favorites. After becoming enthralled with the appendices of The Lord of the Rings, Martin relished building worlds and constructing languages. For more information about Martin and his role-playing game and writing, visit www.martingreening.com.

MOVING ON

CHRIS ABELA

MOVING ON

The doorknob twisted open. *I know I did not forget to lock it*, Hahnee thought. He was sure of it. He peered in through the door's tempered glass, avoiding the decal letters of the shop's name: The Juniper Tree—Native American Arts and Antiques. From what he could tell, the jewelry case and shelves of pottery lining the right side of the shop looked intact and untouched, as did the short glass cabinets and art display on the opposite side.

Hahnee breathed a sigh of relief and pulled the door open. He entered, and a tinny chime sounded above his head. The sage fragrance he'd come to associate with Eyota hung in the air.

"Late start," she called out.

"Bah," he said with a dismissive wave. He fought the urge to snap at his daughter in case her words were not the criticism he took them for but merely observation. "Ten is the time I open." In his experience, opening at midmorning worked better for Sedona tourists. It gave night owls time to sleep in and early birds time to recover from their sunrise hikes.

He heard the closing snap of a hardback book, and his eyes darted to the bronze juniper tree in the center of the shop. The sculpture stood eleven feet tall. The twisted trunk arched back at his eye level and split in two, one half angling left, the other half curving upward. The left splintered into three medium limbs and formed their own cornucopia of bare branches that stretched to the large square skylight in the ceiling. The upward half twisted into two large arms rich with foliage. The sculpture predated Hahnee's shop, so it seemed fitting he'd name the place after it.

Hahnee crossed his arms, and his sharp tone cut through the shop. "Why are you here again?" He loved his daughter, but she came around too often.

Eyota appeared from behind the tree and walked along the circular oak bench surrounding the trunk. She stepped into a patch of sunlight that filtered through the juniper branches, and her deep-brown skin looked ashen. She never looked well to him. Her black hair flowed over one shoulder and hung to her waist like her mother's used to. But that's where the resemblance ended. He noticed her dresses had taken on a modernity lately, with thin shoulder straps and deep-cut necklines. He wasn't used to seeing her dressed this way, and he did not like it.

"You know why I am here," Eyota said. "It's time to move on."

From the adjoining room on the far right of the shop, a mission-style wall clock chimed as if it, too, were urging him on. The clock was a gift from a longtime customer, and it had spent many moons on the back wall behind the cash register. But Hahnee had moved it to the adjoining room with the southwest furniture and Navajo rugs because he no longer cared to think in terms of time. He didn't want to be reminded how long he had been here, and he didn't want to know how much longer he'd have. Even if his life hadn't turned out the way he'd imagined, why should he be glad for it to be nearly over?

"I hate to think of you stuck here like I am," Hahnee said. "You should have something better."

"Hasn't the deal always been that I will take over the shop?"

The door chimed, alerting them of customers.

Hahnee turned away from Eyota. Deal or no deal, he wasn't

ready to hand over the shop to her, and she wasn't going to make him. He uncrossed his arms and tried to shake the tension from his shoulders. With a smile and a wave, he said, "Welcome. Come on in."

"After you," said a man who had spent extensive time in the shop over the last two days. Hahnee recognized the expensive shoes and fresh-pressed slacks, an oddity for summer in Arizona. The man held the door open and gestured to an elderly couple and a woman in black yoga pants. The three performed the obligatory "go ahead" with the head nod, which resulted in the body bump followed by apologies. The younger woman took the initiative and moved inside first.

While they all smiled and exchanged glances and nods with Hahnee, it was only the well-dressed man who held the longer eye contact of a serious buyer. A popular tourist destination, Sedona attracted all kinds of customers. The shop didn't have a particular type that frequented it. Most browsed, like the other three in the shop. Hahnee estimated that only twenty percent were serious buyers. But even those who were serious buyers didn't spend as much time here as this man did.

Yesterday he'd strutted in with those expensive wingtips and meticulously studied the patterns and weaves of the American Indian blankets and the Navajo rugs. The day before that, he had dissected the beadwork on the vests and moccasins. Today he started on the jewelry.

Hahnee walked behind the jewelry counter and gently placed his hands on the glass. "Can I show you something in the case?" he asked.

The man started to raise his head and paused as if fixated on an item.

Hahnee gave him a moment to let his interest bubble before he inquired, "Do you see something you like?"

The man reached into his pocket and retrieved a business card. He placed it on the glass counter. "My name is James Christie. I'm interested in the silver cuff you're wearing." He leered at the spiderweb turquoise stone set in the plain, two-inch cuff. The rectangular stone was an inch and half in length and just under an inch in width, with a sawtooth bezel. Its deep-green consistency combined with its sharp clarity made it an eye-catcher. But it was the rich chocolate and golden lines that made up a tight, uniform matrix that made it rare and valuable.

Hahnee pulled his hand back. "Perhaps you'd be interested in a squash blossom necklace."

"No," Mr. Christie said. "Just the cuff with the spiderweb turquoise."

"I can never sell this," Hahnee said.

Mr. Christie turned his head, peering around the shop.

The door chimed, and they both watched the elderly couple leave.

Hahnee's eyes followed Mr. Christie's gaze as it floated to the woman in black yoga pants. They watched her weave past a front table with ethnographic photos until she reached the line of short glass cabinets and hanging art.

When she appeared to be safely out of earshot, he heard Mr. Christie say, "Fourteen thousand."

Hahnee's eyes shifted back to Mr. Christie. He refused to indulge him with an answer.

Mr. Christie placed his hand on the business card and slid it across the glass counter. He tapped it twice with his forefinger for emphasis. "When you're ready to sell it, call me."

Hahnee watched as Mr. Christie walked out of the shop with an air of confidence. In his experience, collectors like that came back. He picked up the card and read it: Whitehill Auction House, James Christie, special acquisitions. He tore the card in half and thought of Eyota. If he passed the shop on to his daughter, Mr. Christie was going to be yet another problem she'd have to deal with.

"The colors of these paintings are exquisite," the woman called out. "You commissioned these?"

Hahnee stared at the three paintings. "No," he said. "Estate sales." The first was a watercolor, the other two oil on canvas. The colors were striking from a distance as well. Hues of calming blues, radiant purples, and fiery oranges and yellows mesmerized the eye.

He walked across the shop and joined his customer under the watercolor painting. She wore a simple peach top with her yoga pants, and her brunette hair was gathered in a ponytail. He guessed she was middle-aged, even though she looked a bit younger with her natural tan and fit physique. With the uptick in commercial spas and meditation retreats, half the tourists looked and dressed like her these days.

She pointed up to the watercolor with a confused expression. "But the Sedona rocks aren't red in this one." Behind the framed glass was a three-by-four-foot landscape painting of Cathedral Rock with Oak Creek in the foreground. Along the water's edge were the simple shapes of indigenous women and children. Male silhouettes stood farther back, between sycamore and oak trees. On careful inspection, one could see pencil marks under the watercolor paint where the artist had outlined the women by the water.

"In ancient times, the rocks were not red," Hahnee said.

She cocked her head, and her eyebrows drew closer together.

He'd expected that. No one ever realized he was telling the truth. "There is an unwritten history among these pieces," Hahnee explained. He told her of the ancient indigenous tribe that had once lived in the Sedona mountains and their efforts to live within the rhythm of the land. He shared their lessons of respect for all living things, which they believed was at the core of all balanced interactions.

Hahnee pointed to the tiny figures dotted along the mountain ridges. "This painting shows the arrival of a nomadic tribe of warriors on their way to South America. They were looking for food reserves to carry them across the desert when they came upon this agrarian group." As Hahnee retold the story of their invasion, the events played in his head like a cinematic feature.

The nomads had sneaked through the trees and taken the inhabitants by surprise.

He described the nomads' weapon of war and extended his arms to emphasize the size. "The maquahuitl was a large, flat, four-foot-long club with an oak handle. The sides were embedded with razor-sharp obsidian blades." He went on to explain how the nomad warriors first slaughtered the men as they tried to protect their families. The nomad women watched for anyone who tried to flee and stripped the turquoise from the slain bodies. While most of the agrarian women and children died in those first bloody hours, a handful were kept alive for three days to prepare food and serve the nomads.

The woman gasped. "That's horrible."

"Yes," Hahnee said. His stomach clutched. "For three days they grieved and feared for their lives. They cried. They begged for their children to be spared as they served feasts."

"And were they?" she asked.

Hahnee felt his chin tremble. No matter how many times he told the story, he felt the anguish of the tribe. He would have thought recounting the story so many times over the years would make him immune to the grief, but it didn't. The loss still hung hard on his heart. He cleared his throat and swallowed. "No," he finally said. "They were not spared."

"But why?" The woman demanded to know. "Why kill them all?"

He grimaced. "I doubt it occurred to them to do anything else."

With a heavy sigh, she stepped past and refused to look at him.

He was used to customers acting this way when he told the story. By today's standards, those events were inconceivable.

The woman stopped and focused on the second painting, an oil on canvas.

"That's the goddess Aquene," Hahnee said. The goddess was visible from the top of her head to the bottom of her torso, and she held a clay pot under one arm. She was superimposed on the sky and sunset, which took up two-thirds of the painting. Her black hair caught reflections of the cobalt, sapphire, and cornflower blues of the sky. Her clothing became the sunset, with shades of burnt sienna fading into goldenrod and chiffon yellows. The landscape in the lower third of the painting was from the perspective of someone standing on Airport Mesa, overlooking the Sedona valley and surrounding mountains.

"Aquene collected her people after they were slaughtered," Hahnee said. In an open palm suspended over the valley, Aquene held a man whose lifeless arm hung limp toward the viewer of the painting while his legs dangled off the ends of her fingers. The clay pot under her other arm was tipped forward just enough for the pile of slain bodies to be seen.

The woman pointed to a collection of old dolls in the short glass cabinet under the painting. "And this is her?" The dolls ranged in size from twelve to seventeen inches—each on its own stand—and adorned the top shelf. They were all carved from wood, some painted and some with fabric clothing.

"Yes," Hahnee answered. "As are the pendants." The shelf below contained a collection of old silver and copper pendants. They came in different sizes, from one to three inches. Whether they were simple or ornate, the common element in all of them was the female silhouette holding a clay pot.

Hahnee's customer moved under the last painting. It also showed the goddess Aquene superimposed on the sky. In this oil on canvas, she held the rim of the tipped clay pot with both hands as the blood of her people poured over the mountains and colored them red.

Hahnee stepped past the woman. He never felt the need to explain the last painting.

The woman choked back tears as she reached out, her fingers grazing the red mountains. "It's beautiful. No wonder people feel Sedona is a spiritual mecca. So much love and pain drenching the landscape here. And the energy vortexes I've read about . . .

they are in these paintings too. Cathedral Rock, Airport Mesa, and this one is the view from Schnebly Hill."

Her eyes shot to the cuff with the spiderweb turquoise on Hahnee's wrist and then to his face. "Your cuff looks like the one the goddess is wearing in this painting. So that's why you wouldn't sell it to that man earlier."

Hahnee jerked back. "No . . . um . . . " He looked down at the cuff, unable to explain. The woman's acute perception made him uncomfortable. He tried to gather his thoughts and think of something to say.

"I overheard. I'm sorry."

Hahnee looked up as she turned and walked back to the cabinet with the goddess figures. "Do you feel one of them calling to you?"

He watched her open the cabinet and pick up one of the more ornate figures with aquamarine clothing. She closed her eyes and placed it next to her heart. "I love this piece. It speaks to me."

"The spirit of the goddess speaks through the artists, and that is what you hear," Hahnee told her.

She smiled one of those wide smiles that made him think of contentment.

Hahnee joined her at the open cabinet and took the goddess doll from her hands. "Many people confuse these with kachina dolls, which are traditionally made from cottonwood root. These are made from the juniper tree, always resemble a female body, and often include the clay pot or golden staff."

He turned and waved for the woman to follow him to the sales counter in back. "Come. I'll wrap it up for you."

"Wait!" Her voice was loud and sharp. "Something doesn't feel right. What if there's a curse?"

Hahnee stopped. He'd spent more years in this shop than he cared to remember, and this was the first time someone had sensed the curse. *Do I tell her*? He looked down at the cuff with the spiderweb turquoise stone and contemplated his options.

When he looked up, Eyota shook her head at him from behind the bronze juniper tree. *She's right. I shouldn't tell her.*

Hahnee turned and walked back to the woman. "I assure you the doll is not a curse," he said. He took her hand and cradled it in his own. He lay the goddess doll in her open palm, then gently rested his hand on top. "It is a blessing. Because when you carry this piece beyond the shop, you carry the story and the lessons of the ancient people and their goddess, so they are not forgotten."

Her eyes widened. She started to nod but then paused. "But there is a curse," she insisted. "I feel it."

Hahnee moved his hand from the top of the doll to her shoulder. "It is not for you to worry about. Take the doll and remember."

Hahnee spent the next two hours trying to convince Eyota he wasn't going to tell the woman about the curse.

"But you thought about it," she said yet again. "You've been in this shop too long, and it's time for me to take over."

He dragged his feet to the bronze juniper tree and sat on the circular oak bench, facing the front of the shop. He sighed and hung his head. When had his daughter become so obstinate?

Hahnee heard the door chime. In his frustration, he shouted, "We're closed!"

The door lock clicked.

Two men stood at the front of the shop, but Hahnee focused in on only one. He shot straight up. "Pallaton," he said with a shaky voice.

He felt Eyota rush to his side. "What's he doing here?" she asked in panic.

"You can see him?" Pallaton's companion asked.

Pallaton stood fifteen feet from Hahnee in an elk-hide loincloth and calf-length tilmàtli tunic knotted over his right shoulder. His right hand held a maquahuitl, the flat end resting on the same thick, broad shoulder.

Hahnee barely nodded as he moved his hand to the side and tried to push Eyota behind him. His hand caught only air.

"My name is Elan," the second man said. "Chief Pallaton came to me on Bell Rock. I am here because of the cuff with the spiderweb turquoise stone."

Hahnee shifted his eyes to Elan. A shaman, maybe. He was darkly tanned, his deep-set eyes as gray as his hair, which was just long enough to pull into a short ponytail at the base of his neck. His lightweight red shirt hung loose around his canvas shorts.

"You must remove the cuff from your wrist," Elan said.

No, Hahnee thought as he became aware of his increasing heartbeat. He felt rooted in place and said nothing. The last thing he wished was to incite Pallaton's anger.

"Please," Elan said. "It will be easier for all of us if you do it yourself."

Hahnee's eyes darted to the maquahuitl. "As opposed . . . to . . . what?"

"Pallaton does not have a way to remove the cuff from you, but I do," said Elan.

"Proceed," Pallaton said, his voice gravel and dust.

Elan began to chant in a language Hahnee was unfamiliar with. The long, drawn-out "eeees" and "aaaas" rose and fell as he chanted.

Hahnee felt a soft vibration from the spiderweb turquoise stone. He placed his other hand on top of it and felt warmth coming off it. The more Elan chanted, the stronger the vibration became and the warmer the stone got. It became hot to the touch, and Hahnee jerked his right hand away.

"Stop," Hahnee insisted. The silver cuff picked up the heat from the stone and prickled his wrist. It started to burn. "Stop it, now!" From behind him came a whistle that sounded like the shriek of a red-tailed hawk on the hunt. Wind whooshed past.

He saw Pallaton's long black hair twist and flap at his side. Pallaton's eyes moved upward, behind Hahnee, and widened.

Hahnee spun around in a defensive stance. Glass cabinet doors and pottery rattled as white light swirled around the trunk of the juniper. The light rose like a funnel and grew wide around the branches. He felt tingles of energy on his forearms as the vortex of energy reached the skylight and evaporated. The spicy, refreshing fragrance of fine gin and resinous wood permeated the shop.

A woman with skin as brown and golden as the juniper tree appeared from behind the sculpture. Her abdomen was round, as if full with child. Strands of turquoise beads were draped along her ample bosom. Her skirt of thin aquamarine cloth hung low under her belly.

She stepped forward, and swells of white light with an aura of aquamarine floated around her hands. She arched her arms over her head. The two balls of white light met and transformed into a long, golden staff. She twirled it over her head, then swung one end down between Pallaton and Hahnee.

The entire shop rang like a struck bell, the resonant note soon joined by the sounds of wood and glass falling over.

The goddess stood beside Hahnee. "You do not belong here, Pallaton."

Pallaton huffed and lifted the maquahuitl over his head. "Step back, Aquene. Hahnee belongs with his people."

Hahnee scrambled sideways, bumping into the jewelry case. Elan stumbled after him.

"You have kept him long enough," Pallaton snarled. "He is mine again." He lunged, sweeping the maquahuitl so the obsidian blades shattered the golden staff in a flare of light and to the sound of breaking glass.

Hahnee lurched back, his forearms shielding his face.

Elan's clammy hands grabbed Hahnee's forearm. "You must stop them," he said.

"The curse no longer binds him here," Aquene explained to

Pallaton. "His free will keeps him here. And you will not again take what is not yours." White balls of light swelled around her hands. She arched back, and her nimble arms moved over her belly and head. A white line connected the two balls of light like a bola. Aquene twirled, echoing the whirlwind that had delivered her. Hahnee saw her hands dance, and the bola flew from them, snapping around Pallaton's torso, binding his arms to his sides. The maquahuitl clattered to the floor, bits of obsidian skidding across the tiles.

Pallaton grunted and staggered like a lassoed animal. He spun three times and heaved his arms, bursting the lasso into speckled light that pooled in glinting spheres around his hands. He arched his arms over his head and thrust the spheres through the air at Aquene.

The first hit her chest, the second her belly. She rocked and sunk back.

Hahnee gasped and leapt to catch her, but she recovered. She planted her foot, and sprays of light jetted up around her. She circled her arm, breaking the lights into glittering orbs the size of raindrops.

"Stop them!" Eyota shouted.

Hahnee fell to his knees between Pallaton and Aquene. "Please," he begged. He looked at Pallaton first. "As a warrior chief of your people, and"—his eyes shifted to Aquene—"as a mother to your people, please understand the desperation of a father to save his daughter."

The glittering orbs dissolved, and the shop fell into silence.

"Please," Hahnee begged through uncontrolled sobbing. "Let me stay. Spare my daughter, and I will serve her time."

"Would you set your wisdom against mine?" asked Aquene, her eyes remote. "Should not each of Pallaton's people who slaughtered and pillaged mine serve their own thousand years on earth telling our story so our lessons and people may be remembered?"

Hahnee just clasped his hands and bent his head to the

ground, the tears dripping from his face.

"So be it," Aquene said. "I will respect your free will and not force you. But think deep. I tell you it is foolish to release her from this burden."

Pallaton let out a low, primal growl and picked up the maquahuitl. "No! Let this end now. You've cursed my people long enough."

Aquene threw her hands up as the swells of light returned. "If you want to fight, Pallaton, I will not hold back this time." Giant wisps of sky-blue light appeared in the air behind her. They stretched large toward the ceiling, and the sound of cracking came from the skylight. The wisps glided down, swirling like ink in water.

Eyota dropped to her knees in front of Hahnee. "You must let go. I am responsible for my own actions." She brought her face close to his. "Give me the cuff."

Hahnee stared at Eyota and froze. *This can't be happening*, he thought. The amber of her eyes took him back to an ancient time well before their path led to Aquene's people. He had stood in a cold river and speared a fish while she watched from the top of a boulder. She had clapped her hands, and when his eyes met hers, she'd looked upon him with the awe and innocence only a daughter could bestow upon her warrior father. He had been her protector. *But now I am not enough to save her.*

Hahnee grabbed the cuff with the spiderweb turquoise stone but did not pull it off. "I had hoped to have carried this burden for you . . ." He felt a tightness encompass his heart. *What if she's not ready?* What had he done to prepare her? She had visited so many times as of late, and he never warned her about the endless pain of memories. *How will she endure without me?*

"I'll be fine," Eyota said as if she'd heard his thoughts. "It's my time."

Hahnee slipped the silver cuff off his wrist.

Eyota held out her arm with a reassuring nod.

Hahnee lowered his chin to his chest and squeezed his eyes

shut. This was it: the moment to pass the curse and move on. He felt the tremors begin in his chin and held his breath as they spread through the rest of his body. When he couldn't hold back any longer, he exhaled and opened his eyes. With shaky hands, he slid the cuff onto her wrist and said, "I'll always love you, Eyota."

To his surprise, the cuff adjusted to her wrist. The ashen tone of her hand and arm faded, and his eyes moved up to her face to see that her skin was now a rich umber, with a hint of rose on her cheeks. She looked more human than ever before.

Hahnee rose to his feet and extended his hands to Eyota. "Let me look at you."

Eyota grabbed his hands and stood. She smiled and twisted her body. The ends of her dress swirled in the air.

Hahnee heard her chuckle. It was the sound of sweetness he remembered from long ago. It brought a smile to his face and forced the tightness in his chest to release. He suddenly felt open and light, the same way he'd felt the first time he laid eyes on his brand-new daughter, wrapped in softness. He pulled one of Eyota's hands to his face and soaked in the warmth of her palm against his cheek. His hand slid down hers and his thumb caught the thumping pulse in her wrist.

He stilled himself.

Tears lined the bottom of his eyelids, and he whispered, "You're alive."

Eyota nodded. Her hand moved to his chest and covered his heart. A sob escaped her lips as her hand moved through his chest, catching only air. "Yes, but you're not."

"It's all right," Hahnee whispered. "I'm free."

After a long pause, Hahnee heard the click of the door lock and the familiar chime. He watched Elan pull the door open. Blinding sunlight burst into the shop.

Pallaton hoisted the maquahuitl over his shoulder. He stepped through the door first, engulfed by the light, his dark silhouette there one moment and gone the next.

Hahnee glanced over his shoulder just as Aquene disappeared behind the bronze juniper. His eyes then shifted to Eyota, who gave him another reassuring nod. With her blessing, he slowly walked out of the arts-and-antique shop and never looked back.

For hours he walked, easy and unhurried. He followed dusty trails and climbed over rusty rocks, winding past low junipers and sharp cacti, reflecting on his interactions with the environment. He listened to his thoughts and the occasional flute notes carried on the wind until he found himself on top of Belle Rock.

A thousand years he had lived. Cursed to tell the story of Aquene and her people. And in that time, he often contemplated the meaning of his life and the purpose of the curse. He thought it was about remorse and forgiveness. Yet those things were for him and about him only.

He realized as he stared over the vast expanse of red rocks that whether it was taking from the sky, the mountains, oceans, animals, or people . . . it was about respect . . . and rebalancing what one had taken from the world.

Hahnee felt the energy of the ancestors envelop him. As a gentle breeze kicked up and the energy swirled around him, he found himself enrapt in the warm, peaceful comfort of moving on from this earth after a thousand years in the waiting.

Chris Abela started writing when she was nine years old but spent much of her adulthood pursuing other careers just to prove that nothing could be as satisfying as writing. And, darn it, she succeeded. Her other endeavors include psychology, counseling, and usability research. She resides in Maryland with her husband and two children. On weekends, you'll often find their house full of caffeine-and-pun-addicted friends who share a love of books, games, and great barbeque. Visit Chris at www.authorchrisabela.com and look for her other work in the Quoth the Raven Anthology.

JUST ONE OF THOSE DAYS

A.J. MAYALL

JUST ONE OF THOSE DAYS

It was 10:14 PM, and a gun was in my face. The man holding it looked haggard, living off a single small meal a day for about a week and a half, by the looks of it. He wasn't exactly tall, but I wouldn't call him short either. I know it's easy to just say, "average", but I hate the term *average*, no one is average.

I've been through this sort of thing more times than I care to count, so I stopped decades ago. I know this ain't exactly the best way to report information, not much drama to hook the recipient, but I'm an old man, and I don't give a good goddamn these days. I'm just a bitter hermit living in the creepy house on the edge of town, a relic watching relics on the outskirts of South Whispers, Idaho, in the Owyhee Desert.

George, the man currently holding that gun in my face, had tanned skin, half of which came from living in the desert, the other was likely some Hispanic and Native heritage. None of that was why he was holding a gun to my head, of course. Last thing I wanna be is some old man sounding like he's using someone's ethnicity against them. I pride myself on not adhering to some of the unpleasant views held during my upbringing by closed-minded men.

By the look and smell of the man, he'd been wearing the same clothes for the last week and a half: a red shirt and jeans with noticeable greyish brown sediment from use, embedded in the fabric. He held my gaze with a shaken look in his, one that showed desperation and horror.

"The gun's not loaded, George. Sit your ass down. I made some pie, you want any?" I asked.

He pressed the gun against my nose. "I got bullets, old man, now where's the antiques?"

I knew better. Like I said, I've been through this before.

He moved his hand and pointed the gun at the concrete wall behind me, pulling the trigger. It simply clicked, and George looked incredulous, as I knew he would. I looked over my shoulder to all of the bullet holes that littered the warehouse wall. How many times do I have to say that I've been through this before? I really do need to fix the wall, though.

"What the damn hell, old man? You psychic or something?" George asked as he stumbled back, having second thoughts about this break-in of his.

"Not in the slightest. Now, you look hungry. Like I said, I made some pie. You want a slice?" I knew he wasn't gonna take it, but he was in my storehouse, and I had pie. The least I could do was offer a little bit of generosity; a host at gunpoint is still a host.

He shook his head and looked behind him, at the door he had broken open with a crowbar. What little scrapes he'd made were lost in the debris of all the other break-ins.

I shrugged and cut myself a piece of pie—chocolate mousse, my mother's recipe. I took a quick bite and turned away from him. "Okay, okay, I know why you're here. Everyone knows about crazy old Zachary Graves, on the edge of town, with his big, scary, haunted house, and the warehouse behind it that's chock-full of old antiques."

I'm Zachary Graves, by the way, just realized I never actually introduced myself.

"Here's the deal, Georgie boy. I'll let you have one thing from my warehouse, but just one, so you can pawn it for a few bucks. I mean, I'm coming to the end of my life. Goodness knows someone'll be coming in for an estate sale and all these damn things are gonna get sold to a bunch of people who don't even know what the hell they're buying. Worse yet, they do know. But you're desperate. I like desperate. Desperate means you're willing to make mistakes. Desperate means you're gonna make a mistake, which means you're gonna learn from it. Let's see if you're ready to learn from your mistake yet."

George looked incredulous. He had to be about 19, maybe in his early twenties. Hell, the older I get, the more the younguns' ages blend together. For all I knew, he was in his thirties or mid-teens.

Damn kids.

"Maybe I'll just kick your ass, old man, and take what I want!"

We'd come to this part of the conversation. I simply sighed and turned around as fast as I could, which, considering my age, is still pretty damn fast…at least faster than he was expecting. The twin pistols now aimed right at him made him stumble back. The handles looked to be made of gold and ivory. The barrels were some weird bronze or brass color.

My old Occult 45s, best friends a hermit could have.

Anyway, when I first inherited these things, they were flintlocks and changed to the pistols the first time I picked them up. I pulled back two hammers with my thumbs and aimed for center mass.

"These things never carry bullets, George, but they also never run out of ammo, and they never miss their target. You've heard the stories about me and my family; you damn well know what these things can do."

George froze and nodded.

I opened my palms to drop the guns, which simply vanished with a flash and a wisp of smoke.

"Your grandfather was some sort of adventurer, wasn't he?" George said. "I heard he built up this collection over years of breaking into mummies' tombs, temples in the Amazon, and all that."

I nodded. George was pretty much right. You see, in the old days, adventuring was commonplace for the more eccentric upper-middle class. Everyone's read old pulp stories of some doctor traipsing through Asia. I refuse to call it the Orient; don't ever say the old dog can't learn a few things here and there about cultural sensitivity. Anyhow, these were the people running in the dungeons, raiding temples, breaking into long-forgotten pyramids, fighting mummies. Pistols, whips, and cutlasses were the weapons of choice. They were usually accompanied by a scientist, a bodyguard or two, some agents who owe life favors, and some perky, stupid, little kid brought along for the adventure. Oh, come on...Johnny Quest? Short Round? That was me, back in the day.

The thing is, no one ever asks whatever happened to those stupid little kids once they grow up.

My grandfather had been able to fill no less than seven museums with ancient cursed artifacts over the course of all of his adventuring that I helped out with. Seven full museums. Nowadays, museums don't have the pull they used to, and everything had been donated. Not to mention that, hey, exhibits come and go. Gradually, the museums called up the family and wanted to know if we could come to pick up a couple dozen old monkey paws or ancient sarcophagi or strange onyx necklaces that seem to bend light around them.

Grandpa died when I was twenty three. My dreams of college abroad were cut short because I was the only living family member who knew anything about all of these damn items and how to keep them safe and secure.

Oh, hell, I forgot where we are in the story! Let's see...he had the gun trained on me, I offered pie. He said he'd kick my ass, I pulled the guns on him, and then let my Occult 45s go, that's right.

"One item, George. You can have one item from my collection, but," I said, holding up a hand, "I have to tell you what it will do to you first."

George nodded and slowly shuffled closer to me.

I gestured down to the pie. "Last chance for a snack."

He shook his head, as I knew he would.

I pointed to my table and said, "Leave the gun there. It won't do you any good anyways."

George did as he was told, and I gestured to the back of the room. He followed me; there may be hope for him yet. The back of the storehouse had an ornate wooden door that clashed with the concrete wall it was set into. I reached out to the handle and swung it inward, revealing vast darkness. We stepped in, and I felt around for the light switch. When I flicked it up, rows upon rows of fluorescent lights far above illuminated the large room.

"Wait a second," George said, "that's impossible. That room's larger than the whole of the storehouse! I cased this place for an hour."

"I know. And the door won't open for anyone but me. Why do you think no one's ever successfully stolen anything from me?" I paused, looking him dead in the eyes, "I take that back, I did have one robbery."

"What the hell do you have in here?"

"Thought you're the one who cased the place; you tell me."

George shrugged sheepishly. "I don't know. I just thought, you know, antiques and old stuff. Something I could take to one of them roadshows and get appraised for a good chunk of money, or, you know, make a few bucks at the pawn shop."

I smiled, walking over to one of the nearby shelves that had an ornate Venetian music box. It was black, gilded, inset with rubies, diamonds, and huge sapphires. On the front face was painted the Virgin Mary bleeding from her eyes. Next to it, as with all my items, sat a small manila folder.

"Would you like this? Before you say yes, please understand what this is. It's no ordinary music box; this has a captured siren song. Developed in the late nineteenth century by an absolute madman, he built a machine that played anti-music. Anti-music, can you believe it? It could capture sound—not like a recording, but literally capture sound, the pure heart and soul of the tones. Crazy, obsessed fellow went to Greece, found the Sirens, and forced them to sing into the box."

George's eyes lit up. He reached out to grab it, and I smacked his hands with the manila folder.

"You're not listening, Georgie boy. You know what a Siren's song does to you? It compels you to destroy yourself. We've lent out the box, over the years, to various people. Just because no one has managed to steal from me in quite a while doesn't mean that they didn't rob Grandpa or other people who've filled in for me when I've been sick."

George opened the manila folder and immediately dropped it, screaming. Old, yellowed photographs fluttered to the ground. One showed a man who cut off his face and tried to feed it into the music box; another showed a woman who had put a shotgun to her heart.

"A music box is only supposed to play for so long. We're talking about the most beautiful song you've ever heard. But you can't bring yourself to close the box and rewind it, not to mention a siren just wants you to drown, so there's magic in the box. You'd make whatever offering you can think of to bring yourself closer to that music, realizing you can never live without hearing it again. The longest I've known anyone to survive after having listened to the music was 27 minutes, 27 excruciating minutes. He killed himself by driving a dagger into each ear just to make the music stop playing in his head." I smiled again at him. "So, is this what you want?"

George shook his head and backed away. "No way, man! There's no way I'm even messing with something like that!"

I shrugged and kept walking, a smile as big as the zeppelins I used to commandeer with Gramps. I got everything back in the folder and tidied up, whistling a jaunty tune from my youth.

We passed by other artifacts until Georgie was attracted by a quill pen. "How much could I get for something like that?"

"Oh, be careful. See, this old pen's got quite a curse on it as well, but it can be yours if you want it."

He looked at the pen, then the manila folder beside it. He reached for the pen but grabbed the folder instead. I was impressed. Definitely hope for him. He flipped it open and winced at the images of desiccated corpses, pen in hand, surrounded by barren reams of paper.

"The feather came from an angel and was rumored to be kissed by a muse. You know what happens when you take something from an angel?"

George shook his head.

"Depends on the angel, but mostly, you get a blessing you'd never want. If the angel were to give you the feather, that's one thing, but to take it is spitting in the face of that celestial being. Back to the quill, though. It never runs out of ink, and you are forever inspired. It starts slow; smells are more intense, the wind in the trees sounds more beautiful, the play of morning sunlight on dew in the grass becomes a cavalcade of rainbows in your mind."

"That doesn't sound so bad."

"No, it doesn't if that were all. But, it never stops. The intensity just builds. Soon, you have to write about it, but the more you write, the more inspired you get. You'll spend every last penny you have and sell everything you own to buy, you hope, enough paper to capture the beauty of the world around you. You stop eating, stop drinking because that's cutting into your writing time. The worst part? When you die, you take the words with you. The last thing you see, from what I've been told, is everything that you've ever written on those pages vanish. As the pages go white, your vision goes black. I don't even know if you're allowed to go to heaven, having messed with something stolen from an angel. Frankly, I think seeing that much beauty and having it taken away in your last minutes is the closest thing to hell I can think of."

George put the folder back, looked me in the eye and shook his head.

"I mean, you never know; you might be able to hold off the temptation, just write a couple books and make some good money. Grandpa said when he found it, the guy was in the middle of writing…I believe it was a twenty thousand-page epic. Grandpa said it was one of the most amazing things he ever read. He tried to take a photograph of a few of the pages while they still had ink on them. The photos never turned out though. Heaven won't let you take the words of the sinner."

I shrugged and headed deeper into the warehouse, past a few dozen monkey paws that I had expertly tagged and kept in a cage. When George stopped to look at them, I smirked and shook my head. "Trust me, you don't want those. Getting what you ask for with a twist on it is not only overdone but, frankly, by this point, everyone's heard of these darn things. You can probably find a much more powerful one somewhere else. Try eBay, I hear you can get a bargain."

A couple displays down from the monkey paws was an old Ouija board. It was fashioned from a single piece of solid dark-stained redwood. The letters, numbers, and various runes were inlaid with silver. On a small stand in the middle was a planchette with a piece of glass as a viewing window.

"This one's interesting. You see, the wood came from a Native American burial ground that was never meant to be disturbed. I know, I know, sounds hokey. I swear it's the real deal. It's said some form of dark magic was invoked when this thing was made. I don't know if that's true, but even before the slight modification," I pointed to the glass in the planchette, "this thing had already had a death count of about fifty.

"That glass used to be a monocle for some late eighteenth, early nineteenth-century London occultist. Apparently, wearing it lets you see the truth. This fella affixed his damn monocle into the planchette, hoping it would allow him to see whatever was actually attacking people who used it. He ended up taking two curses and made them one really big one."

"What do you mean?" asked George.

I handed him a sizable folder. It was easily 4 inches of notes and paperwork. In it were news clippings of murder-suicides. There were a few notebooks of various tests that had been done by occultists and scholars of the dark arts over the years.

"The power of a Ouija board is actually in the planchette. Once the monocle was put into it, the two objects sort of fell in love. It'll show you everything you want to know, but it needs power, so it draws out your soul. You could probably use the Ouija board a few times with no problem; even the cardboard ones wouldn't pose a threat. See, you never actually summon anything. Most people, when they have a question, already kind of know the answer. You subconsciously answer your own question. This takes it to another level. What this little pointer does is draw out your soul, chains it, abuses and forces it to your bidding. This thing's movement on the board is actually your soul responding to you."

"Uh...cool?"

"The more you use it, the weaker the link between your body and soul gets. It tears it away. You may not even realize a good chunk of it's not even inside you anymore. Eventually, you're going to want to talk to capital O, capital T, Other Things. And that's what ends up happening; you get pushed out, a half-dozen things jump in, and the next thing you know, you're coming to, in the middle of a bloodbath, with a knife sticking out of your own chest by your own hand. The spirit of vengeance and the spirit of pure truth are a deadly combination. I don't know the full details but, according to the notes that have been taken over the years, the only things you see are everyone's foulest truths and a primal urge to eradicate those people for their transgressions. God knows what jumps inside you, and it's more than happy to help you with that bloodshed. The thing is, your spirit is so weak at that point, the only thing it ends up jumping to, once your body kicks it, is that planchette. If you look at it at just the right angle, you can see trapped souls screaming in the reflection of that glassy center."

George calmly closed the folder, set it beside the Ouija board, and backed away slowly.

I laughed and gestured back near the other side of the warehouse. "Okay, I can only think of two more things you might like that people won't ask questions about."

As I patted him on the shoulder, using him for a bit of support, he gave me an awkward glance.

"Don't worry, I'm just an old man. I'm not as sprightly as I was back in his youth. Now, you pay attention," I said, gesturing to a small locker. I opened it and pulled out a pair of well-worn leather boxing gloves. I tossed them to George; he backed away for a moment but caught them at the last moment.

"Touching won't hurt you; bad things only happen if you put them on."

"Where's the folder on this?"

"Funny thing, that. There's not much info on it. Once we found out what they do, we never really wanted to test it that much. These things make you win any fight, but you will want to fight more."

"Doesn't seem that bad, considering."

"True, but when you take them off, it takes a while for that magic to dissipate. Literally, you will win anything you go up against. It's a damn shame, too."

"What do you mean?"

"The last owner was a poor guy in the fifties who just needed some help winning a few boxing matches. He went home after practicing for a good five hours, and his wife asked what he wanted to have for family dinner. Jokingly, he said his favorite comfort food, which was PB&J. She scolded him and suggested roast beef. It was a joke because their three-year-old son was deathly allergic to peanuts. He went out to mow the lawn and came back in to find his son dead and his wife standing there with a rictus grin, holding a plate of the peanut butter and jelly sandwiches. They had to have the family dinner before she could do anything else. He won the argument."

"That's horrifying!" said George.

"Then his wife and him got into an argument; why the hell didn't she call the cops, why the hell she didn't stop their kid from eating? Turns out, because it had to be a family dinner, she force-fed those sandwiches to the kid. Again, they got into an argument he had to win. She was already pushed over the edge after murdering her child. All he wanted to do was fight. When the police finally arrived, they found him sobbing after he crushed her skull with his bare hands. Every finger was broken by the time he was done beating her. He couldn't stop himself."

George tossed me back the Golden Gloves, as I called them. I set them back in the locker and closed it up. "To be fair, as far as curses go, that was actually manageable. You just have to know when to wear them, when to keep your damn yap shut, and how long to stay in seclusion until the magic wears off. My only real regret on that one is we never really got their history."

George shuddered. "There was one more item that you thought I'd be good for," he said, gripping a lump under his shirt reflexively. It wasn't a cross, but it was the same instinctive motion.

"Yeah, that I do. Come on, kid."

"Where is it?"

In the back of the warehouse is a television with one of the VCRs built in, and a glass case with a bare mannequin neck and shoulders within.

"This," I said, chuckling, "is the Necklace of Sang et Honte. I believe this goes back to the 14th century and it was a gift from a jeweler to some—I don't know—empress or something. Basically, they had conquered the homeland, killed his family, but left him alive because he could actually make jewelry the empress would wear. His gift to them for sparing his life was this necklace."

George cocked his brow, looked at the unadorned head, and then to me. "There's nothing there, dude. What are you talking about?"

"I'm not finished yet. You see, it has this really nasty habit. It makes you relive the worst day of your life. Not like it sends you back in time to literally relive it. You have the worst day of your life, and you're compelled the next day to go through the same actions over and over again, with no memory of having done it the day before. You ever have those dull days that just bleed together? This makes every yesterday just fade to the back of your mind and puts you on repeat. The actual events of that worst day, they're in the past, but for you, it's always fresh."

"Where's the damn necklace?"

"I'm getting to that, Georgie boy, hold your damn horses. I'm fairly certain this is the thing you think you could handle, because all of your worst days are behind you, right?"

George shrugged. "Yeah, pretty much. My mom died about a month ago, and I lost my job soon after that, but I can bring myself to go to work, even though I'm pretty much out of money now, and—"

"And you thought you could probably get a good stack of cash by stealing some old antiques. The silly old man's sitting on a pile of rubbish that's worth more than a few million dollars at this point. He wouldn't notice if one or two things went missing, right?"

Georgie nodded. "So, where is it?"

I reached over and pulled open the front of his shirt. "You took it ten days ago."

"What the hell are you talking about? I've never seen you before tonight."

"That's what you said ten days ago, and nine days ago, and eight—here, actually, let me show you who stole it."

I reached over and hit play on the VCR. There was security

footage of me being held at gunpoint by George as I lifted up the case, picked up the necklace, and handed it over to him. As he put it on his neck, you can see I damn near dropped the case as I begged him not to put it on.

"Your gun has no bullets in it because you've already given me about a dozen warning shots. You're compelled to do to the same actions, Georgie. Do you even remember how I know your name? You told me, seven days ago. Have you noticed you've been wearing the same clothes for damn near two weeks?"

He staggered, looking at his chest and then the tape, almost toppling over, "I feel weak."

"You only had a breakfast of crackers and cheese, since you can't really afford much. Why do you think I offered you pie? Kid, you'll starve yourself to death soon enough." I shook my head. "After you die, I could have just stopped by your place and picked up the necklace, but I'm trying to give you a choice, same choice I've been giving you. I said you could take one item with you. You wanted it to be the necklace. You can walk right back out the door with it, I'll see you tomorrow and ask you again, or you can give it back, sit down, have a good meal, and tomorrow, if you wanted to stop by in the morning, maybe I can give you a job cataloguing some of these artifacts."

"That's crazy, man. You're absolutely crazy! I didn't steal this from you. I've always—" George racked his mind. The video could be lying to him, but at the same time...he'd always had this necklace, hadn't he? Maybe it was something his mom gave him, some heirloom, something you can never give away.

"Georgie, I know that look, that face; that's the curse. You never noticed that you're wearing it, and it's why you think you're so miserable. It's going to kill you slowly. Please, Georgie, just give me back the necklace."

He shook his head, turned tail, and ran screaming out of the back room of the warehouse. I heard him grab the gun off the desk and slam the door behind him.

I sighed to myself, alone once again. "Well, there's always tomorrow, Georgie."

I walked out of the back room, turned off the light, closed and locked the oaken door, removed it from the wall and set it against the desk. The wall showed no signs of ever having had a massive warehouse behind it, only bare concrete.

"This damn thing's gonna be the death of me," I said.

The Door of Need always opens to the thing you desire most. What I always desired most was more space for these goddamn artifacts.

I looked at the rest of the pie, shook my head, and tossed it in the trash. I hated letting good food go to waste, but there was no way I was gonna eat the whole thing by tomorrow. I walked out of the storehouse, closed the door, and headed to my estate's kitchen, where I had flour, sugar, butter, and some chocolate already set up. I'd been through this before, like I said. Always best to be prepared.

I began to make a new pie for the next day. It's always good to have something for a guest. I don't get many visitors, and Georgie's the first company I've had in damn near ten years. The least I can do is be a good host when he comes by and puts a gun in my face at 10:14 p.m. tomorrow. I just hope he'll be hungry enough to have some pie then. If he can break one habit, maybe he can break another, and if I can save him, maybe I can save myself.

There is hope for him, but I learned a long time ago that having hope ain't enough to save someone. Vigilance and smarts, with a dash of chutzpah, wins the day. It's how I've stuck around for so long, sheer force of stubbornness.

That's the worst curse of all of these damn things that I have. Knowing what would happen if I weren't there. No matter how much I don't want to be here, I carry on my goddamn, lonely vigil.

But having a stupid kid sidekick by my side might not be so bad.

Not that I know what that was like or anything.

. . .

A.J. Mayall is a storyteller, gamer, and drinker of Cherry Cola. Currently working for the amazing indie e-book publisher Smashwords. For more about A.J. Mayall visit www.ajmayall.com.

THE PARANDADA

HEIDI A. WILDE

THE PARANDADA

Rune Talvik walked toward the village center between crowded rows of houses that seemed to lean against each other for support. His hands were stuffed in his pockets and his head was down, concentrating on the rain-slicked cobblestones beneath his thin soled shoes. The rain had stopped, but the lingering dampness made the air heavy and painted a sheen on his pale cheeks. The fingers of his right hand closed around a filigreed pendant as he pressed his lips together in determination. After a few minutes, he rounded a corner and the narrow street opened into a large square, filled with carts and stalls from which various vendors shouted with enthusiasm.

He made his way past the food vendors with their steam and spices filling the crisp air. He rushed by the trinket vendors loudly shaking their wares of metal and lace. He had nearly walked the length of the market when a brightly painted wagon came into view. A shiver, equal parts relief and trepidation, skittered across his shoulders at the sight of the impish looking man standing outside.

Two days ago, Rune overheard Mr. Janus's maid talking to the foreman about the new vendor at the market and the wonders he had on display. He wasn't sure if he had heard them correctly, but the wagon was there, and the squat man of miracles with it. Rune slipped around a portly gentleman to get a better look.

Mr. Fritjof Foley stood on a wooden bench holding a wooden cane wearing a wooden smile. Rune wondered if it was the man's skin, dark brown and deeply lined, that made him think of him as wooden, or if it was the utterly still way he held himself—as if he were a statue. Not that it mattered. If the man could do what he'd heard he could, Rune wouldn't care if he had three heads.

If this didn't work, he didn't know what else he could do. How could he have been so naive? Twenty years old already and still fumbling about like a child. His father would never have fallen into this mess. He and his sister had been late in planting and an early frost had killed their entire barley crop. Mr. Janus had seemed so worldly and elegant, yet kind. Offering to give them a loan so they wouldn't lose their home, Rune hadn't thought twice about signing the contract. Thinking of the flash of light that had appeared once he'd signed only served to remind him how blind he had actually been.

The afternoon sun filtered through the leaves of the surrounding trees speckling the crowd in a dance of light and shadow. Rune felt the chill once more but shook it off, averting his gaze from the unsettling tint the shadow cast across the little brown man's features. He stepped a little closer to the wagon.

Foley lifted his cane and tapped it on the bench, loudly, three times. The people around him quieted and turned their heads in his direction. Rune moved to stand between two average-sized men in the front, which only proved to make him feel shorter. With his slender build and small stature, he wasn't one to stand out in a crowd. Why hadn't he gotten any of his father's features? He was sure he would have been able to properly take care of his sister if he'd have been more of his father's son.

"Ladies and gentlemen, have you ever made a mistake so great, so damaging that you'd rather die than face the consequences?" Foley began. "Have you ever pleaded as you did when you were a child to uncaring, retreating backs? Of course you have! Of course. Haven't we all? Gather 'round then, ladies and gentlemen, for I have the solution to your problems, great or small. Come closer and take a look." Foley waited for a moment or two, holding a silk covered box above his head, until the crowd shifted closer, pressing against Rune on all sides.

Foley whipped off the silk with a flourish. "Behold, ladies and gentlemen! The Parandada!" Showing off a small cedar chest, he scanned the crowd quickly and, by the way he pressed his lips together, he seemed to not like what he saw.

"Now, you may think this chest is less than impressive, underwhelming even, but I assure you, ladies and gentlemen, this is just what you've been looking for. And for a paltry fee, I can give you the power to change your life!" Foley held up one finger and circled the crowd with his gaze. "One mistake erased. As if it never happened."

Taking hold of the box with both hands again, he continued. "Bad business deal you wish you could undo?" He lifted the chest higher. "Parandada! Thinking of that special lady you let slip away? The Parandada can remove the image of her departure from your life. Anything you can imagine, you can undo. Now, who'd like to try?" Foley spun around on his left foot and grinned at the crowd. "Come on now, don't be shy."

Rune ran his thumb along the edge of the pendant in his pocket, his heart pounding at the man's words. Could his box really save Rahne? An image of his sister in their small barley field, covered in dirt and a bright smile brought an ache to his chest. She loved that field; it was the reason he'd gone to such lengths to save their home.

The squat, brown man brought the box back down to his chest then drew one finger alongside his nose. "I do need to explain; however, you can only have one. So, think carefully about what it is you'd like to change."

Foley gently wrapped the silk covering around the chest and gave the crowd a paternal gaze. "It can be difficult, thinking of which mistake you'd like to erase. I understand, but don't take too long. Your new future is waiting." He stepped off his stool and turned, solemnly carrying the chest up the three steps, through the red and purple paisley curtain, and into his wagon.

Rune watched the curtain fall back into place, a feverish tingle flowing up his back and over his scalp. Could it work? He glanced around at the rest of the crowd and noticed that most were heading back to the savory smells coming from the meat carts. Of those that remained, expressions ranged from skeptical to a desperate sort of hunger. He felt that desperation was certainly on his face as well. He wasn't surprised to see others lingering. What would humankind be without our regrets? Rune felt a longing hang on his heart as he turned back to the wagon.

This might be his only chance to make things right. Clutching the pendant, he muttered, "I will fix it, Rahne, I swear."

Before he could lose his nerve, Rune took a deep breath and closed the distance between himself and redemption. He gave a small hesitant rap on the paneling, unsure if this was where he should be knocking. A clattering of dishes sounded from the other side of the curtain, but no voice beckoned. Rune knocked again, louder this time, and soon the curtain parted, revealing Foley's brown face and lively eyes.

"Come in, come in. Oh, do come in," Foley said warmly, a welcoming smile at the ready. Once inside, Rune glanced around, irresolute. Foley bustled back to the table and motioned to the chair across from him. "Why don't you have a seat and tell me your situation, Mister...?"

"Rune Talvik, Mr. Foley, sir." He paused and then took his seat in a rush. "And I've done something awful." Rune studied his slender, white hands for a few seconds, gathering his nerve. Looking up, he asked, "Do you really think you can help? I mean, can you really erase mistakes?"

Foley reached over and placed his tanned hand on Rune's, confident and comforting. "As if it never happened."

His manner reminded Rune of a vicar he'd known growing

up and he felt some of his tension fade. Though now being this close to him, Rune realized what he'd thought were deep lines in the small man's face were actually differences in skin tone. As if his skin had a grain to it.

Foley lifted his hand, making a fluttering motion with his fingers. "Never happened."

Distracted from his musing by the movement, Rune imagined his problems floating away on the wind as he watched Foley's stubby fingers dance. He nodded then, assuaged by that image. Pressing his lips together, Rune figured he might as well get to the heart of it. "How much does it cost?"

"Your most valuable possession," Foley said in a way one might say "three farthings" or "a bouquet of weeds."

Rune paused. "Most valuable possession?"

Foley nodded, turning his palms up with a shrug. "That's it. Just one item."

Rune studied his hands again, mentally cataloging all his possessions. "But I don't have anything of value." A tightness began to squeeze his chest. What if he was not able to free her? He slipped his hand back into his pocket and rubbed his thumb over the cameo in the center of the pendant for courage, for comfort.

Foley chuckled and shook his head. "I was obviously unclear. The thing most precious to you. Surely you have something that you vowed you would never part with?" The man's lively eyes took on an impish glint.

Rune felt himself go pale. "You don't mean—" He clutched the pendant in his pocket.

"That's the very thing." Foley's eyes gleamed as rested his hands on the table top.

Rune frowned at the little man's quick response. "But you don't even know what I was going to say."

"Trust me." Foley leaned forward slightly. "I've been doing this a very long time. Whatever you were just thinking of, that is the item." He snapped his fingers, the sound of it odd to Rune's ears.

"But I can't! Not that. I—I just can't." Helplessness welled up in Rune's throat, cutting off his speech.

Foley sat back in his chair and tilted his head to the left. He drummed his fingers against the table, giving off a hollow sound. "Either your mistake is not as great as you'd originally thought, or you aren't as full of regret as you need to be to make this change in your life. Either way, I don't like people wasting my time."

"Please, no, I need your help. I just can't give you that." Rune kept his hand around the pendant. Rahne...

"Why don't you tell me what it is you've done? I'm sure we can work out some arrangement, but you must understand, the bigger the mistake, the larger the sacrifice must be. It's just how it works." The little man folded his arms over his belly and waited.

Rune didn't like the casual avarice with which Foley spoke, but he was running out of time and options. "I..." Shame and regret rushed in so quickly, filling Rune's senses it was a moment before he could speak. "I made a deal with a man, if you can even call him a man. More like a demon." He trailed off again, glancing at Foley with an odd sense of déjà vu.

Foley merely quirked an eyebrow and motioned for him to continue, his expression still and expectant.

"We were going to lose our home. I was out of options and this man, Mr. Janus, said he could help. I figured he'd give us a loan and I would work it off for him at his metal shop." Rune paused again, feeling something like inevitability closing in around him as he looked across the table at Foley.

When Rune didn't immediately continue, Foley guided him. "But this Mr. Janus had a different sort of payment in mind." It wasn't a question, but Rune figured that much of the story was obvious.

"Well, yes and no." Rune drew his hand out of his pocket,

pendant still clutched in his palm. He slowly opened his fingers to reveal a beautifully crafted cameo of a young woman with features similar to his own.

"I have been working for him. This was my first piece. It's my sister." Rune's fond smile had sadness curling around the edges.

Foley picked up the pendant and gave Rune a look of confusion. "It's fine work, though I fail to see the problem. If you are working off your debt as you thought, why come to me?"

"You don't understand. That is my sister." The tide of anguish that crashed over him after he spoke those words left him breathless. "I've... That's the first time I've said that out loud." Rune felt his entire body tremble; he was nervous and uncomfortable having his sister in the palm of someone else's hand, literally and figuratively.

"He said she would be free once my term was served, but he keeps adding years to it. I fear he means never to release me. Or her." Rune kept a hold of the chain, fingering it gently before returning his gaze to Foley's. "I heard some of his employees talking about you. They said you could work miracles. They didn't give much detail, but if I've ever needed a miracle, it's now."

The little imp nodded, a suppressed excitement seeping out of him in jerky movements and half-formed smiles. "Oh yes, I do indeed. Yes, yes." He made a soft tittering sound and tapped his shoes on the ground in a little dance. "So, your solution to making a bad deal with a...demon, did you say? Is to make another deal with me?"

"I don't care what you think of me as long as it will release my sister. Can you do it?" Rune's voice was terse and desperate. He could feel how despairing he must appear, and he hated it, this feeling of helpless misery. Caught in a snare where his every movement only tangled himself up tighter.

"Most assuredly. This deal will free her from any arrangements you have made in the past."

Foley's words should have eased Rune's mind, but something

about them was unnerving. He didn't care. Whatever the cost, he owed it to Rahne.

"This pendant is my most valuable possession, but it's so much more than just an object. I can't give it to you. You understand that, right? I can't give you my sister."

Foley grinned then, a wide, creaking grin as his hand tightened its grip on the pendant. "But what use will this be once your mistake is undone? Your sister will no longer be inside it. You will not have created it."

The logic of those words initially comforted Rune, but as his own logic asserted itself, the comfort was quickly replaced with a bone-deep foreboding. He frowned, trying to gently tug the pendant back towards his chest. "Then of what use will it be to you, if it will not exist as you just stated?"

"The energy released in this piece's undoing will be very useful, to be sure. The process is not something you need to worry about or understand. Just know that your sister will no longer be inside. It will be as if your mistake never happened. Isn't that what you want?"

"Yes, of course." Rune looked down at the pendant they were both holding for a long moment. If he used the Parandada, Rahne would no longer be trapped. It wasn't like he was actually giving his sister away. This would free her. With a last loving squeeze, he let go of the chain. "Very well."

"Excellent! Yes, yes. Very fine indeed. Shall we shake on it? Gentlemen's agreement and then we'll get started." Foley's eyes crinkled as he grinned and held out his hand.

Rune took the small hand offered him and shook it once, gravely. He marveled at the texture of the man's skin, unlike anything he'd felt before. Cool, smooth, and devoid of give as he squeezed it.

"Lovely, pale features you have. Your sister, too, I imagine?" Foley cradled the pendant in his hands with a delight that made Rune reach out for it again. Foley drew it out of his grasp, wagging a finger under Rune's nose. "Uh-uh. A deal is a deal."

THE PARANDADA

Foley pushed the box in front of Rune, uncovering and opening it. "Now all that's needed is for you to look inside, your mistake foremost on your mind. Concentrate on the moment you want undone."

Rune bit his lip, and looked between the pendant and the box once, twice, before gripping the sides of the box and looking into its depths. Closing his eyes, he concentrated on the day he'd made the deal with Mr. Janus, the day he'd agreed to put his sister in stasis for collateral. Losing their house seemed an almost laughable problem now. He'd rather lose a hundred houses than give up his sister again.

Rune opened his eyes and was shocked at how much bigger it seemed inside. As he felt himself being pulled into the box, Rune saw Foley smash open the pendant, a white mist rising from it. Rune tried to drag himself back from the box, but his hands and arms refused to cooperate. He tried to shout, to kick, but he only sank further into the box.

Foley took a deep breath, inhaling the mist completely; his features suffused with light that left him decidedly less wooden looking. "I'll have to send Mr. Janus a gift basket; one or two more like this pair should be all I need."

Rune heard him speak as if he was underwater, slow and distorted, and as he spoke, Foley reached over to close the box. Only then did Rune realize he was completely inside. Muffled murmurings sounded all around him and he felt his skin pulled tight. His body flattened out as the air was crushed from his lungs. Everything around him slowed and sped up in turns, rewinding and repeating.

Rune didn't know how much time passed in the dark torture of the box, but he opened his eyes and found himself outside Mr. Janus' estate. A breathless surprise fluttered his heart and he nearly knelt to kiss the ground in gratitude. Before he let the excitement overtake him, he wanted to make sure he had actually been taken back in time and not just transported physically in that strange box. As he was wondering how to approach Mr.

Janus to find out, a petite figure strode up the hill in his direction.

His heart pounded in his chest and a half-strangled shout of joy caught in his throat. Rahne! Rune watched her make her way toward him, hearing her muttering something to herself. He laughed and ran over to her, hugging her tightly. "Rahne! You're alive. I'm not too late. I'm so glad. I'm so glad!" She struggled in his embrace and he pulled back to look down at her frowning up at him.

Rahne pushed him farther away with a soft grunt. "What are you doing, Rune? Not too late for what? Why would I not be alive?" She sighed, a look of despondence tugging the corners of her lips lower. "Never mind that now. I was worried when I couldn't find you. You should have told me you were coming here. Do you think Mr. Janus will give us a loan?"

A bit of Rune's joy dimmed as he thought about that two-faced man. "We're not talking to Mr. Janus. We'll have to find another way."

"Another way? Rune, I thought you said this was our only way." Rahne continued frowning and rested her hands on her hips.

"I was wrong. I—I've changed my mind," Rune said in a rush, his fingers gripping her shoulders. "We cannot make a deal with Mr. Janus."

Rahne scowled at him as she tried to wriggle out of his grasp, the strength of his grip obviously displeasing her. "What happened to change your mind? I know I was hesitant at first but I thought on it last night. I agree with you. Besides, it's not like this is the first loan Mr. Janus has given. He's helped quite a number of people."

Rune glanced up the hill to the estate grounds as a shiver ran down his spine. Turning back to his sister, he asked in a low voice, "And what has become of all those people he's supposedly helped?"

Rahne finally managed to shake him off and took a step

back, breathing out a short laugh. "Well, they've moved on, haven't they? Once they repaid their loan, they got on with their lives." She reached out and patted Rune's shoulder with a worried frown. "Just as we will." She gave his shoulder a gentle shove. "Is it that you don't want to work in his shop, lazy bones? If that's what you're worried about, I don't mind doing the work. You can tend our field." She was certainly teasing him. When would she ever willingly give up working in her field?

Shaking his head and grasping her shoulders once again, Rune gave her an exasperated smile. "Of course, I don't mind doing the work, but—" He sighed and let his head droop. "You wouldn't believe me." Raising his head, he looked into her eyes sternly. "But you must trust me. We'll find some other way. Or we'll move. But we're not taking a loan from that two-face."

"Move? Where is this coming from? I'm not moving! That's our home, Rune. How can you talk about leaving it? Great-grandfather built it, for goodness sake. Who else should live there?" Rahne started backing away from him, obviously very confused, and looked toward the path up the hill. "I don't know what's come over you, calling Mr. Janus a two-face even! But if you won't do this to save our home then I will." Turning on her heel, she quickly made her way up the hill.

Rune hurried after her, begging her to turn around. *Should I tell her I've made this deal once before?* Just as he was considering how quickly his sister would call for a priest if he did tell her, Mr. Janus stepped out of the gate. Breaking into a run, Rune got in front of Rahne, blocking her way. He felt an intense gaze freezing his spine. Without turning to confront Mr. Janus, he urged, "Go home, Rahne. Please, trust me."

It was as if she didn't see Rune at all, her eyes lighting up with hope at the sight of the tall gentleman making his way over. "Mr. Janus! Good day." She brushed past Rune without so much as a glance. "I hope I'm not disturbing you, but I have a matter I would like to discuss."

Rune stared at her in shock for a moment but then tried again to get her attention. It was as if he'd turned invisible.

Mr. Janus bowed elegantly with a charming smile and took Rahne's hand in his. "A visit from you would never be a bother, Miss Talvik. How may I assist you?"

Rahne's blush at Mr. Janus' words caused Rune to reach out for her, to call out to her, but his arms would not obey his command. Opening his mouth, all the words he needed to say congealed into a lump in his throat refusing to be uttered. Widening his eyes in a panic, he looked over at Mr. Janus. The cold knowing smile the other man was giving him turned his stomach.

How could he know? What does he know? Rune tried again to force his limbs to move, to make some kind of a sound. In the end, all he could do was watch as his sister was led through the gates. Mr. Janus tossed him an amused glance over his shoulder before securing the gate with a wave of his hand. The scene was all too familiar to Rune: Mr. Janus's refined speech mesmerizing the listener, coaxing her to make a deal.

Once they were gone from sight, Rune fell forward onto his knees, his body finally able to move. He let out a painful gust of air and clumsily rose back to his feet. "Rahne!" He stumbled forward calling out to his sister, but when he reached the gate he couldn't make it budge, no matter how many times he crashed into it. "Rahne! Don't! Please, don't do it! He's a liar!" His voice was raw, and tears streamed down his face as he cried out and pleaded with her.

Through a window on the second floor, he saw the familiar flash of light and he dropped to the ground. He was too late. He hadn't fixed anything. Glaring up at the sky, he yelled, "You got what you wanted! Why did it turn out like this?" He pressed his head against the gate and choked on a sob.

"You wanted your sister freed, did you not? I'd say we both got what we wanted." A mocking voice sounded above Rune's head.

Rune jerked his head up at hearing that voice and he glared. "What I wanted was this deal to have never happened! But I came back only to have it repeated."

"The deal you made with Mr. Janus was undone. Your sister's soul is no longer in the pendant. I fail to see why you are dissatisfied with your results." The little imp leaned against the wall of the estate, one nimble hand fluttering as he spoke. Rune took a closer look at the little man and was surprised to see his wooden features had faded even more since their last meeting.

With a sigh, Foley appeared unwilling but continued with a gleam in his eye. "However, if you are genuinely unsatisfied, perhaps you would like to make a new deal?"

Heidi A. Wilde is a respiratory therapist by night and aspiring author by day. She spends her nights dragging people back from the brink of death, but she dedicates her daylight hours to the pursuit of writing. She's had an ongoing love affair with words and language since she began reading at the age of three (the dictionary and encyclopedias were some of her most fun summer reading during elementary school). Not only the *what* of what people say, but the *how* has always intrigued her and she hopes that curiosity has informed her own writing. Current projects include a Regency Romance series, a fantasy saga, and even a foray into the realm of Steampunk, as well as the occasional short story competition or anthology piece.

THE GARDEN PARTY

SHANNON FOX

THE GARDEN PARTY

A stone angel clutched a laminated placard between its fingers: 50% OFF! EVERYTHING ON SALE! Moisture had smeared the corner of the red ink.

"Let's go in," Charlie said. He pulled Katie by the hand towards the entrance of the store.

She dug in her heels when she saw what kind of store it was and rolled her eyes at her boyfriend. "Really, babe? Another antique store?"

"Just for a minute. Just to look."

"No," Katie said. "I told you I wanted to go home. My feet hurt from walking, I'm sunburned, and I've got sand all over me."

"You're the one who wanted to go to the beach," Charlie said. He looked her up and down with a smirk. "To get a tan."

Her blood pounded in her ears as she felt the judgment leeching into his words. *Pale people don't tan, so why did you even bother trying?* She wanted to smack the smug look from his perfectly bronzed face.

Charlie let go of her hand and took a step toward the store. "Stay here if you want, but I'm going in."

She watched the door shut behind him and contemplated

storming off towards the car. She wondered if he'd chase after her. Or if he'd even noticed she'd moved from the sidewalk outside.

Katie looked at the sign in the window as she pushed open the door. A.R. Gread. She was sure Charlie was in hog heaven to be browsing a store with a snooty name like that.

Dusty armoires and curio cabinets cluttered the floor, their shelves crowded with curiosities. Paintings of all styles and sizes clung to the walls like fungus. What couldn't be hung up simply leaned against wrought iron tables and rolled up oriental rugs. Statues jockeyed for the last remaining bits of floor space.

Katie wrinkled her nose at the musty odor. She hated that smell. It was the scent of too many afternoons wasted while Charlie haggled over a lamp or an old book.

As she made her way deeper into the store, she was careful not to touch anything. She knew firsthand how serious these shopkeepers were about their you-break-it-you-buy-it policy. With her student loans, she didn't have any extra pocket money to spend on this place.

A group of small, white porcelain figurines lined up on a table caught her eye. Her grandmother had owned something similar. She'd actually left the collection to Katie, but Katie had given it to her little sister. At the time, she hadn't had any use for miniature kittens and puppies with dopey smiles on their faces. Now, though, she wondered if perhaps she should have kept one to remember her grandmother by.

As Katie reached for the tiny white horse in the corner, a disembodied voice startled her.

"Is there something I can help you find?"

Katie looked to her right and spotted a man seated in a red velvet armchair. She hadn't noticed him as she'd walked up. Probably because he looked like one of the antiques himself.

Though the thick bush of white hair adorning his head revealed his age, his blue eyes were sharp and his face was curiously free of wrinkles. His skin had the unnaturally smooth look of a shirt that had just been ironed.

"I'm just looking," Katie said, hoping he would go away. She didn't like the way he was eyeing her. As if she were a chocolate he wanted to pluck from the box. She needed to find Charlie and get out of here.

As if summoned, her boyfriend rounded the corner with a canvas in his hands.

"This painting is incredible. Who painted this?" Charlie turned the canvas around, so the shopkeeper could see it. In her opinion, it looked like a passable attempt at recreating a puddle of spilled spaghetti sauce.

The shopkeeper stood. "That was done by one of our local artists. I can find the name if you'd like."

"Please," said Charlie.

When they were alone, Katie grabbed Charlie's sleeve. "Can we go? I'm tired."

He shook her off without glancing at her. The painting had his complete attention. "Just a couple more minutes."

"I think I got too much sun today," Katie said. "I should lie down. Please, let's go home."

Charlie sighed. He set the painting down and turned to her with narrowed eyes. "You always want to leave."

"Not always," she protested.

"I never complain when you make me go to the mall with you to purchase yet another lipstick that you're just going to lose in the bottom of your purse."

"When was the last time we even went to the mall? We've been to four antique stores this weekend alone!"

"I haven't found what I'm looking for yet."

Katie folded her arms over her chest. "And what's that?"

He threw up his hands. "You wouldn't understand."

"I wouldn't? Do you even know what you want? Where does it end, Charlie? With us spending every weekend arguing in antique stores, over and over again until one of us gives up or dies?"

Charlie pointed a finger at her. "You always turn it into a fight."

"You never listen to what I want."

"Because you don't compromise. If you'd just let me have five minutes to look around…"

"We've been here longer than that. At least ten minutes."

"Because you're distracting me, Katie. How am I supposed to take a good look around with you constantly whining and pulling at my sleeve?"

Katie gritted her teeth. "I do not whine."

"Excuse me." The shopkeeper smiled politely at them. "The name of that artist is Timothy Pollard."

Charlie nodded, as if he knew exactly who that was. Katie rolled her eyes.

The shopkeeper took a step toward her. "You didn't seem very impressed with the painting so I thought you might like this instead."

She heard Charlie gasp as the old man turned the object he was holding in his hands to face her. An antique silver mirror with a filigreed handle, tarnished in places and the surface of the glass spotted with age. But worse than the imperfections of the piece was the face staring back at her in the mirror.

To her horror, Katie now saw that a bloom of pink colored her cheeks and nose. Her freckles, which she tried to keep concealed under layers of carefully applied makeup, had multiplied exponentially in the sun. Strands of blond hair hung limply around her face like greasy noodles.

Katie tore her gaze away from the mirror. She had to get home before someone she knew saw her like this. "Charlie, we're leaving." She tried her best to sound assertive, as if her words brooked no argument.

But Charlie either didn't hear her or didn't care. In his hands, he now held a ceramic elephant, about the size of a grapefruit, stylized and covered in a mosaic of colorful tiles.

She knew why it had caught his eye; Charlie used to have a similar one. Until Katie had knocked it over on their first anniversary and its destruction had seriously brought into question whether they would see another year.

"How much is this?" Charlie asked, turning to the shopkeeper.

"I'm afraid that one's not for sale."

"How much, though? One hundred dollars? Two hundred?"

"I'm sorry, but it isn't for sale."

"Two-fifty?"

"Let's go, Charlie," Katie said. She raised her voice. "I mean it. It's me or that stupid elephant."

But her boyfriend continued to ignore her and took a step toward the shopkeeper. "Come on. Everything's for sale for the right price. Just give me a number. I'm not leaving without it."

A cloud of dark smoke suddenly stung Katie's eyes and made them water. She squeezed them shut and coughed as the smoke tickled her throat.

When she opened them again, the smoke had cleared, and she was alone with the shopkeeper. Charlie was nowhere to be seen. On the carpet, the ceramic elephant lay on its side.

"Charlie?" She looked around but didn't see him anywhere. She hadn't closed her eyes for long. How could he have moved that fast?

The shopkeeper stooped to pick up the elephant from the carpet. It seemed to shimmer as he laid his hands on it. A trick of the light, perhaps.

"Did you see where my boyfriend went?"

The old man shrugged. "You said you wanted to leave. Now you're free to go."

Katie blinked. "You didn't answer my question."

"Didn't I, though?"

"Where's Charlie?" She hated how her voice quivered as she said his name.

In response, the man turned and walked away from her, heading deeper into the store.

"Hey!" Katie yelled as she followed him. "I was talking to you."

The shopkeeper glanced over his shoulder at her but did not stop until he was standing in front of an enormous curio cabinet. He unlatched the doors and Katie could see that there was an empty space on the top shelf, just wide enough to accommodate a ceramic elephant.

"What do you want with this man, anyway?" the shopkeeper asked as he slid the elephant onto the shelf where it belonged. "There are other, better specimens."

The elephant glittered in the late afternoon sun.

"Other, better specimens?" Katie asked. "What happened to Charlie?'

There was a twinkle in the shopkeeper's eye as he smiled. "I think you know what happened to Charlie."

She looked from the cabinet to the man and back again, a pit of dread growing in her stomach.

"What have you done?"

"You gave him a choice. He chose."

"He's not..."

"Dead? No. Not dead. Suspended. Like a mosquito in amber."

"But he's inside that elephant?"

"His soul is."

Her pulse pounded in her ears and she felt dizzy. She wanted to believe the man was lying to her, that his mind was simply addled by age. But what other explanation was there? One moment Charlie was there, demanding the man give him a price for the elephant and then, with a puff of smoke, he was gone.

"He didn't deserve this," she said. "Not at all."

The man looked annoyed. "You're deceiving yourself, Katie.

You were there. You told him to choose you or the elephant. I'm sure that wasn't the first time you've felt as if your own existence paled in comparison to the latest trinket or artifact he happened to stumble upon. No, I'm sure this has happened many times before."

He was right. Katie knew he was right. But she loved Charlie with everything she was.

"Give him back." She felt her hands curl into fists at her sides but forced herself to relax. Attacking the old man wasn't going to make him any more inclined to help her. And she needed his help to get Charlie back.

"I'm afraid I can't. I never intended for it to be reversible." His tone was so certain, so final that she knew he wasn't lying.

Katie stared at the Charlie-elephant in the curio cabinet as tears blurred her vision. What was she going to do now? She couldn't just leave him here. All alone, sandwiched between a gilded tiger and a monkey in a fez hat. Her eyes kept moving along the shelf, taking in the crocodile with its yawning jaws, the parrot with ruby eyes, and on and on. She gasped.

"They're not…all of them?"

The man gave a curt nod. "But don't mistake them for people who deserve your sympathy. Every one of them stumbled in here, blinded by their greed, and quite willingly walked into the trap I laid."

She thought she might be sick as her eyes roamed around the antique store, taking in the sheer number of figurines packed onto shelves. There must have been hundreds of them.

"It's not just the statues," the man said. "Everything you see in this store is enchanted."

Katie put a hand out to steady herself as the blood roared in her ears. Hundreds upon hundreds of people just like Charlie. "Everything? How could you do this to them?"

"Imagine a garden party, Katie. One with plates of finger sandwiches, fresh fruit, colorful macaroons, and pitcher after pitcher of iced tea. A lovely event that can only be ruined by one thing," the man said. "The inevitable arrival of a cloud of buzzing flies, drawn by the aroma of food. You can't stop it from happening. Unless, perhaps, you catch them first. I find a jar of honey to be quite suitable for such an occasion."

"Is that how you describe it? Catching flies with honey? Those are people in there."

She took a breath. For courage. "And I suppose I'm next."

He shook his head. "No, Katie. You're free to go."

She stared at him, searching his face to see if he was joking. "Free to go? Why not me?" she asked.

"Why not you? Because you're a guest at the garden party, Katie."

She squeezed her eyes shut. They'd been planning their wedding. Charlie had told her he was shopping for the perfect ring. She'd begged him to buy her something modern, not anything that came from a glass case in an antique store. They'd fought over it, but in the end, she'd won that round. After all, if she was going to have to stare at the ring every day for the rest of her life, it ought to be something she liked.

They had vacationed with each other's families. They shared a bank account. They'd been looking at condos together. They were planning to get a puppy in the fall. Everything was going according to plan.

And yet. Now she was free to go, free to walk back into a different life. A life without Charlie. Loving Charlie had never been easy. She had always come second to whatever item he'd toted home from the flea market. The brass candlesticks, the first editions, the porcelain figurines, all of it capable of eliciting more affection from him than she ever had. She remembered the stinging slap he'd dealt her after she'd broken his elephant. She could almost feel the way his hand had closed around her wrist, squeezing until she thought he would snap it. The wild look he'd had in his eyes as he'd yelled at her and called her all kinds of vile things. When he kissed her, those words still returned again and again to her mind, no matter how hard she tried to forget them.

A few tears slipped down her cheeks, stinging her sunburned skin. As she wiped them away, she suddenly thought of Morocco. A place she'd wanted to visit for years. But Charlie had always said no, had always said traveling outside the country cost too much.

Katie blinked her tears away and promised herself she would go. She would see the markets of Marrakesh. Visit a sultan's palace. Ride a camel through the desert. Do all the things she'd always wanted to do now that she had no one to tell her no.

"Do not misunderstand me," the man continued. "You're certainly flawed. You're vain and at times, selfish. But you're not disposed to greed. Not as he was."

"Is greedy really the worst thing a person can be? And who are you to judge?"

She watched the shopkeeper's face as he considered her words. He suddenly looked very, very tired and she wondered how old he was. And what he was.

"I have walked this Earth for a long time. Longer than you can fathom. Greed brings war. It tears people apart. It causes love to whither on the vine. Perhaps greed is not the worst of all sins, but it is among the most destructive. As for who I am, it is irrelevant. It does not change his fate."

She took a breath. "I don't understand why you'd let me go, after everything I've seen here today."

He shook his head. "Once you walk out that door, you will never return. This place won't open for you. It was intended for Charlie."

"But I walked in on my own."

"You were accidentally caught up in the enchantment. Like one of those fishing nets you humans are so fond of using. Now I'm releasing you. So, go home Katie."

She hesitated, just for a moment. Then she pointed to the Charlie-elephant. "Not without him."

"I can't let you do that."

Katie crossed her arms over her chest. "You can and you will."

Amusement glittered in his eyes. "Are you threatening me?"

Her insides turned to ice at his words, but she fought to keep her voice steady as she replied, "Not a threat. You said it yourself: what's done cannot be undone. So, it won't matter if he stays here with you or goes with me."

The man rubbed his chin. "It has never been done before. I don't know that his soul will continue to live on if you take him from this place."

"Then I would be doing him an even greater kindness."

The man studied her for a long moment, appraising her like one of his antiques. Katie forced herself to meet his gaze, though her skin crawled from his attention.

After a long moment, he nodded. "You are the first person who has ever been unintentionally caught in my trap. So, I suppose it's only fitting that you will be the first person to ever remove an object from my store. If you understand the risk to Charlie and wish to proceed anyway, I will let you take him with you."

She nodded. "I have to believe he truly loved me. And that he would do the same if our roles were reversed."

The shopkeeper unlocked the curio cabinet and picked up the elephant. He stroked its trunk for a moment, before placing it in her outstretched hands and gently folding her fingers around it.

"It is not my place to speculate on human relationships," the man said. "But I agree he loved you. As he loved all the objects he possessed."

With that, Katie suddenly felt a crushing pressure in her skull as the man and the shop around him twisted, blurred, and disappeared.

She found herself standing on the sidewalk out front, facing an empty storefront, with the elephant in her hands. It was still late afternoon and the sunlight reflecting off the mosaic of tiles that formed the elephant's hide momentarily blinded her. She blinked against the glare and slipped the elephant in her pocket.

The statue of the stone angel still stood out front. Its hands, now empty of the laminated placard, beckoned to her.

The shopkeeper had said that everything inside the store was enchanted. She'd taken that to mean that the figure outside was just a normal statue. But as she stared at the orphaned statue of the angel, she felt a shiver run down her spine and walked quickly away. Perhaps it wasn't enchanted as the others were, but there was still something unnatural about it.

On the way back to the car, a window display caught her eye. The TV screen inside displayed the words, "Nobody loves you like you do" in bright, rainbow colors. She'd never noticed this store before. Perhaps it was new. Katie watched the TV until the words faded out and were replaced with the brand's logo: Vanity Outfitters.

Katie felt as if she'd been plunged into ice water. She glanced down the street toward where the antique store had been.

Could it be?

She closed her fingers around the elephant in her pocket and turned away from the window.

Shannon Fox lives in San Diego, California, though she was born and raised in Arvada, Colorado. She moved to California to attend UC-San Diego where she graduated with a B.A. in Literature-Writing. Her short stories have appeared in the *Plaid Horse* magazine, *Black Fox Literary Magazine*, the *Copperfield Review*, the *Fat City Review* and more. She has also authored over 200 articles and blog posts for online and print publication, including a co-authored piece in *Scientific American Mind* magazine. She owns her own marketing company and blogs about writing and life on her website www.Shannon-Fox.com.

THE BAD JU-JU CRUISE

LAURYN CHRISTOPHER

THE BAD JU-JU CRUISE

"One of my kids—one of your kids, for that matter—might have made that thing in kindergarten," said Kate, tugging Roz away from the artifact vendor booth and the fist-sized clay statuette that squelched on the table like a misshapen toad.

Kate smiled at the vendor, who nodded back at her, his grin revealing a mouthful of stained teeth. She didn't know how much English he spoke, if any, but she didn't want to offend him. During their single day in the Mexican port city of Ensenada, they'd discovered that many people spoke passable English, some of them far better than her own limited Spanish.

Kate leaned close to her best friend's ear. "For all you know, his family is in the back room making more of these ugly little clay statues. What on earth do you want this one for?"

"I don't know," said Roz. "I just do. It's a collectible. It speaks to me—"

"It needs a translator."

"Come on," Kate said. She let go of Roz's arm to check her watch as she walked. "The ship sails in less than an hour. We need to find a taxi and get back, or we'll be stuck here—Oh, good God!"

Roz had gone back to the artifact vendor's booth.

Fine, Kate thought. If Roz wanted to waste her money on fake Mexican artifacts, she wasn't going to stop her. She wasn't her babysitter. At least this time the thing she was going nuts over was something small enough to fit in her pocket.

The last time Roz had fixated on something it was an antique treadle sewing machine they'd found at a flea market. Roz had paid a ridiculous amount of money for the thing—it didn't even work—and then it wouldn't fit in the back of the Prius. They'd had to call Kate's brother, Sam, and wait until he could come out with his pickup truck to take it to Roz's house.

So, she'd wait while Roz bought her little blob of clay. In the meantime, the booth right next door to the artifact vendor sold bargain-priced, refurbished electronics, and she needed another memory card for her camera.

"I'll be right here," she shouted to Roz. When Roz waved, indicating that she'd heard, Kate turned her attention to the electronics booth. She knew exactly what she wanted, and if the vendor had the memory cards she was looking for, she was fully prepared to go to the mat to argue the price down.

Roz waved Kate away and moved back to the artifact vendor's booth. It was probably just junk, but the squelchy toad had captured her attention more than anything else she'd seen during the entire day of touring around Ensenada, and she'd seen plenty.

And bought plenty, too.

None of it was all that valuable, but the whole point of the cruise had been for both she and Kate to take a few days off from the round-the-clock duties of being single moms to energetic preteens, forget their ex-husbands, and just have fun. Roz had gone into full tourist mode and was having a blast. Her oversize shoulder bag was stuffed with long scarves in colorful prints, hand-embroidered sundresses, trinkets for the kids, and tons of cheap silver jewelry.

But the squelchy toad artifact just kept calling to her.

And when something called to her like that, she had to buy it. It was that simple.

"How much?" she said, pointing to it.

"No for sale," said the vendor, shaking his head. He picked up a different artifact and held it up for her inspection. "You like this. Five dollar."

"No," Roz said, reaching for the squelchy toad. "I like this one."

The vendor moved it from the center of the table to the back. "No for sale," he said again. He pointed to the row of small sun god carvings along the opposite side of the table. "All good. Three dollar."

Roz reached into her purse and pulled out a five-dollar bill. "Five dollars," she said, pointing to the squelchy toad.

"No," said the vendor, shaking his head emphatically. He picked up the squelchy toad and put it into a box just behind the table.

Roz could just see the top of its head. Assuming that it was a toad, and that the rounded part she thought of as its head was, in fact, its head.

"Look," she said. "I really want that thing."

She couldn't explain why and didn't even try. Instead, she plopped her purse down on the table and started digging through it. "What will you take for it?" She started pulling things from her purse and extolling their virtues to the increasingly agitated vendor. She pulled out nail clippers and lip balm, reading glasses and a tiny sewing kit. "You can't have my phone – I need that, but I've even got American chocolate." She held up a candy bar that hadn't gone too squishy yet.

The vendor just stared at her like she'd gone mad. If he

understood a word she'd said, he chose not to reply; but he'd inched backward until he was standing near the back of the booth.

"That's right, back away from the crazy lady," Roz muttered. "I get that a lot." Then, louder, she continued. "Okay, you drive a hard bargain." Pulling her wallet out of her bag, she opened it up and tipped it over, coins and bills plunking down onto the table.

The vendor eased closer.

"Yeah, I thought that would get you," she said. "Cold, hard cash, my friend. That should be somewhere in the neighborhood of two hundred and thirty or forty dollars. And change."

Another customer came over and started asking questions about the miniature sun god carvings. Roz ignored him.

And then she realized that she had an opportunity.

Quickly she scooped her things back into her bag—leaving the money on the table—then leaned across, reached into the box, and retrieved the squelchy toad.

"Hey!" shouted the vendor, who turned back and saw her just as she was standing back up.

Roz pointed at the money on the table. "I paid for it," she said, dropping the figurine into her bag and moving away from the table.

"No sell. No sell! Stop!" shouted the vendor in his halting English. When she kept backing away, he started rattling off God-knew-what in Spanish, scooping up a double-handful of the money she'd dumped on the table and thrusting it toward her.

Roz turned and fled. It suddenly seemed like there were many more people crowding the mercado than she'd noticed before. With the vendor still shouting behind her, and several people turning to look, Roz ran to the next booth, and grabbed Kate by the arm.

"Come on," she said, practically dragging her friend away. "We've got to get back to the boat."

"What did you do?" Kate said, breathless, as soon as they made it out of the mercado and were safely tucked inside a little car that claimed to be a taxi. The old car was cramped, smelled of sweat and chickens, and had a heavy rosary hanging from the rear-view mirror. The windshield was so decorated with rickrack and photos of various saints that Kate was amazed the driver could actually see out of it.

"Are we heading toward the harbor?" Roz asked, looking out the window.

"I hope so," said Kate. "I think that's where I told him we wanted to go. So, what did you do back there? And don't think I'm going to let you avoid the question."

"I bought the figurine." Roz was still looking out the window. A bad sign, in Kate's opinion.

"And...?"

"And what?"

"And why was the vendor yelling?"

"Was someone yelling?"

Kate smacked Roz on the arm. "Whatever. Maybe it's better I don't know. That way, when we end up in a Mexican jail, I can honestly say I have no idea what's going on."

"I really did buy it," Roz protested, turning to face Kate. "I gave him all the cash I had on me—"

"How much?" Kate asked warily.

"I don't know. A couple hundred dollars—"

"Why?"

Roz sat there, opening and closing her mouth like a fish before finally mumbling "I don't know. I just had to have this." She fished the artifact out of her purse and sat there, holding it.

Kate looked at the figurine. "So, you paid the guy a couple hundred bucks for a blob of clay and he's yelling at you?" she said, with exaggerated patience. "Have I got it? Or have you left out a detail or two again?"

"He didn't actually want to sell it."

Kate leaned her head back with a sigh. There was no headrest attached to her seat, so she found herself looking up at the roof of the taxi, and the sixty billion postcards of the Virgin Mary and other saints that were plastered above her. She wasn't Catholic, but at that moment, felt a strong desire to cross herself, maybe say a prayer or two. It couldn't hurt.

At least she didn't feel the urge to confess. Roz hadn't pushed her that far. Yet.

"Well, we can't go back. We don't have time," she said, turning her head to look at Roz. "I guess you're stuck with an expensive lump of clay."

Roz fidgeted, stroking the squelchy toad she held in her hands. They rode quietly for a few minutes, before she finally spoke.

"Why do you suppose he was so determined to not sell it to me?"

"I don't know," Kate said. "Maybe his kid really did make it for him and it's his favorite good luck charm. For all we know, it might have been the only genuine artifact on his table. On the other hand, maybe it's like in the movies, and it has jewels or something hidden inside—"

"I'm not breaking it open."

"Didn't say you had to. But if you have it x-rayed and find it's full of precious stones or something, I'm claiming my half now."

"I don't think this is the way to the harbor," Roz said after several minutes—and several turns—later. They were driving through a shabby neighborhood, one definitely out of the usual tourist-trap parts of town.

Kate leaned forward and tapped the driver on the shoulder. "Adonde vamos?" she asked, hoping she was getting the words for 'where are we going?' right. "A el barco grande turista, mas rapido, por favor?"

The driver rattled off something mostly unintelligible in Spanish, his words coming out rapid-fire as he U-turned the taxi and they sped off in a different direction.

"What did he say?" asked Roz.

"I have no idea," Kate replied. "I was trying to ask if we could get to the big tourist boat as fast as possible – but I'm not even sure if I got that much right."

"We're gonna miss the boat," said Roz. She had a sinking feeling in the pit of her stomach that was challenging a rising panic. "Then what will we do? My feet are killing me, and I spent all my cash. Do you have any money? I have my credit cards, but we don't know anyone here and—"

"If we miss the boat, we'll walk into the cruise line's office and ask for help," Kate said simply, cutting her off. "It's just a bit of bad luck, not the end of the world. I'm sure we won't be the first stranded tourists they've had to deal with."

❧

Roz was basking in all the attention. Missing the boat had been a pain, but she'd flirted shamelessly with the crew of the little tugboat, and now they were tripping over themselves to be helpful as they chugged their way toward the still slow-moving ocean liner.

Language barriers be dammed. Some of those guys were cute, and her ex wasn't around to disapprove. Besides, it wasn't like she was ever going to see them again.

And then they reached the cruise ship. The crew had been polite enough about helping them aboard, but the passengers who'd gathered to watch from the rail above cheered enough to make up for the crewmembers' lack of enthusiasm for their unorthodox boarding.

"We made it!" she called out when she finally stepped on

board. Clutching the doorframe, she leaned out of the still open doorway and blew kisses at tugboat crew; then, swooping off her wide-brimmed tourist hat in a grand gesture, waved to the crowd above. "Thank you, thank you!"

"Oh, come on," Kate growled, grabbing her by the arm and dragging her away from the door and disapproving crewmembers and down the hall in the general direction of their cabin. "I just hope that stupid good luck charm was worth it."

"Hey, it got us here, didn't it?"

"After making us miss the boat," Kate said. "If it's going to give out good luck and bad luck in shares like that, I'm not so sure that's a good thing."

Roz pooh-poohed the idea. "Don't be such a downer," she said, stopping in the hallway and balancing herself by grasping the frame of a conveniently open cabin door with one hand while she reached down to tug off her shoes with the other. "I hate these shoes," she said. "Cute, but my feet are killing me."

She was standing there, stuffing the first shoe into her bag, when the occupant of the room—clearly oblivious to Roz's use of the doorframe—let the cabin door swing closed.

On Roz's hand.

"It could have been worse," Kate repeated for the umpteenth time. "At least nothing's broken—"

"We don't know that. The doctor distinctly said he really couldn't tell without X-rays," Roz said, waving her heavily-wrapped hand in the air.

The pain medicine would kick in soon, Kate hoped.

"Is it dinnertime?" Roz asked. "The doctor said I should take the medicine with food."

"Yeah, our seating is in just a few minutes."

Roz grabbed the squelchy toad.

"What do you want that for?" Kate asked.

"Show and tell," Roz said with a grin. "You should bring something to dinner, too."

Kate shook her head. "Don't need to bring anything," she said, smiling sweetly. "I've got you."

At dinner, Roz regaled their tablemates with the story—somewhat modified—of how she acquired the figurine. The pain meds appeared to have kicked in, and Roz was in high form, talking excitedly, and gesturing with her bandaged hand.

"Obviously, I suck at negotiating prices," Roz said, laughing, as she concluded. Everyone at their table was listening and laughing along with her. "But I got what I wanted, and that's all that mattered."

"May I see it?" asked one woman.

"Of course," Roz said, passing the squelchy toad around the table. The man to her right looked at it, but as he handed it to his neighbor, his shirtsleeve dragged across his plate and through a puddle of marinara.

The next person to handle it passed it on without a problem, then burned her mouth on a too-hot sip of tea. As the squelchy toad made its way around the table, a little cloud of chaos followed—a fork fell to the floor, a wineglass tipped into someone's lap. By the time the figurine made it all the way around the table to Kate, people were passing it quickly, not even looking at it before handing it along like a hot potato. The tension at the table was rising with each little accident.

When the squelchy toad got to her, Kate didn't even touch it. She just tossed her napkin over it. "Bad juju," she said, laughing.

Everyone laughed—everyone except Roz—and people started telling stories about lucky charms, cursed artifacts, and mysterious deaths.

"None of those things have been conclusively traced to old curses," Roz said. Everyone had finished eating, and a waiter was moving quietly around the table collecting the empty dishes. "It's all just a series of coincidences."

"Pretty bizarre coincidences, if you ask me," said a professorial man on the opposite side of the large round table.

Kate was listening to the conversation, didn't register what was happening at first when the waiter reached for the napkin covering the figurine.

And then it seemed to her as though everything happened in slow motion.

The waiter picked up the bundle.

Kate turned in her chair.

The waiter stepped back, colliding with another waiter who was passing just behind him.

Their trays flew.

The squelchy toad landed with a thud on the floor, between Kate's and Roz' chairs.

As spilled trays and their contents clattered to the ground around them, Kate and Roz both reached for the artifact at the same time, the tops of their heads brushing, but not quite colliding.

"Put that thing away!" hissed Kate as Roz's fingers closed on the figurine.

And for once, Roz didn't argue, but quietly slipped the figurine back into her pocket.

❖

Much later that night, Roz lay on her bed, flat on her back, with one knee raised. The squelchy toad perched on her knee, its odd little clay face looking at her through narrow eyes.

"Do you really think it's cursed?" she asked.

"Dunno," Kate mumbled from her own bed, not looking up from the e-book she was reading. "I suppose it could be."

Roz didn't want to think about it. She liked the figurine—but didn't like the idea that she'd managed to steal a cursed artifact. Even after she fell asleep, the idea persisted, as hordes of ugly clay squelchy toads chased her through her dreams.

She ran. Away from the toads, toward a huge bonfire.
And then, abruptly, she was awake.

"Kate," she hissed. "Wake up!"

Kate moaned from the other bed.

"Do you feel that? The ship's not moving!"

Roz sat up, turned the switch on the bedside lamp, but nothing happened. She reached over and shook Kate. "Wake up," she said again, more urgently this time. "There's no light."

"That's because it's night and we're supposed to be sleeping," mumbled Kate. "Easier to do in the dark."

"No, don't you feel that? There's no engine noise, either. We're not moving."

Kate finally sat up; Roz could tell because her voice was no longer muffled by her pillow but came from a little higher. "Okay, so what do you propose we do about it?" she asked.

"We go see what's going on," Roz said. She was already reaching for the bathrobe she'd left somewhere near the foot of her bed.

"Right," Kate said. "Because the ship doesn't have any staff to handle things like that, and really needs your expert help, oh venerable cruise ship engine expert?"

"Come on!"

Kate sighed, but Roz could hear her fumbling around. A moment later, a large glowing rectangle shone in the darkness.

"My e-reader," Kate explained, tilting the tablet around, using the screen's glow to illuminate the dark, windowless cabin. "But my phone has a flashlight app on it that will probably work better."

"I have a little light on my key ring," Roz exclaimed, fumbling in the dark to find her bag and her keys. When she ran across the squelchy toad in the darkness, she slipped it into one of the bathrobe's oversize pockets, where it settled like an oddly comforting weight.

A few minutes later Kate and Roz—wearing pajamas, fluffy cruise ship bathrobes, and tennis shoes and equipped with a tiny key light and a cell phone flashlight—were creeping along the hallway.

"It's creepy, how quiet it is here," said Kate.

"I didn't notice the engine noise that much until it stopped," said Roz. "I think that's what woke me up."

"Do you smell that?" Roz said.

"Yeah," said Kate. "It's just like Jake's seventh-grade science project. Burning plastic. Had to keep the windows open for days to clear the air in the house. Was glad the weather cooperated…" her voice trailed off.

"I don't like this."

"You and me both. So why are we heading toward the smell instead of away from it?"

"Because we need to know what's going on," Roz insisted, leading the way down the hall.

They reached the elevators, looked at each other, and passed them without a word, heading for the stairwell instead. The smell of burning plastic and wiring was worse here, and Roz smacked herself in the face with her bandaged hand as she reached up to cover her nose.

They went cautiously down the stairs, peering out into the hallway at each level. Their own cabin was on the lowest of the passenger levels, but the crew-level hallways seemed eerily silent.

The emergency alert sounded just as they reached the engine level, a man's calm voice instructing all passengers to proceed at once to their assigned muster stations on the upper decks. Kate tugged at her sleeve, but Roz ignored both her and the alert, and pushed open the engine level door.

All the silence of the upper decks was made up for here. Crewmembers, panicking in several languages Roz didn't understand, were rushing up and down the hallway, flashlights bobbing at crazy angles. Everyone was coughing and choking in the smoke-filled air.

"Look," Roz hissed, pointing toward the end of the hallway.

Flashlights illuminated clouds of smoke pouring out a hatchway; darkened abruptly as the hatch was closed.

"What are you doing here?" a gruff voice demanded, shining a bright light directly into their faces. "This area is off-limits to passengers."

Roz looked up but couldn't see beyond the light to identify the speaker.

"We wanted to know what was going on," she squeaked.

"Nothing. Just a drill," the gruff voice replied. He swung the flashlight upward as he spoke. "You heard the announcement. 'Passengers are to go upstairs to their muster stations'" He practically pushed them back into the stairwell, closing the door behind them.

"A drill? Like anyone's gonna believe that one," Roz said, pulling the door open. A broad back blocked their way.

"Go upstairs!" It was the gruff voice again.

Roz started to protest, but Kate reached over and closed the door. "Come on," she said. "We can't do anything down here anyway."

They retraced their route back up the stairs, climbing cautiously in the dark, with only their tiny flashlights to guide them. They had nearly reached their own level before the emergency lighting switched on, making it easier to continue up the next three flights. Other passengers, still groggy from sleep, joined them at each level, awakened by the room stewards who were moving from cabin to cabin, knocking on doors and trying to keep everyone calm as other crewmembers guided people toward the muster stations.

"What's going on?" was an oft-repeated question, though no one seemed to have an answer.

"Bad juju," Roz murmured under her breath, the weight of the squelchy toad heavy in her pocket.

The ship limped toward shore on one engine. The cruise director made frequent, entertaining announcements over the PA system, trying to keep everyone's spirits up, but rumors of "bad juju" washed over the ship like a wave.

"It's not the figurine," Roz wailed, standing alone with Kate near the rail, watching the California coast creep slowly closer. "It can't be."

"You don't know that," Kate countered. "You have to admit, things got weird from the moment you first saw it."

"What do you want me to do? Throw it into the ocean? If it really is bad juju, it will boil up a tsunami or something."

"Yeah, and if you stand here on the rail with it long enough, a shark is gonna jump out of the water and eat you," teased Kate.

Roz glared at her.

Kate laughed. "I'm kidding and you know it," she said. "It's not just the figurine—"

"Thanks."

"—it's you." Kate continued. "You're cursed, Roz."

"That's total nonsense, and you know it."

"You drove up to San Francisco and the fog rolled in so thick it shut the freeway down for six hours. You went to Chicago, and a blizzard shut down the airport. When we were in Miami—"

"You can't blame the hurricane on me," Roz said, picking at the bright red acrylic fingernails she'd had done at the beginning of the cruise. "Nobody expected it to head north."

"That's my point. Nobody expected it to, but it did. And three days stranded in a Miami bus station wasn't my idea of fun."

"Some of the guys were cute. Admit it."

Kate just looked at her, one eyebrow raised. "Oh, come on. No showers, no toothpaste, the same clothes for three days, and nothing but vending machine food—"

"You're just focusing on the bad part—"

"Yeah. Because there wasn't a good part."

"It's not like you can blame me for that."

"Sure I can," Kate said. "You're cursed, Roz. Pure and simple. I don't know what you did in whichever past life to earn it, but you've got terrible karma and stuff happens when you're around—don't even try to deny it—and it mostly happens to the people who are around you. The figurine recognized you as a kindred spirit. It's a perfect totem for you, actually."

Roz looked at Kate, mouth hanging open. "You really mean that."

"I'm just telling it like I see it," Kate said with a shrug. "What else are best friends for?"

"You think I'm bad luck, but you hang around with me anyway?"

"Somebody's got to look after you, protect everyone else. Or at least try to minimize the damage," Kate said. She reached over and took the squelchy toad from Roz' hand. "I think Bad Juju Toad here will look great in your kitchen window," she said. "Might scare the mouse out of your kitchen."

"I've got a mouse in my kitchen?" Roz squeaked.

"Like I said," Kate said, leaning on the rail and looking out over the water. "Someone's got to take care of you."

"Humph," Roz said. "I do just fine on my own. Most of the time." Then a sly smile flicked over her lips and she fished in her pocket and pulled out the squelchy toad, holding it up in front of her face. "Whaddya say, kid," she murmured to it. "Wanna help me get even with a certain cheating scumbag of an ex-husband?"

The toad just squelched there on her palm, but Roz could have sworn she felt a tingle run through her that was more than just the breeze off the ocean. She looked over at Kate and raised an eyebrow. "Well?"

Kate laughed. "Count me in. That's a bit of bad juju I can fully support."

. . .

Lauryn Christopher has written marketing and technical material for the computer industry for too many years to admit. In her spare time, she reads a lot and writes mysteries, often from the criminal's point of view. Her "Hit Lady for Hire" series has a second novel scheduled for release in the summer of 2019. Lauryn is a frequent contributor to short story anthologies. You can find information and links to more of her work, and sign up for her occasional newsletter, at www.laurynchristopher.com.

REQUIEM

MARK LESLIE

REQUIEM

Peter Drebonier III clapped his hands together as the auctioneer bellowed, "Sold!" and brought his gavel down hard, signaling an end to the seemingly endless flow of verbal diarrhea. "To the man in the blue suit for three hundred thousand dollars."

Peter's rounded belly hitched with a chuckle he could not contain.

My very own haunted bureau, he thought. For practically a steal.

Getting the bureau home would not be a problem, but he would have to tip the movers an exorbitant sum so they'd be extra careful with it. After all, Peter had been attempting to get his hands on this little bureau — known in certain circles as "Victoria's Cabinet" — for almost eight years. When he'd heard the museum was auctioning off most of the items in their Victorian wing, he'd been filled with delight.

No, more than delight. Rapture.

The tales told about "Vicky's Cabinet" were legendary. This would push Peter's collection of haunted items over the top, making it, by far, the most envious collection in the world. He knew the security guards working at the museum would breathe a sigh of relief to know that the bureau was being removed from the premises. Peter could barely contain his excitement in getting the bureau home and seeing for himself if the legends were true.

As he watched the burly men heft the heavy cabinet into the back of the moving truck, Peter sighed. Though the cabinet was covered, he could still see in his mind the wide decorative drawers that jutted out from where the thick glass of the mirror sat in the intricately detailed wood-carved frame. He couldn't wait to glance into that mirror and see what had frightened more than one security guard from ever entering the Victorian wing of the museum in the middle of the night.

"Let's go, boys," Peter grinned, rubbing his palms together. "There's an extra five hundred dollars in it for each of you if we arrive in the next half hour."

Peter gazed in the mirror at the image of the young woman who was maybe nineteen or twenty years old, with the exact blue bow and matching dress that had been described to him over and over by terrified security personnel. He smiled happily to himself as he looked at the girl the museum personnel had dubbed "Vicky" after the era the bureau had come from.

After all those purchases, he thought, after all these years, I finally own a real ghost. He looked away from the mirror at his classically furnished living room. One of the movers had injured himself trying to get the bureau up the staircase and into the special room where Peter kept all of his allegedly haunted items. And Peter was in such a good mood about owning this bureau that he was willing to let them come back another day to finish moving it upstairs. So he sent them all away, without their tip. "The five-hundred-dollar tip," he'd told them, "is for when you come back after the weekend and finish the job." They offered to return within a few hours with another man, but Peter thought it would be best if he could have some time alone with his new prized possession.

Turning his eyes back to the mirror, Peter intently watched the image of young Vicky in the mirror. He noticed how she gazed wistfully into the mirror as she moved about and fiddled with the bow in her hair. Then, after several minutes, as if still disappointed, but satisfied for the moment with how she looked, Vicky let go of the bow, shrugged and turned from the mirror. Then her image disappeared.

After another moment, Vicky reappeared in the mirror in the same pose she had first been in, struggling with the tiny blue bow. Peter watched, a chill running down his spine, as she re-enacted the exact same scene he had just witnessed.

How beautiful she looked, this ghost he now owned. But also, how sad and forlorn. He felt that he could understand just how she felt as she fixed herself in the mirror. For, many times in his life, Peter too had gazed into his own mirror, trying to adjust the way his suit fit the pudgy body he was cursed with, but ultimately realizing there was nothing much he could do about it.

A tear strolled down Peter's cheek as Vicky stopped adjusting the bow, shrugged, turned and disappeared again.

Then the image replayed itself.

Peter watched her all afternoon.

And all afternoon he cried.

It was beautiful.

❖

After the movers left for the second time and Peter had tipped them generously, he climbed back up the stairs to the large, over-furnished room where "Vicky's Cabinet" now sat.

Having spent so much time with Vicky over the past few days, Peter had found himself drawn to her in many ways. Like a daughter he'd always wanted to dress up and look pretty — nicer than he'd ever be able to look; like a lover he'd never once had and could only watch and yearn for; like a friend which he had only fleeting memories of as a child. He watched Vicky's image and cried for the fact that his one companion in the world was a ghost from a time long past and could not see him.

Vicky was trapped in her own exact ritual, destined to perform it again and again. Never altering, never seeing what was going on around her. Never realizing how she was being watched, how she was being loved.

Yes, love.

Peter had found himself falling in love with Vicky, in every sense of the word. And why not? They were two similar souls. Each caught in their own rituals from which they could not escape. Why couldn't they be a couple? Sure, he would never be able to act upon his feelings for her, but at least he could dream and watch her.

Watch her, and care for her. Care for her, and long for her. Long for her and lust after her.

Watching her move, Peter had studied over and over the way her small breasts flowed beneath the fabric of her dress. Imagining that she was disrobing rather than fixing her bow, he felt the stirring in his loins and the beginning of an erection.

As Vicky shrugged and turned from the mirror, Peter brought his hand down to rub himself.

The image played itself over again, and Peter unzipped his pants to free his aching erection. Watching Vicky's eyes, wishing that just once her gaze would meet his own, he pumped his erect penis inside his fist and imagined her slipping her dress off of her shoulders.

"I love you, Vicky!" Peter cried aloud, wishing she could hear him. "Oh, how I love you." He closed his eyes as he orgasmed.

When Peter opened his eyes and looked into the mirror, he caught the image of a figure standing by the door. "Oh my God!" he yelled, aware of how his softening penis was exposed, sticky and dripping. It was probably one of the movers having returned. But how did he get back into the house past the alarm system?

Stuffing himself back into his pants, Peter turned, trying to come up with some sort of explanation for what he was doing.

But there was nobody at the door.

"What the hell?"

He turned, looked back in the mirror, and there stood the stranger beside the doorway, glaring. Whipping his head back and forth, Peter confirmed that he could only see the man in the mirror's reflection.

What the hell was going on?

Dressed in a navy-blue button-up front and shiny black tights, the stranger stood at the doorway and stared at Vicky. His blue eyes twinkled, and he grinned as he flipped his long flowing black hair from his face.

Just then, Vicky shrugged and turned from the mirror. Only, this time, she didn't disappear. She stopped as if startled by the man. The man's lips moved as if he were saying something, and he advanced on the girl.

"No. Vicky. Run," Peter heard himself scream. He didn't need to know what the man was saying to understand his intent.

The stranger grabbed Vicky by the shoulder and hauled her to the floor. One hand tearing off his own shirt, the man roughly mashed Vicky's left breast with the other. Seeing her pretty lips quivering, Peter guessed that Vicky was crying or screaming or some combination of the two.

In one solid quick gesture, the man tore open the front of Vicky's dress. Her small breasts hitched as she cried soundlessly. The stranger ran a hand along her cheek, down her neck and over her chest, flicking a finger across a nipple. Then he leaned down and covered one of the creamy white mounds with his mouth.

Viciously, the man bit down, drawing blood.

Falling to his knees, Peter screamed.

Something, a bad feeling, woke Peter suddenly.
He sat up in bed.
He listened.
But there was nothing.

Just the same, Peter thought that he should check it out. After all, he didn't want to find that a burglar had broken in and discovered his secret stash of highly valuable haunted artifacts.

As he threw his housecoat on and reached into his dresser drawer to pull out the 9mm pistol which he always kept loaded, Peter again regretted not hiring any full-time help around the mansion. He'd gotten rid of the maid, butler and cook as live-in servants after just three days of service. Though they were good people, Peter relished his privacy. He chose, instead, to call them in during the day to clean and cook and tend to his needs. But that decision had also left him alone every night, and potentially vulnerable.

Well, not really. There was the state-of-the-art security system which he'd had installed that kept even the tiniest of intruders from sneaking onto the mansion grounds. It had certainly cost him plenty, but it was worth it for the piece of mind it brought.

What piece of mind? he thought as he exited the bedroom and walked down the hall, the pistol pointing his way. Despite the illegal security system, with its under-the-table assurance that nobody could have possibly made it even close to the mansion alive, Peter was still nervous. While the programs which kept the house under tight surveillance were foolproof they were still part of a newly designed computer system. And computer systems could sometimes malfunction.

Peter couldn't be too careful. He was a wealthy man. And, though he considered himself a decent person, a wealthy man could have plenty of enemies he didn't even know about; people who hated and scorned him not because he had done anything to them, but merely because he was filthy rich and they were not.

When he arrived at the den, he reached in and flicked on the light switch. The room proved to be empty, except for a large wall unit which hosted half a dozen monitors and a large computer terminal.

Walking over to the security system, Peter surveyed it. None of the security cameras inside or out revealed any movement. The system was activated to the second highest level, so it was impossible to even get onto the mansion grounds without being seriously hurt, or, more probably, killed.

But, what if someone was inside already?

By pressing his thumb into the fingerprint scanner and simultaneously flicking a switch, Peter engaged the highest level of the system — the one which would not allow anyone to even leave the property. That way, if anyone somehow had gotten past the security system due to a flicker or hiccough in the system's program, they would be stopped on their way out — permanently.

Assured, Peter left the security den and then walked, a little more casually, to the closed door of the special room and listened.

Silence.

Remembering the scene he had witnessed that afternoon, Peter was almost hesitant to peer into the room. He didn't think he could bear to see anything more happen to the girl he had fallen in love with. It was too terrible a thing to watch, helplessly, unable to do anything while she screamed soundlessly for mercy.

Peter paused and took a deep breath, trying to erase the image from his mind.

He opened the door and scanned the room.

Except for the haunted objects — the table and chair set, the phonograph, the old wooden rocking chair, the Gaelic sword hanging on the wall, the empty cedar bookshelf, the Russian army boots, the seascape painting, the charred teddy bear, the purple scarf, the gold-rimmed spectacles, the daybed and the newly acquired bureau — the room was empty.

A flash of activity from the mirror caught Peter's eye.

Remembering the startling vision of the strange man attacking and raping the young and helpless Vicky, Peter forced himself to walk over to the bureau. He promised himself that this time he would not run screaming like a banshee if he saw the same horrific scene.

He got close enough to the mirror to peer in.

The reflection revealed that the seemingly empty room was alive with activity. At least a dozen people, of all shapes, sizes, ages, and cultures were either moving around the room or engaging in some sort of activity with one another.

In the corner by the table and chairs, an old gentleman wearing what looked like a military issue suit sat across from a younger man who looked like an extra out of an early 20's movie. They appeared to be partaking in a conversation which required much effort on their parts.

Beside them, on the rocking chair, sat an elderly woman wrapped in a shawl, staring fixedly at her hands, and rocking to a consistent beat.

Next to the old woman, a young man in a Scottish kilt stood in place playing a soundless set of bagpipes.

A few feet past the Scot, a young blonde woman with gold-rimmed spectacles sat with a knife, waving it a few inches above her wrist as if trying to work up the courage to press the blade into her flesh.

Standing above the blonde woman was the same dark maned man who had attacked and raped Vicky. Sweat gleamed off his bare muscular chest as he leered down at the woman while fastening his belt.

Taking another look at the woman, Peter noticed that her clothes hung on her strangely, as if torn and loose. He realized that this beast of a man must have just finished having his way with her.

Just like he'd had with Vicky.

Vicky.

Suddenly worried because he hadn't seen her, Peter searched the rest of the room. The fascination of seeing so many ghosts had shocked him into momentarily forgetting about the object of his recent love.

Beyond the rapist and his latest victim, Peter spied Vicky sitting in a corner of the room. She was involved in some type of conversation with a young boy who clutched at a teddy bear and didn't seem to be responding to her at all.

Poor Vicky, Peter thought, watching her try to communicate with the boy. Then, unable to watch her any longer, because seeing her torn blue dress brought back memories of the horror he'd witnessed that afternoon, he continued scanning the other ghosts.

All of these people involved in so many different activities.

But no noise.

That, more than anything, was what chilled Peter.

❖

Peter awoke a few hours later to a scream.

He clutched the 9mm to his chest and quickly bolted out of bed. Creeping down the hallway, he first checked to make sure the security system was still at its highest level, and then snuck back down to the haunted room.

From behind the closed door, he heard shuffling noises.

"This is it," Peter whispered, checking to make sure the safety was released on his gun. Somebody had somehow bypassed the security system and was after his possessions. Maybe they can get past a glitch in a computer system, Peter thought, but let's see them get past my gun.

Bracing himself against the wall across from the door, Peter prepared to kick the door open, counting in his head.

One, two ...

A giggle from the other side of the door made him pause.

He listened. There was more shuffling.

Aiming the gun at the closed door, he considered simply shooting through the wood. Perhaps it was too risky to chance getting the door open.

He gripped the pistol tightly and squeezed one eye shut, aiming dead center of the door.

Another giggle.

More shuffling.

Then a deep, hearty voice: "Stop that fucking noise!"

An unintelligible response.

"I said, stop that fucking noise!"

"Eat me!" replied a young feminine voice.

"Would the both of you just be quiet," replied the voice of an older gentleman.

What the hell was going on in there?

He listened, but there was only more quiet muffled voices and shuffling.

Peter looked back and forth down the hallway, then lowered the gun to his side and stepped forward.

A scream cut through the silence.

A gun went off.

Peter dove for cover up against where the floor met the wall and fired a shot down the hallway when he realized that the gunshot he'd heard was from his own gun. The scream had startled him enough to squeeze the trigger.

Lying on the floor in the empty hallway and bringing the gun up to train it on the doorway, Peter waited a moment. When all he heard was more shuffling and the murmur of voices from behind the door, seemingly unfettered by the gunshots, he got to his feet, carefully turned the doorknob and pushed the door open.

As before, the room was empty, except for the objects, and, of course, when he looked in the mirror, the ghosts.

He walked into the room, amazed. A collection of muffled

voices could be heard coming from all corners of the room as he moved. Getting closer to the mirror, Peter looked inside and saw the animated figures moving about the room.

But this time, when he saw their feet hit the floor, he could make out the sound of footsteps. This time, when their lips moved, he could hear muffled speech.

He stood and listened. Every once in a while, one of the voices or noises punched through the air with full force.

The scream came loud again, this time with the unmistakable smack of flesh hitting flesh.

Peter spied the room until he found the rapist hunched on the bed over Vicky, his lean muscular arms pinning her own down to the mattress, his naked body heavy upon hers.

Peter screamed as the beast plunged into her.

Vicky's scream met Peter's and together their screams mingled and danced in the air to the savage rhythm of the large man's violation.

❈

"Get your lazy ass out of my way!"

A foreign tongue responded and there was no mistaking the colorful words which had been chosen no matter that Peter didn't understand the language.

"That's my corner!"

"You had it all day. Up yours."

"Dolly, dolly. My favorite dolly."

"You cheater. Put that piece back. Cheater!"

"With one quick pull of the knife, I'll end the pain forever."

The voices came so loud through the night and down the hall to Peter's room that he couldn't shut them out. Even pressing his hands to his ears, the maddening, never-ending torrent of voices rained on him.

No matter where he went in the house, he couldn't escape the sounds of the ghosts. And that, worse than seeing them, was driving him crazy.

Upon fleeing the roomful of ghosts, Peter had run to the security system, hoping to shut it down and run off into the night. But what he found there left him with a cold feeling in the pit of his stomach.

The shot he had fired down the hallway had entered the security mainframe. Whatever else the bullet had done, it had rendered the fingerprint scanner useless so that Peter could not override the system from continuing to run at the highest level.

Making it impossible for Peter to leave his mansion. Since his phone lines were patched through the security system — to ensure privacy from phone tapping, hackers and to monitor all incoming calls — Peter's phone was also inoperable at the highest level without being able to scan his thumbprint. And a quick search through the house for his cellular phone was a waste of time when Peter remembered he had left it in the car in the garage which was separate from the main house and was thus now off limits.

Vicky's scream tore at his heart yet again.

Fixing his top lip tight against his bottom one, Peter lifted the whiskey glass and looked at it before taking the last swallow.

The incessant arguing and screaming and goings on of the ghosts became too much for Peter to handle. The only saving grace of all the intermingled voices was the fact that they helped to blend out Vicky's screams and cries.

But it was taxing.

So taxing that Peter had spent the last twenty hours either drinking or passed out. Remaining in a drunken stupor was the only way he could handle the noise, the constant noise.

But with this, his last drop of whiskey finished, Peter knew that he now had no choice.

He raised the empty bottle like a club and stumbled into the hallway and up the stairs.

He tripped and fell, barely feeling the edge of the wooden steps dig into his forehead as he landed. He laid there, listening to the voices. As they sank into his mind he found the strength and conviction to move again.

He got up, clumsily climbed the rest of the stairs and headed toward the haunted room.

Raising his bottle overheard again, he walked into the room and stood looking at the mirror. His voice was raw from hours of shouting and screaming at the ghosts. But all his screaming had done no good. The ghosts, after all, were not aware of him or of the world that Peter existed in. They merely lived in their own world, a world that Peter had become a witness to.

Thanks to that goddamn mirror.

He'd had enough time to figure it all out. It had never occurred to him before, but now, in a drunken haze, it all made sense. For whatever reason, the mirror was like a window into the world beyond the living. That, in itself, was quite a discovery. But Peter had unwillingly discovered something else about ghosts.

Ghosts were apparently accustomed to having their own space. What Peter had done by collecting haunted objects was force many different ghosts to share the same haunt. Trapped together for all of eternity, of course they would bicker and fight.

And if the bickering were not enough, there was poor Vicky. What had Peter done to her, thrusting her into the same space as that brutal rapist? Well, maybe he couldn't take back what had been done to her, but at least he could prevent himself from seeing and hearing it twenty-four hours a day.

That goddamn mirror.

With the bottle still raised overhead, he let out a hoarse battle cry and ran at the mirror.

Peter awoke to screaming and rolled over.

Strangely, he wasn't in his bed. There was a hard floor beneath him. And something was pressing into his throat. It was painful, and he couldn't breathe, but somehow it didn't stop him from being able to move.

He pressed himself up to his hands and knees and saw that he was beside Vicky's cabinet. Then he remembered where he was when he blacked out.

He'd been advancing on the mirror with the bottle raised when he'd stumbled forward. The last thing he could remember, his head had connected with the surface of the mirror.

Peter looked down at himself, at the huge shard of glass sticking out of his throat. He pulled it out with a sickening slurp and tossed it to the floor. What the hell?

"Hey, you, newcomer! Get the hell out of my way!"

Peter looked up at the bare-chested dark-haired man. The rapist was staring straight at him. He could see Peter. But not only him. All the other ghosts were there, looking at Peter. They could all see him.

"Can you hear me, you stupid ass?" the man said. "Here are the rules: Stay out of my way and I won't beat the crap out of you for fun."

The man moved forward and delivered a roundhouse kick that connected with Peter's head and sent him sprawling across the floor.

Reeling from the blow, Peter realized what had happened. He had accidentally killed himself and become a ghost in his own haunted room.

He stood, dusted himself off and looked down at the piece of glass that had been lodged in his throat. The glass must have been from Vicky's cabinet. Did this mean he was now haunting the bureau with Vicky? Peter then looked up at the man who was advancing on the helpless young woman Peter had come to know as Vicky.

Vicky! For the first time, Peter would now be able to do something to help her. Glancing once again at the shard of glass then again at the dark-haired man, Peter smiled.

"Oh, have I got a bone to pick with you."

Mark Leslie is an author, professional speaker and bookseller with more than a quarter century of experience in writing, publishing, and bookselling. Having grown up with an intense passion for reading and writing, Mark started writing when he was thirteen years old, was drawn to bookselling and has remained in the industry, wearing many different hats, since 1992. But regardless of which hat Mark is wearing, he usually defaults to the title of "Book Nerd." Find out more about Mark by visiting www.markleslie.ca.

Made in the
USA
Lexington, KY